OUR
OWN
COUNTRY

OTHER BOOKS BY JODI DAYNARD

The Midwife's Revolt

OUR OWN COUNTRY

JODI DAYNARD

LAKE UNION
PUBLISHING

Text copyright © 2016 by Jodi Daynard

Published by Lake Union Publishing, Seattle

www.apub.com

ISBN-13: 9781503954809
ISBN-10: 1503954803

Cover design by Laura Klynstra

Printed in the United States of America

Disobedience is the foundation of liberty.

—Henry David Thoreau

I never thought of myself as a very good sort of person. I had no particular gifts, as did my midwife sister-in-law, Lizzie, no taste for rebellion, as did my soldier brother, Jeb. Nor did I possess a sharp pen, like that of my friend Abigail Adams. Yet so powerful were my desires that I eventually defied my family, and even the law, in pursuit of them. In being bad, my friends like to say, I eventually became good—which was fortunate, for they had not much liked me previously.

—Eliza Boylston
Quincy, Massachusetts, 1794

Part I

1

MY EARLIEST MEMORY IS OF LIGHT, THE resplendent light that streamed through our windows in slanted beams and made a kaleidoscope of my small world. Beyond the windows, light filtered through the orchards, stippling the apple and peach leaves and the squirrels that scuttled beneath the gossamer canopies with a lacy web of sun and shadow.

Our estate stood on the road to Watertown, now called Brattle Street, in Cambridge, Massachusetts. We owned about twenty acres that descended gently to the Charles River. Next to us stood John Vassal's house, built in 1759, when I was three and Jeb was five. Every morning that year, at breakfast time, my parents complained about the racket that interrupted their morning sleep.

"I understand he wishes to finish by spring, but must he have them start with the dawn?" my mother complained. Mama was then big with child, and the rings around her eyes bespoke a wakeful night.

"I'll have a word with him," said my father, for he was on good terms with the Vassals and all the other prominent Cambridge families. Before the Troubles, we were always at one grand house or another, and I can still recall the feeling of being lifted up into our carriage and the sound of Papa proudly bellowing to our old

Negro coachman, "To the Borlands'!" or "To the Phillips farm!" or "To the Hutchinsons'!"

The interiors of these homes now blend together in my mind to form a single stunning image: footmen in red wool coats, combed clean and brass buttons shining, stand tall and erect, and I have to look very far up to see the undersides of their dark noses. They dare not smile at me, but allow me to pass through into a grand foyer, which smells of lilies and paste wax. There I stand in astonishment at the living display of fine silk gowns—lilac, emerald green, snow white—all of them direct from London or Paris. Soon enough, however, I grow bored and wend my way to the kitchen, drawn to it as a mouse seeks warmth in winter.

I recall the Borlands' cook. She was a very black woman who seemed to take up a full quarter of the smoky room. Directly after I entered, her giant hands would lift me up and set me upon a table beside a pile of trimmed vegetables. Her voice, dancing with the cadences of a far-off place, would say to me, "You don' wan' deerty yah frock, now." And then came the joke, repeated at each visit: that if I got in her way, she'd bake me along with the meat. This made my chin wobble, which set her heaving with laughter.

We had not the large staff of these other homes, but we did have two stableboys, a coachman, a footman, a lady's maid for Mama, a parlormaid, the nurse, the tutor, Cassie, our cook, and her husband, Cato. Cassie was young when I was a small girl—in her middle twenties. She was not tall, but her strong, lithe body was well proportioned, and from her oval face, with its slightly receding chin and judgmental mouth, a pair of quick brown eyes gazed discerningly upon the world.

Cato I rarely saw, for he was usually abroad chopping or hauling wood, digging the garden, or carrying bushels of hay. He was very tall, thin, and dark. I thought he would have made an excellent scarecrow, and indeed, he often seemed one to me as he stood between tasks in the garden. I did not know the sound of his voice, but when I chanced to come upon him he always bowed gravely. Cassie spoke to me of him with great pride.

•   •   •

I remember laughter, too, which echoed down hallways as Jeb and I chased each other on freshly waxed floors. Beyond the house, our laughter became lost behind the dense shrubbery, only to reassert itself in sudden shrieks as we darted in and out of the trees, on hunts for treasure or in violent games of tag. We lived in our own world, neither needing nor desiring others. Mama and Papa were as distant to us as the gods of Mount Olympus, pushy and irrelevant beings who now and again swept down upon us to insist that we eat, dress, or ready ourselves for bed.

If the grounds defined our kingdom, then the house itself was our castle. It had been built in 1746 and had two stories of five bays, with two fine parlors on either side of a grand entryway. But the house also had closets and dark halls in which to hide, and from these we leapt out at one another at unexpected moments. Or we would race down the stairs, grasp the ornately carved newel post—the unrivaled envy of all Cambridge society—and career through the foyer in pursuit of each other. We would run past the round mahogany table upon which exotic flowers luxuriated in an antique vase, until Mama inevitably cried, "Take care! You shall break the vase!"

Maria was born in the spring of '60, when I was four. Unlike Jeb and me, who were fair, she was as dark as a little Spaniard child. She was, as well, so quiet and contented as a babe that I often forgot she existed. Mama probably did, too, for she held her but a few minutes a day, when our nurse brought the dark little creature into the library for its diurnal petting.

Of all the rooms in our house, this library was my favorite. It housed a pianoforte, imported from Italy at great expense, which no one knew how to play but which Mama thought she might one day learn. There was a mahogany card table and a candlestand upon which sat a large tome of colored floral engravings. Here, my mother could usually be found working on a needlework screen or quietly perusing her flower book until she declared which species of flora she would have that year in her garden. If my father were present, he would frown and say, "Mrs. Boylston, one could as easily grow a palm tree."

"Oh, but I'm sure there's a way," Mama would say, tapping her finger on the book's cover for emphasis. "Surely there exists a special mulch or soil or other."

"There is no way," Papa insisted. Unlike Mama, he knew something about palm trees, since many grew on his Bridgetown sugar plantation. Neither Mama nor I had seen the plantation firsthand, but I felt I knew it intimately from a detailed watercolor in Papa's library, which was painted during the time of my grandfather's tenancy.

But Mama simply would not accept the realities of our harsh New England clime. Each year, having learned nothing from previous disappointments, she blamed the plants' failure to thrive on the servants. "Something simply isn't right," she would say. "Cato must have made a mistake."

I believed everything Mama told me then. About plants and palm trees, and the shameful ignorance of slaves. I believed that a real lady must never "lift a finger," and so I let my stockings fall to the floor to wait for the maid to pick them up. Rising in the morning, I stood in the center of my chamber with my arms above my head, waiting for this same maid to remove the shift from my body. Indeed, beyond holding my own fork and knife, I rarely used my arms at all, and it's a wonder they did not fall off from disuse.

Though just as sheltered as I, Maria seemed to have been born without that natural inclination to adopt the manners of the time, especially those meted out to young girls. She liked to play dress-up, but instead of being caught in Mama's fine silk shoes and trailing petticoats, we often found her tripping down the hallway in Jeb's breeches and heavy black shoes, their enormous pewter buckles obscuring her tiny, willful feet.

Nor would Maria suffer the servants to dress her properly—her little body would stiffen so that it became a Seven Years' War to put the least thing upon her. She brushed her own hair, often coming down to breakfast with half of it pinned and the other half hanging down her back. Mama tried all manner of threats and punishments, eventually leaving my sister to her own devices.

I had but one friend apart from my siblings, a girl named Louisa Ruggles. Her family lived not far from us, just off Brattle Street. Louisa was a pretty girl, plump and slow, with dark hair and languorous brown eyes. I have little recollection of Louisa's house. She was an only child and seemed to enjoy our lively home better than her own.

When not with my siblings or Louisa, I could usually be found in Cassie's kitchen. Neither Mama nor Papa ever entered there, nor were my siblings tempted to linger in its hot and smoky atmosphere. But this kitchen is where I scurried whenever I had been wounded by a defeat at tag, or by Jeb's teasing, or by some other profound unfairness, such as the times Papa refused my request for a new bonnet or pair of gloves. Then Cassie would pick me up and sit me on the table, and handing me a mug of chocolate, would begin an artfully designed tale of woe:

"You tink you got a 'ard life, Mees Eliza, let me tell you about da time on de eye-land . . ."

On and on she went until I would forget all about my own problems and cry, "Oh, Cassie! Dear, poor Cassie!"

Every afternoon, I begged Mama to let me go with Cassie to the market. She would never have considered it had Dr. Bullfinch, our physician, not recently read something of Dr. Franklin's upon the salubrious effects of "taking an air bath." Once we had left our property, I would cling to Cassie, for the world beyond our door seemed so big and bustling. There were loud noises—a constant banging of hammers and sawing of wood—and strong smells, not all savory. The horses and carriages belonged to those adult gods, and I feared they would crush me. I was ready to return home, to watch the filtered light that traveled across the china vases and velvet settees, the Greek-key parquet floors and Turkey carpets, and to be enfolded once more in the soft, quiet safety of our home.

•   •   •

When I was twelve, Cassie bore a child named Toby. Almost from the moment of his birth, I thought of him as my special pet. Indeed, I secretly believed that Cassie had birthed him just for me. Whenever I went into the kitchen, I would cry, "Where, oh, where is my little lamb? Little lamb, where are you?" He was quite shy and seemed to live beneath Cassie's petticoats. But when he heard me, he always giggled.

Later, once he had learned to speak, Toby would emerge from that dark, safe place, crying, "Here I am, Liza!" Then he would run into my arms. Sometimes he would sit in my lap and suck his thumb, the other hand grabbing on to a loose twist of hair.

I liked to hold Toby close and smell his warm baby smell and caress his soft, fuzzy "wool," as we called it. Toby played with the gold cross I wore about my neck. At times, his fingers would leave off the cross to explore my white skin, and I'd laugh and say, "That tickles!" He *was* my little lamb, and I loved him dearly.

By the time Toby was three, he displayed an eagerness to learn. One morning, as I entered the kitchen to ask something of Cassie, I nearly tripped over Toby as he lay on the kitchen floor with a book open before him.

"What have you there?" I asked. I bent down and picked it up. It was my old primer. Smiling at the memory of it, I recited, "'In Adam's fall we sinned all. The cat doth play, and after slay.'"

Toby laughed, and the sound sent an odd thrill through me. "Well, well," I said, crouching beside him. "Do you know what this is, Toby? This is the alphabet. From it, we make words. Would you like to learn the alphabet? I could teach you."

Cassie had stopped her work to watch us. "Maria give 'eem dat," she said defensively. "She say y'all finished wit' 'eet."

It seemed that Cassie feared I would accuse her of stealing it. But I said merely, "He's such a curious little dear. I should like to teach him very much. I could teach you as well, you know, Cassie."

"Me?" Cassie laughed, showing a row of strong white teeth. "What I wan' to read fo'? What I wan' to know mo' about da sufferin' o' dees worl'?"

"Well, suit yourself," I said. "But I *shall* teach Toby, if I may."

Our lessons began that afternoon, after church. I was able to procure one of Jeb's old copybooks from the nursery, and I prevailed upon Cassie to whittle a few cedar pencils, a task which made her mutter indistinct curses, for she was too impatient and kept breaking the tips.

The servants never came in to the family rooms without being called, and so when Mama saw Toby sitting in my lap in the parlor, she said, "Goodness, Eliza. What are you doing with that child in here?"

"I'm teaching him to read."

"Read? What for, pray? Have you discussed this with your father? I doubt he would approve."

"*Please*, Mama," I begged, ignoring her questions. "You know this is the best room to read by, for it gets a most glorious afternoon light."

For a moment she seemed to consider my request. But then she cried, "No, indeed! I have indulged you far too much as it is. If you must teach him, do it in the kitchen."

And so I sat upon the kitchen floor with Toby in my lap, his little hand wrapped around mine as I fashioned the letters. "*A* . . . like so. And then there's *B*," I said, sounding them out as I went along. Soon, in but a few weeks' time, Toby descended from my lap, grabbed the pencil, and began to fashion the letters all by himself. The first time he did so, I exclaimed, "Oh, Toby!" and tears of pride welled in my eyes.

2

ON SUNDAY, NOVEMBER 12, 1772, I AWOKE in great spirits because it was the day Mama and I were to plan my sixteenth birthday party. We began to speak of it over breakfast while Papa, Jeb, and Maria ate silently. Jeb was now seventeen and near six feet tall. He had a fine, aristocratic nose and clear, wide-set eyes. Blond, wavy locks fell carelessly about his shoulders. Maria had descended with her bodice askew and her thick, dark hair a wild tangle. Mama glanced at her with disapprobation but fortunately was distracted by her thoughts concerning my party.

She asked, "And what do you think of a great pair of sugared plum pyramids on either side of the—?"

"Cannot you speak of table decorations in the library?" Papa interrupted. "I find it impossible to concentrate."

Papa had told us all a hundred times that it was not polite to read at table. Yet somehow this rule never applied to him. On Sundays, he looked forward to reading the *Courier* as if it were his divine right. The *Courier's* audience was those men who firmly believed, as did my father, that all the recent public whining about oppression was a lot of nonsense. For years the crown had turned a blind eye to Colonial merchants who did not pay their taxes. What were a few pennies to them now?

I replied, "Well, what *would* you have us talk about at breakfast?"

Papa cast me a baleful look, but we were both distracted by Jeb, for at that very moment he stood up from the table and bellowed, "Yes, by all means! Let us speak of anything but the real world. For it seems that no one in this house has the least notion of what is going on in it."

"Jeb!" Mama cried. "How can you be so rude?"

I glanced at my brother. I knew not to what he referred, though we all had heard of the unfortunate incident that past June, when some wild ruffians attacked and burned the HMS *Gaspee* in Narragansett Bay, killing its captain.

"Well, our son is not far off the mark, Mrs. Boylston. I do not like to trouble our ladies with it, Jeb, but—"

"Then don't," said Mama firmly. "Come, Eliza, let us away to the peace and quiet of the library."

"Yes—be off," said Jeb. "To your flower books and talk of sugar ornaments. Just don't seat me near your friend Louisa, or I shall plead illness and take to my chamber."

I shoved Jeb in the arm as Mama and I rose from the table. "Oh, Jeb, Louisa is a charming person. I know she's not very bright, but she is plump and pretty, and quite agreeable."

"Take heed, Eliza," Jeb said, smirking now and pointing a finger at me as he made his way toward the stairs.

Mama and I moved into the library and sat there for some time, chatting happily away about the upcoming party. We gossiped about all those who would attend, and I asked her whether she thought Louisa Ruggles might someday make a good match for Jeb.

"Possibly," said Mama, looking through her flower book, as we had still not decided on the arrangements for the table. "I for one would not be averse. The Ruggles are a fine family, though I *have* heard rumors of an uncle with liberal sympathies."

"She is madly in love with him, poor thing," I insisted. "But you heard Jeb. He says she is dull and that I mustn't seat him next to her."

"What is wrong with a dull girl, I wonder?" Mama asked. "Any man would be pleased to have a wife with no strong opinions of her own. Well, it's your party. You may seat people where you like." Then she paused and finally blurted, "Why not put Cassie between them?" At this absurd idea, we both laughed.

We went to church and returned. Cassie did not join us, but I thought nothing of that. She, Cato, and Toby often attended but one of the two Sunday services. Usually Toby would be waiting for me just behind the kitchen door, and I would hear his shriek of delight when he heard us return. He knew that his lesson would begin shortly.

This time, no shriek greeted me. Noon came, and then one, but there was still no call to dinner. Wondering whether there had been some mishap in the kitchen, I moved in that direction. It was odd that neither Mama nor Papa had said a word about the lateness of the meal.

But why was Toby so silent? I expected him to come careening out the kitchen door once I opened it, which I then did.

Cassie was standing in the middle of the room, her back bent flat as a table. She supported herself with both hands gripped upon the cutting board. She was moaning, inhaling and exhaling in gulping heaves, as if she would be violently ill. I glanced about. Toby was not in the kitchen, and I asked aloud, "But what has happened? Where is Toby?"

Cassie was unable to speak, but our young scullery maid, whose name I could never remember, turned to me and replied, "He's been taken, miss. To the tavern. Cato and Toby both. There's to be an auction."

"An auction?" I did not understand. I left the kitchen at once, to seek out my parents. I found my father in his library, reading the *Courier*. When he heard my steps, he looked up from his paper and smiled.

"Eliza. Darling. How go your preparations? Are you ready to be admired by near and far? I expect you shall soon have more beaux than you know what to do with. I'm sorry I was so short-tempered about it. I really am most proud of you. Yes, most proud."

As I said nothing, he returned to his paper. But I just stood there. "What has happened to Cato and Toby?" I finally asked. "Where have you sent them?"

My father sighed. He then pointed to the broadside, as if it were to blame. "I can hardly expect you to know the events of the day. But, in a word, I must retrench. Yes, retrench and consolidate."

I gazed about my father's study: hundreds of leather-bound volumes stood within flame-red mahogany cases. A blue damask sofa sat upon a large Turkey carpet.

"What mean you? Toby is my special charge."

"Yes, I know. But Eliza," he sighed. "You've simply no idea of the pressure I am under. A hurricane has hit Barbados, and my crops have been destroyed. My debts grow. It was either the carriage or—"

"The carriage?" I cried in disbelief, hearing only that much. I then turned and fled the room, mounted the stairs, and flung myself onto my bed, where I cried hot tears. My face was red and wet when Mama knocked. She said, "Eliza, Louisa is here."

"Louisa?" I sighed. "Well, all right. A moment." Usually I was glad of Louisa's company, but not today. I dried my tears and descended. Upon seeing me at the base of the stairs, my friend curtsied.

"I hope you've dined already?" she asked courteously.

"No, in fact. Our cook, Cassie—well—" Here, I grabbed Louisa by the hand and fairly dragged her into the library. "Oh, Louisa. Something terrible has happened."

Louisa placed a thick, warm hand on mine and sucked in her breath, her look one of complete absorption in my predicament. "Tell me, dear. Tell me *everything*."

We sat together upon the sofa facing the fireplace. Taking a deep breath, I told her what had happened. At the end of my narrative, she released my hand, and I awaited Louisa's considered judgment. At the time, I heard wisdom in her dull, heavy pauses, and in her parroted adult phrases I was sure that I heard the ring of truth.

"It is very sad about the little boy, since he was such a favorite of yours."

"Yes, yes," I agreed warmly.

Then she smiled slightly. "But Eliza, you may take comfort in knowing that they don't really feel the same way about things as we do."

"What mean you?" I frowned. I recalled Cassie, doubled over in pain, her arm braced upon the kitchen table. And I recalled Toby's delight in learning to read—at three, whereas Jeb was five before he could do so. I said, "I *saw* Cassie. I believe her pain was very extreme."

Louisa smiled knowingly. "Oh, they make a great show of it, I'll grant you. But she'll get over it soon enough, I expect. The key, Mama says, is to keep them busy."

For once, I was not convinced of Louisa's wisdom, but I fell silent on the topic of Cassie. Louisa went on to ask me what she had come to ask, namely, whether she could bring a cousin of hers to my party. This cousin, apparently, would be staying with them through the holidays. I said of course she could, and she left soon after, all smiles.

Once Louisa had gone, I sat thoughtfully in the library for a few moments. I could not remove the image of Cassie from my mind, and this image was soon fortified with the low, real, keening sound of her grief coming from across the hall.

I stood up from the sofa and moved out of the library, determined to seek Jeb's help. For while he was not as close to Cassie or Toby as I was, lately his heart seemed so certain about things, especially upon the topics of right and wrong.

A few moments later, I entered my brother's chamber without knocking. He was sitting on the floor amidst a flotsam of wood and scraps of cloth, his long legs splayed. He was constructing a kite.

Jeb looked up as I entered. "Oh, hallo, Eliza. I'm just—"

"I wish to tell you something that greatly puzzles me," I interrupted him. "I can't rest until I do."

"Tell me, Sister." He stood up from the floor. I then told Jeb everything Papa had said, and where Cato and Toby had gone. Hearing me, Jeb's jaw clenched, and he bent to lace his boots.

"Go you somewhere?" I asked.

Jeb looked at me, puzzled. "We'll both go."

"But where to?"

He took my hand. "Come," he said. "I dare not waste a moment explaining."

Jeb leapt down the stairs two at a time and then opened the front door. A nipping autumn air rushed in, and I hesitated, wondering whether I should don my cape. We heard footsteps, and Jeb grasped my hand tightly. Mama appeared in the foyer, followed by shadowy Maria, who was holding her place in a book she had been reading.

"Where go you at this hour? Dinner is nearly ready. *At last*," Mama sighed.

"Do not wait for us," Jeb said.

We stepped outside. Through the closed door, I could hear Mama turn to Maria: "What can they mean, going abroad like this just now, and with no explanation? Papa!"

"Yes, what mean you, Jeb," I echoed, "dragging me out without my cape? It's cold!" I flapped my arms as Jeb fairly dragged me down the road toward town.

"Papa has sent your 'special pet' to auction. Do you wish to retrieve him or not?"

I made no reply, but merely grasped Jeb's hand as we walked the rest of the way to the tavern. It was a fine autumn afternoon, though a little chilly. The white houses along Brattle Street shone with the bright declining sun. It had been a warm summer, and the maple leaves had just begun to yellow; a few had turned a brilliant orange, and even fewer had fallen. In town, I saw no signs of the duress about which my father had spoken. In the center of town, where the market stood, we came upon people going about their chores: servants stood in lines at the stalls. Ladies peered into shop windows. Coachmen smoked their pipes by the flanks of their tethered horses. We heard the clang of the church bell, marking two.

But the commotion of the market, the sun's glare off the houses, and my inner turmoil all conspired to make my head spin. "A moment, Jeb. Please." I stopped walking and closed my eyes. When I opened them, I noticed that things *had* changed: ladies, many of whom I recognized, strolled as usual with their families; their servants waited in line to purchase fish for supper—yet I could hardly tell the two apart, for they all now wore homespun to show their support for the Cause. How very ugly it was!

We soon passed the bright-yellow courthouse and made our way up the road to Stedman's Tavern, near the Common. Within, it was dark with smoke and dense with men. Jeb inquired of some old fellow standing next to him, whose hands were taken up with a pipe and mug of cider, and was told by a nod of the head that the auction was upstairs. We mounted the tavern's narrow, steep stairs, Jeb going first. Coming up the final steps, we emerged into a great room, also quite smoky, in which chairs had been set in rows.

Here sat farmers, shopkeepers, and the lawyers of merchants who could not be importuned to attend the auction. No doubt Papa's lawyer was here, though I knew not which of them he was. These men spoke among themselves; some wrote in ledgers. Their suits appeared dusty, their thick-soled shoes worn and scuffed.

Before them, a line of Negro men and women stood. The men were in chains that held their arms behind their backs. They stood erect, some staring off toward an imagined horizon. The women wept, their tears making shiny rivulets down their black faces. One woman cried so loudly that the auctioneer gave her a violent poke, and she stopped crying at once. I was astonished that the poor creature's fear of this man was even greater than her grief.

My horror at this scene cannot be described. I knew we had slaves, but I had never considered where they came from, or where they went when they left us. They simply *were*—much like our chairs, or the food on our table.

But there was little time to dwell on these new feelings. My eyes sought out Cato and Toby. I saw them not at first, for they were not in the line. They were safe! Or so I thought for a moment. My eyes wandered to the right, where I noticed a placard nailed to the wall: "Slave Auction TODAY." The word had been painted on its own slat and nailed over the board, hung by a nail. In this way, I supposed, one might easily exchange the slat for others that read "TOMORROW" or "NEXT WEEK." It was then I espied Toby. He was nearly hidden behind the row of slaves standing next to the sign, in the arms of a young Negro girl. I approached her. Jeb placed his hand on my shoulder, as if to hold me back. I shook him off, and he went to have a word with the auctioneer.

"Give me the child," I said to the girl. "He's ours. He's here by mistake."

Recognizing me, Toby ceased his crying. He reached out as if he would play once more with my cross. "'Liza!" He grinned.

I nudged the girl's arms loose and placed mine across the child's thin, naked shoulders. A cloud suddenly passed over the sun, casting the room in almost total darkness. I felt the press of Toby's warm hands upon my throat as Jeb pulled me back.

"It's no use," he whispered. "They've already been sold."

3

I HAD BEEN A GREGARIOUS AND SOCIAL child, but after this event, I fell silent. I lost the desire to speak to anyone—not to my parents, nor Jeb, nor even to Cassie, whom I bade leave my meals outside my chamber door. What might I say to comfort her? Such words had not yet been invented. My heart grieved in a way I did not know how to fix. My gold cross burned me and kept me from sleeping until, one night, I removed it. I kept recalling how, in the tavern, Toby's little hand had reached for it. I could still feel his fingers in the hollow of my neck.

I knew not what had brought about this calamity. But things were far worse when I finally left my chamber to eat breakfast with my family—for there, all was as if *nothing* had happened. Cassie, now upright once more, placed the eggs, the ham, the biscuits, the salted fish, and the applesauce on the buffet, and everyone heaped their plates. Jeb ate wolfishly. Maria wrote surreptitiously in a little notebook on her lap. Her dark curls tumbled over her forehead, and her ink-stained fingers moved quickly, as if she feared interruption.

"What do you do, child?" asked Mama.

"A moment, Mama. I have just one more thought."

"Thought? What thought should a girl be having at table?"

Wisely, Maria made no reply.

"Hello, Eliza," said Papa, noticing my entry into the dining room, though his eyes remained downcast.

Mama said, "I'm glad to see you're feeling better. And very timely, too, for I was wondering what you thought of a sugar swan as a centerpiece for the dessert course. And—oh, did I tell you? The Inmans are coming. Apparently George Inman said, 'I wouldn't miss the Boylston's party for the world.' Isn't that an auspicious sign, Eliza?"

I endeavored to smile—for Mama *was* thinking of me, was she not? But, lips quivering, I managed to say only, "Mama, I fear I haven't the heart for a party."

"Haven't the heart?" She laughed nervously, her eyes flitting toward my father. "Why would you say such a thing? Of course there will be a party. The invitations have been sent and answered. Besides, what would I tell people?"

"I don't know."

"Tell them someone has died," muttered Jeb, "for it would be true enough."

Papa rose from his seat as if he might accost my brother, then sank back down into a feigned distraction. At the thought of what Jeb might have meant, I blinked back tears and could not eat a morsel.

•   •   •

Later, as Maria and I sat in the library, we discussed the matter of the party. Jeb had gone upstairs with his tutor. He had failed his entrance exams to Harvard that July, much to Papa's dismay, and was endeavoring to improve his Latin. We doubted he made much progress. Jeb was highly intelligent, though not studious, and I always thought that the expense of a tutor was wasted on him. The family's true scholar of the family sat right next to me. She had begun to read the *Odyssey*, one of many leather-bound tomes to be found in the library.

Now Maria closed her book and looked at me with her deep, dark eyes.

"Surely you will attend your own party. Mama has gone to such effort."

"I don't know what to do. I don't see how I can smile my way through such an evening. I feel it very keenly, Maria. I know Papa must have had a very good reason to do what he did. He must be in very great trouble of some sort, though I cannot understand it. Can you?"

"Our parents are used to doing what they please with their property. I doubt Papa felt he needed a *very* good reason."

"Papa said it was either the slaves or his carriage."

Maria smirked. "You see. Not a *very* good reason." She continued, "It's a terrible thing Papa did. But whom shall you be punishing by refusing to go to your own party? Our guests are innocent of the crime, and Cassie will not get her family back."

"No." I considered. "But perhaps Mama and Papa will take the opportunity to reflect upon their actions. Yes." I nodded. "Reflect and . . . and *feel* for poor Cassie."

Maria sighed. "Think you Mama will ever consider how Cassie, or Cato, or how any of them *feel*? She'd as soon consider the feelings of her shoes."

•   •   •

We had recently heard the news of the British ships in the harbor and their hostile vigilance of us. We had heard, too, of the throat distemper and the canker rash that had made their way up the coastal routes that fall. These plagues had begun to carry off our Boston neighbors and instilled dread in our hearts: in the former, the sufferer grew a dense, black fur in his throat and eventually suffocated. The latter was more insidious: the victim would seem to recover, only to collapse in sudden death, days—or even months—later.

But our parents seemed little concerned. Papa continued to sit in his study and pore over his papers, no doubt finding more ways to "retrench and consolidate." My mother busied herself planning for my party, and, as there was little else for me to do, I joined her, though perhaps not with the same alacrity I once had felt.

It grew quite cold, and we finally prevailed upon Papa to light the fires: wealthy though he might have been, he was quite frugal in certain matters. Sometimes we went near into December before he let a servant use the wood that had been drying in the bins since the previous year.

At these times, we refused to bathe. Though a bath in the kitchen was warm enough, our hair would turn to icicles by the time we returned to our chambers. Between ablutions, we kept a discreet distance from one another.

Our first snowfall came on Sunday, November 19, three weeks before my sixteenth birthday. It arrived with such sudden fury that we did not go to church, neither morning nor afternoon service. By three o'clock, the snow was two feet high, and soon the gathering wind blew the snow into drifts of five feet and more. When the storm had begun to taper off, Maria, Jeb, and I stuck our noses out the front door in wonderment at the whiteness. We exhaled in unison, to watch the smoke from our mouths gather and disperse. The shrubs and walkways were white, and the pointy tips of gates and fences stuck up like giant, jagged teeth along the road. There was not a soul abroad. We saw only the brown and black backs of our neighbors' dogs bounding up through the snow and heard the anxious cries of owners and servants, calling them back.

Speaking of cold, Mama had come down with one that week and kept to her bed. Jeb eluded his tutor as often as he dared, going abroad—we knew not where. But Maria and I were content to watch nature from our windows. The library windows, though wavy, were newly cleaned both inside and out. From these we saw Mama's formal gardens, not yet pruned back for the winter, frozen in their last colorful bloom: pink, salmon, yellow, and crimson, all made more vivid by the partial layer of snow. Beyond our garden, I could just make out the chimneys of the Vassal house.

We played a game of chess, which my sister handily won within half an hour. I endeavored to play a tune on the pianoforte but gave up after sounding so many wrong notes that Maria covered her ears.

"It's not my fault, Maria," I said. "Nobody has thought to hire a tutor for me. How should I become proficient otherwise?"

"One hardly needs a tutor to learn a thing." Here, my sister rose and approached the pianoforte. She nudged me aside and sat down. Then she gently placed her little hands on the keys and began to play one note after the other up and down the keyboard. She then played every other note, and within ten minutes she seemed to have memorized sufficient notes to play the first bars of "Over the Hills and Far Away."

Mama appeared in the doorway and cried, "Stop at once, Maria!"

"Why should I? Is this not an instrument, meant to be played?"

Mama had no ready reply but needed to have the last word. "Well, but—do be careful!" she said. Once she had left, Maria and I laughed out loud. We thought it was amusing that Mama should not interrupt me but waited until Maria played something melodious. After this, we settled into solitary pursuits—I, a book; Maria, her diary. Papa had given her a large, heavy account book several years earlier, and she carried it everywhere, often writing stories in it. We were thus engaged for perhaps an hour when my sister set her diary in her lap, blinked quizzically, and swallowed hard.

"Maria, what is it?" I asked. "Are you unwell?"

"Oh, it's nothing. I felt a sudden—something." She reached a hand to her throat.

"Allow me to tell Mama," I said, rising.

"If you wish. I think I shall go lie down for a few minutes."

Upstairs, I knocked loudly upon my parents' door. "Mama! Maria is unwell. I believe we must call the doctor." There was a rustling, and Mama came to the door, tying her dressing gown about her. Her face was pale, and her nose was red and chapped.

"What needs she a doctor for?" she asked, reaching into her pocket for a handkerchief. "It is but a cold. We all of us have it."

"I fear it is no mere cold, but something else. She said—she said she felt something *here*." I touched my own throat, in the hollow where my cross had been.

"It is early yet. Let us wait till suppertime. I doubt very much but it is this same dreadful cold we all have."

"Yes, Mama," I said. But, espying Cassie in the hallway approaching with a tray for Mama, I said, "Cassie, bring Maria some tea as well. She is poorly."

Cassie nodded. Above stairs, we remained correct with one another. And, since Cato and Toby's departure, I had not ventured into the kitchen at all.

"Yes, Miss Eliza." She curtsied.

I went to Maria. She was sitting on top of the bedcovers, fully clothed, engrossed in her book, her legs crossed beneath her.

"Oh," I said. "I thought to find you in bed, not on it. Are you better?"

Maria put a finger in her book to hold the place and looked up at me.

"Not worse, thankfully."

"That's a relief! I nearly had Mama fetch Dr. Bullfinch." Just then, Cassie entered with her tray.

"Look, your tea arrives."

"How nice. Thank you, Cassie," said Maria.

"But *brrr*—it's cold in here. Cassie!" I called, just as she was leaving. "We need a fire."

"You know Mr. Boylston don' let me touch da wood, Miss Eliza. Not befaw he say so."

I silently cursed our father for allowing the fire to go out. He had his barouche and four, yet my sister was to go without a hint of warmth!

"Well, you shall do so now, Cassie, and if there's a price to pay, I shall pay it."

She nodded and left the room.

In short order, the fire was lit and raging. I sat upon the bed next to my sister and caressed her hair.

"You're truly not worse?" I asked.

She leaned her head against my shoulder. "I am tolerably well, Eliza. Let us discuss something else. I find the subject of illness—especially my own—so tedious."

"Very well. What should we discuss?"

"I believe . . ." she considered, "I believe I should like to discuss our dreams. You go first."

"My dreams? Why, I—"

Maria turned to me and frowned. "Surely you have them, Eliza. We all do."

I blushed. "Why, I suppose I have thought about the things Mama has said. Mama says I shall make a brilliant match and be the mistress of a large and stately home . . . Oh, but I *should* like to remain in Cambridge—"

"Stop." Maria frowned. "Have you so little imagination as to dream only that which Mama has allowed? Surely you must have your own ideas about your future happiness?"

"Indeed I do. As I was saying, I should like to remain in Cambridge, or Boston at the very farthest."

Maria sighed.

"Well, what do you dream of, Maria?"

My sister closed her eyes. Her hands rested in her lap.

"I see a large house."

"Ha—you see!"

"Nay." Maria reached out her hand. "A large house in the country."

"In the country? Not far, I hope?"

"Yes, Eliza. Far from here. In the western parts of our county, perhaps. A large house filled with women."

"Women?" I cried, appalled at the thought.

"Women friends. We shall write, or paint. We shall prepare our own meals and wear what clothing we like. At table, we may talk about art, or the books we read—or write."

Maria's talk shocked me. "This is your dream?" I asked bewilderedly. "No husband, no children?"

"I don't see them when I close my eyes. That doesn't mean they won't happen. I see the other, however." Maria then changed the subject.

•   •   •

"Would you like to read one of my stories?" She reached for the diary on her bedside table.

"Oh, yes. I love your stories. They are always so full of adventure."

"Here. Read upon this. It's about an Athenian woman who cares for wounded enemy soldiers during the Peloponnesian war and falls in love with one of them."

Taking up the heavy ledger book, I looked askance at my sister, for the subject was slightly daring.

"And you say you care nothing about love, Maria. Humph!"

"It's just a silly story, written for my own amusement. Read it."

I read Maria's story aloud until I noticed that her eyes were closed. Gently, I put the book on the side table and went round to the fireplace, where I quietly added a few logs. Then I kissed my sister's forehead before leaving—how she burned! Perhaps it was the proximity of the hot fire—*Yes, certainly, it was the fire,* I thought.

Maria did not descend that day for supper; Cassie brought her a tray but found her asleep and tiptoed out of the room. I did not worry overmuch, but I slept ill and, the following morning, bolted from my bed to check on my sister. She was turning fitfully, but her eyes were closed. She had thrown the covers off herself in the night and when I pulled to adjust them, I noticed a bright rash across her neck and chest. I leapt back in fear and ran to tell my parents.

"Maria has a rash! A bright-red rash!" I cried, having entered their chamber without knocking.

"Have Cassie fetch Dr. Bullfinch," Papa mumbled. I did so at once. Cassie left the house and returned half an hour later with Dr. Bullfinch, the family doctor. He did not stay long, which relieved me greatly. After he had left, I entered Maria's chamber and found her sitting up and staring at the flickering fire. Her cheeks had lost their hectic redness.

"Dearest," I said, sitting myself next to her. "How are you? What was that rash? Was it not the canker rash? What did Dr. Bullfinch say?"

"Oh, the rash has paled. Look." Maria pulled the bolster off to reveal her neck and shoulders. They were nice and white, with just a thin streak of ruddy pink on one side of her neck. I sighed with relief. "I shouldn't like to complain, but I am *bored*. Dr. Bullfinch says it is but a cold, and that the rash has not the telltale bumps of the canker rash. I shall soon be well, he says, and yet he has forbidden me to read or write or do anything!"

"Shall I open the curtains?"

"Oh, yes. With any luck we shall see something interesting."

"We may be so fortunate as to see Dinah shaking out the carpets." Dinah was a young servant girl belonging to the Vassals. We often saw her knocking the dust out of a carpet by the side of the house.

"Oh, look!" Maria pointed. There, in our maple tree beyond her window, against the bright white dusting of snow that clung to the branches, stood a brilliant-red cardinal. "Eliza, isn't he gorgeous? Do you suppose he knows he's so gorgeous, and so very red?"

"I hope not." I laughed. "For Lord knows our males are puffed up enough with pride as it is. Oh, Maria," I said, embracing her, "I'm so glad you're better. I'm so relieved." After a few moments, I had a thought. "Dr. Bullfinch has not forbidden *listening*, has he?"

"I believe it slipped his mind." She smiled mischievously.

I opened the *Odyssey* and took up where my sister had left off. Then for several precious hours, we were travelers to a glorious, ancient world, where our beloved hero battled monsters and survived by his wits.

Maria fell asleep while I was reading, and I left her seemingly much improved.

That afternoon, my sister surprised us all by coming down to dinner. My sister had dressed herself as usual and done a smart job of it. Her blouse was properly buttoned; her petticoats fell straight down, not hitched up on one side or inadvertently tucked into a stocking, as they often were. She had even brushed and pinned her hair. It looked so glossy that it shone. And yet something seemed not quite right about her. Maria's dark complexion had a pale, waxen cast to it. Her walk down the stairs was too slow, and she needed to grasp the banister for balance.

"Are you certain you are well enough to stir, Maria?" I asked. "It is cold—Cassie can bring you something in your chamber."

"No, no," she objected. "I'm bored to tears. Truly. I'm resolute that I shall sit in the library and read." She proceeded to drink some tea and smilingly accepted a kiss on the side of her head from Jeb, who had loaded his plate with ham, biscuits, and Cassie's special brandy sauce.

"Sister," he mumbled after having already taken a huge bite of ham, "I made something for you."

Jeb proffered a J-shaped wooden item that lay in his lap.

"Oh, no. Not another pop gun." Maria rolled her eyes.

"The very same."

"You're very sweet, Jeb. Perhaps this time I shall find a use for it. You know I dislike shooting things. Well, perhaps I can load it with bread and shoot pellets out to the ducks."

Maria smiled while she spoke, but I saw that she ate nothing and merely poked at a lone slice of ham.

"You take no nourishment," I remarked unhappily.

"I suppose I'm too excited to eat. Come—if you have finished. Join me in the library."

Our parents, reassured that Maria was on the mend, announced their plans for the day. Mother said that she would spend the day creating menus for Cassie, and did we fancy fish or fowl for Sunday dinner?

"Well, since we all seem to be announcing our plans," Jeb stood, "let me announce that I plan to go abroad. It is cold but sunny, and they have cleared the main road. I shall walk about town pretending to be a college lad with a fine parson's job ahead of me, paid well to spout nonsense."

"Jeb! Have a care, will you?" Our father frowned and glanced at Mama, who had just stepped into the dining room.

"What?" Jeb laughed in astonishment. "Are we to pretend that I am fit for a scholar's life? Oh, we are all so *dull*! I shall die of our dullness!" Jeb cried. "Eliza, do you wish to walk with me?"

"I've told Maria I would sit with her in the library," I said regretfully, for I should have liked to go abroad.

"Oh, yes, I forgot. Well, adieu! I am heartily sick of this house. We all behave as if there were nothing of importance beyond it."

And, apparently finished with his tirade, Jeb departed. Our mother ran to the door and called after him fretfully, "Your cap!" But he was already far down the road.

"That child gives me a headache," Papa sighed, shutting the door against the cold.

I took Maria's hand, and we walked to the library. She sighed. "I wish I had the energy to go abroad. I wish it were spring, and doing so were not such an ordeal."

"I know," I said. It was not so simple for us as it was for Jeb. We had petticoats to drag through the snow and ice, boots to lace, bonnets, mitts, and capes to adjust. The very thought was exhausting. Of course, no one had the least idea of Maria's going abroad just now.

We installed ourselves in the library by the large windows. The afternoon sun, in its decline, was brilliant, and melting ice from the tree branches refracted a rainbow of colors before dripping out of sight. I had hoped to see Mr. Cardinal again but did not. That was a disappointment, for his careless beauty gladdened my heart, igniting within me every sort of foolish hope.

Maria and I played a game of chess, which I won after a struggle. I might have exulted more had I not been alarmed by her sluggishness, her pallor. We then read companionably for near an hour: I, *A Midsummer Night's Dream*; she, the *Odyssey*. After an hour, however, she grew fatigued.

"My eyes close, Eliza. Perhaps I shall lie down for a bit."

"Oh, do, dear. You're not yet well."

She smiled, her lids fluttering shut. "This story transports me so, with its palaces whose brazen fires 'make night day.' Oh Eliza, by such magical means am I able to travel the world! Do you think everyone understands the magic of books? Of seeing not what *is*, but what *might* be?"

"But you're so very good at seeing what is, Maria. Without you, I would hardly know what was real."

Maria sighed and considered my words. "It is a burden always to see things in their true light. Books—they are such a wonderful escape, don't you see?" But even as Maria said these words, I saw her shoulders roll forward. I set my own book down and helped her up the stairs. She paused upon the landing. "But how I am out of breath!" Maria placed a small hand on her chest.

"Come, darling. Let us get you out of your gown. Shall I call for Cassie to bring you something? A dish of tea?"

"Oh, yes, I would like that."

We entered her chamber. It was such a pretty room, with its tiny pink flowers on the wallpaper; a gossamer crocheted canopy hung above the mahogany bedstead. From her chamber, my sister had views north, across our orchards, and east, to the Vassal house and the same ice-slicked maple tree we saw from below.

Her room was quite cold once more. Cassie and I got the fire going and managed to undress Maria and get her into bed. The bed was cold, too, and Maria shivered. Cassie left the room to get the tea. I lay myself down on the bed beside my sister and wrapped my limbs around her, to warm her.

"Oh, yes, that is good. That is better," she said, snuggling into the warmth of my body. She closed her eyes. "I believe I shall be able to sleep now. And when I wake, I'll fly back to the isle of Helios, to see what the fierce sun god has done with the poor hungry sailors who have eaten his beeves. It will transport you, Eliza."

"I look forward to it," I said.

"I'll finish it by the Sabbath, I am sure, and then it shall be yours." It was then Thursday. Maria shut her eyes, and her breathing slowed; I sat up. Cassie entered with tea and a biscuit, but I shook my head, mouthing that she was already asleep. Cassie set the tea down on the bedside table. Beyond the window, the sun continued to turn the ice to sparkling rain. I heard the church bell ring. Suddenly I saw the cardinal again! He was just there, beyond the window, standing on his gray stick legs and snip-snipping with his triangular black beak. I drank the tea meant for Maria and left soon thereafter. Behind me the fire glowed brightly. All seemed well.

I descended the stairs and sat in the library, looking out upon the whiteness. I dreamed of spring and lively gatherings. But I was jolted out of my reverie by a piteous shriek from above. I ran at once to Maria's chamber to find Cassie standing over a dropped tray and broken china. Maria lay on the bed, eyes open, lips blue, breath gone. She had left Odysseus and his men forever, on the isle of Helios.

4

THE FUNERAL WAS HELD THAT MONDAY AT the new church. The snow had turned to ice in places, and we slipped precariously as we walked behind the funeral carriage to the chapel. We suffered the pitying stares of shopkeepers and farmers who seemed surprised to learn that those who lived on Brattle Street were not, in fact, immortal.

Our parents walked ahead of us, side by side but not touching, worlds apart. Papa broke down periodically; Mama's eyes seemed not to blink, and Jeb and I leaned on each other as we walked behind them. "I don't see how we shall go on," I whispered. "The pain is too much."

"What choice have we, Eliza, if God wishes to give an eye for an eye?" His tone was bitter.

"What mean you, 'an eye for an eye'?"

"What else would you call it?" Jeb laughed mirthlessly. "God would have them know what it feels like to lose a child."

"Surely that cannot be." I frowned.

"What? Do you not believe in a vengeful God, Eliza? Have you been asleep at services all this time?"

"Vengeance against whom, pray, and for what?"

"For Cassie, of course."

My brother's anger, and the town's anger, and the shock of his pronouncement, was all too much: I burst into great heaving tears.

"Oh, Sister, I'm sorry. I'm so sorry." He grabbed onto my shoulders. Mama and Papa turned around to see what had happened.

"Of what do you speak?" Papa asked accusingly. His eyes blazed, though he could not have heard us.

"Nothing," I said, wiping my own eyes indecorously with a sleeve. "Let us continue on."

Reverend Winwood spoke about the fragility of life and the need for readiness. No doubt he meant to be a comfort. Mama and Papa nodded at his every sentence, yet I found it vexing to be lectured—nay, scolded—on a topic we understood all too well. What's more, the reverend had a terrible stutter, and his p-pronouncements up-pon the f-fragility of li-li-life always made Jeb want to explode in laughter. On this day, however, I knew that, were I to so much as glance at Jeb, I would laugh and cry simultaneously, and I shielded my eyes from him with one hand through the entire service.

From the church we then moved into the graveyard, where we stood in the frigid cold. Our stiffened fingers grasped the newly upturned dirt to throw into the grave. Mama swooned and sat down upon a large rock. Jeb and I hugged each other and wept.

On the way home, Jeb, who had been walking silently by my side, paused when we reached our snowy garden by the Charles. I turned toward the house, but he moved the other way, pushing through the mounds of snow down to the partially frozen river. There, he took something from his pocket and hurled it ferociously across the water. "Damn Dr. Bullfinch!" I saw the object sail into the air and land with a plunk. It was the pop gun he had made for Maria. I turned in a panic, fearful that our parents had heard my brother's cry.

"Come on, Jeb," I called. He turned and looked up at me, his shoulders shaking. Tears ran unchecked down his red face. "Come on," I repeated. "Let us be a comfort to one another."

"There is no comfort in me, Eliza," he said. "Only rage."

"There is no rage in me, only misery," I replied. "I thought her well. Her neck was . . . pale. Dr. Bullfinch said it was *not* the throat distemper."

"It was," Jeb said. "He admits as much now."

But my mind had traveled back to the day before Maria died. "We spoke of our futures, our dreams"—I broke off, weeping. "Oh, Jeb, surely anger would be better than *this*?"

Jeb shook his head. "Be careful what you wish for, Sister."

• • •

Mama cancelled the party. Jeb's lessons were suspended, and he and I spent the daylight hours dully playing cards in the library, finding games less painful than speech. Our father sobbed periodically throughout the day, always turning his back on us and pretending a sudden need to blow his nose. In our mother's eyes, however, we saw tears only once: when Maria's coffin had been lowered into the ground, and she had sat upon the rock to keep from falling.

We ignored Thanksgiving entirely, though perhaps it was wrong of us to do so. Surely there was something to be thankful for. Maria would have found something. My sixteenth birthday came and went. The house, shrouded in black crepe, remained unlit. Jeb spent more and more time away from us, and when he was with us, he and Papa argued. Papa grumbled that he didn't see why he'd bothered to work all his life when Jeb despised wealth and planned to give it all to his beloved "common man." Jeb retorted that he didn't know how Papa could support the crown when every day even he, Papa, had fewer and fewer rights. Mama and I stayed clear of them both—we had no strength for quarreling.

The March thaw finally came. I had not heard from my friend Louisa, and I wondered what had prevented her from condoling with us. Perhaps there had been illness in her house as well.

In April the purple crocuses popped their heads up in the lawn. Daffodils in all their frilly finery made an appearance, and Mr. Cardinal came around once more, bringing his pale-pink lady with him. O, brilliant pair!

One morning I was awakened by the sweet perfume of hyacinths coming through a crack in my window. I rose from my bed and descended the stairs, still in my shift, to follow the smell. It lured me out of doors. To passersby, I must have appeared a ghostly figure. Closer I came to it; I sought it out—here? No. There? When I finally found the hyacinths—oh, that first, fragrant, blue clump of life—I buried my face in them, weeping in gratitude for my senses, and for Maria.

· · ·

I spent the spring, and indeed much of the summer, on the banks of the Charles. I followed the sun as it traveled from Boston into the heavens and then westward, past Watertown. I felt myself caught in its consoling light as children played catch, couples strolled, and families ate their dinners on blankets, *en plein air*.

It was nearly autumn before Mama revived. One bright September morning, as we sat at breakfast, she announced, "Eliza, it will please you to know that you are to take dance lessons from Mr. Curtis, of King Street. I have heard it from Mrs. Ruggles that Louisa shall be attending as well."

"Indeed?" I said without much enthusiasm. Once, the idea of traveling to Boston for such a purpose would have delighted me. Now I felt only a faint dread of society. What's more, I was quite tan, having spent all summer in the sun. But accepting Mama's proposal did mean that I would need a new gown or two, a new bonnet, and a suitable pair of shoes, and such a thought, while it did not send me into the ecstasies of expectation that it might once have done, did lift my heart in a consolingly familiar way.

"Thank you, Mama," I said. "It's a marvelous idea." I ran to Papa to request the new items at once.

Mr. Curtis's dance studio stood at the top of King Street near the Town House. It was a busy market area with shops and taverns, and foreign goods fresh off the ships in the harbor. Inside the studio, an old crone with palsied hands, dressed in an unfashionable gown, sat at a spinet. Many girls I knew were there, and one by one they curtsied to me, expressing their mourning duties. Louisa stood among the girls in a lovely violet gown.

"Eliza, how are you?" she said, clasping my hands with her usual earnestness.

"Very well."

"You are tan," she remarked.

"Yes."

"Oh, I suppose it shall fade soon enough." After a moment, she cast her eye to the other side of the room. "Regard the boys. There is not a single one with whom I should be delighted to—"

Louisa broke off, and a sudden hush came upon the crowd. I soon saw why: Mr. George Inman, the veritable crown prince of Cambridge, had arrived. He stood at the studio's entrance beside his valet.

Mr. Inman was not particularly tall, but his limbs were comely, his posture erect. Perhaps three or four years my elder, he was dressed in the finest blue cutaway coat, and in the shine on his boots, one could see a fair likeness of oneself. He had a long face with a long, rod-straight aquiline nose. A cleft chin leant distinction to an already handsome face, and his eyes matched the blue of his costume. He smiled, perfectly aware of the effect he made among us ladies.

Murmurs of "Ooh, look!" and "What's he doing here, I wonder?" flew about the crowd as each girl pinched her cheeks and sucked at her lips. Soon Mr. Inman's valet moved off to sit at the back of the room, while the paragon himself joined the crowd.

For the next forty minutes, I was insensible to all but our instructor's voice as Mr. Curtis cried, "And one and two, step right and left!" I was not a natural at dancing, and I had to concentrate so as not to fall on my face. At the end of the hour, as I sighed with relief, Mr. Inman approached me.

"Miss Boylston. I see you've survived the hour—barely."

"Yes, barely." I returned his smile. But I wondered: *What had I done to merit his attention?*

Mr. Inman looked at me thoughtfully. "But allow me to introduce myself. Mr. George Inman." He bowed.

I curtsied, and then Mr. Inman said, "Miss Boylston, would you do me the honor of allowing me to call upon you in Cambridge?"

The others in the room heard Mr. Inman's request. Louisa's mouth actually gaped in surprise. I took a spiteful pleasure in her envy and then frowned at myself.

But I said, "You may," and then curtsied most prettily.

The moment I arrived home, I swooped down upon Papa, who was at his desk. "Papa, the most amazing thing has happened, and I'm afraid you must order me a new gown at once."

"Afraid? Why, pray?"

"Oh, Papa."

"Well, does the queen arrive? Are we to have a royal visit?" Papa smiled at his own wit but did not look up from his papers.

"Nearly. Mr. Inman wishes to call upon me Saturday next."

"Hmf." He shrugged, but I could tell that he was impressed. "I suppose things could be worse. Well, well." Papa finally looked up at me, and though his voice had been teasing, his eyes were sad. "You've hardly asked for a thing all year, so I won't deny you. Mr. Inman, you say? Shall he get his degree at last? It's been about a decade, I believe. Well, I suppose if one has wealth, brains are hardly necessary."

"Oh!" I flew back out of his study to find Mama, whom I knew would make more of a fuss over my news. After all, she had sent me to Mr. Curtis to catch a big fish, and I had obliged her by doing so.

· · ·

From the first, Jeb seemed determined to ruin my chances with Mr. Inman. For one thing, he refused to go to church with us that Sunday, an absence that would surely be talked about.

We had breakfasted as usual and stood waiting for him at the door when he arrived in the foyer only to say, "I'm very sorry, Mama, Papa, but I can't tolerate one more sermon by that p-pedantic p-parson or his blasted p-prayer for the k-king."

"What mean you by that, Jeb? Surely you cannot mean to remain behind," Mama objected.

"Indeed not," Papa agreed.

"It does seem cruel to mock him," I added, though at the very thought of the man I had to purse my lips to keep from laughing.

"I shan't go," Jeb said, folding his arms and looking steadfastly at the floor.

Mama cried, "But what shall we say to the Inmans?"

Jeb shrugged. "Perhaps you could say I have strained my back and cannot sit."

"Jeb, that is hardly credible," I objected.

"Well, then, tell them that I am dead and lie in state. What do I care what you tell the Inmans?"

Out of nowhere, a hand came through the air and slapped Jeb across the face.

"How dare you speak to your mother like that," Papa said. "Go to your chamber."

I grabbed Jeb's arm and led him aside as he massaged his stinging cheek.

"Jeb, you *are* cruel. Only think how Mama has suffered," I whispered. "And really, your timing could hardly be worse."

"Why is that?" Jeb looked at me questioningly.

"Haven't you heard? Mr. Inman plans to pay me a visit on Saturday."

Jeb frowned but made no reply. To Mama, however, he turned back and said, "I'm sorry, Mama. But surely you must feel the winds of change. Our citizens will fight for the rights denied them. Perhaps you women are content to remain children, being told what to do, but our men will be men. Very likely, we shall soon be at war."

Mama took a step away from Jeb. "I don't know how you can say such things," she replied. "I shall say to anyone who asks that you are unwell."

"Say what you like." He shrugged. "I shall go neither to church nor to my chamber." Taking only his cap with him, Jeb pushed past us and walked swiftly toward the stables. "Juno! Ready my horse!" he called. Then, as an afterthought, he turned to us and said, "Do not wait for me for dinner, for I shan't return before tomorrow."

Mama, cold and hard a moment earlier, now burst into tears. Papa bellowed, "Blast that confounded child!" and moved to console her. I was left to wonder why Jeb disapproved so of Mr. Inman.

•   •   •

The following Saturday, Cassie spent the better part of the morning preparing me for Mr. Inman's visit, beginning with a bath, then a powdering that masked the remains of my tan.

"Cassie, you'll make me look like a statue."

"Den 'ee worsheep you like 'ee *should*." She nodded for emphasis.

I glanced behind my shoulder at her and sighed, upon which Cassie trussed me tight as a turkey. Then she helped me into a new blue silk damask gown, whose fluttery sleeves were the very height of London fashion. I sat upon my bed and, on my feet, Cassie placed a pair of brocade shoes so new that they posed a slipping hazard on our freshly waxed floors. Carefully, I stood up. "How do I look?" I asked her, circling slowly about.

"Good enough to eat, Miss Eliza. You just watch he don' try 'eet."

"Cassie." I frowned. "Mr. Inman is a gentleman."

"Dere no such ting, Miss Eliza."

"You're a little fool. Go back to the kitchen and get ready." Cassie bowed her head and was off. Over the summer, we had let go a number of servants, and Cassie was now but three remaining ones, not counting the stableboy, Juno, and our old coachman.

·   ·   ·

I was soon demurely waiting for Mr. Inman in the front parlor. Mama paced the foyer.

"Mama, would you kindly find an occupation? You shall embarrass me by hovering about like that."

"Oh, but this is so exciting, is it not?" She smiled warmly at me. Such smile from her was a rare occurrence.

"I don't know," I said. "I feel quite nervous, somehow. Cassie says he might try to eat me, and the truth is, I do find his pale eyes rather wolflike."

Mama's smiled vanished. She glided quickly over to me as if her feet had turned into wheels. "Cassie is deranged," she said. "And I'm beginning to think you are, too. How could one not like Mr. Inman?"

I shrugged. "I don't know, but—*please* go. Papa!" I cried. At the threat of Papa's intervention, Mama wheeled herself out of the parlor and disappeared up the stairs. Five minutes later, I heard the clop of horses' hooves. I peered out the window to see a very fine carriage with two sleek pacers and an ebony coachman stop before the house. Mr. Inman descended, and I turned back quickly, so that he would not see me waiting for him.

Our butler went to open the door, and in Mr. Inman strode. He looked about him, and I watched with bursting pride as his gaze came to rest on our glorious staircase. Mr. Inman turned, and I stood to greet him. "Mr. Inman," I began with a curtsy. "It's very good to see you." From the corner of my eye, I caught Mama peering down at us from the top of the stairs, and my heart thumped with irritation. "Please, have a seat. Have you been well, Mr. Inman?"

"Indeed," he grinned. His cool blue eyes assessed me boldly, which made me blush. "I'm infernally busy, though, what with our upcoming exams, and a declamation I must give for the Speaking Club."

"Oh? A declamation? Upon what topic, pray?" Here, thank goodness, was something to discuss.

But Mr. Inman replied, "I've no wish to bore you, Miss Boylston. At least, not on my first visit."

"No, sir," I smiled encouragingly, favorably impressed by his willingness to poke fun at himself.

"Very well, then. It is on the story of Dionysius and Damocles. Do you have an opinion on that?"

"Indeed, I do. Do you wish to hear it?"

Mr. Inman was all astonishment, whether feigned or no, I knew not. "Do you mean to tell me that you know who those men were?"

"Of course." I laughed. "My brother, Jeb, would say that such a legend about the evanescent nature of power is an apt one for our time."

Mr. Inman nodded thoughtfully, and I believed we would then discuss the topic. But he changed tack. "I was sorry not to have the pleasure of attending your party last year. Am I to have the pleasure of attending another?"

I could not at first reply, so swift and unexpected was the pain he caused me. Surely he knew why we had cancelled the party? I managed to say, "We haven't discussed such a thing as yet."

Seemingly unaware of my change in tone, he said cheerfully, "Well, I have already begun to plan my graduation party next summer. Or, that is, Papa has. Everyone shall be there. Including you, I hope." I knew he sought my eyes, but they were fixed upon the pattern of my brocade shoes.

"If you wish it," I said.

"Well, then, that's all settled."

After making a few easy remarks upon Mr. Curtis's dance studio and the poor pianist, Mr. Inman took his leave. I remained sitting in a whirling vortex of emotion for several minutes.

Jeb returned just as Mr. Inman's carriage left. Upon entering the house, he accosted me at once. "Eliza, how can you be so foolhardy as to entertain that fellow?"

I looked up out of my fog. "Why, what can you mean? Mama says it's an honor that he has chosen to single me out. The girls at Mr. Curtis's school were green with envy."

"Know you nothing at all? Is that pretty head filled with air?" he replied.

"What should I know about Mr. Inman that I do not? He is a student at the college and shall graduate this summer. He has plans to work for his uncle in Boston." I recalled how Jeb had failed his Harvard entrance exams and now, it seemed, refused to take them again. How he planned to support himself was an endless topic of concern for our parents.

"Eliza." He grasped my arm and then whispered, "His reputation is by no means stellar. He plays at cards and loses a great deal of money. He is at the bottom of his class, or very near it—"

I laughed. "You are not even *that* high!"

Jeb took no offense; he merely shrugged, as if to say that school was for boys, and he was a man.

Out of the corner of my eye, I saw Mama's skirts on the stairs above, swishing as if they would descend.

"Eliza." Jeb grasped my hands. "There are other things as well. Rude things not for a sister's ears."

"*Things*," I said dismissively. "You know nothing for certain, do you?"

"I know that Mr. Inman's distinguished uncle, as you call him, aids the East India Company, which shall soon enough be our mortal enemy."

"Our mortal enemy? Come now, Jeb. How can a company selling tea, of all things, be anyone's mortal enemy? Mama is right, I think, when she says you tend to exaggerate."

Suddenly, Mama was beside us, having heard but a few words. "I am right? In what respect, pray?"

Jeb ignored her question and continued, "You must know by now that our town is entirely divided, and that Mr. Inman and his family shall soon be pariahs."

"By that measure, so shall ours," I replied. "At least we shall be on the same side."

"But not on mine," said Jeb.

Mama, ignoring Jeb, turned to me and inquired, "So, Eliza, how did Mr. Inman's visit go?"

5

SO LONG AS I ORBITED MR. INMAN, my star rose into the heavens. But the rest of our country seemed to be heading in quite the opposite direction. Five days after Mr. Inman's visit, a band of men with faces painted like Indians mounted three British ships and dumped three hundred and sixty cartons of tea into Boston harbor.

"They've gone mad. Completely, utterly mad," said Papa at dinner, reading the broadside about the event the following Monday. "Honestly, I know not what shall become of us."

Neither Mama nor I had any comment to make. Jeb was absent, having spent the past several days in Boston with friends.

"Perhaps we should write Jeb to come home," Mama said at last. "I like not that he's in town just now. It's not safe."

"Oh, I imagine he's safe enough. Besides, it would serve him right to get into some trouble," grumbled Papa.

"Oh, but what now? They'll close the port altogether, and then we shall all starve."

"That is going too far, Mr. Boylston." Mama frowned.

"We shall see," Papa answered her, unconvinced. But even I had begun to notice that the atmosphere in Cambridge had grown tense. When once our family had been at the apex of society, we now had to lower our eyes on the way to church as the cool, unfriendly eyes of local militia and townsfolk followed us the entire way. How unfair, I thought, that *we* should be blamed for taxes imposed by a distant king!

Toward the end of that afternoon, Jeb arrived home. He was filthy, and upon his face were faint traces of black tar. We all ran out to greet him as he, scant of breath, confessed, "Mama, Papa, I fear I'm in danger."

"Son, what has happened?" asked Papa, reaching to pull him indoors. He had not noticed the tar, as I had, nor reached my alarming conclusion.

Jeb paused in the doorway, as if unsure of how to continue. "I have—I have been involved in something in Boston, and I hear they pursue us."

"What have you done, Jeb?" I approached him, moving between him and our father, who seemed slow to comprehend.

"Hear me out. I may be arrested at any moment." We quickly entered, and Jeb paced restlessly in the foyer as he spoke. He would not remove his cape. Mama looked as if she might faint. Jeb kept glancing out the windows every other moment.

"Tell us," Papa said sternly. "We will know the truth!"

"Then you shall have it!" Jeb replied angrily. "For near two years, I have been a member of the Sons of Liberty. It was I who dumped the tea into the harbor. I and my mates. It was high time for *someone* to take a stand."

"Oh, Jeb!" I cried, reaching out to him. I had heard of the Sons of Liberty. They were the same dastardly group that had set fire to the *Gaspee* the previous June.

Mama and Papa were perilously silent. Papa finally looked at his son. "I shall protect you as far as I am able, because to do otherwise would be *our* ruin. But be it known that henceforth you are no son of mine."

"Papa, you can't mean it," I said.

"I can and do." He turned away, and Mama followed him.

"Jeb, why?" I grasped his arm. I fervently wished to understand my brother's frustration, but I could not. All I could see was the danger, the foolhardiness of what he did. "You might have been killed."

"I follow my beliefs, Sister, as each of us must do."

"Surely you understand that we can bear no more heartbreak. Promise me you shall stop these treasonous, dangerous activities."

He leaned into me and whispered, "I love you very dearly, Eliza. But I can make no such promise."

•   •   •

We every moment expected a knock at the door. Henceforth, we would live in constant fear of reprisals, and we suspected everyone of knowing what Jeb had done. Thankfully, however, Papa did not make good on his threat to disown Jeb. He might have, once. But I believe he simply had not the heart to lose another child.

I ceased going to Mr. Curtis's dance studio; it was now late November, and the weather was growing cold. What's more, Mama did not like the idea of my visiting town under the circumstances. I was gratified to know that she cared more about my life than my marriage prospects, if only slightly. In any case, Mr. Inman visited me several times during his vacation from school. Each time, my feelings were most puzzling: as he descended his carriage, my heart contracted with excitement. Yet within moments of speaking to Mr. Inman, this positive impression faded, and I was left with the uncomfortable sensation that I can only describe as . . . something cold and rapacious in his eyes, at odds with his words, smiles, or erect bearing.

It was to avoid those eyes that, on Mr. Inman's third visit, I asked him if he cared to play a game of chess.

"Maria and I often played. And I often lost," I added, guiding him, under Mama's watchful gaze, to the library. "But then winning or losing hardly matters, does it?"

"Certainly not." Mr. Inman grinned. "Unless one happens to like winning."

"Do you like winning, Mr. Inman?"

"Of course," he laughed easily.

Ten minutes later, however, he was not so smug when I removed his queen and said, "Check."

"Blast!" He lifted himself off his seat slightly, the better, perhaps, to see what he had not noticed before. Then Mr. Inman, beginning to panic, searched for a way out. He evaded me but two more turns before I said, "Mate."

Mr. Inman stood up abruptly and gave the table a little shove with his thigh. The pieces clattered and shifted, and for a moment, I thought the entire board would come crashing to the floor. However, it just managed to right itself in time to avert disaster. "Confounded luck!" he said.

"Precisely," I said mildly. He turned toward me with an unfriendly, almost hostile stare.

"Beaten by a green girl. Not every man could take it so well as I, you know." Mr. Inman endeavored a smile, though I thought it not quite sincere.

"I'm sure you'll have better luck next time, Mr. Inman." Then I thought that perhaps there would not be a next time, for it was almost certain that I had offended him by winning. I silently cursed myself for being so tactless.

Mr. Inman soon took his leave, but he returned twice more during his vacation and then later, in the spring. Each time we played chess, I made sure to let him win.

•   •   •

Mama could not have been more pleased by my growing connection to Mr. Inman. She prevailed upon Papa to buy me two more gowns. Louisa, drawn to my rising status, began to visit again as well.

"You are the luckiest girl in all of Boston," she said one day as Cassie helped me into a new gown.

"Do I look very fine?" I asked, smiling. I already knew the answer.

"That color suits you well. And, oh, your waist! If only I had such a waist!" Louisa did not have a narrow waist, but she did have an ample bosom, which I lacked. She whispered, "I have a secret to share that will greatly improve the fit of your bodice."

"Do tell," I said, amused.

When Louisa had taken her leave, Cassie turned to me: "Dere is nutteeng wrong wit' yah bosoms, Mees Eliza. Yah got the sweetest little bosoms I ever seen, and a man would count himself lucky, 'ee get his hands on dem."

"Cassie!" I cried. "You're incorrigible."

She nodded solemnly. "Yes, Mees Eliza."

●　　●　　●

Papa's wild predictions from the fall turned out to be prescient, for in March, Parliament voted to close Boston Harbor and demand reparations. In June, General Gage, our governor, sealed the harbor tight, using the formidable British navy to do so. But instead of being angry with England, Papa kept muttering, "This is our own son's doing. If only the damned Rebels would let things alone! Let us pay the fine and be done with it."

What shipments arrived now had to make their slow way down from Portsmouth. Staples of our existence such as tea and meat became scarce. Papa announced over dinner one afternoon that he would let go of the butler.

"Who is to answer the door, pray?" asked Mama.

"With any luck, we shan't have to answer the door," said Papa wryly.

For those in Boston, it was far worse: people soon took to the town middens after market, in search of food. Our circumstances were not so dire, although going without tea did give me a terrible headache.

As for Mr. Inman, the closing of the harbor put a damper on his high spirits, for the Harvard overseers had decided to cancel commencement. Normally commencement was a giddy, weeklong debauchery, something the students looked forward to almost from the moment of their entrance to college.

I was disappointed for the boys, but Papa said it was just as well to rid our town of such havoc, since the real thing was nearly upon us.

"Oh, Mr. Boylston, you exaggerate," said Mama. "At least the Inmans shan't cancel their party."

"Perhaps they should, though."

Mama was right, however. When next I saw Mr. Inman, he mentioned the party once more.

"Mr. Inman," I asked, "how is it your family is able to host such an event when goods are hardly to be had at any cost and must be hauled all the way from Portsmouth?"

"Oh," he replied, "that is no very great obstacle for my family. We have ships in Portsmouth."

"I see."

Mama suddenly entered the parlor where we sat conversing. She turned to Mr. Inman, and my heart pounded, for I could not guess what she might wish to say to him.

"Mr. Inman." She smiled warmly. "I am very glad to see you again."

Mama behaved as if we had always socialized with the Inman family, but we had not. She had been great friends with the first

Mrs. Inman but didn't care for the second and current one, finding her a "poseur" and rather "vulgar." However, this did not change her conviction that the younger Mr. Inman would be an excellent match for me.

"And I you, madam." He bowed.

"My husband—Mr. Boylston and I were very sorry to hear of the college's decision to dispense with commencement this year." This I knew to be a lie, for Papa had only that morning expressed his relief at this turn of events. "I know it is an event to which you all look forward."

"It's true, madam. My fellow students and I were ready to get ourselves up to all sorts of mischief." Mr. Inman winked at me, as if to say, "Oh, but you know I am not that sort of fellow."

"Mischief—oh!"

"Mama." I sighed. "I'm sure Mr. Inman is joking."

"Oh, yes, of course. But if I may . . . we should like to invite you to dinner Saturday next. To condole, as it were, with your disappointments. We shall, of course, be inviting your parents as well."

Mr. Inman bowed once more. "It is an honor, and, for myself, I accept with alacrity." He flashed me a complicit grin, and I returned the smile, though dinner with the Inmans put far more terror in my heart than joy. I had little doubt but that it was for them to observe—and approve—the merchandise.

·   ·   ·

Saturday, June 11, 1774. Dinner with the Inmans began pleasantly enough. Mrs. Inman complimented Mama's new summer gown, and Mama congratulated the Inmans on their son's graduation. Earlier, Mama had been in a panic when a shipment of quail that we had been expecting at market was unexpectedly delayed somewhere in Newburyport. All morning she fretted that we would go without meat for dinner. At the last moment, however, the quail arrived, saving the day.

As we ate the quail, the topic of the tea-dumping arose, and while Jeb was thankfully not in attendance, having wisely chosen to remain in town that day, Mr. Inman, believing himself to be in like-minded company, insisted that the perpetrators of the event "be hung by their necks in the square!"

"Just so, just so," said Papa, after which an uncomfortable silence reigned, for which no amount of quail could compensate.

After dinner, the men chose to have a brandy in the library. We ladies took our cranberry tea in the parlor. When I chanced to look in at the men, I noticed that Mr. Inman senior sat smoking—alone. I moved toward Papa's study and heard voices. The door was closed, but I knew both voices well. What could Mr. Inman want with Papa? I suddenly feared that perhaps Mr. Inman knew something about Jeb and his activities in town. Was he warning Papa about Jeb, or threatening to expose him? I knew not. When he finally emerged, however, Mr. Inman was smiling, and Papa said quite affably, "Come, let's have a smoke." I returned to the parlor to finish my tepid cranberry tea with Mama and Mrs. Inman.

After such a long dinner, I wished little more than that they would all depart. George Inman had been casting me knowing smiles all evening, and I was tired of smiling back at him. But I was to suffer one more scene with him. Papa, in a jovial spirit, announced that he considered it "no very great evil" were the "young folk" to have a few minutes to themselves. I did as Papa bade.

We sat in the library while our parents took themselves into the parlor, entreating us only to "leave the door open as wide as a holy Bible."

Mr. Inman had begun to speak about his plans after graduation when Cassie entered the room with a tray of sweetmeats and two cordial glasses. As she moved to set the tray down upon the table, Mr. Inman's attention shifted to the book that rested there. As it happened, it was Homer's *Odyssey*, the same tome that Maria had read and that I had not opened since her death.

"Oh, Homer—most marvelous," Mr. Inman intoned. "Though you know Homer himself never wrote a word of it. Nor was he its creator. Not *per se*."

I knew all this and more about the blind poet but thought it prudent to say nothing. Mr. Inman, however, misunderstood my silence.

"Pardon me. Perhaps you do not like to read. Some ladies find it taxing on the eyes."

"But I do," I said quietly.

Cassie, having set the tray down beside the *Odyssey*, seemed unwilling to leave me alone with Mr. Inman; she stood sentry by the door. Catching sight of her lingering presence, and perhaps frustrated by my sudden reserve, Mr. Inman said, "*She's* a pretty little thing. Not young, though. I'd say about thirty. Am I correct?"

"I don't know," I said.

Mr. Inman now turned to our slave. "Come in, come in. I won't bite."

"What would you have with Cassie, Mr. Inman?"

He grinned. Perhaps he felt a certain proprietary right over both of us, now that our fathers had shared a glass of brandy. "Why, only to know whether she reads. Some of them do, these days, you know. They hide it from us. Here—" Mr. Inman lifted the tome and held it before Cassie. "Now, what does this say?" he asked, pointing a long, thin finger to the gilt letters on the cover.

Cassie glanced at me briefly before lowering her eyes. "I don't know," she replied.

"Come on, now," he objected. "I know you do. Read it. What's this word? Homer. That's right. And this letter. What is it? Surely the Boylstons have not been so negligent as to leave you in *darkest* ignorance?" He laughed at his own joke.

"I don't know, sir. Maybe an *A*," Cassie guessed. I saw tears well in her eyes, yet still I said nothing. Oh, why wouldn't Mr. Inman leave her alone?

Mr. Inman turned back to me. "They're all such good liars, Miss Boylston. Terribly good. We have something to learn from them, surely, if only we would suffer to be close to them long enough." Here, he actually pinched the nostrils of his nose.

I stood up. "Cassie," I said, masking my annoyance with Mr. Inman by my harshness toward her, "you may return to the kitchen."

Mr. Inman laughed. "Loyalty to your old mammy—it is most fetching. Most fetching, indeed."

"Mr. Inman, I'm sorry, but I have a frightful headache coming on. Please excuse me." I curtsied and left the room, leaving him to bow and join our families. I heard the rustlings of concern among them. Mortified, I ran into the kitchen just as Mr. Inman made my excuses to his parents.

Cassie was clearing up after us, and we both soon heard the carriage pull away. "Oh, Cassie! Dear Cassie!" I flew into her arms. "I have been such a fool. Such a terrible little fool."

She held me to her breast as I cried. I suppose I expected her to give me words of comfort, but instead she said, "You expectin' an argument, you won' get none from me, Miss Eliza."

6

I DID NOT SEE MR. INMAN THE following week, and it was with some relief that I thought courtship together a thing of the past. Consider my surprise, then, when a messenger appeared at our door carrying an invitation from the Inmans. It was lavishly engraved in blue ink and read, "Mr. and Mrs. Ralph Inman request the Honor of your Presence at a Soiree for their Son George Inman."

"Mama!" I called from the foyer. She entered from the library, where she had been discussing something with Papa. When I saw her, I proffered the invitation and said, "I can't believe it."

"What is it you cannot believe, Eliza?" asked Mama.

"I cannot believe that Mr. Inman would continue to pursue my acquaintance after everything that has happened."

"Why, what has happened? I heard you told him that you had a headache."

"He was abominably rude to Cassie. I hold it not gentlemanly to mortify a poor servant for no good reason. Surely you must have overheard."

"Oh, somewhat," she said vaguely, shrugging her narrow little shoulders. "But one mustn't make more of things than they are."

I moved away in slow and stately fashion, only to fly to Cassie the moment I was out of Mama's sight.

She was placing a loaf of bread in the oven. The kitchen was hot, and perspiration dripped from her forehead.

"Cassie?" I asked. "What think you of Mr. Inman? Be direct with me."

Cassie shrugged.

"Well, I myself find him everything elegant and charming. And yet—is there not something self-satisfied and cold in his eyes? That is my question."

She turned to me, set her bread down, and stood to her full five feet. Then she shivered.

"You wan' Cassie tell you what she tink? Really tink?"

"Of course."

"Well," she began. "'Ees hollow. Dere nutteeng inside." She tapped her own breast. "Maybe some garbage."

I smiled. Cassie's judgment came as no surprise. "And in demeanor? Some days I think him quite handsome."

Here, Cassie made her feelings known by a *frisson*. "'Ee's as white as milk. And 'ees bot-tom 'ees *flat*. 'Eet 'ees da sorriest bottom I evah seen. A woo-man must 'ave someteeng to 'old *on to*, Mees Eliza."

Cassie's pronouncement on Mr. Inman's bottom was so passionate and so grave that I let out a sudden snort of laughter.

"Oh, Cassie," I said. "You are priceless!"

• • •

Mama began to prepare us all for the Inman's party. While I had a fine new gown to wear, she fretted that my brocade shoes were "not quite the thing." Louisa came to our rescue with a pair of her own, just my size.

Jeb would not attend, not even under another threat of disinheritance. One night, when I nearly collided with him in the dark hallway before retiring, he said, "Eliza. How can you think of attending such an event when the people of Boston starve? Those who strut their wealth while others suffer shall soon be hoist on their own petard."

"You're too *extreme*, Jeb," I whispered, as our parents had already retired, and I feared waking them. "I see no evil in the fact that the Inmans wish to celebrate their son's graduation."

"You sound like our mother." He smirked. "No, you don't see, I agree. But your blind eyes shall be opened soon enough. Mark my words, Sister."

Rebuked, I felt tears come to my "blind eyes" and blinked them back. "Oh, let's not quarrel. Please."

"All right." Jeb placed a hand affectionately on my shoulder. "Well, in any case, I have arranged to stay with friends in town for a few days. That should provide a good enough excuse for Mama. But Eliza," he said and suddenly grasped my arm. "What if he asks your hand in marriage? You're not tempted to say yes to Mr. Inman, are you?"

"I've received no indication that he is thinking anything of the kind. However, do you not think that a woman be a fool to deny him?"

"A woman would be a fool to accept him! Listen, Eliza." Here, my brother pulled me into his room. "I have since made inquiries. Mr. Inman has led a debauched and careless life. He has all the faults of his class, and then some."

"Are we not of the same class?"

"Perhaps. But I have decamped, and I pray you will come to your senses soon. We are on a sinking vessel, Sister, one not worth saving."

I was thoughtful, recalling Cassie's words about Mr. Inman. "Cassie likes him not."

At this, Jeb laughed. "So, you take your opinions from Cassie now, do you? Well, Cassie happens to be right."

I grasped my brother's hand and leaned in to him. "Cassie says his bot-tom is too flat, and that a woman must have something to hold on to. Is she right in this as well?"

"Sister!" Jeb shut the door, which had been slightly ajar.

"Shhh! Well, *is* she?"

"How would I know such a thing? Lord, Eliza, how you surprise me sometimes. But if the thought of Mr. Inman's flat 'bottom' is enough to keep you from marrying him, then know it to be the truest thing in the world."

7

THE MORNING OF MR. INMAN'S PARTY WAS quite hot. We had enjoyed a temperate spring, but summer had arrived with a vengeance. Mama fretted that our satin gowns were too heavy and that stains would form beneath my arms. She insisted I wear pads of wool batting there, which I refused to do. How would I dance, having to worry at every step that the soaking wool would fall to the floor?

"Oh, but what, then, shall prevent those unseemly stains? It is dreadfully hot!"

"Mr. Inman will simply have to accept the fact that in hot weather women perspire, just as men do, Mama."

Jeb, who passed us in the hall, placed his hand on his rear end, and I warned him away by lifting my eyebrows.

When it was time, Papa called for our finest carriage—that same barouche and four for which he'd sold Toby and Cato. It appeared before our house with a strange coachman, black as an Ethiop. He sat quite rigid and stared directly ahead, as if he wore the same blinders as did the horses. Perhaps he worried that his powdered wig would slide off his head.

"Who is that?" I asked Mama, as we stood poised on the front steps.

"He's one of the Royalls'. Isn't he fine looking? Your father borrowed him for the evening." Isaac Royall Jr. and his family lived at a grand estate called Ten Hills Farm, in Medford.

Just then, Papa joined us on the stairs. "Evening, my lovely ladies. Now, isn't that a fine sight?" He glanced at the coachman with a self-satisfied air. "There are now merely nine hills at Ten Hills Farm. For I have taken one."

"Apparently, he was a prince of some sort," added Mama. "Or so he avers to Mr. Royall."

"Poor man," I replied. "He was once a royal prince, and now he is but Prince Royall."

Papa snorted at my joke, but Mama did not find humor in it. "Indeed not. The Royalls feed him excellent well and even give him his own room in the slave quarters."

"Luxury, indeed," I said.

The day's sun descended beyond Watertown; the church bell rang six times. The streets were dusty from the extreme heat, and my mother glanced at her shoulders to see whether any dust had settled upon her. She flicked two fingers against her shoulder, did the same against mine, and finally seemed satisfied that we were both dust-free.

The coach took us through the center of town and then east, toward Charlestown. We passed the market, where vendors were packing up for the night, and the little octagonal courthouse, shining brightly yellow in the declining sun. We passed the meeting-house and Harvard College, now emptied of its students. It seemed odd to find no sailcloth tents, no mountebanks selling snake oil, no fat babies or boneless men or drunken groups of boys singing in the streets. The college was eerily quiet, and a little sad.

I espied a lone tutor, hardly older than I, walking between buildings, calico gown flapping. Suddenly I felt an unbidden panic at the thought that I might have to dance with Mr. Inman. I had

had only three lessons before my parents thought it imprudent for me to return to Boston.

"My ankle hurts," I said.

"Oh, nonsense, Eliza," Mama replied.

"It is stiff from sitting, I expect," said Papa illogically. "Roll it about this way and that. It shall pass."

By the time we arrived at our destination, however, it seemed that my ankle had managed to break itself between West and East Cambridge. I walked with a distinct limp, which I half believed to be genuine.

"Oh, gracious, Eliza. Straighten up," Mama said. "You look deformed."

My father grinned awkwardly as the Inmans' broad red door opened onto an elegant tableau.

•   •   •

I had been in many grand homes, but never had I seen anything quite like the Inmans'. The foyer was octagonal in shape, its floor not marble-painted wood but actual marble, laid in a black-and-white diamond pattern. Upon a carved center table flourished a bouquet of exotic flowers. And, as for our staircase, of which I'd always been so proud, it was nothing compared to that of the Inmans'.

I soon took leave of my parents to wander on my own. Sipping a glass of refreshing citrus punch that had been placed in my hand, I glided into the parlor in Louisa's shoes. Boys and girls milled about the punch bowl. I recognized many of them, though I could not recall their names. One of the boys I thought particularly handsome: he had dark, wavy hair and lovely hazel eyes. When I passed him, he raised his glass to me and smiled, but no one introduced us, and so I moved on into the garden. There, tiny lanterns were strung in rows upon the elms; they glowed in the dark like lightning bugs. Folding garden chairs, painted bright white, encircled perhaps three dozen round tables, each covered in Irish linen. Upon each table a cluster of candles flickered crazily within a hurricane lamp. By the light of the lamps and glowworms, children chased each other around the vast yard. The girls' white dresses and bobbing curls flashed in and out of sight. The boys, in dark costumes, were nearly invisible, so that one had the impression of several dozen little girls being chased by darting shadows.

I found a place among the tables where other girls my age already sat, accompanied by a chaperone. Ours was the new Mrs. Inman's sister, a sweet and smiling creature entirely ignored by us.

The girls at my table were in the midst of a conversation about homespun.

"Disgusting," one girl was saying.

"Indeed," said another.

"I shouldn't wear it if my life depended on it," said a third.

Then the first, who wore an aqua gown, changed the subject.

"Mr. Inman is handsome, is he not? His eyes are so very blue."

"They match your dress perfectly," said the second girl, in an emerald-green gown.

The girl in the aqua gown, whose name was Hannah Appleton, giggled, "Oh, you're right! They do!"

"Regard what a fine figure he cuts," the one in the emerald gown added, as the fine figure himself walked past our table, affecting not to notice our admiring stares.

This might have been the moment to reveal that Mr. Inman had been paying court to me, but I knew not what to say without sounding boastful, so I remained silent.

It was soon time to move to the parlor, where I found my dance card upon a table strewn with rose petals. I eagerly put it to use, my ankle having miraculously healed once I realized that I would be safer from Mr. Inman's attentions on the dance floor than off.

Papa had little use for dancing. After a requisite minuet with Mama, he went off to the library, where he was able to smoke a fine cigar and drink a glass of aged brandy with Mr. Inman.

Finally we heard the bell-like sound of crystal being struck by a silver utensil. Then, more and more glasses were struck, building into a cacophony of wavering notes, until the musicians ceased playing and George Inman took center stage. I took a place by Mama at the room's entrance. "My head pounds," I said. "I should like to go home."

"Go? Not before he speaks, certainly," said Mama.

"I'll call for the carriage," said Papa, suddenly behind us.

"Five minutes," hissed Mama, casting my father a significant glance.

Mr. Inman proceeded to thank his guests, his mates from school, and most of all his beloved family. Something about the jaunty way he stood, the way one hand made flourishes in the air, and the slow, sonorous intonations of his voice, filled me with abhorrence. *How smug he was!* I thought. *How vain! But why had I not seen this all sooner?*

"Let us go, Mama," I said. "I'm falling down."

Papa moved to call for our coach, but just as the butler opened the front door—just as I felt a warm, welcoming wind of freedom, the icy hand of fate held me back.

"Miss Boylston!"

I turned to find Mr. Inman moving swiftly toward me. Could I pretend not to have heard him? Impossible.

"Miss Boylston," he repeated, inches from me now. "In vain have I sought a moment alone with you. Might you do me the honor now?"

I looked about me for means of escape. Too late! "It is late, and my family—"

Mama nudged me in the small of my back with a hard, pointy elbow. Still, I did not move. My feet grew roots; my body became a tree, stolid and silent.

"Very well," Mr. Inman cried, full of brash good humor. "If Mohammed will not come to the mountain." Then, before all those who stood waiting for their carriages, Mr. Inman fell to one knee and grasped my hands in his.

"There is one thing I lack," he began. "One thing that shall make me complete. It is not a diploma, nor lodgings in Boston, nor a loving family. It is your hand in marriage, for you are the most charming woman of my acquaintance. Eliza Boylston, will you marry me, and make me the happiest man on earth?"

I swayed in place. Lightning had struck. I suddenly thought of Jeb, my beloved brother. To think that I had compared him, my fine and noble patriot, to this wretched specimen, this shallow dandy!

With as winning a smile as I could muster, I said, "You catch me off guard, Mr. Inman. I shall have to think about your kind proposal, if that is acceptable."

"But of course." He continued to smile. Was it only I who saw the mortification in the sudden tensing of his jaw? Murmurs of disapprobation spread through the foyer. And then, before any other disaster could occur, I was whisked out of that house and fairly thrown into the barouche.

If Mama's feelings could have wrapped themselves around my neck, I would have died in the coach before ever reaching home.

Papa said, "I simply cannot believe it, Eliza. I was under the impression that you fancied Mr. Inman. Hadn't he come to court you all winter? Why did you allow it if you liked him not?"

"I did like him—somewhat," I said. "But I thought—oh, but Papa! It was hardly prudent of Mr. Inman to ask my hand in marriage when he could have no assurance of my accepting him."

Here, my parents exchanged glances. Mama placed a forestalling hand upon Papa's arm. She might have hid the truth forever, but Papa was no liar.

"He did have reason, Eliza. Mr. Inman requested, and I gave him, my consent."

"You what? But—"

"Do *not* speak," Mama said.

I shivered at her murderous tone and lapsed at once into silence.

•   •   •

"How was the party?" Jeb asked me the following morning at breakfast. He must have returned sometime during the night. He ate ravenously, though I merely sipped my tea and picked at the edges of a single egg.

"Are you to marry Mr. Flat-bot-tom, then, and eat sweetmeats while Boston starves?"

"Don't you know? I should think all of Boston knows by now," I replied glumly.

"Apparently we Rebels do not travel in the first circles."

"No," I sighed. "I shan't marry George Inman. But he asked. He asked me before everyone. Mama and Papa, his friends—oh, Jeb!" Here, I leaned over and allowed myself a consoling embrace. "I would not give him a private audience, so he knelt in the foyer by the front door and asked for my hand in marriage."

"You would have done well to offer him your hand and nothing else."

"Jeb, don't tease."

"Well, what did you say?"

"I told him I'd think about it."

Jeb slapped his thigh. "Well done, Sister. Not clever, perhaps, but a genuine insult! A radical blow for the Cause!"

I was in no teasing mood, however. "Brother, how could he have imagined I loved him?"

"I'm sure he didn't imagine any such thing. Mr. Inman no doubt believed you would marry him despite your antipathy. Many girls would, you know."

"You're right. I hadn't thought of that."

Jeb looked at me, both humor and sarcasm gone. "It hardly matters, Eliza. Your rejection of Mr. Flat-bot-tom will soon seem a mere trifle."

"What mean you?"

"Sweet Sister," Jeb looked at me pityingly, as if I were a mere child. "We are nearly at war. People such as the Inmans have already begun to flee. The British ships patrol our waters and await the least provocation to attack us."

"Why do Mama and Papa not leave then?"

Jeb looked at me gravely. "Because they know they should have to leave me."

•   •   •

Jeb was right: by August of '74, a mere two months later, the Inmans' party seemed a century in the past. My anger at Papa, while it lasted well through the summer, soon faded in the face of far worse problems. The Royalls fled to Nova Scotia. Back in May, Governor Hutchinson had fled to England and was replaced by General Gage. That month, our own pastor, Reverend Winwood, fled, and Christ Church shut its doors. We were thus compelled to attend the First Parish meetinghouse just next door to our old church. It had a radical parson by the name of William Emerson, whose sermons in favor of independence had been published far and wide. Mama said that only "common folk" went there in their "vulgar homespun," and that she wouldn't be caught dead inside its walls. Thus, Papa and I found ourselves without her but with Jeb, who had been attending it for several months.

I could not believe that we would take up arms against our mother country, much less that she would attack us unprovoked. Yet on the morning of September 2, 1774, just as we were finishing breakfast, I heard a rumbling roar abroad. It sounded like the ocean had reached us and that an enormous wave was about to break. We stood up and moved to my father's study, where we watched through a window. The sound grew closer, more menacing, and in a moment we saw a sea of men pushing and jostling, their fists in the air. Many held sticks; a few held muskets.

"Cassie," Papa called, "fetch Juno and the coachman." The two Negroes soon appeared at the front door. This was a novel sight, but Papa seemed not to notice. "Run to the stables," he told them. "Bring back whatever wood you find. We must nail shut the doors and windows. At once!" The terrified coachman and young Juno fled as if they would ne'er return. But they soon reappeared carrying planks of wood, which they and my father then set to nailing across the doors and windows.

The massive tide of men had grown: I saw neither its beginning nor its end. As I stood by the window, one young farmer stopped, turned, and unleashed something from his hand. A thud pounded violently just to my right. The rock missed the window and bounced off the clapboards. We quickly retreated to the interior of Papa's study.

"They move. They move!" Papa informed us. "They stop not for us." Indeed, the tide rolled westward, though we learned of its destination only later, when news reached us that four thousand people had surrounded Lieutenant Governor Oliver's estate, Elmwood.

As soon as the men had passed our home, Papa went out in search of news. It was near noon when Jeb descended the stairs. In one hand he held an iron poker.

"Where go you like that?" Mama cried.

"To join them, of course." He then disappeared into the fray.

8

IF MY PARENTS HAD EVER DENIED JEB'S participation in the rebellion, they could not do so now. Papa watched Jeb through the parlor window and bit his own forefinger, the fleshy part, to keep from shouting. Mama ran to her chamber and did not reemerge till supper.

As I watched my brother disappear into the roiling tide, my heart lurched just as if he had been swept away at sea.

He was being swept away from us, that much was certain. For by August of '74 he had already met Elizabeth Lee. Within the month, he would leave us forever, to take up residence with his new wife in Braintree, Massachusetts.

Jeb didn't tell me he had met or fallen in love with Miss Lee, but I saw it for myself one day at meeting. We were sitting in our pew with Papa, who was already fanning himself with his hat, as it was quite close in the meetinghouse. I was doing my best to listen to Mr. Emerson's sermon when Jeb sneezed so loudly that one could hear it in the back row. A girl directly in front of us turned around, her brown eyes bright with mirth.

"Shh!" she said. But the way she looked at Jeb told me everything he had failed to tell.

The girl with the bright eyes was Judge Lee's daughter. She and her brother, Harry, lived several estates down the road to Watertown. Our families had never socialized with one another, for Judge Lee was known to be a liberal thinker, sympathetic to the Cause.

In brief, a match with Elizabeth Lee would have been a catastrophe. Jeb must have known as much, and yet the following day, he brought Miss Lee home. Mama did not wish to receive her.

"But you must see that you have no choice in the matter," I said to her.

"Oh, but I do! I do, indeed!" she cried, wagging her finger at some imaginary solution as she paced the library.

"Perhaps." I shrugged. "If you're willing to lose him."

"Lose him." Mama snorted. "How could we lose him?" But Mama relented, receiving Miss Lee in the parlor the following day. Mama, Papa, and I sat on one sofa, like grand inquisitors, and Jeb and Lizzie sat on a smaller sofa facing us. Jeb kept putting his hand on her knee, and she kept gently removing it. I tried to catch Jeb's eye to stop him, but he had no eyes for me.

"And your father?" Mama was asking. "Does he find himself thinking of leaving our shores?"

"Indeed, he leaves on the twelfth." Miss Lee smiled ruefully.

"That is very soon." Mama said it as if she would have liked to scold Judge Lee for fleeing so precipitately.

"Too soon," Lizzie agreed. "But there's nothing to be done. He must go."

"You mean you remain here without him?" Mama asked.

"I'm afraid so. My brother, Harry, leaves as well. He is determined to go to sea on a privateer ship." Lizzie's voice was sad, but she glanced at Jeb with a tender smile.

• • •

While the interrogation of Miss Elizabeth Lee continued, I endeavored to probe the mystery of her cheerful, confident air. Clearly the girl cared nothing for her appearance: Her shoes were scuffed, and she wore a homespun frock. She breathed and laughed far too easily to be corseted, and I shuddered to think that there might be nothing at all beneath her gown. Lizzie's ample bosom was but partially hidden by a lace neckerchief, and her hair—well! Those thick auburn waves seemed to have been pinned by a witless ape.

All this I saw, yet nothing did I comprehend. Rumors in Cambridge were that Mrs. Lee, Elizabeth's mother, had been the descendant of a king, yet here her daughter sat, having renounced all the superiority of her class, and corset-less as a milkmaid!

I sat there in my somber crepe gown, feeling old and vulture-like. Indeed, I felt like an old carrion bird beside a cheerful lark, though I was but seventeen. Partly this was because Cassie had pinned my hair so tight against my scalp that a headache threatened, and also because my corset allowed me only shallow breaths. I longed to stand up.

"And what, pray, shall you do with your papa gone? How shall you manage?" Mama was asking.

"My dear," Papa interjected tactfully, "I'm sure Judge Lee has made provisions."

"That's quite all right." Lizzie smiled warmly. "Papa has many friends."

"And Lizzie has me," Jeb stepped in. For the tenth time in as many minutes, he placed his hand on his beloved's knee. At his incorrigible touch, Lizzie suddenly burst out laughing.

"What's happening?" Mama inquired. "What is so amusing?"

"Nothing, Mama," I said gloomily. "Nothing at all."

• • •

"Well? What think you?" asked Jeb, once he had returned from walking Lizzie home. He sat by my side in the library.

"She seems a fine girl, and I'm very happy for you, Jeb," I began. I hesitated a moment before adding, "But I would be remiss if I did not follow my conscience and say that I am also concerned."

"About what, pray?" he asked. Oddly, Jeb did not seem surprised.

"I fear you're about to be drawn into a society from which there will be no returning. I fear we'll lose you."

Jeb regarded me. "You're right, Eliza. But it's a choice I make willingly. The truth is, it's been a long time since I felt myself at home here. A long time since I felt that I belonged."

"Oh, Jeb!" His words broke my heart, though I was not fool enough to think them untrue.

• • •

Several days after this conversation, Jeb bounded cheerfully up the path and into our parlor with news to share. "It is all settled. I have spoken to Judge Lee, and to Lizzie herself. What do you know but she has agreed to marry me! I have already written to Uncle Quincy, and he has just replied with a most wonderful offer."

The name of Uncle Quincy made Papa's eyes flash. We rarely mentioned the Quincy name in our household. My father was related to that notorious family, though he no longer acknowledged the connection. Apparently the colonel had offered Jeb and Lizzie a cottage on his property, in Braintree.

"We leave immediately after the wedding," Jeb said. "Oh, Eliza!" He grabbed me and twirled me about. My father, always a gentleman, proffered his hand, which Jeb shook gravely. "Thank you, Papa," he said. Jeb then approached our mother for a hug, but Mama had turned a cold shoulder. In Lizzie, I knew, Mama found everything she ardently disliked in a woman. Independence of thought, defiance of fashion, an outspokenness that bordered on the scandalous.

I agreed with Mama's judgment, and yet there was, mixed up in my disdain for Miss Lee, something akin to envy.

"Cassie!" Papa called. "Cassie! Can you fetch us the good Madeira? You know the bottle. The black one, with the thick punt? And some cordial glasses."

Cassie appeared in the foyer. "What happen?" she asked, confused by Papa's happy request and Mama's gloomy countenance.

"Jeb is to be married," I said.

Cassie flashed a broad grin at Jeb, who lifted her off her feet. "I'm all grown up now, Cassie," he said.

"I get de Madeira," she wriggled out of his embrace and departed, returning shortly with the requested items. My father poured four glasses.

"Well, my son, I don't know that I would have chosen her, but I wish you every joy." We toasted, and then Jeb embraced Papa. "Oh, Father. Just you wait. You will soon love her as much as I do. She is so—so very lovable!"

"Indeed, indeed. I am sure she is," Papa muttered.

Jeb kissed me affectionately on the side of my head and rose to leave. Once he was gone, I moved to console Mama, who was in a bad way. She paced and fretted in an agitated manner. "He and this Lizzie person will make the acquaintance of John and Abigail Adams, and the despicable Quincys shall have them round for coffee to discuss us as if we were vermin to be exterminated!" I had nothing to say, believing that Mama was entirely correct in her assessment of the matter.

·   ·   ·

One week later, we stepped forth for the first time since the riots, to attend Jeb and Lizzie's wedding. At first Mama refused to attend, but I pleaded with her until she came to her senses. There would be no celebration afterward—the couple planned to go directly to Braintree, for Cambridge was by this time too unsettled.

Without, it was fine and warm, but Cambridge town felt deserted. Saturday was typically a bustling market day. Now the market itself was empty save for a few local farmers selling their early harvests. I walked cringingly, my eyes cast down. At any moment I expected for us to be attacked. But Mama and Papa, in their wedding finery, strode with heads held high.

At the meetinghouse a small crowd had gathered. These were Lizzie and Jeb's friends from town, young people wearing home-spun and brown-stuff suits. Judge Lee stood beside Reverend Emerson, his bearing at once dignified and anxious. Lizzie's brother, Harry, stood beside his father. He was a handsome, restless youth who kept glancing about him. I turned into a front pew as Papa and Jeb approached. Finally, Elizabeth Lee stepped through the meetinghouse doors. She was dressed in a cream silk gown, with a sprig of fresh lavender in her hair. She smiled warmly at Jeb, whose eyes glistened with tears of joy. My father could barely contain his emotions, and when Mr. Emerson pronounced them man and wife, Papa blubbered like a child.

9

IMAGINE SILENCE, INTERRUPTED ONLY BY THE CREAK of old stair treads, and darkness. The scenes of happy ruckus and chases, the laughter and shouts punctuated by stern parental warnings, were now but a memory.

The silence and darkness were real. My parents and I seemed to have acquired a genteel distaste for one another, and I spent my days in Cassie's kitchen or in my chamber. As for the light, we didn't dare waste our candles on anything save the evening meal—if bread, butter, and a little tea can be called such a thing.

Without, nature was hardly kinder to us. Ceaseless snow and rain, rain and snow, all that autumn. Or perhaps Nature condoled with us, sending down her ceaseless tears.

At least Jeb was a faithful correspondent. He wrote us twice per week, letters addressed to all three of us. These letters were happy but vague, written to avoid offending rather than to impart information. For what could be said of Braintree, or of Lizzie, or the Quincys and Adamses, without giving offense? He thanked Mama and Papa for their wedding gift of Star, a beautiful Narragansett pacer whom Lizzie already put to good use, and he shared news of their various crops.

Toward the end of December, I received a letter addressed to me alone. In it, Jeb allowed himself to express his truest feelings:

Dearest Eliza,

Dare I speak of the firelight, and of the view over the sea from our window? You have never seen such beauty, I assure you. The Quincys are very kind—you would adore them. The colonel can be blustery, but he is sensible on all subjects concerning our present state of affairs, and most generous with his firewood and provisions of every variety. Lizzie misses her brother greatly, as he has recently set sail on the *Cantabrigian* and she doubts whether she shall have a letter from him anytime soon. I have met Mrs. Adams but not Mr. Adams, as yet, though I'm told he returns for Christmas. Mrs. Adams is a very useful sort of woman, unafraid of farm work. Her mind is equally active, and little escapes her shrewd attention. Yet she has a warm and passionate heart. I think you would like her a great deal, Eliza . . .

"Like Mrs. Adams!" Mama, who had been reading over my shoulder, exclaimed.

"Can you not give me a moment's privacy, Mama?" I shoved her slightly and continued reading.

But I must leave off now, since I think I hear the Great Lady herself at the door . . .

"You see. It is just as I predicted. The situation is most dire. Great lady, indeed!"

I set the letter down upon the hall table and turned to my mother. "Dire? Why, he sounds quite happy, Mama."

"Yes, well. We shall see how long *that* lasts."

•　　•　　•

It snowed all Christmas Eve and Christmas Day. I was languid with boredom, which remained unbroken by any sort of feast, games, or song. Nor was there a special meal to delight the senses, though Cassie did make an excellent stew. But a few days after Christmas, I received a most remarkable post. It was an invitation to a party in honor of the queen's birthday, addressed to me personally—by none other than Mr. Inman!

I was relieved that he harbored no grudge against me. I thought to decline the invitation, but the idea that I might enjoy good and plentiful food decided me in Mr. Inman's favor.

Mama, having been so fearfully burned in her previous attempts to marry me to Mr. Inman, affected indifference.

"Go if you like," she said. "Or don't."

"I think I shall go." I smiled at her. "Since he was so kind as to invite me."

•　　•　　•

On the morning of January 19, 1775, I found myself standing on the wet path before the house, basking in the sunshine. Indeed, it was so warm and bright it felt like spring.

Mama said I should wait indoors for the carriage, but I wished to feel the sun on my face, the warmth on my body. It had thawed, and great torrents of water continued to pour down from the trees and rooftops.

I arrived before Mr. Rowe's house around noon. Mr. Rowe was Mr. Inman's uncle and now employer. This house, which stood on Pond Street overlooking the harbor, was newly built and gleamed with fresh white paint. A party approached from the other direction, and a lively group—two boys, two girls—descended a carriage. They nodded to me coolly, and I recognized Hannah Appleton, the girl of the emerald-green gown, and the handsome black-haired boy with the hazel eyes. We went into the house together, I going slightly ahead. I heard the girls giggle behind my back. What did they laugh at? From within came the smell of savory cooking; my stomach growled. A butler took our capes and bonnets as we entered, and I looked about me: the parlor was prettily appointed with rich Turkey carpets and mahogany furniture. If there was starvation in Boston, one saw no sign of it here.

Mrs. Rowe, a plump, cheerful woman aged fifty or so, greeted us warmly. Then she announced, "I'm sorry to be the bearer of bad news, children, but Mr. Inman has taken ill and does not leave his bed—it is only a cold, but it came on too suddenly to send word to anyone." A murmur of disappointment went up among the small crowd. But Mrs. Rowe said, "Do stay. There shall be merriment and good things to eat. We mustn't let it all go to waste." Sighs of relief sounded all about me, and my joy at this news, so unfortunate for Mr. Inman, was very great indeed. The situation seemed to have been designed by Providence: excellent food and cheer and no Mr. Inman.

Almost the moment Mrs. Rowe left us, I was approached by the handsome lad with the hazel eyes, which now looked at me bemusedly.

"Hello," he bowed. "I'm Tad Hutchinson."

"Yes. You were at Mr. Inman's party." I curtsied, gave my name, and then inquired, "Would you be related to our former governor?"

"He's my uncle. Mama's brother."

"Ah. Well. I hope he had a safe journey?" There was nothing else to ask under the circumstances. The governor had fled in haste to England, having become—like all those then in power—a target of the people's rage.

"He did. We received word of his arrival only yesterday."

"It's a shame about Mr. Inman," I changed the subject.

"Indeed," Mr. Hutchinson replied. "It seems that illness, given this dreadful weather we've been having, is impossible to avoid. I expect he'll be up and about in a day or two."

A servant brought round some dressed oysters on a silver tray. I took one. It was savory and delicious. I took another, wishing that I could claim the entire tray for myself. Just then, the invalid appeared in the entrance to the parlor. He wore his robe and nightcap, and cut a silly, almost endearing figure. Miss Appleton and her friend pouted their sympathies for him.

"Dear friends," Mr. Inman announced with a wan smile. "Welcome. I'm most dreadfully sorry for this inconvenience, which I hope is more to myself than anyone else. This blasted cold has robbed me of the pleasure of your company. Please make free to enjoy yourself. I suspect that a few of you might be perfectly happy without me."

He cast his gaze about the room as the well-mannered young Tory children smiled and tittered. Mr. Inman suddenly withdrew a handkerchief from the pocket of his robe and sneezed into it. "Excuse me. I shall remove to my lair, so as not to importune you with my excretions." Espying me at last, he singled me out with almost ostentatious fondness: "Eliza, how good to see you. I see you've met my good friend Tad." I could not help but wonder why I, of all people, merited such kind attention, having treated Mr. Inman so unpardonably. Perhaps he was not so bad as I had thought.

"Yes. We're just now getting acquainted," Tad replied. Here, I caught what seemed to be a knowing look between himself and Mr. Inman.

Once Mr. Inman had returned to his chamber, Mr. Hutchinson excused himself with a bow. I thought he had gone off to flirt with the other ladies, but he surprised me by returning with a glass of wine.

"Why, thank you," I said. "You're very kind."

He then whispered conspiratorially, "Look." From behind his back, Mr. Hutchinson produced an entire plate of oysters.

"Oh, aren't you clever!" I cried.

"My tutors at Harvard didn't think so, alas," he laughed.

"How did you accomplish this?"

"The cook fancies me," he said wryly.

"Shocking!" I laughed, lips already closed indecorously about the oyster.

We continued in this easy vain, like old friends. Then, at a quarter to one, Mr. Rowe called for the carriages, and the party retrieved their hats and cloaks. We would all ride the short distance to the state house and then return from thence to our own homes. People exited in a bustle of excitement, for the ships would offer a grand salute at one o'clock.

"A moment," Mr. Hutchinson said. He made his way down the front path toward the waiting carriages. He said something to my coachman and then returned to the house. "Your Negro shall meet us there by and by. I'll take you in my own carriage. There is something I wish to discuss with you before we join the crowd."

By now I was puzzled but by no means alarmed. That this young man, nephew to our former governor, chose to single me out, flattered me. Perhaps he wished to ask me something of a personal nature, such as whether he might call upon me in Cambridge. With a gloved hand touching the small of my back, he led me up the stairs.

"Why do we go up?" I asked, turning round. The servants were nowhere in sight. Presumably they had gone to the kitchen below stairs to enjoy a moment's peace, now that everyone—or so they believed—had gone.

"I thought we might cheer the poor patient up. But there *is* something most particular I should like to ask you, Miss Boylston."

"Indeed?" I smiled. "I shouldn't like to miss the cannons."

"Oh, you shan't miss the cannons. Mark my words."

We had arrived at a chamber door halfway down the hallway. Mr. Hutchinson opened it. Before we entered, I thought, *Why has he not knocked?*

•　　•　　•

Mr. Hutchinson planted a kiss on my lips. My eyes were open, and I saw Mr. Inman in his dressing gown.

"Mr. Inman!" I objected, but instead of intervening on my behalf, he reached out and grabbed me roughly from Mr. Hutchinson. I screamed, but there was no one to hear. The servants were far below stairs. After a moment, Mr. Hutchinson said, "That's enough for you, chap," and drew me back to him. He leaned me against the bed, but I would not stand. My knees bent, and I sank to the floor. Mr. Hutchinson then fell directly upon me, and his hands moved roughly to pull up my petticoats. Mr. Inman stood up from the bed. He said, grim-faced, "Easy there! Enough!" I thought he would then stop his friend, and that this absurd prank, or whatever it was, would end.

It did not.

The chamber was warm from the fire. The shutters were closed upon the window, and the candle gave a lurid cast to the red Turkey carpet, upon which I lay. I felt the room spin above me as Mr. Hutchinson fumbled with his breeches buttons and then fell upon me.

"Oh, get off! Get off!" I cried.

But he would not budge. He held my wrists hard to keep me from pounding and scratching at his back. I shall never forget how he continued to smile with pleasure, even shutting his eyes at one point, as I sobbed and continued to shout my protest.

Mr. Hutchinson's attack upon me was of mercifully short duration. Afterward, he rolled off me, scant of breath. From the corner

of my wild eye, wet with tears, I saw that Mr. Inman, who now sat
at the edge of the bed, rubbed himself beneath his dressing gown.
He soon finished with a grunt, coughed, and then said, "Remove
her from my sight." Just then the cannon off the ships exploded;
the sound reverberated through the floor.

"You see," Mr. Hutchinson said, buttoning his breeches. "I told
you that you would not miss the cannons. It is just one o'clock. Let
us go."

I could hardly stand. But I would not ask for his help. I was
in pain. There was blood on my petticoat. But I crawled to the
door on all fours, then stood and fled the room, crying, "You think
I'll tell no one? Is that what you think?" Mr. Hutchinson hardly
seemed to notice my threat. But Mr. Inman, who had gotten back
into bed and pulled the covers over himself, replied.

"No. I don't think you will. No one will believe you. And, as for
myself—I've done nothing very wrong."

"Nothing very wrong? How dare you say so?"

"By rights you were mine, Eliza. *Mine*."

But I had already fled the chamber, disheveled and trembling.
Reaching the bottom of the stairs, I suddenly felt cold and faint. I
leaned on the newel post and considered calling for the servants.
But what would I say? Why was I there, alone? Why looked I in that
ghastly state? I found my cape, which hung in the hall armoire, and
was about to step abroad—to go where, I knew not. My carriage
had gone ahead. I had no money, no friend, and was ten miles
from home. In another minute, Tad Hutchinson came up behind
me, and I hurried out the door. The dirty, bustling street seemed
far safer than those elegant rooms within the Rowe house.

Mr. Hutchinson's coach pulled up before the house.

"Allow me," he said, offering to help me up into the carriage.
I shunned his proffered hand, and eventually the coachman, an
old Negro in a powdered wig, descended to help me up. The ride
was short, and we sat in silence. Upon arriving at the state house, I

mustered the courage to ask Mr. Hutchinson, "How long have you planned this? That is all I should like to know."

"Seven months," he said. "Since the night of the party. Apparently your fiancé was quite dismayed at your reneging on an agreement before all his family and friends."

I was about to say that I knew of no such agreement but then considered it beneath me to say a single word to my attacker. He noticed it not, however, but went on cheerfully, "I'll confess to some improvisation on my part, however."

I might then have leapt out of the carriage and suffered a broken ankle, when once more the coachman came to my aid. I hazarded in a trembling voice, "Would you be so kind as to fetch my coachman and carriage?"

"Certainly, miss," he said. "Follow me." I felt the old Negro's gloved hand press my elbow in support, as if he knew Mr. Hutchinson were not to be trusted, and I had a most terrible thought: perhaps the old coachman had witnessed other ladies in my sorry state . . .

"What? Not staying for the festivities?" Mr. Hutchinson called to me in a loud, petulant-sounding voice. I did not reply. Perhaps he wished to humiliate me further; thankfully, the cannon blasts and the general merriment all but drowned him out. No one noticed as I gratefully mounted my own carriage and sped off down Tremont Street, toward home.

10

MAMA MET ME IN THE FOYER. "GRACIOUS!" she cried. "You're home early! Why, what has happened?"

"Nothing, Mama. A slight indisposition, is all."

"No, indeed. You look as if you were run over by a carriage. Has something happened? Were you robbed?"

"No, no. I tell you, I am simply indisposed," I said, though I hardly managed to remain upright. "I shall ask Cassie for one of her teas." And, escaping as best I could, I went to find our slave. She was kneeling by the hearth, having just set something upon the coals. She turned; seeing my stricken face, her own drew tight. I lowered my eyes for shame. She put her rough little hand upon my forearm and felt my trembling through my cape. Then, slowly, she looked up at me and said, "What dey do to you?"

"Oh, Cassie!" I threw myself into her arms. She gently led me to my chamber, undressed me, and let down my hair. She left me for a time and returned with a foul-smelling tea. Sanicle, she said. I knew not what it was, but I drank it. Only when Cassie had succeeded in making me comfortable, and after shooing away my concerned parents, did she sit and take my hand. She stroked my cheek. Cassie then asked, "Who did dis?"

I could not reply; I wished to, but their names would not form on my lips.

"I shall poison dem. You trust Cassie. She know 'ow to do 'eet." With these words in my ears and her rough hand holding mine tight, I soon fell asleep, finding brief comfort in oblivion.

Cassie woke me early the next morning with more of that foul concoction. She said I must drink it if I was not to get with child. Setting her tray down on my little dressing table, Cassie gently shut my chamber door and patted my legs. "You be well soon, Mees Eliza."

I was able at last to tell her who had attacked me. At the mention of Mr. Inman, Cassie began to spit curses in her strange tongue.

"Oh, Cassie. I feel so ashamed. So—stupid. And Mr. Inman—he stood by the bed, watching—rubbing himself." I grimaced and shut my eyes once more, this time against the image I feared would never leave my mind.

"Peegs," she said. "But you *knew* what men can do, didn't you, Miss Eliza? Did your Mama nevah tell you dis?"

"No," I admitted. "I had no notion that men would ever, would ever want—"

"You are but a babe," she said, though not harshly, caressing my hair as she said so. "You know nutteeng of de world. So, now I tell you a story, a real story, and you learn how we wee-men suffah. You learn how we are *strong*, too."

Cassie proceeded to tell me the story of when she first came from Africa to my father's plantation in Barbados. She was but twelve years old. She spoke of her first days and weeks on the plantation, in a shack with her mother, sister, and a dozen other people. Her papa had died aboard the ship. There was no floor in the shack, no beds, no shoes. Thankfully, the weather was temperate.

Papa employed two vicious overseers at the time, and Cassie feared them. She tried to be invisible and for some time thought she was. But one morning, she was so overcome with fatigue that she fell back asleep after the bell had already rung. Everyone had left for the cane fields.

Cassie awoke to dark shadows above her: the overseers. They were white men with lean bodies and cruel eyes. Perhaps thirty or even older. She sat up to dress, but one of them reached out and pressed her back onto the floor, his hand braced between her small breasts.

They reached under her shift and groped between her shaking legs. Then they took turns with her body. When they were finished, they told her to get dressed and into the fields, and that if she breathed a word they would kill her. Ten months later, at the age of thirteen, she gave birth to a baby girl, but the babe died within a few days.

"Oh, Cassie," I said, forgetting my own misery for a moment. "These were my own father's men?"

"Yes, Miss Eliza. Your own fadder's men. But he don't know what goes on when he not dere. 'Ee don't even tink about 'eet."

"Well, I shall make him do so," I said with conviction, though I had not the strength to stir from my bed.

I lay back on my pillows. Cassie caressed my hair, combing her rough fingers and long, ragged nails through it. Her nails gently scraped my scalp and made it tingle.

"You shall be well 'een time, Miss Eliza. You not de first, nor de last, woman who have dees happen. And some day soon you meet a good man. Like my Cato was. A good, *decent* man—"

Suddenly, there was a knock at my door, and we started. It was Mama.

"Oh, Cassie. I didn't realize you were already here. Are you better this morning, my dear?"

I grasped Cassie's hand. "A little, I believe. Cassie has made a tea that has eased me greatly."

"I'm glad. Shall we see you at breakfast?"

"Not today, Mama. Tomorrow, perhaps. I shall no doubt be much better tomorrow."

"I'll tell Papa you are better. He worried all night."

My dear papa, who allowed little girls to be ravished on his own property. Once Mama had left, I entreated Cassie to tell me the end of her story.

"So, what happened to those men? Were they ever punished?"

"Punished?" Cassie's eyes widened. "Oh, no." Here she flashed her broad white teeth. She said, "Mama and I make dem someteeng good to eat. *Very* good. Dey puke for two days. And den dey die."

11

WITHIN A FEW DAYS, I WAS OUT of bed, and in a week's time I was to learn that I was not with child, for which I thanked God in Heaven. But I was beset by terrible cramps, and so retreated to bed once more. Cassie told me several times, "Bring dem heah. Cassie give dem someteeng very good to eat."

The two culprits, however, vanished directly after the party, and we knew nothing of their whereabouts until spring, when we learned that Mr. Inman was with General Howe and the British army in Boston, and that Mr. Hutchinson had left our shores to join his family in England.

Our situation by this time—February of '75—was quite degraded. The weather was dreary, the markets were empty, and there was little to eat except for cod, biscuits, eggs, grain, and what preserves Cassie had been prudent enough to store that summer past.

My seventeenth birthday had come and gone without fanfare. Mama now thought it all but hopeless that I should marry, as those men who had not fled had either joined the army or stood in wait to fight.

Thanks to my dear Cassie, I survived the attack upon my person. Yet my soul was in turmoil. I had nightmares, and feared leaving home. Upon stepping abroad, my breath caught in my chest, and I thought I would faint. Worst of all, I had begun to feel a roiling anger that knew no outlet—toward Papa, once more, who'd given Mr. Inman his consent without informing me. Toward Mama, who, I now believed, surely knew of this consent.

And yet, he had been right about my not telling anyone—for who might I tell who would believe me? Who might I tell without doing irreparable damage to myself? I knew the answer well enough.

When, two weeks after the incident I have described, my mother announced that Mrs. Gage, wife of Governor General Gage, was hosting a ball, for the Loyal and Friendly Society, I replied coldly, "I shall not go."

"You *shall* go," she said. Mama then called to Papa. "Mr. Boylston!" She moved out of the front parlor to knock on his study door. Papa was at his desk, peering through his spectacles at the day's broadside. He wore that look of dismay we had come to know quite well. "Eliza says she will not attend Mrs. Gage's ball."

Papa removed his spectacles and gazed up at me: "I should think you'd be glad to stir from this house; I imagine there'll be good food and fine wine. Good society, too. May I ask why you avoid the event?"

"Papa," I began, my voice quavering with emotion, "those boys who remain in our midst are criminals and cowards. The very dregs of your so-called good society. They—"

But before I could say more, I felt a swift jab at my ankle— Mama had kicked me! I opened my eyes wide and stared at her.

"Eliza. I begin to think there is something profoundly wrong with you."

I turned to face her squarely. "Being your child," I said with slow, cold fury, "I would not be surprised."

As I fled up the stairs to my chamber, I heard my father ask, "Do you think that was really necessary, Margaret?"

"Indeed it was," she said. "Have you not noticed how intractable, how incorrigible, she has become of late?"

"But to say that our boys are criminals and dregs—perhaps there is a reason. Perhaps she was insulted by one of them at the Rowe's house. The child looks far too pale . . ."

Here, I ceased to hear them, having reached my chamber door in tears, my ankle still smarting from where Mama had kicked me.

•   •   •

Mrs. Gage's event was the last such event my parents were ever to attend. Every day thereafter, we expected an attack—instigated by Mrs. Gage's own husband—and remained as prisoners within our own home.

Our provincial congress was ready for war. It had already authorized the purchase of guns, munitions, powder, and cannon. Then, on February 26, a confrontation occurred between General Gage's troops and the Salem militia, under the command of Timothy Pickering. That such a confrontation might soon occur in Cambridge, we had no doubt. Once more we nailed the planks across the windows and doors.

The following week, we received a disturbing letter from Braintree:

> . . . as we were able to clear two fields before winter, I find myself free to focus on the fate of our country and shall likely soon join the Cambridge militia. This shall bring me in closer contact with you. Before then, however, I hope to plant two gardens. Apples we have in abundance, and flax as well. Lizzie shall be kept busy in my absence. She already loves Star greatly and rides him near every day.
>
> Rest assured, Mama, Papa, that my joy in choice of partner is complete. She is my helpmeet, my dearest friend.

I have little doubt that my wife could run the entire North Parish on her own, were circumstances to require it of her.

Then, scrawled across the bottom of the page, the paragon herself had written,

Dear Mama, Papa, and Eliza—

I am flattered by my husband's lavish compliments, but what he could mean I know not. Let it not be a mote in your mind's eye. I shall scold him roundly for it by and by. Ever yours, Lizzie

Mother found this letter vexatious in the extreme. "Run the North Parish? What can he mean? Richard," she said, turning to my father, "know you what he could mean by this? Imagine, leaving a woman alone on a farm—I doubt very much whether they even have a servant! Oh, how he must secretly suffer!"

"Secretly suffer?" I objected, picking up a spoon. Cassie had served us a dinner of stewed cod and vegetables. "Jeb seems perfectly contented. Nay, more than contented. But he shall fight, if there's a war."

Mama ignored this last statement, which perhaps was just as well. "But only think, Eliza—a cramped little house, and no maid. How slovenly, how chaotic, it must be."

"Perhaps Lizzie makes up for her slovenliness with her industriousness. I expect Jeb believes there's more virtue to a woman than keeping a neat house."

"Indeed, there is not!"

Mama's fervency had an unfortunate effect: my father and I looked at each other and began to laugh, which neither of us had done in a long time. It was good to see that I still knew how.

12

ON TUESDAY, APRIL 19, 1775, WE WOKE to cries in the street that the British army was coming. There was pandemonium without as a crowd of men raced to the bridge across the Charles, to remove its planks.

We remained inside, breathless with anticipation, until that afternoon, when Papa made for Wood Street, Mama shouting after him not to go. There, he learned that the British had replaced the planks on the bridge and crossed over. They were now north of us, where General Heath's men had confronted Rebel militia, and several men had been killed, among them one we knew: John Hicks, a local tradesman.

My father did not return to the house immediately, but first went round to the stables. Papa owned several muskets and must have decided that the threat of his own slaves turning against us was less great than the British menace, for he armed our old coachman and our young stableboy Juno. Three other young Negro men Papa welcomed into our home.

"Cassie! Make up the beds!" he called. Cassie approached Papa, who stood in the hallway by the kitchen.

"Sir," said Cassie. "What beds do I make, sir? We have only Master Jeb's and dose of de girls."

I knew Cassie's concern: Was my father actually requesting that she make up the family beds for our slaves?

"Yes," he replied. "We have 'em, let's use 'em! By God, I'll not stand on ceremony now."

Slaves in the family beds! I never imagined I would see such a thing. Cassie made up the beds with the family's fine linens and bolsters. Of course, Cassie bathed the boys first and gave them clean nightshirts to wear—she was having none of that stable filth in the house. I happened to enter the kitchen at an inopportune moment and caught a glimpse of two slick, black bodies, heads bent down, knees up, in two tin tubs, like steaming puddings.

That night, my mother insisted that I sleep in their chamber. Though I could not step abroad without quaking, I felt no fear of our stableboys.

"I am hardly worth hanging for, Mama," I sighed, staring with dismay at the narrow sliver of bed next to Mama.

But Mama, who was sitting up with her nightcap on, was not to be gainsaid. "Some of our citizens have lost all compunction about committing hanging offenses," she fretted.

"It's well they're not citizens, then."

"Shhh! I sleep!" Papa complained.

I slept restlessly for several hours until Mama sat bolt upright, eager to make certain that the tall chest we had shoved against the chamber door had not budged.

We survived the night unmolested, but the news that reached us in the morning unsettled us all. Men were fighting and dying in Lexington. We knew not how many Rebels had been killed but heard that eighty regulars had perished.

At last, the worst had happened: War had come. On April 20, thousands of men descended upon Cambridge to camp on the Common. From them, my father learned that Rebels had taken possession of Roxbury. Men we knew had died. But I don't think we truly believed we were at war until the following day, when the wounded began arriving in wagons, and neighbors began to fashion makeshift hospitals in their homes.

Lizzie wrote to us at once, begging that we do the same, but Mama would not hear of it.

"And invite smallpox and all manner of disease within? Certainly not."

My heart went out to our brave militia, and my impulse was to help them. Yet, unlike Lizzie, I should not have known where to begin, even had Mama allowed it. I had never tended the sick, or dressed the wounded. I imagined I would faint at the sight of their blood.

·　　·　　·

Every day, my parents spoke of leaving; every day, I wished even more that we would stay, that I might pluck up my courage and help those boys. Then, on the nineteenth of May, a messenger came to our door with the news we had so dreaded: Jeb was in Cambridge. He had arrived at Colonel Prescott's regiment the night before and would find a way to visit us that afternoon. Meanwhile, we heard from another source that twelve thousand Rebels surrounded Boston, essentially making prisoners of all those within.

Jeb did not visit that afternoon, or the next, but let us fret and pace until I determined to set out to find him. Then, late that Friday, just as we had sat down to a dish of tea and stale biscuit, I espied him through the wavering windowpanes, musket and canteen across his back, loping happily up our walkway. He seemed older than I remembered, more manly. His fair hair, loosely plaited, had been tied with a linen string. Oh, he was a welcome sight!

"Mama! Papa! It's Jeb!" I called.

We all ran out to meet him, even Cassie. Jeb lifted Cassie off the ground as he embraced her. "Oh, I'm surprisingly glad to see you all."

"Jeb, where have you been?" I scolded him. "We waited and waited."

"We've been camped in Cambridge, but I've been loath to come. Smallpox has broken out among the men, and you've not been inoculated."

"Nor have you," I reminded him. But he shrugged this comment off, adding, "Our boys are at a fever pitch and are ready to fight."

"Oh, do not talk about war!" our mother cried.

"But tell us," I said, grasping my dear brother's hand, "tell us all about married life. For if Mama is right, I shall never know those joys myself."

"Eliza, it is the most marvelous thing." He sat down there on the stoop and gazed toward the river. All the trees were in pale-green bud, and the stalwart daffodils had pushed their way up through the hard dirt. Everywhere in nature, life was ready to burst forth. "More marvelous than anything—we are wildly happy. Half our days are spent laughing, and the other half—"

I nudged Jeb just as Papa raised his eyebrows.

"I was only going to say that the other half is spent figuring out this farming business. Sister, our failures at farming send us into peals of laughter. But Eliza—you must come to see our farm. It is so lovely. The ocean is just there, beyond our window." Here, Jeb waved one hand out to our own gentle Charles, as if his mind's eye saw a vast coastline. "We have all manner of birds and sea creatures. And we can even make out the ships in Boston, and the North Church spire. The Quincys are very kind, and we have now finally met all the Adamses—"

"No Adamses, no Quincys," our father waved away the unsavory drift of the conversation.

"Very well, Papa. I have only to say that they have been most amiable."

"And Elizabeth, she is well?" I inquired. It pained me for Jeb that Mama had not asked after Lizzie, though it gave me little pleasure myself to do so. Each time I heard of Lizzie nursing the wounded, or digging a field, or delivering a child, a strange, sinking feeling invaded me.

"Oh, yes," Jeb grinned. "Marvelously well." Jeb looked as if he would be happy to elaborate, but I grunted an acknowledgment and said, "Come, let us go in. Cassie. Make us some tea." She nodded and left us. Mama and Papa followed her.

"Oh, my Lizzie!" said Jeb once they were gone. "A finer woman could not be found. She is perfect, my dearest friend. If only you knew."

I could not contain myself a moment longer.

"Lizzie, Lizzie, Lizzie!" I cried bitterly, and burst into tears.

"But Eliza, what on earth's the matter? I thought you liked her."

"I do like her—well enough."

Jeb embraced me warmly. "You poor, poor dear. You're depressed. I knew it when I first beheld you, so tired and pale. Are you very unhappy?"

"Oh, no," I said, wiping my eyes. "I would not burden my brother with my misery." *A little lonely without you, perhaps.*

"What word have you of the invasion?" I changed the subject. "What is it they say? Oh, it would be so good if they all returned to their ships and the sea."

"No," Jeb shook his head. "We've put the day off long enough. It must come. I, for one, am ready."

"I shall never be ready for the day you put yourself in harm's way."

Jeb turned to me as he moved toward the door, eager to be off. "Promise me one thing," he said. He took my hands.

"What is it?"

"Promise me you will get to know my Lizzie. It is my particular wish, Eliza."

Jeb's request surprised me, but I said at once, "I will. Of course."

I had little to offer Jeb, but on an impulse I removed one of my gloves. I kissed it and gave it to him. "They say objects can have magical powers. I pray this one does."

"I shall keep it close, Eliza. As I will your loving spirit."

I hugged and kissed him tenderly. He soon bade Mama and Papa good-bye. I watched him jog off down our path, his golden plait dancing behind him.

13

THURSDAY, JUNE 15, 1775. THOSE FAMILIES THAT had not already fled did so now, and our own family began to prepare for departure. We would remove to my Uncle Robert's house. Uncle Robert, my mother's brother, was a wealthy widower who lived in Portsmouth, New Hampshire. Mama told me that they had procured some crates, which would be delivered on Saturday.

"I shan't leave Jeb," I said.

Mama replied coldly, "Jeb has left *us*."

I said nothing, but a wild thought occurred to me: that I might decamp for Braintree and stay with my sister-in-law. But it was a thought I quickly discarded, for what might my flight serve but to hold her back?

The Ruggles family was leaving the following day, and Louisa came to say good-bye. I had entirely forgotten to return her shoes after the Inman party, and she had not requested them. Now, when I went to retrieve them, the very sight of them filled me with disgust.

"Thank you for loaning these to me," I said. "I apologize for having kept them so long."

"Oh, that's all right." Louisa smiled. There followed an awkward silence. Things unspoken hung heavy between us. I asked

Louisa did she wish to sit, but she said that her family's departure was imminent. She had but a few moments to spare.

"It seems everyone is leaving. I'm surprised your family remains."

"We stay for Jeb."

"Oh, yes," she said. "Papa says that anyone who remains now deserves his fate."

"Does he?"

"Well," she continued, oblivious to my stiffening posture, "everyone we know has departed. The Olivers, the Royalls, the Brattles. Why, just last week I was grieved to learn that Mr. Hutchinson has already departed for England."

I stared at her. "You know him?"

A look of pleasure spread across her soft face. "Oh, yes. I have twice enjoyed his company this year. His hazel eyes I shan't soon forget. And he is so very charming. Do you not think so? But, oh—perhaps you've not met him."

I now found myself in some danger of revealing what I knew, and was held back only by the conviction that Louisa would sooner blame than comfort me. However, I felt an urge to speak at least a partial truth:

"Louisa, Mr. Hutchinson is not who you imagine him to be. I'm glad he has departed."

"Glad—Mr. Hutchinson? Why say you such a thing?"

"I dare not reveal my reasons. But you may trust my good word."

"Well, Eliza," she stared at me, as distant in spirit as she soon would be in miles. "I wished to end as friends, since we are parting, perhaps forever. But I must say, our friends were all very shocked that you rejected Mr. Inman. Some of our friends even began to whisper that—that you would wind up an old maid." Here, her plump little nose turned up to confirm her courage in telling me the truth.

At this, I let out a shrill laugh. "Old maid? I'm glad you think so. I've known precious few men, Louisa, and I care for none besides my Jeb. As for women," I looked pointedly at her, "I find myself less inclined to like them, either."

"Oh, Eliza!" she cried. "I take my leave of you."

"There is nothing I would more willingly part withal," I said, stealing a favorite line from the Bard.

Once Louisa had left, I thought, *Yes, I am very glad she is gone from our midst.*

•   •   •

Saturday, June 17, 1775. The morning sun blazed through my chamber windowpanes; it would soon be very hot. I emerged from my room to find several large crates in the hallway.

When I descended the stairs, I found yet more crates. Our stableboys were in the house once more, their rough hands rolling our fragile china in kitchen cloths. They then stripped our beds of their linens and coverlets; these would be used to wrap fragile items as well. Mama and Cassie moved from chamber to chamber, gathering up as much as the crates would hold. Those items we could carry would go in our trunks; the rest we would store out of sight in the cellar, in hopes they would remain unmolested while we were gone.

In the dining room, I took a dish of tea from the sideboard.

"Out of the fat, into the fire," Papa said. "Portsmouth shall have no more food, and no more love for us, than Cambridge does."

"But what of Jeb?" I insisted.

"Your brother's a fool," Papa replied. "But, as he's chosen his path, so must we choose ours."

I turned my back upon Papa and moved out of doors. There, heedless of the bilious yellow blanket of pollen that covered our steps, I sat myself down. Not eight in the morning, and the air already felt too heavy to breathe. The trees swayed with a slight breeze, shaking more pollen dust down upon me and everything beneath them.

Small boats upon the river sailed languidly by, and a couple or two strolled the road, heading toward the village. A child darted in front of us, chasing after a red ball that gathered speed and bounced across the street, toward the river. He laughed and shouted to some friend, unseen by me. These simple, natural sights might once have gladdened my heart, but they did no such thing now.

I soon moved off toward our apple orchard. As I perched on a stool and was watching the robins peck the grass, I heard the first cannon. I stood and ran inside, through the kitchen door and into the parlor, where I found my father, mother, and the three stable-boys huddled together. At their feet a vase lay shattered. It seemed the shock of hearing cannon had made one of the boys lose his grip upon it.

"Cassie!" Mama called. Cassie came and picked up the shards and swept the porcelain dust that had flown across the floor. But when she finished, she remained in the parlor with us. Mama did not object. Papa then went into the foyer and grabbed the musket by the front door. He said he was going to town for news.

Papa was gone a long time—an eternity. When he finally arrived back at the house, his countenance was grim. "Howe and Clinton lead the attack upon Breed's Hill. The Rebels have run out of ammunition. Reinforcements stand at Charleston Neck but will go no farther. It is said—"

"Enough!" Mama put her hands over her ears, then balled them into fists and squeezed her eyes shut. "I shall hear no more. No more!" She fled the parlor, leaving us to await further news.

•　　•　　•

We waited in silence. Cassie, needing something to do, went back and forth with refreshments, which we did not touch, until she finally sat herself down on the sofa to wait. She took my hand in hers. Together, we bent our heads in prayer. At around five, the sounds of cannon fire tapered off. By six, all was quiet. Too quiet. The world felt suddenly empty, and in the silent void I felt my heart bang against my chest.

The sun had gone down, the heat of the day had abated. Papa said he would go into town once more for news. He had just opened the front door when we espied a dirty young lad running up the road toward us. The boy, breathless, stopped before my father, glanced at our house, and then pulled a folded paper from his pocket. Papa gave the boy a penny and watched him move off down the walkway before he unfolded the paper.

Papa read the writing on the paper. Then he sank down onto his knees and crawled about helplessly. "God in Heaven," he looked up, "why?"

I stood and stared at my father, unwilling to move toward him, as if news could not reach me from such a distance.

Papa made as if to rise, then fell back again upon his knees. "I can't . . . can't tell her."

He began to howl, and at this sound I unfroze.

"Papa!" I cried.

"Never, never," he repeated. Then, seeing me, he grimaced. "Oh, go away, Eliza!"

"No, Papa."

I bent down to touch him but he withdrew from my touch. Cassie gently pulled me away from him.

"Come," she said. "Leave 'eem alone." She took me by the hand and led me up the stairs to my chamber.

Suddenly I felt as if I were choking. I put a hand to my throat.

"Cassie, I can't breathe."

"Don' speak, Miss Eliza. Da breaf knocked clear out of you."

I let her undress me and put me to bed. Then, instead of leaving, she removed her shoes and climbed upon the bed and held me as if I were a small child. She caressed my hair and I curled into a tiny ball and put my thumb in my mouth. I closed my eyes and would not open them.

Sometime later, perhaps several hours later, hearing a noise below, Cassie woke, waking me as well. She exited my chamber. I placed a dressing gown about me and entered the dark hall, to catch a glimpse of Lizzie's limp form endeavoring to climb the steps as two men half carried her toward Maria's room.

"I am well," she kept saying, "I am well." But she was covered in blood and dirt.

•   •   •

Cassie descended into the kitchen, returning with a bowl and pitcher. With these she disappeared into Maria's room. I should have gone to help, but my will was paralyzed. Soon I heard more feet upon the stairs. Looking down, I saw Papa at the base of them. He held Jeb beneath the arms, and a man I did not know held my brother's dusty feet.

I moved to the stairs, but Papa, breathless, called up to me: "Eliza, return to your chamber. I beg of you." I saw my brother's face, eyes closed in eternal sleep. His chest was bloody. A white kid glove, stained red, stuck out of his waistcoat pocket.

I returned to my chamber but did not sleep. I sat upon the bed, in a paralysis of indecision and shock. Should I go to Mama? Lizzie? I wanted Cassie to return to bed and hold me in the dark. But Cassie did not return to me, and I knew she was giving what aid she could to Lizzie. The moment dawn lightened the sky beyond my window, I rose and went to Jeb.

He lay on the bed in clean clothing, his hair combed, his hands crossed upon his chest. Someone had done this. *Cassie*, I thought. No one else could have.

Papa sat by the side of the bed. He had been weeping; tears ran down his face, unchecked.

"Where is Mama?" I asked.

"Dr. Bullfinch is with her. He has administered something, I believe. She sleeps sweetly—" and with this thought, he began to weep again.

I glanced back at Jeb. He looked as if he, too, had fallen asleep and would soon wake. But never had he been that tidy or that still. I moved toward him and put my head on his chest. I touched his hair, which had been combed into a neat plait.

"My darling, my darling," I murmured. I kissed him: he was quite, quite cold.

Papa wept. He then pulled himself together enough to murmur, "If you see Lizzie, tell her I should like to have a word in the parlor."

By ten o'clock, when there had still been no sign of Lizzie, I finally knocked upon Maria's chamber door and entered. Lizzie was still asleep, her long auburn hair flowing all about her white shoulders.

Hearing a noise, Lizzie abruptly sat up. She looked about her, disoriented, and murmured, "I was just dreaming that Jeb and I—"

With no warning, she began to sob.

"Papa wishes to see you in the parlor," I said, for her tears, rather than move me, turned me to stone. There would be no telling what depths of despair I might feel, had I allowed myself to mourn as freely as she. "Cassie is cleaning your gown. It was—very soiled. In the meanwhile, you may take one of mine."

"I wish to see Jeb."

"Papa is with him."

She stared up at me, her eyes wild.

"I *shall* see him, and I shan't wait to dress. If your father wishes to see me in my shift, so be it." She stepped from the bed, hair loose, her ample bosom showing beneath her shift. I fled at once, to warn Papa that Lizzie, undressed, arrived.

I decided to check upon Mama and found Dr. Bullfinch within, sitting by her bed with his hand upon Mama's wrist. Her arms lay helplessly by her sides, and her eyes were now open, though she appeared to see nothing.

Dr. Bullfinch stood to greet me.

"How is she?"

He shook his head.

"Very low, I'm afraid. And you, Miss Boylston? Do you wish me to attend to you? I have laudanum—it is very effective."

"No, thank you. I am well enough."

I curtsied and left the chamber. Standing in the dark hallway, unsure of where to go next, I suddenly felt as if I were in a small bark, lost upon a dark sea, unmoored, and that those around me were as flickering candles upon a distant shore.

•   •   •

Tuesday was Jeb's funeral. It was held at King's Chapel in Boston. Other families of fallen boys were there as well. Colonel Prescott arrived toward the end of the service and condoled with us a short while. Before taking his leave, he handed Lizzie a letter. She read it, hardly breathing. I should have liked to know the words she read, to hear the voice she heard speaking to her from the page. Perhaps, hearing Jeb's voice, I would begin to feel—for nothing touched me then. In this I shared something with Mama, who walked ramrod straight, as if she had ceased being human altogether.

Many guests gathered at our house after the funeral. No one seemed to care that crates stood everywhere. Papa's library was half-packed, and piles of books were strewn about in tall piles. I drifted silently among the guests, thinking how our friends—those who remained in Cambridge—must have pitied us our Rebel son. Once the guests had left, Papa spoke to Lizzie for a long while, periodically weeping with her. They were as one in the openness of their grief.

I stood at the base of the stairs, peering into the parlor, unseen by them.

"But I insist," Papa was saying. By the slow shake of her head, I gleaned that Lizzie refused whatever Papa had offered.

Cassie soon passed me, coming through from the kitchen. She did not stop but moved to attend Papa and Lizzie. When she left the parlor, holding two mugs, I moved to her and asked, "What do they speak of?"

Cassie hesitated a moment. "He tell her she must come to Portsmouth. Braintree 'ees too dangerous now. But Miss Elizabeth, she refuse. She say she has women to tend, and a farm to run."

"Thank you, Cassie."

"Your papa 'ees right, but she won' listen."

"No," I said. "She wouldn't." I turned and mounted the stairs to my own chamber. There was little more to be said to anyone.

Later, when I came downstairs to bid Papa good-night, I found him at his desk, his head in his hands.

"Come, Papa," I said. "Rest awhile." I took him by the shoulder and we mounted the stairs together. Only then did I notice that Lizzie's chamber door was ajar. I peered in, holding my candle before me: the bed was neatly made. The gown she had borrowed lay primly upon it. Papa, revived at once by fear, descended the stairs two at a time, heading to the stables. Star, the Narragansett pacer my parents had given the couple as a wedding gift, and a little mare, which we later learned belonged to John Adams, were gone.

"Damn that woman!" Papa said as he climbed the stairs. "She's gone off!"

I said nothing. Two days later, dressed in black and wearing an armband, I left with my parents for Portsmouth.

Part II

14

JULY 1775. IN PORTSMOUTH, THE WOODEN HOUSES from olden days still stood by the marshy riverbank. The paths dipped and swayed, and only the very center of the town flattened out to accommodate a market and shops. Three churches formed a triangle in the town's center. An old fish market stood near our new house, on Spring Hill. From the parlor window of Uncle Robert's house, I could watch the fishermen as they coasted in to shore after a good morning's haul.

My chamber was a pretty, sunny room with two windows looking onto Deer Street and two facing east, toward the river. From those windows, I had a broad view of the Piscataqua, Kittery Point, and Badger's Island. If I stood close to the easternmost window, I could make out Pest Island, where Portsmouth's citizens went to take the cure for smallpox. Uncle Robert slept in the room across from me, and my parents occupied a large, quiet chamber in the back of the house, behind the staircase.

Above me, in the old nursery, lived a mousy girl named Phoebe. She was about sixteen or so and served as a chambermaid. Recently she had been keeping house as well, since Uncle had let go several house servants. In a small chamber across the hall from the nursery lived a man whom I presumed to be a lodger. But I did not meet him before near two weeks had passed, as he rose before dawn and returned after dark. However, I heard his footsteps upon the stairs.

A ban was in place in the town, and we were to eat no meat at all, and fish only twice a week. It hardly mattered, for I had lost my appetite. I grew so thin that Cassie was at her wit's end, and even my mother noticed. She had only that week found her voice after near three weeks of silence. It was exactly the same voice, yet I could not rid myself of the sensation that this rigid being at our table was but a clever simulacrum of my mother.

"It's not fashionable to be so thin, Eliza," the automaton remarked one evening.

"Oh, leave the poor girl alone," said Papa. "Can you not see how ailing she is? Lord knows I would be, left alone with the pair of us." I caught my father's eye and smiled wanly. Papa, though having regained his senses, seemed to be ailing as well. Since we'd left Cambridge, he had developed a slight cough. He kept clearing his throat as if something were stuck in there.

The week of our arrival, the town was buzzing with news that Governor John Wentworth had fled his mansion and was holed up at Fort William and Mary, just a few miles south of town. Then, late on the second of July, we learned that George Washington had taken command of the new Continental Army in Cambridge, lodging at the Vassal house. Had we been there, we no doubt would have made his acquaintance. I could not help but think how overjoyed Jeb would have been to meet the general.

The news of Washington's arrival in Cambridge served to galvanize Portsmouth into two camps: those of us who dared not leave our homes, and those audacious men in the streets who celebrated His Excellency's new command.

One might be tempted to think that the loss of a son on Breed's Hill would have made my parents eager to embrace the Cause. But instead, Jeb's death pushed them in the other direction. They cared nothing for the ideology of Independency. To them, the war was a senseless plague best cured by an immediate return to the status quo.

Mama no longer felt comfortable going abroad and kept mainly to her chamber. Uncle lived to eat and speak of his son, my cousin George, a lieutenant under General Gage in Boston. I thought my uncle's proud talk about his son tactless given our recent loss, but many families found themselves, like us, in the awkward predicament of having fathers or sons behind enemy lines, and it was difficult to pretend otherwise.

Uncle Robert was older than Mama by several years. Life had been good to him, apart from the death of his wife several years earlier. He was a broad-shouldered man in his prime, perhaps forty-five years of age. His hair, though white, was yet intact. He enjoyed the pleasures of life and had a particular fondness for food. The results of this fondness were less noticeable than they might have been, since a London tailor cut him very smart costumes, made of the finest silk and wool.

I spent most of my time in the kitchen. Unlike in our home, my uncle's kitchen was spacious and bright, though often quite smoky. All of the servants, save Cassie, smoked tobacco in clay pipes. Sometimes the smoke grew so thick that my eyes stung, and I would beg Cassie to open the door. The back door provided a shortcut through the garden to Front Street and the Whipple property, whose slaves came and went as if our kitchen was theirs.

My uncle's coachman, an old slave named Jupiter, liked to linger in the kitchen as well. He might have been seventy or ninety—impossible to tell. When Cuffee Whipple, a young slave known as the best fiddler in all of Portsmouth, came over, he and Jupiter played music together. Sometimes, Cuffee brought his violin; at others, he drummed with spoons while Jupiter twanged out notes on his Jew's harp. The two of them playing together was a comical sight, as Jupiter was a tall, skinny beanpole of a Negro and Cuffee was smaller than I. They made a stirring ruckus until Jenny, Uncle's cook, sent them packing with a shrill cry.

Jenny was a plump, red-faced woman of about fifty with thick legs and arms. She had her own cottage at the back of the property, having lived with her husband, the caretaker, until he died several years earlier. Jenny was used to the Whipple slaves entering her domain, but she resented Cassie, whom she clearly saw as a threat to her authority. It was painful to watch Jenny scold Cassie as if she were a green scullery maid.

While the kitchen was smoky and hot, and while Jenny's bully-ragging made me sometimes wish to intervene, the kitchen's conviviality consoled me. There, I felt less alone.

In the evenings, after the heat of the day had passed and the sun had descended behind the westward end of our hill, I would walk down to the edge of the water and watch the ferryman bring the shipwrights home from their long day at the shipyard. I would squint at the water, turned red by the declining sun, and at the sight of the approaching men—tired, dirty, and scorched—I finally allowed the tears to come. The sight of these young men, one of whom might have been Jeb, thawed my heart. The pain was welcome, in a way, for there were times I had feared that I had become as unfeeling as my mother.

One such moment that first week of July, when tears nearly blinded my vision, I collided with one of the disembarking shipwrights.

"Oh!" I said. "Excuse me." I wiped my tears and looked up, where I found the bluest eyes I'd ever seen. They were not cool sky blue but almost aqua, like the blue of an Old Dutch painting. And these eyes were set in a very tan, handsome face.

The shipwright nodded and looked away at once. Was this out of deference to my tears? I thought it odd that he did not at least introduce himself, having careened into me. Instead he walked quickly up the hill. My eyes followed after him: He was young, though perhaps not in the flush of youth. Twenty-five, I guessed. He was not tall but shapely, his arms and shoulders made hard by his trade. He had a broad nose and full mouth, and his hair hung loose about his shoulders in very tight curls. It was brown yet with a top layer of sun-streaked gold.

I saw this man every day for the next several days as I took my walk before supper. Once, he was just descending from the ferryboat; several other times, I saw him walking along Front Street or heading up the hill. Always he nodded but said nothing, never gave his name.

I began to look forward to my solitary walks and the moments I would see the shipwright disembark. Seeing him—his strong form and handsome if somber face, his intelligent eyes in which I fancied I saw a certain pride, even superiority—my pain ceased for a few seconds.

Some time that sad, solitary July, I realized that I had been thinking about this shipwright as I lay in my bed at night. When I set my mind free to go where it would, I imagined the scene in which this shipwright stopped, bowed, and introduced himself. I curtsied and smiled, whereupon I could in good conscience offer my name and residence (just up the hill) and ask his name in turn.

I played this scene over and over in my mind, deriving the keenest guilty pleasure from it. But he would *not* introduce himself, and it was unthinkable that I should do so. I resolved to stop walking to the ferry at that hour, and it was with both relief and a crushing loneliness that, somewhere toward the end of that month, I ceased to see him.

I did not cease dreaming, however. It was as if my soul had grappled on to this lone source of pleasure, and I had not the will to let it go. All my fallen hopes, all my passion and heartbreak, I heaped upon the slender dream of this poor stranger! I knew it to be foolish—utterly so—and yet I could not help myself.

But perhaps such mad hope is not entirely wasted on the dreamer, for one salutary result was that I began to eat once more. The color returned to my wan face. Both Mama and Papa remarked that they were greatly relieved. They had feared I would literally die of grief, which surely happened in those days.

One hot morning in July, as we were finishing breakfast, a messenger came with a letter for my father. Papa paid the boy a few pennies, retreated into his study, and donned his spectacles.

"Hell and damnation!" he cried. Mama and I ran to find him standing with the letter in his hand. He turned to us and said, "There's been a revolt on my plantation. My overseer has been murdered—his throat slashed! Half a dozen slaves have escaped. The estate's in turmoil. I must go."

"No," Mama said. "You can't leave us. Not now."

"I don't see another way."

I left Papa's study, and Papa closed the door upon me, though I was able to hear their continued argument through the door.

Three days later, Papa was on a ship to Virginia and thence to Barbados. He told us he hoped to return in time for Thanksgiving, but as it was a poor time for sea travel, this was not certain. Papa meant the heavy winds at this time of year, but we knew about the ships of war dotting our coastline, and we trembled for him.

Soon after Papa had left, we heard of a possible British invasion just to the north of us, and the people of Portsmouth began to flee inland. On this same night, a violent storm hit, making day of the night skies. The lightning, unremitting, sounded like trees cracking in half. In the kitchen, I came upon little Phoebe huddled in the arms of Jenny. They gripped one another in terror, believing that the world was coming to an end.

On this fearsome night, my mother made Cassie sleep in the hallway outside her chamber door. Uncle Robert, waking in the middle of the night, tripped over her and tumbled forward onto his hands and knees, frightening Cassie half to death.

"For God's sake!" he cried. "Who's this?"

The ruckus woke me, but somehow, Mama had managed to sleep through the commotion. I soon remedied that by rapping loudly on her door. "Mama! Mama!"

"A moment. I'm coming." Mama opened the door to find Uncle Robert and myself, our candles flickering.

"Mama. Uncle nearly tripped and killed himself over Cassie."

"Well, Brother, why did you not take a candle?" she scolded.

Before my uncle could reply, I cut in. "Why do you have Cassie lying on the hallway floor, like a dog?"

"We can talk about it in the morning."

"We certainly will," I replied. I then knelt down by Cassie, who was crying softly.

"Cassie have such a fright!" she said.

"Go back to sleep." I hugged her. "Things shall be better in the morning."

Suddenly I looked up to behold someone standing in the back stairway with a candle. His hair was undone and it fell in dark, tight curls about his shoulders. Dark legs stood out from a linen nightshirt that came to his knees. The light of the candle illuminated a pair of aqua-blue eyes. Our eyes met, and his flared at once in recognition. It was the shipwright!

15

I REFRAINED FROM INTERROGATING POOR CASSIE THEN and there about the shipwright. *Surely he rented the chamber from us,* I thought. But I lay awake much of the night, nonetheless, in anticipation of speaking with her about him. At the crack of dawn, I set out to do so.

Cassie had cleared away her bedding, and there was no sign of her in the hallway. I descended the stairs to seek her out. It was yet early, even for her, but I could not fault her for wishing to remove the traces of her degradation before the family rose for the day.

I found her in the kitchen, alone. She was peeling carrots—such menial service as Cook Jenny would allow. My heart filled with pity for her. After all, what had Cassie to call her own, save the small dignity of her kitchen domain?

Cassie did not look at me, though she knew my presence. She placed the kettle upon the coals. I edged closer to her.

"I am very sorry for you, Cassie. It is unacceptable, what Mama does. With Papa gone, she has become slightly unhinged."

"Tank you, Miss Eliza," she said. I saw a silent tear run down her cheek.

"By the way," I began casually, "who was that fellow on the stairs last night? I've not seen him about before, though I have come across him on my walks."

"Watkins, you mean?"

"Oh, is that his name?" I asked with feigned nonchalance. "The servant. Tanned, very blue eyes."

Cassie nodded. "Dat Watkins. But he not a servant, miss. He Master Robert's slave."

"Slave? But he's white." Cassie must have misunderstood.

"Not white, miss, 'alf-breed. Don' make no difference, though."

"But he's a shipwright. I've seen him on the ferry from Badger's Island. He must be very well skilled."

"Oh, 'ee well skilled, all right. Light skin, well skilled." She shrugged.

Cassie's tight-lipped responses irritated me. I would know more, and so I turned squarely to face her and endeavored to meet her shifty eyes.

"Cassie, what do you *know* about Watkins? About his past, I mean?"

"Why you want to know?" she challenged.

"I'm, well—curious. He seems—if he is indeed a slave, as yet I doubt, he is unlike any slave I've ever known."

"Well, you right about dat, Miss Eliza. He not like us. No, miss."

Cassie told me that Watkins's mother had been a light-skinned Negro from Jamaica. Purchased by a former royal governor of New Hampshire, she bore a son and a daughter. The governor's wife, enraged to discover that her husband had fathered two children with this Jamaican, sold the girl "downriver." The boy was later sold to a Mr. Watkins, from whom Uncle purchased him several years earlier.

"He tink dat make 'eem white," Cassie concluded. "I don' mean de *out*side of 'eem, Miss Eliza. I mean, he tinks he a white man, and dat your uncle will set him *free*."

"Well, maybe Uncle Robert will," I said.

Cassie smirked. "Master Chase? Nevah. 'Ee know a good ting when 'ee got it. Master make plenty of money off 'eem."

But before my curiosity regarding some last point could be satisfied, Watkins himself emerged from the back stairs and entered the kitchen. He glanced at me, and by our sudden muteness he must have gleaned we were speaking about him.

Cassie handed Watkins a gunnysack filled with provisions for the day. "Thank you," he nodded to Cassie. His voice was deep, and of a fine, clear timbre. He glanced back at us and then fled through the back door.

·   ·   ·

Now that I knew who this Watkins was, there seemed little danger in meeting him on my walks. Our relation to one another was suddenly quite clear and unambiguous. He was my uncle's slave. It was thus with a clear conscience and a light step that I set about to take my walks down to the river once more.

I now saw this Watkins several times a day, just as if my knowledge of who he was made him visible. He was in the kitchen to fetch his sack, racing down the front stairs or slipping down the back. Those mornings I woke as dawn broke, I saw him emerge directly into our hallway and stride down the front steps, pausing to look out the Palladian window, perhaps to assess the weather. I thought this behavior presumptuous—had he been one of ours, and Papa noticed such a thing, he would have received a severe scolding.

Watkins passed through the kitchen to get his gunnysack each morning, and I sometimes saw him there, if only very briefly. He seemed ill at ease among the house slaves. He never joined in their easy banter, never stopped a moment to hear Jupiter and Cuffee kick up a lively tune. I would occasionally come upon him at some house chore—fixing a latch or hauling wood—but in these moments he let nothing distract him. I might have watched him unperceived for an hour or more, so focused was he on his single task.

Now that we knew who the other was, Watkins began to acknowledge my existence. At first, I thought his glance insolently direct, but perhaps that was because of the color of his eyes. They would linger a moment—not rapaciously, as Mr. Inman's had, but curiously—as if there were something about me he did not quite comprehend.

• • •

Meanwhile, Mama simply refused to relinquish her grip upon poor Cassie, and for weeks I cast about for a solution. In the kitchen, "Yes, ma'am" and "No, ma'am" was Cassie's lot all summer long as she obeyed Cook Jenny. At night, she was made to lie her tired body down on the floor in the hall, without so much as a blanket beneath her. She slept there all through the extreme heat of August, with no relief from even the smallest breeze through a window.

September approached when I finally put my foot down. We were at dinner, and Mama had begun to speak about a letter she had just received when I interrupted her.

"Mama, I'm sorry, but I can hold my peace no longer. It shall not do to have poor Cassie sleep in the hallway after she has been used to her own bed. It is cruel, and I don't see that it is necessary."

Mama replied, "Cassie is no longer needed in the kitchen, Eliza, and as I've had no maidservant for ages, I don't see why I shouldn't use her."

"Well, at least let her sleep in her own bed."

"Then she won't hear me if I call. Besides," she insisted, "I am very comforted by her proximity."

"I shall find a way to make her a feather bed, at least."

Mama shrugged. "You may do as you like in that regard, so long as you don't remove the feathers from *our* beds. But, oh, I have failed to mention what I planned to say . . . there has been a letter from Papa."

"What does he report?" I inquired, pleasantly surprised.

She shook her head. "All is not well. Papa is ill; he still coughs . . ." Here, Mama perused the letter once more to get to the part intended for me. "Oh, yes, here it is. He says someone must go to retrieve Star in Braintree. He says he has you in mind to do this."

"Me? Go where?"

She sighed. "Papa wishes you to bring Star back to Portsmouth." This news was most unwelcome.

"Why me? And why retrieve Star? Is it not unseemly to take back a gift, once given?"

But instead of replying Mama handed me Papa's letter so that I could see the request for myself:

My darling Eliza. Circumstances make it necessary for me to ask a great favor of you. I must beg you to go to Braintree as soon as you receive this letter, to retrieve Star. I trust you above any servant to do me this service. What's more, I think it shall be a kindness for you to visit with Lizzie, as we have not seen her in many months. The situation weighs greatly on my conscience . . .

I set the letter down on the hall table without having finished it. "So, I am to rob the grieving woman's horse but do her the kindness of visiting her? Has Papa lost his senses?"

"I'm sorry, Eliza, but there simply is no one else."

"Well, at least let me take Cassie for company."

"You shall not. I need her."

By this point, I was near tears of frustration. "You would send me upon the roads alone, where every day we hear of confrontations and fighting?"

"I need her," Mama repeated. "You may take Phoebe, if you like. Juno shall be with you as well, and what's his name—the old one."

"Jupiter! His name is Jupiter, for goodness' sake. Why can you not remember it?" I stormed off to my chamber.

•   •   •

The following morning, we were up early; Jupiter had already placed my trunk in the carriage. The horses awaited, shifting and snorting. We were just about to set off when a messenger arrived with a letter for Mama. She opened it, but I paid scant attention and signaled for Jupiter to be off. Mama raised a forestalling hand.

"A moment!" she cried, approaching me. "Thank goodness. This came just in time. It is an odd request, but then your father's family *is* odd . . ."

"Who's it from?" I inquired impatiently.

"Colonel Quincy." She drew her upper lip to her nose as if smelling a bad odor. "It seems Lizzie has been ill, and he has procured a servant in Boston."

"Not very ill, I hope?"

Mama equivocated. "Well . . . no. She was, but she is recovering slowly. Her strength has not yet returned. The colonel has located someone, but he does not wish to act out of turn. He feels that Lizzie will accept this servant if it comes from us, though apparently he is quite willing to pay."

"Very well. But what does this have to do with me, or my leave-taking? I am anxious to be off, Mama."

"You shall fetch her on the way. Her name is Martha Miller. The colonel says she is from good, loyal parents recently deceased.

Poor girl." Mama shook her head. "Anyway, she stays at a friend of the colonel's on Marlborough Street. It is very convenient, as you shall go directly past the house."

"Ugh," I groaned. "This grows worse and worse."

"Nonsense. There is nothing to it."

I wanted to say that if there was nothing to it, why didn't she go? But I bit my tongue. Mama pursed her lips and proffered a cheek, which I dutifully kissed before muttering a terse good-bye.

Juno wished to stop briefly at Stavers's tavern before leaving town.

"If you *must*, Juno," I sighed. Would we never get clear of Portsmouth? As I waited impatiently for him to emerge from the tavern, I overheard two elderly dames speaking to each other. They were waiting for the Flying Stage Coach to take them to Boston. Stavers's had placed a peeling wooden settle upon the stone pavers that served as a sidewalk, and the ladies sat upon its edge, not wishing to dirty their capes.

"I simply must have a new cook," one of them was saying. "Our Minnie has grown quite infirm."

"What an inconvenience," said the other.

"It is indeed. But Sarah, not a day goes by that the poor thing does not drop a dish or burn herself." Sarah made sympathetic clucking noises. "But where is one to get a new cook in these times?"

"Excuse me," I interrupted. "I could not help but overhear your conversation. As it happens, I may know of an able cook in need of a position."

The women looked at each other, and I continued. "Jenny, my uncle's cook, has long been seeking another situation. Since we arrived from Cambridge with our own cook, Cassie, Jenny is, well—we don't need *two* cooks, you see. Assuming you can pay her reasonably," I added, for that was the key to the whole enterprise.

I had in fact heard Jenny complain that my uncle had not paid her in many weeks.

Just then, Juno emerged from the tavern. He passed me by, smelling of rum.

"You may inquire at the home of Mr. Chase, on Deer Street."

"Oh!" They looked at each other, impressed. Everyone knew my distinguished uncle. "And who shall we say . . . ?" they called after me, but Juno was already helping me into the chaise, and Jupiter immediately whipped the reins. I waved to the ladies, smiled, and rode off. Several hours later we arrived in Newburyport, where we stopped the night, moving on to Boston early the next morning.

We arrived in Boston town at last, late the afternoon of the following day. Miss Miller was waiting for us in the hallway of Mrs. Adams's uncle's house. She was dressed entirely in black, with a broad hat that obscured her face. She was a tiny thing whom I guessed to be no more than thirteen years of age.

"Hello, Miss Miller." I curtsied as Juno and Jupiter entered, bowed, and took her things.

"How do you do?" Her voice was so soft as to be barely audible. Miss Miller's speech, coupled with her fine clothing, gloved hands, and erect posture, made me doubt whether she had done a day's service in her life.

On the way to Braintree, the girl sat across from me in silence, and I looked out upon the landscape. All around us the maple leaves had turned brilliant tones of red and orange. Most had not yet fallen, but the few that had now swirled about us in the wind. The sun was still warm by day, though mornings were crisp, and I was obliged to ride with two blankets, one draped across my shoulders and the other across my lap.

Boston Harbor was filled with boats of every variety, and also battleships. At Boston Neck, we passed by the militia and suffered their questions for several long minutes. We were eventually allowed to pass through and, with a brief stop for refreshment in

Milton, were clopping down the main street of Braintree's North Parish as the sun set behind us.

The North Parish of Braintree was quite charming, nestled as it was so close to the sea. It consisted of some shops, two churches, and a cemetery. Jupiter, engrossed in conversation with Juno, had missed the turnoff, and we were obliged to turn around. At last, squinting against the burning orange light, I espied Colonel Quincy's stately home on the right, behind a long row of privet hedge. Beyond the great house, down toward the wavering dunes, stood a small cottage. My breath caught and tears pressed behind my eyes to see my brother's home. The view over the bay toward Boston was just as Jeb had described it.

Around the cottage, signs of industry were everywhere: baskets sat askew beneath maple trees, sheaves of flax stood upright in a nearby field; corn, unhusked, lay in an unruly heap in the kitchen garden.

"Miss Miller, it is a pretty piece of land, is it not?"

Martha gazed upon the extensive grounds. "There is a great deal of work to be done," she remarked.

"Lizzie will need to hire a man, if she hasn't already, for there are such tasks here as you cannot be expected to do."

I recalled Jeb's last letter to me, in which he wrote that he hoped to plant two new gardens come spring. Now, as we came closer, I saw all of the projects that Jeb had begun and that death had interrupted: a broken fence, a chicken-coop door off its hinges. By the barn, hay piles drifted will-he-nill-he in the wind.

We descended our carriage just as a pale, thin form, swaddled in a homespun shawl, greeted us. I knew not who it was at first, but when I saw that it was Lizzie, involuntary tears of pity swelled my throat. Fearful lest I fail in my task, I came directly to the point. "Juno," I called, "have Mrs. Boylston's stableboy ready Star. As you know, he's to return with us."

"Ready Star?" Lizzie's voice was a raspy whisper. "You shan't do any such thing." She then shut the door upon us. I thought that this was all the greeting we were to receive when Lizzie, coughing, opened the door once more. "Pardon me—this cough," she said. "Well, you're here now, so come in."

Once indoors, Lizzie took our cloaks. She set our things upon her one great chair in the parlor. It was cold in this room. No fire was lit, and we all moved toward the warmth coming from the kitchen. I introduced Miss Miller to Lizzie. Lizzie said, "Oh, but pardon me. I'm not myself—I shall make us some coffee at once."

"I stay not long. It is only to retrieve Star that I am come. And to deliver Miss Miller," I added.

Lizzie stood erect, her silhouette a thin black shade against the kitchen window. Her voice, though a whisper, had a steely edge to it. "Star is going nowhere. He was a gift to us upon our marriage."

"You could hardly need him *now*," I objected.

"But I do need him. People here rely on me, people whom I must visit because they've no one else to care for them. Besides, what use could your family possibly have—" She stopped mid-sentence, looked at my gown, now slightly frayed at the bottom from use, and said, "Oh. I see."

I turned away in shame. Worn and fragile, we were both near tears, yet we were each too proud to show them. We stood in awkward silence as Lizzie heated water for the coffee. All the while I thought, *In this chair Jeb sat.* Or, *through this window Jeb looked upon the sea as he wrote about the gardens he would plant come spring.*

I could bear it no longer. Lizzie's illness had exposed a vulnerability in her that I found somehow threatening; it made me cling even harder to my old coldness toward her.

"Jupiter!" I called. When he didn't reply, I strode into the parlor to find him sitting in the great chair, his head bowed, sound asleep. Hearing my footsteps, he sprang to.

"Jupiter, ready Star. We're leaving in a moment."

"There's no horse in the stable, Miss Eliza."

"No horse? What mean you?"

"I looked. Juno and I both looked, and we didn't find any horse. We seen some chickens and a cow," he offered, as if these might do in the horse's stead.

"Well, think no more on it, Jupiter. Get Juno and ready the carriage."

Once Jupiter had gone, I confronted Lizzie heatedly. "Where is he? My father wrote to us expressly from Barbados to request that you return his horse."

"It is not *his* horse." Lizzie's eyes flashed from her thin face. "It was a gift, and he shan't get it. He'll sooner get *me*."

"Papa shall be quite vexed."

"I'm sure he will, and I'm very sorry for him. It must be demonishly difficult just now in the towns. We ourselves would starve were it not for the gardens, and help from our—friends."

I saw Lizzie pull back from this last statement, since we both knew she had not counted my family among the latter, nor would she ever.

"Miss Miller," I turned to the girl. "I must take my leave. I hope you'll be most comfortable here."

O, hypocrite words! Comfort would form no part of Miss Miller's life in Braintree. No, nor of Lizzie's. Yet I merely turned to my sister-in-law and said, "Well. Papa shall hear about this."

"Please send him my best regards and tell him I am well. Good-bye, Eliza."

Just as I had departed and the door was shut behind me, I heard Lizzie exclaim, "Oh, but your coffee!"

16

"I HAVE BEEN MOST IMPORTUNED," MAMA SAID the moment I alit from the carriage. She asked me nothing about my trip, nor anything about Lizzie or Miss Miller. "Papa shall be extremely vexed," she said. "He had counted on the sale of that horse to pay for a good many unexpected debts."

"She hid it from me, Mama," I said quietly.

"Hid a horse? How does one hide a great animal of sixteen hands?"

I shrugged. "Apparently it was brought elsewhere."

"Well, well, but I can hardly concentrate on that now. I am alone, without any maid whatsoever."

"Why? Where's Cassie?" I asked, suddenly alarmed.

Mama ignored my question. "Oh, I can tell she's *beside herself* with contentment—Lord knows why. You'd think that kitchen of hers was Heaven itself, the way she carries on."

"What have you done with Cassie?"

"Done?" Mama looked at me sharply. "Why, I've done nothing. Cook Jenny up and left us! Hired away by that scheming old Mrs. Pritchett! Cassie's now our cook and takes the dairy for her chamber. Oh, will my ill fortunes never cease?"

After Cassie returned to the kitchen, life regained a modicum of stability. I could not say I was happy, but my days assumed a consoling rhythm: Every morning, after breakfast, I would walk down to the market to watch the boats come and go. Sometimes I would rise early enough to watch the ferryman as he rowed Watkins out to Badger's Island. Cassie told me that for the past year Watkins had worked there as a shipwright, for Colonel Langdon. She also told me that my uncle made five pounds each month on his labor.

I then would return home to take up my needlework or a book of stories for young ladies, neither of which held my attention for very long. What's more, sitting in the parlor with little to do, my mind kept casting back with great dissatisfaction to that scene with Lizzie. I felt something like remorse, which nothing quelled save arduous activity. I soon rose and found my way into the kitchen.

There was always a great deal to do, even when Uncle or Papa was abroad: pots to scrub, floors to wash, chamber pots to empty, wood to chop, linens to soak and hang to dry, chambers to air and dust, vegetables to boil, and meat and fish to smoke. At first I merely stood and watched Cassie work. But one morning, she turned to me and said, "Well, Mees Eliza, don' just stand dere." She handed me a bowl, and I began shelling brown-spotted beans, throwing the empty shells onto the floor by my feet. When I was done, Cassie stuck her nose in the bowl as if she expected to find a bloody finger in there.

•   •   •

By now, it was late October or early November. One chill morning, while I was still in my chamber, I heard a hasty rustling above me; then boots clomped heavily down the stairs. I was still in my shift but hastened down the hall to the Palladian window that faced Deer Street. I soon saw Watkins striding out the front door like one of the family. Over his shoulder he carried a musket and large gunnysack, and around his waist he had tied several heavy ropes.

Watkins's bearing was resolute, purposeful. Upon his head he wore a wool cap, from which an unruly curl or two escaped. He headed west down Deer Street, and I lost sight of him. I returned to my chamber, dressed, and made my way to the kitchen, where Cassie was preparing breakfast. I entered and tied a smock about my waist.

"Where was John Watkins off to, so early this morning?" I asked.

"Why you call 'eem *John* Watkins? 'Ee's just Watkins, to you."

"Oh, Watkins sounds like an old butler, Cassie. You know, in one of those musty manses where skeletons are found in the attic. *John* Watkins, now that's much better for a young fellow."

Cassie was unimpressed with my reasoning.

"He's not a young fellow to you, neither, Miss Eliza."

"But you haven't answered my question. Where goes he, dressed like that, and with a musket?"

"'unting."

"Hunting? But for what, exactly?" I asked, impatient for details. I might actually have stomped my foot.

"Food. Maybe 'ee catch squirrels or voles. Maybe 'ee catch a boar."

"A boar? To what use will we put a boar?"

"Tanksgiving."

"Oh, yes—of course. I'd entirely forgotten." That I should be surprised by the idea of a boar and not squirrels or opossums amused me. When I first learned back in summer that we ate those repulsive creatures, my shock was very great. But Cassie was so skilled at tenderizing and spicing these meats that I soon put aside my squeamishness.

I left the kitchen to tidy my appearance and sit myself at the breakfast table. Uncle Robert soon appeared, whereupon he announced, "Good news, all. I have just had a letter from my son, who says he shall join us for Thanksgiving."

"How delightful," I said flatly. "When can we expect him?"

"His letter informs me that he will stop in Connecticut and take a coach from there on November twenty-fifth, or thereabouts."

"Happy news." I did not begrudge my uncle a visit from his son, but it could afford me no pleasure. First, because my cousin was a British officer now. Second, because I recalled him as an arrogant, teasing youth. Cousin George once stole a silver saltcellar and blamed it on a servant who had been impertinent to him.

Later that day, Mama began to plan Thanksgiving dinner. She and Uncle had invited the Peirces, one of Portsmouth's most prominent families, to dinner. Apparently they had a son of marriageable age, though thankfully he was on a trip and would not be joining us.

As Mama wrote her menu, I sat with her in the parlor, reading upon a book. The sky grew dark. Cassie entered and said that supper was ready. Mama stood, stretched, and turned to me. "Are you coming, Eliza?"

"Yes, of course," I said, but I had not yet stood. I had begun to feel uneasy for a reason I could not define. I went in to supper, however, and returned to the parlor before Mama. There, I espied her foolscap on the table. I lifted it and read,

THANKSGIVING WITH THE PEIRCES
November 30 1775

Salade au Crab
Creamed Turbot
Roti du Boeuf au Jus
Minted Peas
Fruit Platter
Floating Island

Mama returned to the parlor minutes later. I held the menu up before her. "Mama. What is this?"

"Why, the menu, of course. Do you approve of it?"

"Approve? The king himself would approve. But surely you realize there'll be no beef for us this year. Or fruit. Or turbot, for that matter. Surely you understand this?" My voice had an edge of desperation to it.

"I understand no such thing. Your father will be home any day now, and he'll arrange it all." She punctuated the sentence by sticking her narrow little chin in the air.

"Father is coming home from a rebellion. It's doubtful whether he'll have managed to keep his plantation from ruin, much less turned a profit on it."

"Nonsense." She moved to sit down, but I stopped her with an outstretched arm.

"We are even now struggling to put food on the table. Have you not noticed what you eat? We've not had beef these six months. Squirrel and opossum and God knows what other vermin have been our daily fare."

Just then Uncle Robert appeared in the doorway. He looked about him. Suddenly I realized the source of my anxiety: Watkins had not yet returned.

"Where is that blasted nigger?"

Mama shrugged her ignorance, but I said, "He has gone hunting."

"Hunting? In the dark? After his curfew? As like to shoot himself as anything else. Blast it. If he comes back, let me know at once. I'll whip him to within an inch of his life."

"No, indeed!" I exclaimed. My mother and uncle stared at me in amazement. "I mean . . . only that he does us a service. I overheard the servants talking, and it seems Watkins has gone to find game for our holiday."

But Uncle was implacable. His three chins jiggled with rage: "Well, I didn't give him leave to do so. Last I knew, *I* was master of this house. He shall be whipped in the square in the morning."

His authority reestablished, my uncle marched off, perhaps to have stern words with the other servants. I doubted they would have the courage to tell Uncle Robert the truth: that it was thanks to Watkins that we had been eating meat at all.

My courage—a momentary flare—had fled, and I said nothing more. Mama endeavored to resume her work, but my outburst had ruined the fantastical mood. After a few minutes, she rose, coldly bade me good-night, and left the room. I said good-night but remained in the parlor. Cassie came in to check that the fire was safely gone out and found me sitting there still, though it had grown cold and dark. It was now near eleven o'clock.

"What? Still awake? And in da cold and dark?"

"I'm perfectly well. Some tea and a bit of fire would be good, though."

"Tea and a fire, at dees time of night?" Cassie looked at me askance but did my bidding. For, even though we now spent our hours side by side in the kitchen, I was still Miss Eliza in the parlor, and she was still my parents' slave.

Cassie set my dish of tea on the stand by the wing chair. After she had placed a log on the fire and gotten it going, she remarked, "Drink yah tea and get yah'self off to bed. You up, I up, too." She made as if to leave the room but then, on its transom, turned to me: "It won' *do*. You know 'eet."

"I don't know what you mean," I said coldly. "Go to bed, Cassie. I'll make certain the fire is out before I head up."

She curtsied and left me alone. Ten minutes later, the log burning low, the room going cold, I stood to extinguish the fire when in through the front door burst Watkins.

"Oh!" I said, cringing lest the noise wake everyone in the house. Watkins might then get his beating sooner than Uncle Robert had planned.

Watkins stood in the hall for a moment. His cap was gone and his hair had come entirely out of its plait. His coat was rumpled, and over his shoulder he carried a heavy sack. From it, two curled tusks stuck out quite six inches.

I said, "Uncle Robert is in a rage. I'd steer clear of him if I were you—"

I thought he would thank me for warning him but instead Watkins asked, his eyes challenging, "Where would you have me go, Miss Boylston?"

I opened my mouth to speak, but he had already moved off down the hallway.

"Oh!" I blurted in frustration once he was gone. My eyes smarted at his insolence. At last I removed to my chamber where I tossed and turned, feeling a fool for having waited up.

I awoke early the next morning, just past sunrise, to find Constable Hill at the foot of the stairs. He was a consumptive-looking man, though hardly past forty, with the nervous gestures of one who took little pleasure in his work.

Constable Hill was in the process of leading Watkins out the back door, toward the marketplace. Watkins's head was down, and he gave no resistance. Hastily, I donned my clothing and cape and ran out across the backyard, through the Whipple property and down Front Street to the square.

Cassie was among a small group already there. When she saw me, she scowled. "What you do here, Miss Eliza?" I said nothing but watched as Watkins was stripped to the waist in the frigid cold. The constable's man counted the lashes for all to hear: "One! And . . . two! . . . and . . . three!" Never had I witnessed such a thing before, nor had I ever known my father to punish his slaves so.

I saw not what transpired on the plantation, but the whipping of John Watkins gave me a small, unwelcome taste of it.

Watkins wept not; he flinched not. He was as stone. Blood flowed down his back, staining his breeches. At one point, his knees folded, yet still he did not cry out.

I did, however. Hearing the cry, Watkins glanced in my direction. His body may have been unresisting, but his eyes blazed with rage and defiance.

That afternoon, we stripped the squirrels and rabbits Watkins had caught for us and hung the meat to dry. If Cassie saw the tears on my face as I did so, she mercifully said nothing. She and Phoebe gutted the boar and stripped it and salted it and hung it to cure in the smokehouse for our Thanksgiving celebration. But I knew I would not eat that meat, not if it was the last food on earth.

17

FOR TWO WEEKS, WATKINS DID NOT GO to the shipyard. From above, I heard only a soft, repetitive chorus of moans. Cassie went up and down the back stairs to tend to him, sighing almost as loudly as he moaned.

I was angry with my uncle, to be sure. But I was also furious at Watkins—why did he need to strut about the house as if he owned it? Why had he defied the curfew without so much as a request to do so, or an apology after the fact? Did he wish to get himself whipped? It seemed so. Cassie's words echoed in my memory: "He tinks he a white a man."

Thankfully, I was distracted from my concern with Watkins when Mama burst into my chamber to tell me that Papa was in Boston and would be arriving in two days' time. She then began perusing the gowns in the room's corner closet. "These styles are woefully *démodées*," she said. "They must be altered, and I'm afraid it falls to us to do the work. Cassie is run off her feet, and the seamstresses tell me that they are all far too busy this time of year."

I suspected that my mother was not being entirely truthful. We had no money for such work, but even had we, many of Portsmouth's seamstresses, now of a radical bent, would sooner have sewn our shrouds. And so, with my dead aunt's old sewing basket between us by the fire and our gowns in our laps, we set to work. We removed the ruffled sleeves and replaced them with buttoned-cuff sleeves. It took a great deal of trial and error to square the shoulders and plunge the neckline so that it bared a seemly amount of bosom. I felt myself to be highly inexpert at this art and sighed continually.

Meanwhile, other preparations were underway as well. Old Jupiter had been given the task of trimming the hedges and clearing the walkway. Poor Phoebe had to drag the heavy Turkey carpets into the yard and beat them free of dust and dirt. As for Watkins, Cassie told me that though his wounds were healing well, he would not return to the shipyard for several weeks more. Instead, he had been put to use as a house slave. It was obvious from his smallest movement that he resented it. He banged down the stairs, kicked at carpets, and came—I thought—perilously close to being beaten once more.

"Cassie, I'm ashamed I've said nothing to anyone regarding Watkins's whipping, which was so unfair, so un-Christian. I am heartily ashamed. Indeed, my soul burns with anguish."

"You jus' keep dat burning angueesh inside of you, Miss Eliza, and don' go telling it to Master Chase."

"Why do you say that?"

But Cassie shook her head as if only another slave would understand.

The following morning, Mama and I chose to resume work on our gowns in the parlor, for it was the only room with a lively fire. We had just donned our gowns to check the placement of the necklines when, suddenly, into the parlor stepped Watkins. There we stood with our open bodices and no stays, the morning light streaming in upon us.

"Oh, pardon me." Watkins looked away.

"Get out!" Mama cried, though he had already done so.

I grasped the bodice of my gown and laughed.

"What, pray, is funny? To have the slaves see you half-naked?"

"Oh, Mama, it *is* funny, even you must admit."

"I don't have to admit any such thing, and I shan't."

"Don't, then," I said, and giggled once more.

•   •   •

That same morning, we received a message that Papa's ship had been spotted at the mouth of the harbor.

"Your papa!" Mama cried. "He arrives. Hurry!"

We ran upstairs to dress. Then Mama, Uncle Robert, and I walked down to the wharf and waited for his sloop to make its way through the harbor. I thought I could just perceive its distant form, like a feather quill in a vast pool of ink.

"Mama, look! Just there!"

The seas being rough that day, the winds and tide unobliging, it took them near another hour to anchor and then to row passengers over to the dock.

At last, Papa stood before us. Tired, stooped—and far too pale.

"Cursed ship," he said, hugging us to him in the cruel breeze. He coughed. "Appalling conditions."

We walked up the hill, Papa still coughing and clearing his throat. Two men from the wharf brought up his trunk, making better time than we did. When Mama inquired how things had fared, my father would not meet her eye. "A bad business. Very bad."

"Come, come, my love," said my mother, drawing Papa closer, as the wind was fierce. "Cassie shall draw you a bath and make some hot tea."

"Oh, for a bath," he sighed as they made their way up the hill. In the foyer, Papa removed his dirty, heavy overcoat and Mama moved to find Cassie. He called after her, "Tell Cassie she'll find some real tea, in a blue tin, in my trunk."

"Real tea!" Mama turned and flashed us a rapacious grin. "That will go so nicely with the cake." Cassie had made some sort of cake in honor of Papa's return, though I dared not set my expectations too high, since we'd had no flour for several months.

Just then, I saw, through the foyer's narrow window, old Jupiter bounding up the path on bandy legs, toward the back door. With him was a tall, young Negress, nearly as tall as he, though far blacker than any of our slaves. She was wrapped in a heavy wool cape, and I could not see her face. Papa allowed himself a mischievous smirk.

"What is it?" Mama asked as she returned from the kitchen.

"You'll see. It's a special gift, my love." We moved into the parlor, and Papa bade Mama sit. He coughed again. In another few minutes, Cassie came into the parlor with the young Negress on her arm. Though dressed in shabby, besmirched petticoats, and weary, this was a healthy girl of perhaps seventeen or eighteen. I stared at her. How beautiful she was! Never had I seen such a regal Negress. Her limbs were long, her neck as long and graceful as a swan's. She might have been Cleopatra's daughter, so proudly did she bear herself. *She could not have long been a slave,* I thought.

"This," my father said, as if he were unveiling a sculpture, "is Linda." Linda curtsied shallowly.

"Does she speak English?" Mama asked.

"Oh, yes, though I imagine she's a little shy, and fatigued from our horrendous journey. We were held up many days because of the rough sea. I know you've long been desiring your own maid, since Cassie was so cruelly taken from you last fall." Here, Papa leveled his gaze upon me, as if somehow he knew I was to blame. "Anyway, Linda is yours if you wish it. If not, you can put her to work with Phoebe, I suppose."

Mama assessed Linda carefully. She circled her, gazing intrusively upon her every part. Impulsively, I stood up and moved to

Linda's side. The girl seemed surprised by my gesture and shifted her feet.

Mama frowned. "Eliza, why stand you beside the girl? That is hardly appropriate." She turned to Papa and smiled. "Thank you, my love. She will do."

"Mama," I objected. "Only imagine what she has been through. The voyage nearly carried off Papa—it's a miracle she even survived."

"Yes, well."

"And, Mama," I continued, my disquiet growing, "I hope you aren't planning to make her sleep in the hall, as you made Cassie do last summer."

"Of course she shall sleep in the hall. Where else should she sleep?"

"Why can she not stay in the nursery with Phoebe? There's plenty of room, and she'll have company, at least."

"You are too indulgent, Eliza. This girl looks proud. As it is, it shall take some work to break her in. I don't see how you'll ever manage a home of your own."

"By your account, I never *shall* have a home of my own!" I left the parlor in haste and, in my failure to look where I was going, nearly crashed into Watkins. I bruised my shoulder on the heavy bundle he held.

"Are you all right, Miss Boylston?"

"Oh, yes. Excuse me!" I said, blushing deeply as I passed him.

Mama spun about and opened her mouth to upbraid Watkins for his impertinence, but he was long gone.

•   •   •

My wishes regarding Linda's quarters prevailed. I knew not why, except that perhaps Mama did not want to importune poor Papa by fighting with me. It was no longer possible to ignore the fact of his persistent cough, although we all endeavored to do so. Jupiter brought Linda's trunk up to the nursery, and we did not see her again that day.

That afternoon, Cassie served a very nice apple pandowdy. Such a sweet did not require a great deal of flour, and it went marvelously well with the real China tea Papa had brought back. I drank it gratefully, though I could hear Jeb's voice in my ear: *Those who strut their wealth while others suffer shall soon be hoist on their own petard.* I thought, *My dear Jeb, we already have been. Or nearly so.*

Cousin George arrived the following day, in poor fettle. Apparently a band of zealous citizens, espying my cousin on the road, blasted him with armfuls of eggs. Cousin George was thankfully unharmed, but his poor horses and carriage were covered in yellow runnels of egg.

My cousin, also dripping yellow, endeavored to keep his dignity as he descended the carriage. He straightened his waistcoat and bowed to us. Uncle Robert, greatly dismayed at the sight, cried, "Jupiter! Juno! Clean this carriage at once!"

Mr. Chase had grown fat since I knew him as a cunning lad. His cravat looked uncomfortable, stretched taut across his thick neck. His small, close-set eyes looked at me. Then he grinned suddenly and cried, "Cousin Eliza! I didn't know you. You've grown up."

"Yes. I believe I was eleven when you last saw me."

"Indeed. You were different altogether! And how do you like living here with Papa?"

"Very well. It is a lovely situation. I find I can see all the way to Kittery most days."

"Splendid," he said. "Nero!" Here, Cousin George turned to his coachman. "Put my trunks in my room and then return to help with the carriage."

"Perhaps Nero would like a mug of cider and a chance to rest a few moments. You, too, Cousin George," I added.

My cousin looked at me in astonishment. However, he replied, "Capital idea. Nero, set my bags in my chamber and stop in the kitchen before returning here. Warm yourself a few minutes by the fire," he added for good measure. Nero, an old, gray-haired Negro of Jupiter's vintage, grew wide-eyed at my cousin's words, as if they had been spoken in a foreign language.

Mr. Chase was soon settled in. Our relations were easy enough, so long as no one spoke about the war. Sometimes, however, especially at meals, I did not like the way those small, close eyes lingered on my person. Once, leaving the dining room at the same time, our bodies touched, and I thought he pressed himself to me deliberately. I turned to glare at him.

"Oh, pardon!" he said, looking down.

But it happened again, and I became so jumpy that I stole one of Cassie's carving knives and placed it beneath my mattress.

Cassie noticed the theft almost immediately.

"Someone take my knife. Now why would someone do dat, I wonder? How'm I suppose to prepayer anyteeng wit' no good knife? What kind of person do such a ting?"

"Oh, all right. For goodness' sake!" I pulled her into the former dairy, now her chamber, where no one could overhear us. "I took it. But if you want it back, you must give me some other one."

"What you do wit' my knife, Miss Eliza? I don't like da sound of dis. No I don'."

"It's just—Cousin George has been looking at me most unpleasantly. He stares at me so."

Cassie considered my words, then shook her head. "No. I don't see dat in 'eem. Course, you never know wit' men. But I 'spect he likes 'em coarser—dem who don' mind a bit of coin for dere troubles."

"Cassie!" I exclaimed. She looked at me and then seemed to understand something. She put her arms about me. "Oh, you poor ting. You poor, poor ting. You still frightened as a child. Well, go get me dat knife befaw you hurt somebody wit' 'eet."

I did as Cassie asked, resolved to find another means of self-protection. Cassie gave me a bit of twine and told me to wrap it about my chamber doorknob. I then fastened the other end to one of the pulls on my tall chest of drawers.

Now each night when I retired, I became a prisoner in my own chamber, and from my cell I heard the easy laughter of the slaves getting to know one another above me.

18

THANKSGIVING 1775. AT THE LAST MOMENT, THE Peirces were unable to attend, much to Mama's dismay. Instead, the Atkinsons came. Mr. Atkinson was the proprietor of Portsmouth's rope-making enterprise; we hardly needed our inexpertly altered gowns for *him*. However, Mama observed that the gowns might do double-duty for a Christmas dinner or New Year's party.

It had taken near a month of preparation to create our Thanksgiving dinner. In previous years, such dinners were a weekly occurrence. Uncle Robert hired a butler for the evening, and the Atkinsons were served a fine wine and oysters. The silver was polished; fires blazed in the dining room and the parlor. Cousin George looked quite the courtly gentleman in his regimentals, and little Phoebe and regal Linda moved about so quickly that it gave the impression of there being more servants than there actually were.

Passing Cassie in the hallway, I asked her where the butler had come from.

"A friend in debt to Master Robert loaned him."

I smirked. How absurd, to go through such a charade—and all for the Atkinsons!

Mr. Atkinson, in his middle forties, fidgeted with his cravat, intimidated by his surroundings. Mrs. Atkinson thought it safest to wear an unvarying grin that did not always tally with the drift of the conversation. What's more, she wore a gown nearly identical in style to ours before we had altered them. I endeavored to avoid looking at Mrs. Atkinson, for fear that I might burst out laughing.

Once we were all seated around the dining table, my father began a solemn prayer. After it, he said, "And now, I would like to thank my dear brother-in-law Robert for his gracious hospitality."

Uncle Robert, moved to say something, said, "I'd like to thank my son, George, for leaving off his military duties to join us."

The Atkinsons' little girl, Annie, wishing to participate somehow, said, "Thank you, Mama and Papa, for my new puppy!" at which we all laughed good-naturedly. Mama's smile and bright eyes told me that she was contented with how the party unfolded. The ice had been broken, as it were, and we had only to enjoy our repast.

The fish in cream sauce, though not turbot, was excellent. After several glasses of wine, everyone conversed with easy animation, steering carefully around Cousin George's thoughtless praise of a recent British success at Falmouth. I was thankful for Mrs. Atkinson, who engaged us in a lengthy conversation about the table decorations.

At last, my uncle's "butler" presented the boar. Cassie had planted the tusks upright in the center of the platter, which made a dramatic display; murmurs of appreciation went round the table. Uncle Robert carved the meat, and the butler offered the platter to each member of our party. But when my turn came, I pulled my plate away with a quiet, "No, thank you."

Papa looked at me. "What? Are you unwell, my love?"

"No, I am well," I assured him.

"Well, then," my mother said cheerfully, looking about the table at her guests, "have a morsel. For surely we do not have such a fine roast every day." Assenting twitters flew about the table. But my gorge rose at the idea of taking even one bite of that meat. My feelings had not changed, had not been dampened by the conviviality or the wine. I kept seeing Watkins, tied and stripped to the waist in the square, blood coursing down his back. No, I could not put this flesh to my lips.

"I'm sorry, Papa. I can't eat it." I had said the words in a whisper, hoping he would let my turn at the meat pass. But he persisted.

"Why not? It is perfectly good." His voice fairly boomed, as it did when he was agitated. The butler stood as immobile as a garden statue. Was it my imagination, or had our guests shifted their postures imperceptibly away from the now-suspect meat upon the platter? Little Annie's mouth was open, her eyes wide at this wholly unexpected scene.

And then I spoke. "I cannot eat this meat because the man who was good enough to hunt it for us, he who set out to forage all day and night in the cold and dark, to put food on *our* table, was whipped until his blood ran. All for having missed his curfew. As I am a Christian woman, I cannot eat this meat!"

"Eliza!" my father exclaimed. My uncle set his utensils down and cleared his throat. Cousin George's face swelled, his cravat becoming so tight that it seemed to be strangling him. My mother, rising slightly off her seat, announced, "You *shall* eat it!" She then skewered a slice of the roast with her fork and slapped it so forcefully onto my plate that the juices flew everywhere. I covered my face with my hands and fled the table.

19

I WAS SHUNNED FOR TWO WEEKS. NO one spoke to me, and I was forbidden to come to table. I took my meals either alone in my room or in the kitchen with the servants. I knew not what had transpired until later that evening, when, as Cassie and I supped in my chamber, she recounted the early departure of the Atkinsons and the subsequent convening of my family in the parlor to discuss "what to do about Eliza."

It was oddly peaceful to be shunned. I lay on my bed, day-dreamed, read, and watched the movement of the boats from my window. I listened to the sounds of the blacksmith's hammer and the sawyers working somewhere down the street. At times, thoughts about Watkins invaded—his whipping, his eyes when they looked at me, and his whispered question, "Are you all right, Miss Boylston?" Six words that I reduced to their smallest parti-cles, examining them for hidden meaning.

I watched the bruise on my arm, the one I had received when Watkins bumped into me, slowly fade from a greenish black to pale yellow. Time faded like the bruise, and after a while, I knew not the day of the week. Then, one morning, my father entered my chamber. He sat on the side of the bed. "Eliza. You've made a ter-rible mistake, painful to all involved. I understand your soft heart, which is commendable. But as this is your uncle's house, surely you can see how he has every right to impose his own rules in it?"

"Yes, Papa."

Papa, cheered by my docile reply, nodded. "Well, after some discussion, Uncle has offered to forgive your offense if you make a sincere apology and show true remorse." Here he paused, a look of eager, almost childlike hope on his face.

After a few moments, I replied quietly, "It is he who should apologize."

"Incorrigible girl!" Papa bellowed. He stood up, wiped his sweaty brow, and caught his breath. "You don't seem to comprehend the situation. He means to send you from us if you do not beg his forgiveness."

"Send me where, pray?"

"He has not divulged that to me," Papa admitted.

"A hollow threat, then." I smoothed my bedcover with my hand to hide a wicked smile.

"Don't doubt it, Eliza. Your uncle is yet a powerful man, with powerful connections."

"My uncle is in danger of being arrested."

We all knew this to be true, though none of us spoke of it. Only the week before, a letter from General Washington to General Sullivan appeared in the papers. It announced, ominously, that Tories who continued to reside in Portsmouth would soon "meet their fates."

Papa sighed. "You used to be such a sweet, agreeable girl," he said plaintively.

"Sweet? Agreeable? Surely you speak of someone else. Ignorant, perhaps, but I've grown up. You would not wish me to remain a silly child forever?"

Papa patted my hand in silence. But, as he left my chamber, giving a defeated little cough as he did so, I had the impression that this was precisely what he would have liked.

•   •   •

I never apologized to Uncle Robert, nor did he send me away. But for several weeks, I feared it earnestly. Each time a coach passed by, I was seized with terror. Each time a servant trod upon the stair, I feared it was to deliver me a trunk in which to pack my things. Yet no one came for me.

Meanwhile, Cassie told me that news of my refusal to eat the meat at Thanksgiving had spread like fire among Portsmouth's slaves. I thought she exaggerated, but, after Cousin George's departure, I began to notice a subtle change in the way the neighboring slaves treated me.

One day, when I brought Cassie upstairs to show her a stain on one of my gowns, we found the gown missing.

"Where on earth is my gown?" I cried. "I hope this is not some silly prank, Cassie. You know how I dislike those."

"You'll see," said Cassie, smiling.

Indeed, the next day, I saw Dinah crossing the field behind our house as if she'd just left it. I ran to my closet, where I found my gown, returned to me. The stain was gone.

Cuffee Whipple, knowing how much I enjoyed music, began stopping over on his way to events and warmed up by playing me a tune. He knew I loved the song "Chester" and played it often. The song, reminding me of Jeb, always brought tears to my eyes.

Let tyrants shake their iron rod,
And Slav'ry clank her galling chains,
We fear them not, we trust in God
New England's God forever reigns.

One afternoon, after a particularly somber rendition, I was moved beyond mere listening. I leapt up from my stool and hugged

Cuffee. So surprised was the poor soul that he dropped his violin upon the kitchen floor and nearly broke it.

•　　•　　•

Christmas was quiet that year, and our dinner included no special meat. It featured a chicken that had annoyed Cassie once too often by pecking at her herbs and that now found itself resting crisply on a bolster of mashed potatoes, adorned by a necklace of rosemary.

We ate our meal. Afterward, we planned to attend meeting at the North Church. My family was not happy about attending this church, surrounded by the likes of Colonel Whipple and John Langdon and other "rebels," but as St. John's had closed its doors several years earlier, we had little choice. Then, just before we left to attend meeting, it began to snow. In the distance, I heard the voices of children singing. Perhaps they were rehearsing for the service. Without, the sky had darkened, and we wrapped our cloaks more tightly about us.

I made my way down the path ahead of my parents, chin tucked down against the cold, and was surprised by Watkins rounding the path from the street. I had not seen him since Thanksgiving. For a moment, we were alone together. Watkins looked up and his eyes met mine. Surely he knew by now, like every other slave in Portsmouth, how I'd refused to eat that boar. I blushed with the knowledge but willed myself not to look away from him. Nor did he look away from me. And when our eyes met, my heart leapt with a joy that he could not help but perceive.

In January, Dr. Jackson gave Papa the news we already suspected: he had the consumption. Dr. Jackson told him that he was to rest, to be bled regularly, to avoid fatty foods, and, if possible, to remove himself to a warmer clime.

Upon hearing the news, my mother became so distraught that she did not leave her chamber until February. When she emerged, she looked oddly calm, and I had little doubt that she had convinced herself that Dr. Jackson had been entirely mistaken.

I myself could not deny my father's illness, but neither could I give up hope of a cure. Perhaps he *would* get well. God granted my mother's denial and my own several months' grace, a time in which Papa seemed no worse. Then the blood came—copious amounts when he coughed. His cheeks were perpetually flushed with fever, and I could no longer deny the truth.

Mama could, however. "Oh, you'll see. These doctors always deliver the worst news—they know we would not pay them for anything less."

The town of Portsmouth seemed ill as well. But this was more a moral fever. Passing through the market, one feared for one's safety. Customers accused vendors of weighting the scales and offering maggot-ridden food. Others got into political rows. A few came to blows. We feared that my uncle might decide to flee. If he did, we could not remain behind, for his house would certainly be confiscated. But Papa refused to board another ship, believing that such a voyage would be his last.

By the end of March 1776, I began to think of the boar, which I had so nobly rejected at Thanksgiving, with a deep pang of longing. Had that same boar been served to me then, I should have clasped it in my bare hands and gnawed at it like a she wolf. So much for righteous indignation!

Meanwhile, Watkins, Cassie informed me, was laying the keel of the *Raleigh*. I woke at his rising each dawn, and, once he had gone past my chamber door, I observed him through a crack as he paused at the Palladian window and looked out upon the day. Once I even saw him stretch his limbs luxuriously, loosening them from the stiffness of sleep before heading to the kitchen, where Cassie filled his gunnysack.

•　　•　　•

On some days, though, he did use the back stairs, and on these days I would not hear him and would sleep until eight or even nine in the morning. By then my family would be awake, and Cassie would be too busy to share the day's gossip.

Cassie never failed to tell me what good friends Linda and Watkins were becoming.

"Every day she tell me how much she admire 'eem. 'Ow clevah 'ee is."

Indeed, I often heard them laughing above me and soon believed, like everyone else, that Watkins and Linda were in love.

"I imagine they'll marry, if Uncle allows it," I replied gloomily.

"And you be very 'appy for dem, I'm sure." Cassie smirked.

Offended, I replied, "Papa says that sarcasm is man's poor substitute for wit."

"Den it's a good ting I not a man, Miss Eliza," she said, ending the conversation.

· · ·

One morning, as the family sat at breakfast, Papa, much to my surprise, inquired after Watkins. None of us had seen him about of late.

"Oh," replied my uncle, "I've hired him out once more to that infernal John Langdon."

I had heard talk about this Colonel Langdon. People in town said he was quickly becoming one of the great leaders of the Cause.

"Uncle, why is it you dislike Colonel Langdon so much?" I ventured to ask. "People say he's an honorable man."

"Honorable? Aye, a 'great patriot.' One who'd be pleased to confiscate this house and throw us all in jail. Well, all right. But if he makes a Rebel of our nigger, I'll kill 'im."

"I don't see how that would be in Colonel Langdon's interest, as there is so much yet to do here for the war effort."

Uncle Robert glowered at me. He did not like his logic being challenged by a woman, certainly not by his own niece. I knew he had not forgiven me for my shocking defiance at Thanksgiving. However, he said nothing further.

After breakfast, everyone repaired to his chamber. I went into the kitchen. Upon entering, I noticed an old, tattered gunnysack on the table. Cassie was outside breaking up the hard soil in the garden for some potatoes. I opened the back door and felt the chill morning air assault me. But the sun was strong, and the air smelled of spring.

"Cassie, is that Watkins's sack upon the table?"

She nodded. "An' it my fault, too. He was jus' turning to leave and I open my fat mouf about someteeng. It made 'eem forget."

"Never mind whose fault it is," I said. "The point is, what is he to eat all day? Will you have the man starve?"

Cassie set her shovel against the side of the house. She wiped her hands on her apron. Then, slowly lifting her head, she let her eyes rest upon my face.

"No you don', Miss Eliza."

"No I don't, what?"

Cassie approached me until we stood only inches apart. "No you don' go puttin' yourself somewhere you don' belong. The devil, 'ee follow you and take our Watkins back to 'ell wit' 'eem."

"What on earth do you mean, Cassie? I simply wish to take the poor man his victuals. The day is fine, and I'm not otherwise engaged."

"So, you *go* be udderwize engage, Miss Eliza. I send Linda to 'eem. She 'appy to go. What business is 'ee to you?"

I did not reply but returned, feelings hurt, to the kitchen. She followed me there like an angry wasp.

"You want to see 'eem 'anged like a ham in de smoke 'ouse? You tink your uncle, or even your faddah, won' do 'eet?"

"I wish to bring him his sack, as a Christian kindness," I said, hurt turning to indignation. Why needed I to argue my case with our slave? "It will do me good to stretch my legs. I've been indoors for too long and am restless."

"Restless, yes. I shore agree wit' *dat*." Cassie nodded. "You plenty restless."

"Cassie," I said warmly. "I know of no other slave who would dare speak to her mistress so."

Suddenly, Cassie picked up the gunnysack, thrust it at me, and said, "Well, go, go. But 'ave a care what I say. Cassie know white folk and dere ways."

Delighted to be in possession of the sack at last, I kissed her on her angry cheek, found my cape, and departed. I strode down Deer Street toward the ferry, shielding my eyes against the bright sun, my heart filled with effervescent hope.

The coast was alive with activity. Carts rumbled down Front Street to the market, and, as I approached the road, my nose was treated to the fecund smell of horse dung, hay, and rotting fish. The ferryboat had already left when I arrived at the wharf. I had to wait near half an hour with a cold wind blowing. Two rough-looking men soon joined me. They were sawyers, also waiting to make the short trip to Langdon's shipyard. They nodded politely, no doubt wondering what a lady was doing with a reeking gunnysack slung over her shoulder. After several moments of awkward silence, I spoke.

"Our man, Watkins, forgot his sack this morning. I thought I'd bring it to him."

"We're happy to bring it for you, miss," one of them said. "We know the one."

"Oh, thank you. But I was hoping to get a look at the shipyard. How goes it? The *Raleigh*, I mean?"

"She's coming along. We've got 'er up on staging. Your man'd be up there now, I expect, layin' the planks."

"He won't be hard to spot," the taller one said. Then they laughed.

"Yep. Only slave we've ever seen at Langdon's. Even though he's near white—from a distance."

The older one laughed again. "Oh, but he's a good worker, I'll grant him that."

"A very good worker," the younger one agreed. "Knows his place, though."

The boat approached then, and we readied ourselves to board. During the crossing, the men fell silent, and I enjoyed the sensation of the wind whipping my face. I knew not why, but having one's breath taken away by a strong wind seemed to take away all fear.

The boatman helped me out on to the rocky shore. From where we landed it was easy to spot the hull of the *Raleigh*, raised high in the air.

"Just there. See him?"

Indeed, I did: His shirtsleeves were rolled up, exposing fine, tan arms upon which blond hairs glistened. He gripped a hammer, and a pouch of nails was tied about his waist. He stood in profile, hair across his face, eyes focused, brow prominent, full lips pursed in concentration. I thought him the most handsome man I'd ever seen.

The two men bowed slightly in my direction and went off to the pit. It was a covered pit—freshly made, to judge by its pale-yellow planks.

Everywhere, men labored at one thing or another. There was a tremendous amount of dust in the air. It floated over everything in swirls and eddies, at the whim of winds that shifted constantly. I coughed, and from the blur of dust I saw a tall, fair-haired man approach. He looked to be in his mid thirties. He had a long face and long nose, and his eyes shone with keen, quick intelligence.

"Hello," he said, bowing. "Whom do I have the pleasure of meeting? I'm John Langdon. You must be shipwrecked, to find yourself here." He smiled at me with such an easy grace that I blushed.

"I'm Eliza Boylston, sir. My family and I are staying with my uncle Robert Chase just now."

"Ah, yes," he said, and his eyes flit away from me, giving me to understand that he placed my uncle among the enemy ranks.

"We arrived last June after—after the engagement at Charlestown. My brother, Jeb, was killed there."

I felt a swift pang of shame. Had I spoken of Jeb so that the colonel would think better of me? Oh, vanity!

Colonel Langdon pursed his lips and murmured, "No one should have to die fighting to keep his God-given rights. Yet it *is* a cause worth dying for. I'm very sorry, Miss Boylston. One grieves no less for heroes."

"No," I agreed.

"I'm afraid you've come to Portsmouth at her lowest moment. But she shall rally."

"*Raleigh*, sir?" I smiled up at him.

Catching the pun, he laughed. "Clever girl. Well, yes, in fact. We'll put Portsmouth on the map, and she'll have her glory back, by and by." Colonel Langdon then noticed the dirty sack on my shoulder. "I somehow think that sack isn't yours, Miss Boylston."

"Indeed not. It belongs to my uncle's man Watkins. John Watkins."

"Yes. Well. I wouldn't want him to starve. He's one of our best shipwrights." The colonel led me to the hull and called up. "Johnny! An angel has arrived with your dinner!" The colonel turned to me and bowed. "It was a great pleasure, Miss Boylston. I hope we meet again." And, giving a familiar wave to "Johnny," he was off.

Watkins had been too focused on his work to notice my presence. Now, however, he stood up, and then slowly descended a steep wooden ladder to the ground. Though it was cold in the island wind, Watkins's white shirt was translucent with perspiration. The muscles of his arms were outlined in sawdust and grime. His hair, dark beneath and golden above, was wound in tight curling locks that fell across his forehead. He wiped his face with the edge of a rolled sleeve. "Miss Boylston," he said, bowing.

The sound of my name upon his lips sent an unwonted thrill through me.

"Watkins." I nodded. One did not curtsy before a slave, but I had nearly done so. I then proffered his sack. "It seems you forgot this."

"Cassie, blast her!" He looked annoyed. "She distracted me. She always does, for hardly has one epic tale ended than another begins."

I would have liked to agree with him, for his words described my dear Cassie perfectly. Instead, I found myself saying, "Is it her fault, then, that you forgot your sack?"

"Entirely." He sounded quite grave, but then he smiled briefly, revealing a pair of dimples so fine they stunned me into silence.

I handed him his sack. As Watkins took it, I happened to notice his hands. There were angry red sores upon his palms. "Your hands!" I exclaimed. "Allow me to see them."

Instinctively, he took a step back and put his hands behind him. "There's nothing wrong with them."

"But there *is*. I insist." I quickly grasped his wrists in a proprietary manner. He flinched as I turned his palms up. Two, nay, three sores bled freely on each palm. The blister on his right hand was quite inflamed. I'd heard that such wounds could become putrid and require the amputation of a limb—or worse.

"Watkins, how can you—how can you be such a fool?"

"Your uncle likes it not when I do not earn my keep," he replied.

"That's an odd notion." I released my grasp. "My uncle makes a tidy profit off of your labor. The least he can do is keep you alive to work another day." Then, without listening to his rejoinder, I went off to complain to Colonel Langdon.

"Miss Boylston," Watkins called entreatingly, "if you insist on telling anyone, let it be Mr. Hackett. I have no wish to importune the colonel. *I beg you.*"

I nodded my assent without turning round. Several rods off, a man I guessed to be Hackett stood over a sawpit. A short, florid-faced man, Hackett was growing redder at what he saw in the pit.

"No, no, man!" he cried to the bottom sawyer, one of the men who had accompanied me on the ferry. "Can you not see that you are far off the mark?"

I half expected him to leap down there and blurted, "Mr. Hackett! A moment of your time, if you please." At the sound of my voice, Hackett turned. "As I was bringing my family's slave his victuals, I've discovered him to be in most egregious condition." How easily I adopted the superior tone Mama might have used!

It was quite effective. Hackett was officious as he led me away from the pit. "I know your uncle. A fine man," he said placatingly.

"Indeed."

Together, we approached Watkins, who stood at the base of the staging. He shifted from foot to foot, impatient and annoyed. Then he removed an apple from his sack, took a bite, and was about to take another when he saw us approach.

"Your hands," barked Hackett.

After some hesitation, Watkins finally opened his hands for Mr. Hackett's inspection. Seeing the open sores, Hackett made a face, spat on the ground, and growled, "By God, Watkins. Three days off! Now get out of here and take care of those sores. I'll send word to your master."

Hackett had turned to go back to the sawpit when I interjected, "I should think his duties must be more varied if the same thing is not to happen again." Instead of replying, the shipmaster now merely grumbled something and went his way.

"Well, Watkins," I said with a cheerful lift in my voice, "you may as well finish your lunch while we wait for the ferry."

Suddenly, and with vicious force, Watkins threw his apple core toward the shore. He mounted the ladder, put his tools in a sack, carried them down with him, and took them to a nearby shed for safekeeping. Then he joined me with obvious reluctance.

The shore was windy, and, as the ferryman had not yet arrived, Watkins sat himself beside a beach plum and opened his gunny-sack. Finding a biscuit, he bit into it noisily.

The silence became uncomfortable. I said, "Cassie shall have some kind of salve, no doubt. She'll make you well in a few days."

"Undoubtedly."

His sudden coldness, so different from the smile I had received when he first had greeted me, wounded me. I almost felt like weeping, but instead I asked, "Have I—have I given offense, Watkins?"

Watkins turned, smiled at me oddly, and said, "My mother, a most excellent woman, died when I was nine."

"I'm very sorry for it. But what mean you by that?"

The ferryman approached. Watkins waved to him and hastened to finish his biscuit. He then rose, dusting the sand off his breeches.

"Only that it has been a long time since I've had a mother, and I have no great wish for one now."

The rebuke, so unexpected, made me turn away. "That is a cruel thing to say." Tears pooled in the ledges of my eyes.

"No, not cruel"—he hastened to reply, just as the ferryman approached. "It's just, I—"

"Comin' aboard?" The ferryman was upon us.

"A moment." Watkins turned his shoulders to the ferryman and looked at me, but I could not read his eyes. I understood with dawning horror that I neither knew him nor knew how to speak to him, and that my attempt to do so had been a grievous error.

We returned to the other shore in silence. There, I cursed myself roundly for having had the clever idea to bring Watkins his gunnysack.

20

THE INCIDENT WITH WATKINS UPON BADGER'S ISLAND unsettled me for several days. A profound remorse followed me everywhere. Each time I recalled his words, I cringed with shame. The others had been grateful for my kindness. Where had I gone wrong with Watkins?

I saw him not after that, and so did not learn whether or by what means Cassie treated his blisters. He seemed to vanish even from the background of my life, and our bizarre encounter on the island eventually took on the wavering unreality of a dream.

In May, the *Raleigh* was launched. Many of the townspeople strolled down to the shore to see her off. There was a formal ceremony, Colonel Langdon presiding, and then to great cheers and celebration the *Raleigh* unfurled her square-rigged sails and turned down the Piscataqua, lifting, with her sails, the hopes of our Rebel citizens.

It was not until June that I next came upon Watkins. This was out on the plains west of town, at the annual Negro elections. Cassie and the Whipple slaves had been speaking of nothing else for near a month.

"Miss Eliza, there'll be music and dancing, and everyone has such a good time. Everyone will look beautiful," gushed Dinah one morning. "Oh, please come, Miss Eliza!" She pressed her slender fingertips together.

"But won't I—stand out?"

"Maybe a little," Dinah admitted. "But other white folk come to watch. Oh, do come!" Here, she gently grasped the sleeve of my gown, and I assented.

It was a fine, warm day when I first espied a scene that made me doubt my own vision: A huge crowd of Negroes had gathered on Middle Street. These must have been men and women not just from Portsmouth but from all the neighboring towns. King Nero Brewster, their elected leader, and several of his officers, all dressed in brightly colored tunics, led a procession that included Negroes on horseback—with guns and swords!

I followed the crowd down the street, onto Middle Road, and into the plains on the outskirts of town. Many sang to drums and lively music. All the while, I tried but failed to understand what these elections were about—and why families such as my own allowed them.

When we arrived at the plains, I saw that there were already near two hundred Negroes waiting there, all dressed in their best and most festive clothing.

Standing behind the crowd, I watched the solemn ceremony in which the new officers were elected and sworn in. King Nero stood on a hastily erected podium and called out each name in turn. After each name, murmurs went up among the crowd. To my surprise, John Watkins's name was called, and he emerged from the crowd to claim his title as a newly elected deputy.

"It is a very great honor for one so young," said someone beside me.

King Nero Brewster spoke a few words in praise of Watkins, and the audience clapped and cheered. Watkins descended the makeshift podium, and though I stood at some distance, his eyes lit on me. He seemed deeply surprised at my presence, and I actually imagined he might speak to me, when all at once he veered to his left and smiled at Linda.

She wore a bright-red turban and a simple red gown, which made her lovely, dark skin glow. A turquoise stone sat at the hollow of her neck.

Linda, shy and silent with my family, laughed easily with Watkins and their mutual friends who had gathered around him. I soon left for home, imagining how they would dance till early light, at Bell's Tavern, to Cuffee's lively violin.

It was right and good for Watkins to love Linda. But as I walked home from the plains, I grew unaccountably morose, and I found myself wishing that a gentle wind would blow Linda out to sea.

The following morning, having made my way to the kitchen after breakfast, I asked Cassie, "How did you enjoy the party?"

Cassie put a worn brown hand to her head. It was creased with wrinkles, though I doubted she had seen her thirty-fifth birthday.

"I drank too much, and now I 'ave a 'eadache."

"Poor Cassie. Have you no remedy you can take?"

"Oh, yes. I take 'eet already. 'Eet doesn't work." Here, she gave me a sheepish grin.

"And—and the others? They had a good time?"

"Oh, dey all have a fine time. Linda, she dance with Johnny till Cuffee can't hold da bow no longer. Dey keep beggin' 'eem for 'one maw, one maw.'"

"I'm glad you enjoyed yourself, Cassie. Truly." I kissed her on the cheek and let her get on with her work. I then quietly repaired to my chamber, where I allowed myself an hour of exquisite misery, replete with copious tears.

•   •   •

On Thursday, July 18, the Declaration of Independency was read from the western steps of the State House on King Street. To many, it was a vindication of all our suffering. Those Rebels whom my family had so long derided were now our leaders. This was now their country.

My family reacted to the news with silent dismay. Uncle Robert paced his house as if it were a prison. Were it not for us, he would surely have fled. But the confiscation of homes was escalating; soon, his physical presence was all that stood between us and homelessness. When, the following week, my uncle was asked to swear his loyalty to the Cause by signing the Association Test, he refused, rendering his position even more precarious.

Papa, however, signed it, much to my surprise. When I asked him why, he shrugged and said, "It is useless to swim against the tide—eventually, one will tire, and all will be lost." But one night that same week, I overheard Papa arguing with Uncle Robert about it. In this argument, Papa sounded far less pragmatic than he had with me.

"We would do well to avoid this topic, Robert," I heard Papa say. They were in his study, but the door was only partly closed. I stood in the hall, barely breathing.

"I've a right to be proud of my son, Richard. Just as you are."

"Just so. I am vastly proud of Jeb. If I could take back our bitter arguments, I would. Surely you can appreciate that I begin to resent those warmongers who killed my son. I begin to think I lacked vision . . ." Papa's voice trailed off.

"Vision? Of what, pray? A Rebel victory?" Uncle Robert laughed derisively.

"A vision not of war, Robert, but of eventual peace," Papa said. "A vision of how we might be—better."

Uncle Robert sneered, "As if anything could be better than the Empire! Honestly, Richard, I find your shift in attitude most worrisome."

My father did not reply, and as he left his study, I snuck off to the kitchen, unperceived.

Just as the people celebrated in the streets, the smallpox invaded. It spread quickly. A smokehouse and guard were established at the great swamp. Everyone coming in to Portsmouth had to be "smoked." We ourselves did not set foot abroad.

•   •   •

I recall only with difficulty those weeks in the summer of '76. While it was a time of vast unrest without, within Uncle's house there was only tedium, genteel discomfort, and mounting tension between Papa and Uncle Robert.

Mama forbade the Whipple slaves to enter our home. Without Dinah's sweet and youthful energy, without Cuffee's music, the house was doubly dull. I had not enough to occupy myself and began to feel quite low. Then, on September 22, we were awakened by a loud rapping on the front door. I peered out my chamber door to see Uncle descend the stairs in his robe and bare feet. Soon there came a piteous groan.

Mama emerged from her chamber. "Brother, what is it? What news?" she cried from the top of the stairs. We all emerged from our chambers. A messenger had arrived from New York. There had been a terrible fire, and my cousin, Lieutenant George Chase, had perished. I had moved out into the hall and heard Mama shriek, "Oh, poor Brother!"

"An act of God, Margaret," Papa replied with some conviction. Mama took this as consolation, but in it I heard an almost spiteful sense of vindication.

For many weeks, the house lay draped in somber black bunting. The pendulums of the clocks were removed. We wore black armbands and jet mourning rings that Uncle Robert brought back from New York. He had been unable to bring the body of his son with him, however. Our Committee of Correspondence, the local

Rebel governing body, determined that doing so might cause a riot, the truth of which I did not doubt.

It was never known who started the fire that decimated half of New York in September of '76, but recriminations on both sides were bitter. As for what happened to my cousin, it was said he had left his ship and gone into a building to help his fellow officers. But I subsequently heard that this building was in fact a house of ill repute, and that Cousin George had been a frequent patron of it.

After Uncle Robert returned from New York, he spoke little. His once portly body lost flesh. Each morning, Cassie brought him her most special tisane and bathed him. She spoke to him soothingly, and I marveled at how she could be so kind to the man who at best ignored his slaves and, at worst, whipped and humiliated them. Indeed, Cassie was so kind to this sad specimen of a man that one day, as he sat in a steaming tub in the kitchen, he grinned at her as if she were the only good thing left on earth.

Mama was certain that her brother had gone soft in the head. She spoke to him as if he were a child: "Shall Brother have a walk today?" Or "Shall Brother come with me to market?" Uncle Robert always looked at her with a blank gawking stare and said, "I shall go with Cassie, this afternoon." The town soon began to take note of old Uncle Robert strolling into town with little black Cassie by his side.

In the kitchen one morning that autumn, as Cassie made an apple crumble, I asked her why she was so kind to Uncle Robert. She looked at me sternly. "What dey teach you at meeteeng, Miss Eliza? I tink maybe your ears is plugged wit' wax."

"I only meant that—"

"I know what you meant. You tink I owe him nutteeng. That he's not a good man. But only tink how *alone* 'ee is. Not a soul in de world care about 'eem. I could not treat a dog so." She clutched at her neckerchief and I was about to interject a word when Cassie, warming to her subject, continued, "When it hurt inside you like dat, dat's a good ting. Dat pain open your uncle's eyes. He *see* Cassie now."

"*Sees* you?" I smirked. "One more day of such kindness, and my uncle shall be hopelessly in love with you."

"Pshaw, dat won't nevah happen."

"Why not? You think no master has ever fallen in love with his slave?"

But Cassie would hear no more such talk.

"Out! Out!" She shooed me away. But, leaving the kitchen, I wagged a finger at her.

"We'll see, Cassie. We'll just see." An apple came flying toward my head, but, thankfully, I ducked in time to miss it.

In November, Congress ordered the building of nine ships of war: five enormous brigs of seventy-six guns, three ships of seventy-four guns, and a smaller ship of eighteen guns. Our town soon became an anthill of frenzied industry. Watkins was sent once more to Badger's Island, this time to lay the keel of the *Ranger*.

Watkins, Cassie informed me, had now risen through the ranks not merely of the slave community but also of the shipyard.

"Dey say he become master shipwright now dat Colonel Langdon has gone off. He very busy now, but after meeting he like to walk with Linda."

Linda, Linda, Linda. Ever since the Negro elections in June, Cassie had been narrating in tiresome detail the growing romance between Linda and Watkins.

"Yes, dey love to walk about town after meeting. Out to da windy point past the ferry. Oh, you should see dem, Miss Eliza. A more beautiful pair of niggers you nevah seen."

"I don't doubt it," I said sourly, "though I myself have discerned no special understanding between them."

"Dat because dey keep it a secret," she whispered. "You know de master wouldn'a want no black babe around here. Not dees days. He knew, he'd maybe sell Linda. Maybe even sell Johnny."

I frowned. "Mama is quite attached to Linda now. And Uncle Robert would be a fool to sell Watkins—"

"Dat may be. But you know I speak the truth. You know dey sell us when dey want."

Oh, I did know it. I suffered greatly to remember Toby, and Cassie fell silent. But while it pained me to see Cassie absorbed in unhappy recollections, I was grateful for her silence upon the vexatious topic of Watkins and Linda.

21

THE DARK WINTER MONTHS PASSED SLOWLY THAT year. There was little to do, and even less to eat. I spent most of my time in the kitchen, with Cassie. During this time I only rarely saw Watkins, and I became convinced that he cared as little for me as I did him. My fleeting interest had been a product of loneliness and depression, nothing more.

One cool, early morning in March of '77, I awoke to the sound of the birds making a ruckus outside my window. The sun had not yet risen, but the birds seemed insistent that I rise. With a great sigh, I obliged them.

Cassie was already up and preparing breakfast. As I entered the kitchen, she was peeling potatoes so sprouted they looked like giant spiders. I took one and attacked Cassie with it, making as if to bite her neck, when I was startled half to death by a knock on the back door. I turned to the window, to see a Negro boy standing there, shifting uneasily from foot to foot.

He was a skinny youth of perhaps nine or ten. The boy's eyes were clear and bright, his face long and sensitive. He was not familiar to me, and for a moment I assumed he was on some sort of errand. Then, moving closer to the window, I noticed his feet were wrapped in torn, filthy rags. A tattered sack slung from one shoulder. This was no local slave child.

"Cassie," I whispered. Cassie turned, frowned, and, catching the vagrant in her sight, was on the verge of shooing him away when she changed her mind and opened the door a crack.

"What do you want, child?"

The boy said nothing.

"To whom do you belong?" I asked, kneeling down to face him. Still nothing.

"Well, then, what's your name? Surely you must have one?"

Cassie whispered, "'Ee look like my Toby."

"A little bit," I admitted. "But his eyes are not so dark. They are almost green."

She regarded the child at arm's length. Her mouth turned down with indecision, which made her look unusually dour. The poor child stood stiffly, no doubt certain that we'd push him back into the miserable world.

"Well, what shall we do with him?" I asked aloud. "We must at least feed him." I motioned for the child to come in and sit on the chair. I then poured him a glass of milk. Cassie looked at me dubiously, then shook her head.

"Come on, Cassie," I urged her. "The child needs a bath."

With reluctance she set a large pot of water on the coals. The boy took fright at this, as if he believed we might boil him to a tender, edible consistency.

After he had eaten, Cassie went to undress him while I stood sentry by the kitchen entrance. We saw, to our horror, weeping, fresh scars, thick as my small finger, all down his back. We said nothing, but Cassie's chin trembled as she helped him to step into the tin pail. He felt the water with his fingers before carefully stepping inside.

"Child, where do you come from? How did you get here?" I asked. Nothing. I said, "Well, but at least tell us how you arrived at our house."

I saw his mind working. For, though mute with fear, I knew from his eyes that he understood us.

"Next door." He shrugged. "What call themselves Whipples. A girl was out front, and when I tell her what I did, she pointed here. She said there was a good white lady—here."

"Me?" I said, turning to Cassie.

"Well, it in't me," she replied.

. . .

After his bath, warm, dry, and full, the child closed his eyes and was asleep before Cassie had set him down upon her bed.

"Poor little fellow," I said, turning to leave. "I don't see what we are supposed to do. I don't see how we can keep him."

"No," Cassie agreed. "Master Robert, he barely keep us."

"Then—what can we do, Cassie? We can't set him to the wolves. You saw him when I asked where he was from. He'll never tell us. I suppose we must find out to whom he belongs."

"And den?" she challenged.

"I don't know. Let me think."

My frock was wet all down the bodice, and I wished to change out of it. "I must go. I shan't be long. Reveal nothing to anyone. And if he wakes, for goodness' sake, entreat him to be silent." Cassie nodded, and I left her alone.

I was in a heedless rush when I nearly collided with Mama on the stairs.

"Why, Eliza, you're soaking wet!"

"Yes. I was attempting to . . . wash a soiled pair of stockings."

"Wash stockings?" she exclaimed. "Why on earth? Really, Eliza. What do we have servants for?"

"It was a trifle. Phoebe was busy with the silver, and Cassie is just making breakfast."

"Well, hurry up and put something on. You'll catch your death like that."

"Yes, Mama." I moved to my chamber, changed out of my frock and donned a dry one. My heart beat so quickly that I grew short of breath. The child could not long be hidden, but I knew not what to do, nor whom to approach.

I sat upon my bed and stared out the window. The child had been deeply frightened—but was it from the whipping, or something else? If we turned him out, he would take to hiding in the woods. He could not last long out there.

I spent near an hour on the bed, thinking it over. I strove to recall what I had been taught at meeting. Was a sin committed for some greater good yet a sin? I wished I had paid more attention. But it was no use. The lofty precepts of theology were of little use to me at that moment.

I then turned my brains to our current troubles. In the war against our motherland, did our men not kill for a greater purpose? There must be such a purpose, I believed, for otherwise our actions would be inexcusable. My reasoning was hardly canonical, but it would have to do.

I rose and approached my uncle's chamber across the hall. I heard him clear his throat and knew he was within. I knocked.

"Who's there?" he said, startled.

"Cousin Eliza, Uncle Robert."

"Well, come in."

I entered my uncle's chamber. He was sitting by the window overlooking Deer Street. He had a benign, contemplative air. His body had wasted away, and he looked far older and more fragile than when we first arrived. For a moment, I imagined he had no strength to deny me anything. I even allowed myself to imagine that he had softened. I came directly to the point.

"Uncle Robert, a child has appeared at our door, a poor Negro child who has been whipped to within an inch of his life. We could not wrest the name of his master from him, but I have no doubt that he has escaped from hell itself. I should like to keep him. For a time, at least."

"Certainly not," Uncle said without hesitation. "I have no means of feeding an extra mouth. Besides, God knows to whom this child belongs. I should by rights report him."

Nothing moved save his mouth, but I had heard the force of will behind his breath. Uncle Robert may have loved Cassie, but his feelings toward slavery had not changed.

Some moments passed between us in silence. Twice I moved to leave my uncle's chamber. But my heart pounded in my ears and would not let me slink away like a miserable coward. I turned to my uncle and asked God to forgive me for what I was about to do.

"Uncle Robert," I began. "I am sorry to give anyone pain, but I must admit that I am privy to the tragic nature of poor Cousin George's death—I speak of the house in which he died. To put it plainly, I know the circumstances."

Uncle's mouth gaped at the mention of my cousin's secret. Had the Devil himself entered my breast? His face told me it was so. I continued:

"I shouldn't like to imagine his excellent name besmirched and ridiculed among the good people of Portsmouth—and perhaps beyond."

This time, as Uncle Robert looked up at me, I saw the dart of pain lodge in his breast, and I swooped in to take my advantage: "The boy may apprentice under Watkins, at Colonel Langdon's shipyard. They sorely need workers there now. Only think how, in but a few years' time, you shall make a good return on his indenture."

My uncle looked up at me without a word; his legs had ceased their restless pumping, and I do believe my willingness to blackmail him in this way came as a shock to us both.

"Uncle," I softened my tone, "I am not insensible to the fact that you have taken us under your wing these two years. I know not how we would have survived without your aid. You are a good, Christian man and shall reap your rewards in the next life. Or perhaps even yet in this."

The fog in Uncle Robert's eyes cleared. Never would he have thought me capable of such villainy. He turned from me with a dismissive wave of his hand. "Well, have your nigger child if you must. Only keep him out of my sight. And if anyone is to go with less food because of it, let it be yourself."

I curtsied deeply and left the chamber. Once in my own chamber, I felt my heart pound wildly. Yet no shame tainted my exultation, though the battle had been a dirty one.

It was just after eight the following morning when, taking up a shawl for me, a blanket for the boy, and an old canteen borrowed of one of the stableboys, I walked out the kitchen door heading for the ferry. The poor child was reluctant to leave the house. Tears pooled in his round eyes. Desperate for Cassie, he ran back into the kitchen and emerged a moment later grasping a small doll she had made for him out of an old rag and buttons. He held it as if it was the only thing he fully trusted.

Cassie stood in the doorway. She said, "Dat doll have powerful magic. He protect you."

She proffered a sack, and I took it. Before leaving my uncle's house, however, and with Cassie remaining in the doorway, I crouched down and held the child by his shoulders.

"I know you're frightened," I said. "But we plan to keep you safe and take care of you. It would be much easier for us if we didn't have to call you 'boy' or 'you there.' Yes, it would be far easier if we had a name to call you. You need not use your old one, you know," I encouraged him.

The child looked at me, then at Cassie.

"I like the name Isaac," he said.

I took the child's hand and said, "Very well, then, Isaac. Let us go before we miss the ferry." And off we went down the hill, toward the ferry and the bright rising sun.

On the skiff, the child clung to me in terror, but we made it safely across the river and were soon on the island. All around us, men were busily engaged in their tasks. There was such an overall feeling of industry—the noise of hammers, anvils against stone, and the rasping of saws—that Isaac forgot his fear, and his eyes widened in amazement.

"You see that?" I pointed to the hull in the distance, its ribs curved like the carcass of a whale. "That's the ship these men are building. It's a big warship. It's called the *Ranger*. In another month, it will have guns upon it and flapping sails. Wouldn't you like to help these men build a ship of war?"

The boy turned to me, his eyes eager. Then some anxious thought occurred to him, and he shrank back in fear. "Miss, I don't know how to build a ship." In his voice I heard the fear of bloody whipping. I knelt by his side and whispered, "No one shall whip you here. If they do, I'll *shoot* 'em with our musket." At this outlandish thought, Isaac grinned. "Besides," I added, "you shall have a big brother to watch over you now."

"Who? Who'll watch over me?" he asked dubiously. Isaac cast his eyes about the many white faces. He would have been foolish to believe me without further proof. Which white man would protect him? Nary a one.

I took the child by the hand, and together we approached the *Ranger's* hollow hull. She had not yet been mounted on staging, but around her, half a dozen men were in the process of building the frame upon which she would soon rest. As we approached, I cast about for Watkins.

He was not among the shipwrights but stood by a lean-to, staring down at an architectural drawing. His figure was silhouetted against the rising sun. He stood with his weight on one leg, in an attitude of indecision. His forefinger rested on the drawing, and he had a dissatisfied air. He then turned quickly, as if to seek someone out, and found me instead, holding the hand of a Negro boy.

Watkins was surprised to see me, but he approached at once and bent down to address the child. His hair was loose and fell in tightly twisted coils about his shoulders. He had grown a small goatee, hair such as may be worn only among shipwrights and sailors. But it lent his fine features an appealing ruggedness.

"Hallo, there," he said to the boy, then nodded civilly to me. "Well, sir," he continued as he knelt upon one knee and addressed the child. "Who might you be? You're not by any chance King George, are you? They say he's very short."

Isaac giggled and shook his head.

"No? I'm relieved to hear it, for otherwise I should have to chop off your head. Here, shake my hand. They call me Watkins. And you are?"

The boy looked at me.

"This is Isaac," I found my voice. "He's going to be staying with us."

"Well, it's very good to meet you, Isaac," said Watkins. The child reached to keep his new shirt from ballooning in the breeze. Collarless, and made of fine linen, it billowed around the child. The shirt must've once belonged to Cousin George.

"I would give you a tour," Watkins continued, "but I'm afraid I can't break away from work just yet. Would you come back tomorrow? If you come at eleven, I could show you what important work we do for His Excellency. Would you like that?"

Isaac nodded. He glanced at me, and I knew his question.

"I'll come as well, if I may," I said. "Isaac, I need to speak to Watkins. Perhaps you could look for shells on the beach? You may keep the ones you find. But don't go too far—I shall call for you shortly. Do you understand?"

He nodded. "But—"

"Yes, Isaac?"

"I'm *hungry*."

I smiled. Children's needs were so simple, compared to ours! "As it happens, Isaac, Cassie packed some provisions. Go find a rock to sit on so you don't dirty your trousers. If you eat everything Cassie packed for you, you can then fill your rucksack up with shells."

The child looked at me twice to make certain I was sincere; he then ran off to find a flat rock.

I led Watkins off in the other direction, out of the child's earshot. Alone with him, I grew suddenly awkward. He stood several feet away from me, head turned to the side, glancing now and again at the strange child I had brought.

"There's a story in that boy," Watkins said, "but I'm sorry I cannot hear it just now. I dare not stop, when so much is in my care."

"I understand," I replied. "We've not as yet pried much from him, but I'll willingly tell you all I know."

"Tomorrow, I have a few minutes at eleven, then an hour at two in the afternoon. I usually eat with the other lads—"

"Yes," I said, leaning in to whisper. "But allow me to say what presses so upon my mind. It won't take a moment. Cassie and I, we are praying the boy may apprentice here, at the shipyard. He's a runaway, and we have little doubt that his owner looks for him as we speak. The boy landed on our doorstep just yesterday. Isaac is not his real name—he won't tell us it. I believe his life, his survival—"

"Say no more," Watkins replied. He then glanced back toward the *Ranger*. "But I must go." Then, suddenly, Watkins took my hand in his, looked gravely at me, and departed.

I sucked in my breath and just stood there a moment or two, while Isaac ran up and down the beach gathering shells.

22

THE WIND WHIPPED MY FACE; MY HAND still felt his hand on mine. My ear still heard his soft voice in my ear. I allowed myself a moment of purest joy. The sun was descending and cast its long shadow upon the shore. I felt myself cast in shadow, too. What did I hope? I dared not answer. But his touch had given the lie to my belief that he cared nothing for me or I for him.

Once home, Isaac fairly skipped into the kitchen, eager to show off his shells. A moment later, Cassie opened the kitchen door with her foot and hip.

"Miss Eliza," she scolded. "What you tink lettin' 'eem in wit' all dees *sand*. Here . . ." She thrust a pail at me and waved us both off to the well to wash the shells clean. "I just wash de floor, and 'ee goin' to track sand all ovah de house. Your Mama is already in a terrible way . . . she gone to fetch de constable."

I stood motionless, believing that Mama had reported Isaac. But Cassie, with one look at the child and a slight shake of the head, gave me to know I was mistaken.

"Wash dose shells, den I tell you. Oh, dees 'ees too much for one day. Poor Cassie heart gon' stop 'eets bee-tin' . . ."

I ran with Isaac to the well and, in my haste, splashed water all over my petticoat, which Isaac found vastly amusing. As a reward for his laughter, I poured the rest of the bucket on his head.

"Ai!" he cried. "Miss Cassie!" Cassie came out and was not pleased to have to dry Isaac off and fetch another of Master George's old shirts.

The shells were soon clean enough to gain admittance to the house, and Cassie set Isaac up with them on the floor in her chamber. She then turned to me. I asked, "Why has Mama gone off to fetch the constable?"

Cassie could not suppress a guilty smile. "What do you know, Miss Eliza, but Linda has gone and run off wit' Bristol Wood'ouse!"

I dropped the bucket and stared at her. Bristol Woodhouse was the slave of that same Mr. Atkinson whose ill fortune it was to be invited to our Thanksgiving dinner. Now he, a goodly carpenter by reputation, had gone off with our Linda. I turned and fixed my eyes upon Cassie, who shrank from my gaze.

"I thought you said Linda and Watkins were a couple. Indeed, you have spoken of little else these six months."

Just then, my mother burst into the kitchen with Constable Hill, Uncle Robert not far behind them. They both looked greatly disconcerted. He had lost a valuable piece of property, and Mama had lost her lady's maid—she would not find such a one as Linda anywhere in the colonies.

"And here I thought her so pliant, so amiable!" Mama was saying to Constable Hill.

"Oh, Sister, those people run deep!" added Uncle Robert.

"Mama," I rejoindered, standing in front of Cassie, "you can hardly blame a slave for wanting to be free."

"I don't see why not," Mama objected. "What else could she do? Where could she possibly *go*?"

I thought it prudent not to reply. Suddenly we heard the faint clack of Isaac arranging his shells on the floor of Cassie's chamber.

With a gasp, Cassie ran to her room and shut the door behind her. The clacking ceased.

"What on earth's the matter with *her*?" asked Mama. Clearly Uncle Robert had not as yet told Mama about the boy.

"I have no idea." I glanced at Uncle Robert, who made as if not to notice me.

I held my breath in the awkward pause before Cassie returned. Such good and ill fortune at once! Emerging from the old dairy at last, Cassie wiped the perspiration from her brow and, to Constable Hill's query, said she knew nothing of the clandestine affair. I for one believed her. While Cassie was an able liar, I did not believe her capable of convincing me of an attachment between Linda and Watkins when she knew of another.

"But Mama, we mustn't keep Cassie from her work. Let us away to the parlor, where we may offer Constable Hill a seat."

"Oh, goodness, you are right." And we left the kitchen for the relative safety of the parlor. Once there, and seated, however, there seemed little to discuss, and I suggested we look in upon the nursery. The four of us tromped up the stairs to the attic, where we discovered Linda's bed neatly made, her Sunday frock draped over a chair.

"Seems she had it planned well," observed the constable. "To my way of thinking, she must have had help."

•   •   •

Signs went up all over town about a pair of runaway slaves. Guards were posted on the roads north and south leading out of town. Stoodley's coach service was notified, though we doubted any coachman would risk his neck for a pair of slaves. But, after a few days, the couple did not appear, and it was determined that they'd managed somehow to escape the net cast around Portsmouth.

For six months I had suffered Watkins's growing attachment to Linda. It had been an exquisite pain, clear and cleansing, each stab telling me that he was ne'er to be mine. Now I recognized the danger to me that came with the freedom to hope. I knew not whether I would have the strength to create another impediment.

Up to this point my attraction to Watkins had been of a fairly superficial nature. But the week Linda escaped, I learned certain facts that had a powerful effect on my feelings toward him.

That Sunday morning before meeting, I was standing in the kitchen helping Cassie prepare our dinner when I heard my uncle in the hallway just beyond us. He was speaking to Watkins. I missed the first part of the conversation, but when it grew louder I clearly heard Watkins say,

"I'm sorry, sir, but I've spent it."

"Spent it!" my uncle cried. "On what, pray, did you spend my money?"

I cast a look at Cassie and moved quickly to stand behind the kitchen door, where I peered out to see Watkins, head bowed abjectly as he stood before Uncle Robert.

"On shoes," Watkins said. "These ones are nearly spent."

I looked down at his shoes. It was true, they were very worn. Why then, I wondered, did he not wear the new ones?

"I should whip you, boy!" said Uncle Robert. "But the people don't approve of that anymore—not even thieves may be whipped these days. Oh, well, but you may keep your shoes—I suppose you need 'em. But you must request a pair next time, not simply take matters into your own hands."

"Yes, sir," said Watkins humbly.

When they had both gone, I turned to Cassie. "That was very odd, Cassie. Watkins just told Uncle Robert that he'd gone and bought shoes with the money he made at the shipyard. Yet he is not wearing them. Why is that, do you think?"

Cassie looked at me as if she considered lying. But a clever reply did not come to her, and so she said,

"Dat money in Linda's pocket, dat's why."

"Linda's pocket! Why, Cassie, he might have been whipped once more—or worse! It was very foolhardy of Watkins to risk his neck for a pair of runaways."

Though feigning annoyance with Watkins, tears of pride had welled involuntarily in my eyes.

"Here," said Cassie flatly, proffering a handkerchief from her pocket. "Dry your eyes."

• • •

On Monday morning, I accompanied Isaac to Badger's Island for his promised tour. It was cold and windy when we arrived, somewhere before eleven. Once upon the island, I wrapped a blanket around the both of us, and we climbed the dunes.

Isaac emerged from the blanket and ran after the gulls. I chased after him, he running even faster to keep away from me, until we found ourselves laughing and breathless at the northern tip of the island. At eleven we were far down the beach when we heard the bell announcing break. Isaac then raced back toward the shipyard. My feet tripped over the blanket that I kept about my shoulders, and I was out of breath by the time we reached the *Ranger*, my bonnet having flown off not once but twice, requiring me to run after it.

Back at the shipyard, one hundred or so men had put down their tools and gathered around makeshift boards for their grog. They eyed me and the Negro boy. I did not see Watkins but heard him call Isaac's name. Isaac grinned.

There he stood, this John Watkins. He was every bit as hale and handsome, alas, as he had been the day before.

"Hallo, there," he addressed the child. "Here, have a sip of grog. No? If you're to be a proper shipwright, Isaac, you've got to have yer pint."

Watkins's hands and shirt were covered with a dark substance that looked like gunpowder. Why would he be working with such a thing at a shipyard? He went off for a moment and returned with a mug, which he proffered to Isaac. Isaac took it in both hands, sipped, and then made a face as he spat the grog into the sand.

Watkins laughed, his face revealing a pair of fine dimples. "You'll get used to it. Come on." He took the boy's hand. "I'll show you what it takes to build a real warship." Having stooped down for Isaac, he glanced inquiringly at me and whispered, "Do you leave at once for home?"

I had no wish to leave, but it was too cold and windy to remain long on the island. I nodded. Then I added formally, "I shall return to fetch Isaac at two." Then I whispered, "If anyone asks, you might say he's Cassie's son."

Watkins nodded slightly, and there followed a silence. What came from me next surprised both of us.

"Perhaps, Watkins—perhaps I might bring a fishing line tomorrow. Yes"—I warmed to my subject—"I should like to learn to fish, and be of use to my family."

Watkins nodded once more: "Certainly. Bring a rod, and, if you wish, I can show you how."

•   •   •

"Have we a fishing rod about?" I asked Cassie casually, upon returning home. She was on the stairs, heading up to see Mama, who had taken to her bed at the shock of Linda's escape.

"You're not having Isaac fish? Da fish bigger'n 'ee is."

"No, no. Don't be uneasy. It's for myself alone I inquire."

"Master George had one," she said. "What you want with 'eet?"

"What I want with it is my business."

"Well, then, you may fetch your own business your own self. Master George kept it in the stables."

"Thank you," I replied curtly, and off I went to procure the rod. I found the pole covered in cobwebs, propped against a corner of the barn. It was quite long: near eighteen feet—an old, noble pole, fashioned several generations ago, made of fir and flexible as a whip. As I left the stables, Jupiter called after me, wagging a black, bony finger, "Caution, Miss Eliza. You're as like to trip and kill yourself with that as catch a fish."

"Oh, no." I smiled. "I'll manage." But, despite my attempts to keep it on my shoulder, the rod bent and dragged on the ground. Its long horsehair line and hook kept coming unraveled. I finally found a means of tucking the line securely beneath the pole on my shoulder, but in the commotion I left the blanket behind, which I soon regretted, as the wind bit shrewdly.

The ferryman muttered something about the pole being longer than the boat, but he helped me set it over the rim of the vessel so that it dragged behind us. Once we had nearly reached the island, he looked at me and said, pipe still in his mouth. "Where's yer bait?"

"Bait!" I cried, having forgotten all about it. "I—I believe one of the men has some. He means to teach me."

The ferryman snorted derisively, waving his pipe for emphasis. "Why, you can barely lift the thing."

"Indeed I can."

"Ha. Well, good luck to you, miss." Here, he let out a phlegmy laugh.

I continued to be an object of ridicule as I dragged the enormous rod up the dunes. Yet such is the power of a being to deceive himself that I truly believed I wished to fish.

Some of the men ceased their labors to observe me, and Watkins himself came striding over, one large hand grasping Isaac's head as one would a melon, and Isaac kept rolling his eyes up and giggling. Watkins said, "Miss Boylston. Have you your lures? If not, I can provide some." All this was said in a perfectly audible tone. Watkins then turned to a young mate who had sat down on a rock with his gunnysack, ready to tuck into his dinner. "Jim, would you mind keeping an eye on this lad while I attend to Miss Boylston? Isaac, be very good, and do not stray. Can I trust you?"

Isaac nodded, for he was by now entirely smitten with the kind and able shipwright.

Watkins then strode off to the master's lean-to, where he rummaged through a pile of refuse and found several bits of discarded meat. These he placed in his handkerchief and returned to me. He then took my rod and held it up by one arm, resting it on his left shoulder.

"Where to, Miss Boylston?"

"Some good fishing spot, obviously, Watkins."

With a parting wave for Isaac, Watkins led me down a narrow deer path to the eastern side of the island. The crowd of men, all eagerly devouring their dinners, took little notice of us, and we soon left them behind. My heart pounded furiously. I had never been alone with Watkins for more than a moment or two. Oddly, I had no fear of him—only of myself.

After several minutes in which we passed through dense brush, sand drifting into my shoes, we emerged onto a wild and empty coast. We stood together upon the dunes, with only the wind and seabirds for company.

Watkins looked about him and then drove the pole into the sand, against a piece of driftwood. "Right," he said, then took a piece of meat and attached it to the hook, from which dripping maggots fell, leaving plenty within the meat for a greedy fish. Watkins's hands worked deftly. Yet he did not cast the line in the water for me, as I had expected. Instead, he turned and said, "I don't have long. Before I leave, I'll cast the line."

"Very well." But I did not understand his intent.

He turned to face me squarely, then suddenly became hesitant, as if there were something in particular he wished to say.

"Speak your peace, Watkins," I said, praying my voice did not betray my pounding heart. With one hand, I held the pole upright; with the other, I shielded my eyes from the sun, the better to see him.

Those blue-green eyes glanced toward me and then away. He began, "I have felt a great deal of remorse, speaking to you as I did the last time we spoke, just here, upon this island."

I hid my shock, saying only, "That was a long time ago, Watkins. It does you credit to remember it, though sometimes, I find, it is best to forget."

"Can you? Forget, I mean? I—cannot. In such cases, time seems unwilling to pass. I've grown unused to kindness," he went on. "Life has made me unforgiving. Wary. You meant only to be kind."

My breath was hardly above a whisper when I replied, "I wished to, perhaps, but I knew not how."

"No," he said. "We neither of us do. How could we?"

A thrill ran through me at that word, as small as it was dangerous: *we.*

Watkins's eyes filled with a sudden humor, which he did not attempt to hide. In a louder, less intimate tone he said, "I suppose you heard about Linda and Bristol."

"Yes. How astonishing. They fooled us all," I said, baiting him as I soon would a fish.

"Not all, perhaps," he remarked.

I glanced at him. "Why, Watkins, did you know of Linda's plans?"

He did not reply but glanced toward the water, as if he happened to see a fish leaping there.

"Come now." I smiled. "I know for a fact that you did."

Watkins turned back around, his eyes alarmed. "How is it you know? I told no one. Oh, wait—*Cassie*."

"I saw you with Uncle Robert. I heard that silly lie about your shoes. You are fortunate that Uncle Robert has not a razor-sharp mind."

Watkins looked distressed. "But I had not intended for anyone save Langdon to know the details of their escape."

"And so no one shall," I said. I sought to change the topic. "Anyway, are they well and truly gone now?"

"Yes."

"Good. I'm relieved."

"Are you?" he said, moving closer to me.

"You know not how much." I turned away from him. I was looking to my left, where Kittery's shore showed a beige strip upon which red warehouses shone in the sun. Old women in their gundalows rowed quietly toward our port, followed by raucous seagulls.

"Perhaps I do."

The wind was strong. I turned back to find Watkins standing closer to me than he had before—or did I simply imagine it? This time, upon meeting his eyes, I had no more strength to hide my deceit, and I burst into tears.

"Eliza."

I took a step toward him. He moved toward me. His cheek pressed slowly, gently, against mine. He smelled of fresh wood, gunpowder, and sweet, warm skin. After a long moment, he finally placed his arms around me. Another long moment passed, after which he pulled away and regarded me, as if to make certain I was real. I shut my eyes and let myself feel his lips on mine. When he pulled away that final time, I held on to his rough hands and kissed them both as if they were the dearest things in the world.

"I must return," he said. He then cast the line and told me what to do should I catch something. I hardly understood a word of it. Yet my conscience bade me speak of Isaac before he departed:

"You cannot know how grateful I am that you've taken Isaac under your wing."

"I saw the welts upon his back," Watkins replied. "I saw everything about the child within moments, though I know not the full story."

"No," I agreed. "He's terrified of his former master, and we don't wish to press him. Cassie is giving thanks to God every two minutes."

"Cassie, thankful? I should think she'd resent the child's presence. The poor woman is run off her feet as it is."

"Papa sold Cassie's own child five years ago. She's convinced that God in his everlasting mercy has sent her this child. That, somehow, their souls are connected."

"Perhaps they are," he murmured, looking at me. With that, he grasped my hands a final time, then left. I picked up the rod and, five minutes later, caught a large perch, which I unhooked and wrapped in Watkins's handkerchief, to take home.

23

I HANDED CASSIE THE FISH, WHICH WAS still in Watkins's handkerchief. She let it rest in her upturned palm and looked at me levelly but said nothing, and I said nothing to her, either. It was the quietest exchange of a fish in the history of mankind.

At dinner, I finally told Mama about Isaac, saying only, "Uncle has agreed that we should keep him, and that he's got the makings of a fine apprentice."

"How irregular. Uncle Robert?" she spoke across the table to her brother. "Know you about this?"

Uncle grunted. "Indeed, indeed."

Mama shrugged. "Well, I suppose since it's Uncle Robert's house he can do as he pleases. Yet I don't wonder but he begins to feel he runs an almshouse."

I stifled a smile. It amused me to hear Mama speak of her brother as if he were not there. It amused me that I had engineered Uncle Robert's grudging acceptance of the boy. But then everything amused me just then. I believe that the British could have won the war and that would have amused me just as well.

After dinner, I did not help Cassie but removed directly to my chamber, where I endeavored to reflect upon what had transpired on Badger's Island. Was I mad? Shame or remorse I had none.

Indeed, I could not wait to feel his arms around me once more, and I lay awake a long time, dreaming of it.

The following morning, I returned to Badger's Island with Isaac. It was a very fine day, with little wind, and this time I remembered to bring my own bait. I dragged the rod through the brush to the eastern end of the island, but I did not see Watkins as I passed, nor did I seek him out. Arriving upon the desolate shore, with the screaming birds all around me, I baited the line as Watkins had shown me, and I cast it. Then I waited, jumping at the least sound. I cast the line in and out and caught two fish, which I placed in a linen sack.

I did this for near an hour, certain that he would come at any moment. I smiled at the idea, believing he might jump out of the dunes to surprise me or clap his hands over my eyes. But then I grew impatient. This impatience was followed by anger, and eventually, by the devastation of knowing that he wouldn't come.

I set my pole by the side of the shack and, looking neither right nor left, neither up nor down, I found Isaac, grabbed his hand, and headed to the ferry.

Isaac was excited. "Miss Eliza, Miss Eliza! I learned so much today. Johnny taught me—"

I listened and nodded without hearing. As we walked up Deer Street to the house, I said, "Isaac, from now on I think you should go with Watkins directly in the morning. I shall send Phoebe to get you in the afternoon."

"You don't want to fetch me? Why?"

I bent down and took him by the shoulders. "Of course I want to. It's just that—Papa is ill, you see. He needs me more than you do. You're a fine, big boy."

At the notion that he was a big boy, Isaac stood taller.

"That's right, Miss Eliza," he said. "Why, I don't need Phoebe, neither."

"I know that. But it's nonetheless safest if I send her to fetch you."

After we arrived home, I could not settle into any pursuit and so took supper with Papa in his chamber.

"You seem rather glum, Eliza," Papa remarked.

"Oh, no," I said.

"You lack the society of those your own age. I would be glum, too, were I forced to remain with such family as you now have."

I cringed at Papa's reference to our diminished family, though it was the truth.

"Allow me to read to you, Papa."

"Oh, do, please."

I picked up his favorite broadside and began to read until he drifted off to sleep. Heading back toward my chamber, I heard Watkins's boots upon the stairs—had I emerged from Papa's chamber a moment sooner, we would have laid eyes upon each other. I wondered what his expression might have told me.

I slept ill and thus awoke quite late. When I finally descended, Mama had already gone out. The day was bright, but I would not go abroad. Instead, I lodged myself by Papa's side once more. I remained there half the morning, reading to him from a book on Roman history. I read him the day's broadside as well. That gave Papa pleasure, and me the means of reading the notices. I looked for one that read "Escaped: Negro boy, about ten years of age. Handsome reward." Thankfully, there was no such notice.

"You are most kind, Eliza, to spend your leisure hours in an old man's sick-room," said Papa.

"Well, Papa, you're not just any old man. You're my dear Papa."

"Yes, yes, be that as it may." Papa waved a hand at me. His nails had not been clipped, and my heart lurched with pity that we had all somewhat neglected him. "But, now go—enjoy yourself. You've done your penance here."

I kissed him and left the room, unsure of what I might do next. I then espied Phoebe in the dining room. She was polishing Uncle's table with rags that reeked of linseed oil.

"Phoebe, I need you to fetch Isaac, our new boy, on Badger's Island."

Her eyes grew wide. "You mean take the ferry, miss?"

"It is but a short trip. Ten minutes at most."

"I never was on a boat—"

"Oh, Phoebe. Just do it," I said, angry not at her, but at having been abandoned the day before. Phoebe nodded and scampered out of the room in tears.

●   ●   ●

I was determined not to visit the island again, and so cast about for a new pursuit. We had recently learned that a regiment of Connecticut militia was camped to the west of us. Rumors had it that the soldiers were sick and starving, nearly abandoned by their own command. I plucked up my courage to help them.

Cassie and I prepared a basket, and I snuck out of the house early one morning. Mama was gone to the market—had she known my destination, she would have forbade me absolutely to go, for there was smallpox and all manner of disease among them.

To see young boys die of wounds inflicted in war is one thing. But it is quite another to watch their suffering and death from lack of provisions. There was nought but maggoty biscuits and no fresh water. The boys suffered from diarrhea and nausea, and there were many moments wherein I thought I might puke. Then I spoke harshly to myself: *Be sick if you like,* I said, *but you shall* not *turn tail and run.*

Several other women, whom I recognized vaguely from meeting, aided the soldiers as well. I nodded to them and continued to make my way through the camp, endeavoring not to breathe through my nose as I did so. I handed out what small items I carried, sat by the sides of those who were sick with fever, smiled at them, and held their hands. A cool towel placed about the forehead gave relief to some, and my revulsion fell away once I realized that these poor boys were mere children. Suffering, far from home. Some were dying.

Toward the end of my first day at the camp, I came upon one boy of perhaps fifteen. He was very fair and thin, and had a grievous wound to his side. It was red and angry-looking. As I sat down beside him, he raised his head and looked at me. His eyes widened for a moment before he looked away. Around us, all was wilderness and the enemy, lying in wait.

"Hello. I'm Miss Boylston. It's good to meet you." I smiled. "Is there something I might do for you? A mug of cider, perhaps? A cool towel?"

"Oh, cider would be nice," he said. I turned to pour some from the pitcher at my feet, but he reached out to me. "Say," he added, "you're so pretty. I hope I'm not being rude."

"Indeed, that is quite rude," I said with mock severity, pouring his mug of cider. I helped him to sit up slightly; he groaned.

"Sorry," he muttered, abashed. He sipped his cider, then placed it on the ground and turned away. I saw the bloody pus ooze from his side onto the pallet.

"What's your name?" I asked.

"Stephen. Stephen Harper. Militia from Stonington." I helped him as with trembling hands he sipped the cider.

"Well, Stephen Harper, I must be off."

"Will you return?"

"I shall return tomorrow, expressly to hear your rude comments."

The boy grinned, and I was moved by the rise in his spirits.

I returned the next day but could not find him. When I asked, someone pointed to a corner of the camp. His corpse was there, but not his soul. That had fled during the night.

I came to the camp near every day for the next several weeks, bringing what food and aid I could. I was saddened only by how I had balked at this task back in Cambridge. How many young boys might I have aided!

When Mama discovered my whereabouts, she nearly died of apoplexy. But I was able to convince her that there was no small-pox at the camp, thus no danger to myself. As for my helping the Rebels, Mama had grown resigned to that, for women everywhere were giving what aid they could, and even my mother was moved to pity by the reports of the soldiers' suffering.

"Come see the boys for yourself," I said, inviting her to join me. She stared in horror and by a shiver let me to know that she would sooner ride naked through the market.

During all this time, did I cease to think of John Watkins, or of our kiss on the eastern shore of Badger's Island? Not for a moment. But I was no longer hurt and angry, for Watkins had behaved most wisely, where I had been foolish.

And yet, sometime in mid-July, what seemed a most excellent and charitable idea came to me. We were just finishing our break-fast. The day promised to be parching. I said to Mama, "I should like to bring cider and biscuits to those poor lads who sweat and burn to make our ships of war. Perhaps I might catch a fish or two as well." And, as proof to myself of my indifference toward a cer-tain shipwright, I added, "Would you care to join me?"

"I dislike islands immensely," she said. "The sand gets in one's shoes and undergarments and everywhere. Nor do I like the wind, which wreaks havoc upon one's hair. But—do go, if you've a mind to."

"I do have a mind to, Mama," I said, delighted. And, impul-sively, I hugged her tight.

And so, on a hot, mid-July morning of 1777, I found myself awaiting the boat once more at the North Ferry landing. In one hand I held a large sack of fresh biscuits; in the other, a gallon of cider. At church, I had shrewdly reminded several elderly shop-keepers of their Christian duty, and in that way received these generous donations.

After a few minutes, my items grew heavy and I set them on the ground just as a flamboyant-looking stranger strode toward me. He wore a cocked hat and the costume of a naval officer—a British naval officer! I would have been alarmed had I not known that our men often stole costumes from the enemy and reused them. Besides, he looked somewhat familiar. I had seen his likeness in a political cartoon in one of Papa's broadsides.

The man smiled jauntily at me and offered to help with my provisions.

"Thank you." I curtsied. He bowed, removing his hat before the strong, hot wind had the chance to blow it away. His face was quite swarthy, his close-set eyes bright and shrewd. So bright was his presence that I did not at first notice how small he was—hardly taller than myself.

At that moment, the ferryman approached and gave a hearty greeting: "Hallo, Captain Jones."

Captain John Paul Jones? I had heard a great deal of this captain. The papers said he was mad, though I gleaned no madness in him. His voice was soft, having a slight brogue, and his manner was courteous. He picked up my sack and jug and put them in the boat.

"Heavy, eh?"

Then—he winked at me!

"What, something from the nuns in the convent?"

"I know not what you mean, sir," I said.

He winked again, and I knew him to be flirting with me. Hateful man! But I added, "I'm bringing a treat for the boys."

"Well, let me see if they deserve it first!"

Ten minutes later, Captain Jones inspected the *Ranger*, having first set the cider and sack by the master's shed. He then climbed up the staging.

"Hell and damnation!" he cried, looking at the *Ranger*. "You call this seaworthy? Langdon! Where the hell is Langdon?"

Colonel Langdon appeared, followed by Watkins. I saw both Watkins and the Colonel approach the little man, bodies tense.

"He's here, as am I," said Watkins.

In his feverish anger, Jones shoved Watkins out of the way, the better to reach Colonel Langdon, and Watkins nearly fell off the staging.

"Help!" I shrieked, and all fell silent. The carpenters ceased their work and stared at me. Colonel Langdon and Captain Jones glanced down at me and then descended the stairs, moving swiftly toward the hut. But the colonel stopped a moment and said, "It's all right, Miss Boylston. I'm sorry we frightened you."

"*You* didn't," I said, staring at the wee little goat-man.

I then carried my sack of biscuits and jug and set them upon one of the boards. Isaac, espying me from a goodly distance, ran up and threw himself into my arms. He buried his head in my bosom.

"Well, hello!" I hugged him hard.

He stared at the biscuits, torn over which one to take.

"Oh, take two, Isaac, or you shall never decide."

He grinned and took one in each hand.

"Shall you stay, Miss Eliza?" he asked, nibbling at a biscuit. "Oh, please stay."

He pulled at my arm. Seeing his pleading expression, I said, "All right. Just this once. I can do a little fishing while I'm here, I suppose, and fetch you in an hour."

"Yay, yay!" Isaac leaped in the air.

I smiled. How well the child fared—how changed from the silent, terrorized boy he'd been but a month before. We still did not know his story, or to whom he belonged. The time was nigh when we would insist that he tell us.

Soon break was over. The men, grateful for their treat, lifted their mugs to toast me. I blushed and curtsied. Watkins, however, was not among them, and I was hurt that he did not at least partake of the food. After all, it was for him that I'd brought it. But this thought led me to another. I soon dried my eyes and inwardly laughed at myself for having thought I had been moved to return to the island out of Christian charity. I then moved off to find my rod and bait and walked through the tall dune grass to my usual spot.

The wind was strong, but the sun was quite hot above me. I knew my skin burned. My feet became intolerably hot, too, and after a while I set down the rod and removed my shoes and stockings. Oh, sweet release! But the sand was broiling, and I walked directly into the water—icy, exquisite. It lapped against my toes and splashed my petticoats. I allowed myself a moment to wade in the water. I reached down and wet my hands and brought some of the icy water to my face. The water spilled down my bodice, and I cried, laughing happily out of shock and relief, "Oh, Lord!"

When at last I moved to take up my line again, I saw a shadow move in front of me. I turned to find Watkins standing upon the dunes. How long had he been there, watching?

"Eliza." He descended, and in a moment I felt his hair on my neck, his cheek against my cheek. "Oh, God," he whispered. "God, what test is this?"

I couldn't help it. I put my fingers through his curly hair and kissed him. We sat down together on the sand, not speaking. After a while I asked, "What was it about, all that yelling?"

"Mr. Jones is alarmed at the condition of the *Ranger*. He's right: I've been insisting the same all along. She's top-heavy and will keel over in a major wind. What's more, Jones assumed she'd be outfitted by now. It's not Colonel Langdon's fault, though. He has been greatly occupied and left things in the incompetent hands of Mr. Hackett."

"But this Captain Jones seems—brutish," I hazarded.

Watkins considered my words. "His manner, I agree, leaves a great deal to be desired. But he's a good man, at heart. An excellent man, even."

I turned to him. "Good man? Excellent man? Why say you so? He nearly broke your neck."

Watkins smirked but said nothing. "I must return."

"That's no answer."

"It's better you were out of it—but oh, I'm so glad you came! You know not how miserable I have been." He continued to hold my hands in his.

"Your attempt to divert my curiosity won't work. I will find out what you hide, by and by." Then I could not help but add, "But why did you not come to me that day? I waited for you."

"You know why."

"Yes." I nodded, looking out to the water. "But it hurt."

"I know. But we'll speak of it tomorrow. Now I must go."

I lingered awhile before retrieving Isaac. I continued to feel Watkins's kiss on my lips, and I marveled: There are lines that cannot be crossed, and yet we do so. In spite of everything we're told, in spite even of what we tell ourselves.

24

I RETURNED TO THE ISLAND THE FOLLOWING day determined to find out what Watkins concealed. I fished in my usual spot and awaited his arrival. He finally appeared at about two o'clock. He came to embrace me, but I pushed him away. "Tell me what you're hiding," I said.

"There are things about Langdon's Yard you know nothing about, and about which you should remain ignorant."

"You can't tell me half the truth and expect me to be content with that. I'm not a child."

John looked about him. "All right, then. On your own head be it. Come on. But let's hurry." He took my hand and led me quickly up the dunes toward the north end of the island, where several small merchant ships had anchored. He stopped before a French brig that was moored at the end of a long dock. The brig's masts were furled, and her deck was crammed with barrels and sacks of every variety.

"What do you show me?" I inquired. "It's a merchant ship. Not a great one, either. Sugar, perhaps. Or grain."

Watkins leaned toward me and whispered a single word. "Guns," he said. His warm breath on my skin made me shiver.

"Where?"

"In the barrels. Buried in the grain."

"Does Colonel Langdon know?"

"Of course. As does Captain Jones."

Watkins then returned me to my safe fishing spot, but I kept glancing back at the ship. A thought occurred to me as I did so. "That would be an excellent means for a person, say, a person who sought their freedom to escape. Yes, an excellent means. But one would need help, would one not? One can't simply steal a ship from its mooring, can one?"

Watkins was silent. I did not expect him to reply, but after a long moment, he finally said, "I implore you—I care little for myself, but the colonel does such very great work for so many . . ."

"You trust me so little," I said. "But then, why should you?"

"I have little experience in trust," he replied.

"I shall tell no one. But it strikes me that you place yourself in danger far too easily."

"I do what God grants I may—though blast it, it is not enough! Why, I would blow our enemy to the moon, if I could!"

I smiled, reflecting upon the familiar tone of his words. "You remind me of my brother, Jeb," I said.

"I've not heard you speak of him," Watkins said, surprised. "Is he with a militia just now?"

"He was. He is dead. At Breed's Hill."

"Oh. I'm sorry. You must have . . ."

"Yes." I looked up at him. "I did."

He soon left me, but I had not the heart to fish. I listened to the terns shriek and watched the plovers run up and back with the tide. Then, after twenty minutes, I brought my rod to the shed, gathered Isaac up, and returned home.

•   •   •

It was good to know that Watkins had such a very great ally in Colonel Langdon, but I had a bad feeling about this Captain Jones. I had no opportunity to mention my feelings to Watkins, however, because he began working round the clock to make alterations to the *Ranger*.

By July, there was no grain to be had anywhere. Food became so scarce that even shopkeepers had nothing to give us for the soldiers or shipwrights. Our militia were by now not merely starving, not merely sick, but every moment expecting an invasion. I did not see how they would have the strength to fight were such a disaster to befall them.

Meanwhile, arrests were imminent for those who had not signed the Association Test. Papa suggested we move to his plantation without him. Although Papa had signed it, we lived under the same roof as Uncle Robert, and our fate was tied to his.

"We're going nowhere without you," I objected.

"I can be of little use to you, I'm afraid."

"Useful or not, you shan't be left."

Nonetheless, Papa insisted that we pack our trunks and be at the ready. I lived in terror, not only for my family but for Watkins who, were we to flee, would certainly be sold.

•   •   •

One night I heard Watkins's boots venture into the hallway. It was quite late—past midnight. The boots paused by my chamber door. I didn't dare open the door but sat upon my bed, hands braced upon the bed, elbows locked, for it was all I could do to keep myself from running to him.

Each night for several nights I heard the boots in the hall, and I began to press my cheek against the door in search of his sounds. At times, I imagined I could hear him breathing, hear him shift from one foot to another. Once he had left, I remained wakeful for many hours.

After a week of such torment, I could bear it no longer. I rose from my bed and opened the door. I looked up at him—O, pitiable creature!—and placed my hands in his rough ones. We stood like that, in the hallway. Silent as the grave, hands entwined, dark silhouettes breathing in each other's scent and feasting on each other's eyes.

Some nights, he came to me like this—so I could hold his rough hands and inhale him silently in the dark hallway. But on other nights, I heard only his boots fleeing up the stairs, and I would open the door to catch the shadow made by the candle he held before him.

Soon I no longer even had this much, for Watkins began to work even longer hours at the shipyard. The *Ranger* was now being outfitted night and day: new cannon, new mast, rum, Windsor chairs, even a backgammon set for the officers. The only item no amount of money could purchase was canvas: the ship would have to go to sea with gunnysack sails. There were fewer men to work at the shipyard as well, as Colonel Langdon left with his battalion, the Light Horse Volunteers, to fight at Bennington.

For several weeks, I had lived on shadows, or on the sound of my love's boots upon the stairs in the dead of night. All the while, I thought, *Surely this foolishness shall pass. Surely I will wake up one morning and wonder what I had played at.*

Yet, something akin to the opposite happened: I woke up one morning with a physical yearning that would not be put down. Rather, this sensation grew more intense throughout the day. I waited impatiently for him to return home all that day. Then, at long last, after we had supped, I heard his boots upon the stairs. He ascended, then, minutes later, descended.

Cassie would give him a bath. I knew she would undress him, strip him of his filthy clothing. She would douse his hair with a pitcher of water, and he, wiping his eyes, would complain of her harshness. She would scrub his curly head with soap, after which he would suffer another ablution from the dreaded pitcher. Finally, Watkins would stand and, his back to Cassie, would let her drape a robe about him and tell him to be off so she herself could get to bed.

Then he would mount the stairs. And it is here that I imagined how it might feel to embrace his warm, clean body. Could one be sent to hell for such thoughts? Mere thoughts, I knew, were the least of my problems.

I waited several minutes after I heard him return to his closet, standing by my door in my shift, heart furiously pounding. My entire body throbbed. Mama had retired an hour earlier; Papa was long since asleep.

Taking my candle, I stepped into the dark hall and gently shut my chamber door behind me. The floorboards creaked upon the joists, and I froze in terror. I then fairly slid toward the stairs, the boards continuing to squeak slightly, and mounted them.

In the attic, the air was close. To the left, in what was once the nursery, little Phoebe slept alone, door ajar, for the heat was stifling. I could hear her soft breathing. Watkins had shut his door, but beneath it I saw the dim yellow glow of candlelight.

I knocked softly. No answer. I knocked again, so fearful now that I had begun to tremble. I had nearly turned and fled when the door opened.

"Eliza," Watkins whispered, those bright eyes blazing with shock. He was dressed in his linen nightshirt. He pulled me into his closet, for he could not risk making a sound in the hallway. Once inside, he silently took my candle from me and set it on the table by his bed, alongside his. I noticed his bare collarbone and feet. Now that I was there, I knew not what to do or say.

"Eliza," he whispered again.

"John," I replied. "For, since you call me Eliza, I should by rights call you John."

"Eliza," he repeated, undeterred. "You cannot stay."

"A little while yet," I glanced at him entreatingly.

"But if your mother should seek you out, or your father call for you . . ."

"They never do."

"But if they *should*."

"Just a few minutes more." I must have appeared desperate: Watkins reached for my hand, and I gave it to him. He pulled me closer until his long limbs enveloped me, and I could smell his clean, warm skin. My cheek felt the pulse of life in his neck, wet curls against my face. We stayed like that for some moments: not kissing, not speaking, just clinging to each other, my need having grown most powerful.

I sat down on his narrow bed, awaiting him. He sat beside me, unsmiling. I lay myself down and coaxed him to lie down beside me. The bed was so narrow he had to lie partly on me, and I wrapped my limbs around him and said, "Oh, yes. This is what I want. Only this." Impulsively, he kissed my neck, placed his head between my breasts, pulled my shift down, and kissed me there. My eyes closed, expecting more.

Abruptly, he sat up and closed the neck of my shift. "You must go."

"Why must I?"

"You well know why."

"Yes. But—what else?" I asked. For I had caught something unspoken in his tone.

John was silent a long while. He would not look at me.

"I'm going away," he said finally.

"Going? Where to?" My voice rose.

"Shh! It's all arranged. I dare not tell you how or when. Not for several months at least, I should think. But I shall be *free*, Eliza."

"Free, you say?" My tone was pitiless, sneering. "Dispatched by the enemy in our own harbor? Free to drown in a storm at sea?"

"Surely you're not so blind!" he whispered harshly. "Do you not see that death would be better than this? Do you not see my rage at loving a woman and yet being counted nobody to do so? Every day, part of me hopes I will fall, drown, be blown to bits. Oh, Eliza, do you not *see*?"

The tears fell unchecked from my eyes then. I had not truly seen, but now I did, and I was speechless at this heartfelt expression of his misery.

"Eliza," he said more gently, endeavoring to heal the wound he had made, "let us speak in the light of day. Surely you must want me to be a free man. Were I to think otherwise"—he broke off this thought. "Like this—like this, I'm no one. You know that."

"What good is *knowing* anything?" I stood up and took hold of my candle.

Watkins held my arm. "You know I mean to return."

"Oh, let me go!" I opened the door and passed through it.

25

"SHE'S BEEN THIS WAY SEVERAL DAYS," MAMA was saying to Dr. Jackson. I had eaten nothing, nor emerged from my chamber, since that Sunday past. "She improves not. I cannot think what to make of it."

"Well, we shall see, we shall see." The good doctor, a bent and kindly fellow, perhaps a few years older than Papa, continued to examine me. He would not be put off from his task on account of Mama's fretting. He took his time, palpating my every soft spot with his long, surprisingly strong fingers. Finally he turned to my mother and said, "My considered opinion is that she suffers no physical illness. I believe it to be merely a touch of melancholia."

"Melancholia?" exclaimed my mother. "What has she, pray, to be melancholic about?"

"It's not uncommon for unmarried young ladies to suffer melancholia from time to time. I should think that all the celebrations surrounding our recent—er . . ." Dr. Jackson pulled himself back from the brink of the sentence, suddenly aware that his words might not find a sympathetic ear among my Tory family.

"Recent victory?" I was suddenly awake and wanting to know the news.

"At Bennington, miss." The good doctor grinned. "Colonel Langdon's Light Horse Volunteers and some others from Massachusetts—they defeated a battalion of Hessian soldiers."

"And the colonel—is he well?"

"Oh, yes, miss. From what I hear, he's gone to pursue Burgoyne's troops over in Saratoga."

At this news, I smiled. Once Mama and the doctor left my room, I heard Mama say to him, "You did her some good, I think, Dr. Jackson. But I like not her low spirits. She has been very up and down in this regard, and often sleepless. This latest episode, combined with your recent urgings, have worn me down. I fear the next invasion of the pox will carry her off. I shall send her to take the cure as soon as may be, though I shan't go myself."

"Madam—" the good doctor began, but Mama interrupted him.

"No," she said. "I care nothing for myself, and Mr. Boylston had the pox as a child."

"All right. I shall arrange for her to go as soon as may be."

I sighed and pulled my head back under the covers. I was miserable where I was, but I didn't see how taking the cure on Pest Island would render me any more so.

•   •   •

September 1777. Just as Mama had predicted, the smallpox arrived in full force, and I thought it only a matter of days before I would be shipped off to Pest Island.

Mama commanded me to remain indoors, but as I had hardly stepped abroad in several weeks, I had a sudden desire to do so. One morning Cassie said that she needed to go to the Whipple house.

"Excellent," I said. "I shall come along."

It was a glorious morn. The heat had abated, and while the leaves were still mainly on the trees, a few loose ones, gold and yellow, fell, cascading and swirling in the strong sea breeze. The Piscataqua glistened in the strong sun, and my spirits lifted with baseless hope.

"Cassie," I said, as we walked companionably down the hill. "Know you when the *Ranger* plans to depart? I imagine they must be nearly outfitted by now. Captain Jones will be eager to set sail for France, I'm sure." Cassie stopped walking and turned to me.

"Soon. Isaac tell me maybe next week."

I had meant nothing in particular by my question, but something in her eyes—or rather, in the way her eyes shifted away from me, made me ask, "Cassie. What do you know?"

We stood in the road, and I pulled her to the side in time to avoid being run over by a cart.

"I can't say." She placed a hand involuntarily on her heart. But now that I knew she harbored a secret, I would not rest until she divulged it.

"You must tell me. At once."

"Oh, Miss Eliza! He means to leave on board de *Ranger*. 'Eet all arrange." Cassie began to cry.

"How long have you known, Cassie?"

"A few days—oh, I am greatly fearing for 'eem!"

"I knew it," I said. "Knew, and yet he said it would be several months yet. We fought . . . oh, we had a terrible row."

Cassie put her arms around me and held me hard. It was obvious that she needed no explanation. She knew what I knew, and perhaps more. And while she had no answers for me, how comforting it was to reveal my suffering at last!

Cassie took my arm, and we walked on in silence. We mounted the stairs to the Whipple property, up through the carved newel posts, past the walnut tree that Prince Whipple, one of Colonel Whipple's slaves, had planted several years earlier. We walked around back and entered the grand home through the kitchen door.

Before the massive, blazing hearth stood Prince and Cuffee. Cuffee, normally filled with good cheer, was grave-faced. He kept shifting from foot to foot; he drummed his long fingers on the wall. Cassie kissed him on the cheek, and I nodded. It would not do to curtsy to a slave, though I had grown fond of Cuffee and the open spirit that shone through his music.

Suddenly the kitchen door banged open and in strode Watkins. He carried a heavy sack over his shoulder, which spilled ears of corn. The sight of him, so unexpected, made me lean on Cassie. Why was he here, absent from the shipyard, delivering grain to the Whipple house? He glanced at me briefly but then looked away. I might have run to him right there in the Whipples' kitchen, surrounded by the slaves and the colonel and his family, had not Cassie pressed her hand against my arm.

Watkins leaned close to Cuffee and whispered in his ear. Cuffee nodded and left the room. Soon, with the help of Prince, Watkins fell to removing the corn from the top of the sack. He then proceeded to withdraw half a dozen flintlock rifles.

"Ai!" Cassie gasped. Just then, the master of the house strode into the kitchen. Seeing the guns, he glanced sharply at me.

"Miss Boylston. You've come at a vulnerable moment for us. I trust you're sympathetic to our cause?"

I curtsied deeply. "Be easy, Colonel Whipple. I lost a brother on Breed's Hill. I'm as eager as you are for a Rebel victory." I said the words, but I did not truly *feel* them, feel the vital significance of this victory in my soul. That would not happen for several months yet.

"Then I may trust that this information will not find its way across the field—to your uncle's house?"

"Certainly not. We are here for a—cup of sugar."

Colonel Whipple nodded and turned to Prince. "Check 'em over. Then get 'em into the barn. Beneath the hay. Don't forget the powder."

"Yes, sir," said Prince.

The balls and powder lay in cartons at the bottom of the corn-filled sacks.

"We leave before dawn. Make sure you're ready," the colonel said to Prince.

"Of course, sir."

Colonel Whipple nodded, bowed toward me, and departed.

"Where go you?" I asked Prince once the colonel was gone.

"Saratoga, Miss Eliza. To engage Burgoyne." Prince pronounced these words gravely, proud to bursting to have been invited along. I then looked toward Watkins, who did not return my glance. Rather, he seemed assiduously to avoid my eyes. He examined the guns' mechanisms, his jaw set hard against the news that Prince had been chosen to go to Saratoga with Colonel Whipple. That would eat at him, I knew.

Watkins retrieved the powder and bullets, emptied the sack of the corn, replaced the guns in the sack, and carried them off to the barn.

I resolved then that I would go to him, beg forgiveness, and applaud his choice to seek his freedom, as I should have done from the first. That night, I listened for the sound of his boots on the stairs until well after midnight, but I heard them not. Nor did I hear them the next morning. Had the *Ranger* already departed? It couldn't be.

As soon as dawn broke, I sought Cassie out. She was preparing breakfast for Mama, myself, and Uncle, and a tray for Papa. I whispered to her, "Cassie, I have neither heard nor seen Watkins today."

She said, "Some men—dey stay on de eye-land."

"Stay on the island? Why?"

"Workin' all tru de night. 'Ee want to do 'eet. Your uncle, he don't object—more wages for 'eem."

"Thank you, Cassie." I turned to prepare my toilet, but Cassie seized my arm in a clawlike grip.

"I can 'ear your thoughts buzzin' around in your 'ead. Wait."
She interrupted her other chores to pack a sack. Cassie packed a bit
of salted beef and several biscuits and poured cider into a canteen.

"Give dees to Isaac. Tell 'eem to share wit' Watkins. Don' be
foolish. Don' try to speak to 'eem. You don't know de evil eyes dat
may watch you, tell on you."

"Thank you," I said, and I kissed her on the cheek for her
troubles.

As I strode to the ferry, the streets were oddly quiet. The ferryman was surprised to see me. "Going fishin' again?" he asked.

"No. Just delivering something for our boy, Isaac."

Once on the island, the ferryman handed me my sack and
tipped his hat. I began to climb the dunes.

What progress the *Ranger* had made! She was painted and
tarred and had been outfitted with cannons. The four on the lee-
ward side were visible as I mounted the dunes. It was, I thought, a
fitting ship for a bold escape.

Isaac was nowhere to be seen, but I was unconcerned. It had
been near six months since he had run away, and I assumed that
his master, wherever he was, had long since given up on catching
the child.

The shipyard had been tidied since last I'd been there. The
sawmill had been abandoned, and the glaziers had gone. What
men there were worked mainly on the ship's decks or in her hull.
The wind on the island was very strong. It moaned and shrieked,
and I draped the blanket I had brought around my shoulders.

The minutes passed. I looked out at the sea, now iron gray with
curling, white foam tips. I paced back and forth, trying to keep
warm. After about ten minutes, I saw Watkins emerge from the
ship with Mr. Hackett and Captain Jones. They argued and looked
as if they might come to blows. Then, quite suddenly, Captain
Jones burst out laughing.

Watkins saw me. I raised the sack to show him my reason for being there. Behind him and to his left stood a ragged row of gunnysack tents. Remains of a communal breakfast lay on boards that had been set upon low makeshift legs. There was a sudden, strong gust of wind that carried the reek of a latrine. Watkins disappeared momentarily and emerged from the hull with Isaac. Isaac flew down the ladder, and I feared he would trip and break his neck. I thought he was glad of the sack, but, to my surprise, he ignored it entirely and flung himself into my arms. "I thought you'd never come here again. Oh, I've missed you, Miss Eliza!"

"I've missed *you*," I said, hugging him. "But look—Cassie has packed some nice things for you, and for Watkins." Watkins slowly descended the ladder, though it was long before break time. He ambled over with persuasive ease.

"What have we here?" he asked, casually resting a hand on Isaac's back.

"Regard what Miss Eliza's brought us, Johnny!" Isaac looked up adoringly at Watkins.

The boy fell to removing his treasures from the sack. He lifted each item and showed it proudly to his beloved mentor. Watkins crouched down, one knee on the sand.

Now was my chance. There would be no opportunity of getting him alone, not with this impress of activity before the *Ranger's* launch. I knelt down upon the sand, as if to help Isaac remove the articles from the sack. I touched Watkins's arm lightly. He turned, and I looked straight into the face of the man I loved.

"I'm sorry," I said. "Will you forgive me?"

"Sorry!" Isaac cried, laughing and jumping up and down. "Why, what're you *sorry* for, Miss Eliza?"

Watkins said nothing; perhaps he nodded imperceptibly. I no longer knew what he felt, but the recollection of my desperation that night made me sick with shame.

Isaac needed an explanation, and so I said, "Only that it seems you boys could have used me long before now. The state you live in is frightful!"

"Frightful?" Isaac said, all astonishment.

I ruffled his soft hair. "What a little man you are. All men feel perfectly contented when they're living like pigs."

"Not all," Watkins added quietly.

Over the next few days, I set about improving the shipyard, cleaning tents and bringing several chamber pots to the island. I now had no illusions about my motivation: It was all so that I could be in Watkins's proximity during his last few days. There was no opportunity to speak to him, but at least I was able to glance at him from time to time. By his own appearance of indifference, he cared nothing for me any longer.

Such coldness, whether real or feigned, hurt. But I was determined not to waver. I made the men dig a pit in the sand, where I had them empty the reeking latrines. The men laughed good-naturedly at my efforts. One cheeky shipwright shouted, "The whole world's our chamber pot, miss!" At this witticism, they all roiled with laughter.

That Wednesday, we received most exceeding good news: Burgoyne's army had surrendered! All fifty-seven hundred of them now marched eastward, toward Cambridge. Supper on the island that evening became a raucous celebration. Cassie and I had earlier that day made a fish stew, enough for the dozen or so men who tarried on the island. As the sun declined in the sky it bathed the river and Portsmouth town in a warm, red light. Men danced and banged on trenchers with their forks. Those who had a whistle played. Others sang bawdy songs with lyrics so shocking I had to stop Isaac's ears. But he pulled my hands away, saying he'd heard those songs a hundred times before.

The men hugged one another and lifted each other off the ground till their feet dangled in the air. They then reached for me.

I was hugged to within an inch of my life. Finally it was Watkins's turn to lift me up. I had not felt his touch in several weeks. When he put his arm about me, I shuddered even before he whispered my name. I felt his arm about my waist, felt his breath upon my ear, for the rest of the day.

That night, after I had just managed to doze off, there came a faint knock upon my door.

"Eliza?"

I knew not how to speak, for his voice touched my deepest feelings of both hope and despair, paralyzing my tongue. He was set to leave in three days' time.

"Would you not bid me good-bye?" he asked, his voice now fully audible. It echoed clearly down the hall.

Terrified, I pulled open the door and fairly yanked him into my chamber, shutting it after him. "Do you wish to be sent to prison rather than to sea? Lower your voice, or you'll soon have your wish. Mama's ears are very keen."

"Eliza," he repeated, cupping my face in his rough hands. "Be still a moment and look at me." I would not. "Look at me and tell me that this is not as hard for me as it is for you." I looked at him at last. Truly looked. Tears threatened to pour from his eyes; all the admirable strength of his body seemed on the verge of collapse.

"You must go. I understand. You are doing the right thing—of that I have no doubt," I said. My voice quavered, but I stayed the course. "Now kiss me, and tell me you love me. Promise me you shall court me properly, as a free man."

"You *know* I do, and shall." He embraced me tenderly. When he had gone, I felt too empty even to cry.

•　　•　　•

Saturday morning arrived. I readied myself to walk down to Long Wharf with Mama and Cassie. Phoebe had agreed to stay with

Papa so that Cassie could see the launch. My posture was stiff and upright, my face, though wan from lack of sleep, composed. Everyone who could walk, and even some who couldn't, came to the pier that morning.

It was cool and windy. Leaves, fallen from the trees, swirled in great gusts all about us. Women, children, old men, slaves, maids, and what few young men remained in Portsmouth all gathered on the pier. The excitement mounted, and at half past nine a hush caught and rippled through the crowd: Captain John Paul Jones would speak. We were silent for him, respectful, moved as we listened to his words of thanks, and of our future glory.

The *Ranger* held her sails half-furled. The crowd could see her sinewy power ready to be unleashed. Sailors waved happily from the deck to loved ones. Every shopkeeper left his shop and stood without to watch the proceedings. The applause and shouts became a roar, drowning out even the moaning wind. There were already cheers and toasts and spilled jugs of cider. Captain Jones untied the rope from the cleat and climbed aboard. Cassie hugged me, and even my mother clapped her hands together, having caught the contagion of the crowd. The church bell rang as the *Ranger* set off to meet her fate, moving ever more quickly downstream.

My head was buried in Cassie's breast, and I could not contain a shuddering sob. When I finally lifted my head the *Ranger* was out of sight. But there in the crowd, on the edge of the pier, was John Watkins, holding his case and seeking me out with his eyes.

26

I LEFT FOR SHAPLEY'S ISLAND, THEN CALLED Pest Island, the following morning. There had been no opportunity to speak to Watkins in the intervening hours, but when I saw him standing on the pier searching for me, my eyes were opened, and my soul was as shaken as Abraham upon the return of Isaac. I knew not what lay ahead for us, but I would not turn back now.

We rowed out to Pest Island six or so at a time. It was an island consisting of about nine acres, wild and uninhabited save for Shapley's mansion, where many of us would stay. There was also a warehouse on the north end of the island, which was used as a hospital. In this warehouse they lodged the slaves and servants who took the cure.

At this time, it was the custom for parents to send their children to be inoculated while they themselves remained at home. There were chaperones, to be sure, but these young ladies, hardly older than their charges, mingled amongst themselves, enjoying an unaccustomed freedom.

Thus, for three weeks, the island became filled with gay youths set free from parental boundaries. We had little to do but to compare pustules and be merry. We ate in a common dining hall, and the food, though plain, was tolerable. We even had meat on Sundays.

Immediately upon landing, we queued up to receive our inoculations in the warehouse. For most of us, inoculation resulted in a mild fever and a few pustules, nothing more.

The day after my inoculation, I walked the shore. I felt slightly feverish, but I was oddly relieved to be upon an island surrounded by the buffering river. I felt as if I had left myself back in Portsmouth and could rest from the tumultuous feelings I had suffered for so long.

I passed by the landing. A boat was just approaching. I shielded my eyes from the sun and gazed out to it. There was Watkins sitting in the back row, among other slaves come to take the cure. He looked lost until he saw me, and then he brightened. I dared not remain to greet him.

That night, though, I saw Watkins lingering at the edge of the woods. We had supped, though I had hardly eaten. Nerves and a continued fever had rendered me indifferent to food. The sun was setting. It had grown cold, and the wind was strong. I had about me a cape and a blanket, too.

With an imperceptible nod, Watkins beckoned me. I approached, but like a ghost he then disappeared. Suddenly I felt a touch upon my arm, immediately accompanied by a voice.

"Shh! I'm here. Follow me."

I reached for him, found his hand, then the rest of him. We walked through the dunes; it was dark and cold, though the wind had died down, and the tall grass scratched at my calves. Watkins unfolded the blanket I carried and draped it around us both. The center of the island was dense with shrubs, and there was no clear path.

The moment we arrived on the eastern shore, I felt Watkins's hand press the back of my head, bringing me to him in an urgent whisper.

"Do you think me a coward? It's what I think of myself, Eliza."

"*You* may think that, but I don't," I whispered back.

"My will failed me. I always believed, despite all, that I was strong—"

My heart burst with pity for him, yet I would not reveal it. I took his hand and sat him down upon the sand.

"Allow me to say what I feel I must. You *are* strong, Watkins. The way you helped us to eat that time, though you suffered a whipping for it. The money you gave to Linda, though Uncle Robert might have punished you. Is this not strength?"

He shrugged, as if it mattered not. "What have I to offer *you*, Eliza?"

"You have offered me yourself—can a man give more than that? I for one can ask for no more." I gripped his hand and thought of that moment on Long Wharf. "When I saw you standing on the pier, searching for me, oh, you know not how my heart leapt for joy!"

Suddenly we heard a whooping cry. John turned abruptly. We heard further shouts, but soon enough ascertained that the revelers were not heading toward us.

"I fear it's not safe to linger," he said, the spell of our connection broken. "Someone may notice my absence, if not yours." Having bared my soul, I had no wish to leave John, but I saw the wisdom of his words, and he guided me through the dunes, where we parted.

On the morrow, I was quite ill. I had a high fever, and did not leave my bed. Several pocks had flowered on my torso and arms. My head pounded, and I wished I had my Cassie with me to rub my back and give me one of her potions.

It was only after two days of complete rest that I felt well enough to leave my chamber. Thankfully, thence began an unseasonable warm spell. Without, the sun was bright, and it felt like spring, and in bright daylight I had no fear to walk through the shrubs. Once on the eastern shore, I sat myself upon the sand, a blanket about me, and shut my eyes. A warm blanket of orange light shone through my lids. After perhaps ten minutes, I started at the touch of a hand upon my shoulder. Watkins stood beside me and kissed my head.

"This is too bold," I said. "One of those old crones in her gundalow may see us." Indeed, just off the northern shore of Shapley's Island, the gundalows from Kittery passed us by. They were a dozen rods off, but I feared that one might veer close enough to perceive us.

"Perhaps you're right. Here, let us move down the shore a bit." We stood and walked south through the dunes, until the boats were silver flies upon the water. I went to sit, but John suddenly grasped me to him. He lifted me off the sand and pressed me to him. Then he nuzzled his face in my neck, his arms wrapped tightly around me.

He had not shaved his goatee, and I felt it prick my neck. "That tickles." I laughed. Warming to the idea, John began to tickle me in earnest, and we struggled. I laughed, eventually managing to grasp his fingers and pull them away from me. I remembered the first time I had seen his hands and the blisters upon them. There were no such blisters now.

I grabbed a handful of damp sand and threw it at him.

Giggling, I pulled him back toward me—he had already grabbed a handful of sand, which he instantly relinquished at my touch. Then I brought Watkins's hands close to my face, as if to inspect them.

"The palms of your hands are white," I observed.

"You examine them as if you might purchase me."

"I would purchase you, if I could," I said mildly. He looked at me tenderly, for honest words were our one precious luxury.

"I remember when you first saw the wounds on my hands," he said. "I was furious with you."

"You had every right to be. I was patronizing. I knew not how else to speak to you."

"And I already knew that I had—improper—feelings toward you. It was my own hopeless frustration that enraged me."

"Improper, indeed! If Mama only knew . . . but, well, your wounds have healed, at any rate."

John smiled. When he did so, his face changed. He became someone who might have won not merely my heart but the hearts of many—a leader of men such as Colonel Langdon. But I would not let my lurch of pity reach my face.

"I'm so grateful for my craft, Eliza," he said. "You can't know how it sustains me, to have built our ships of war. To have helped with the guns—"

John came closer and whispered, "I have carved my initials beneath the planks, where no one can see. Thus, I feel I'm on the ships, in a way."

"You *are* on those ships, John. Were it not for you, those ships would never have been built."

"Perhaps not," he shrugged.

We sat upon the sand and let the sun warm us. I told him about Cambridge and my life before the war. I told him about Maria, and also about Jeb. Then I added thoughtfully, "You and Jeb would have liked one another. He wouldn't have given a fiddle about either your color or your status in society. He would have loved you as a brother and moved heaven and earth to help you."

"If all our citizens were like that," he muttered, "we could actually win this war."

We said nothing for a few moments, and then I hazarded to speak of a tender subject. "Cassie tells me that your father was the former royal governor. Is it true?"

John glanced at me guardedly, which look softened after a moment. "That's what Mama told me. He never acknowledged me, though. In fact, my sister and I were treated worse than the others once his wife saw how much we resembled him. She refused to call for a doctor when Mama was ill—oh, how Mama suffered! She could not breathe, yet for the longest time she would not die. She didn't want to leave us . . . after she died, the governor's wife made her husband sell us."

I sighed and pressed myself closer to him. "We're a grievous race. I see not why the Lord has seen fit to populate the earth with us. It would be better were the earth inundated by wolves. Or wild boar. At least they don't kill out of malice."

"Come," he said. "Let's walk down the beach a bit and forget our grievousness."

"All right."

We held hands and strolled the vacant shore in contented silence.

27

AFTER OUR RETURN TO PORTSMOUTH, I DID not see Watkins for several weeks. I slept very ill, and my sleepless nights must have begun to tell upon me, for one morning at breakfast Mama set down her fork and said, "Eliza, your eyes are positively ringed with black. Are you quite well?"

"Oh, yes." I smiled wanly. "Quite well, Mama. A little hungry, perhaps."

She darted me a warning glance, but Papa rescued me.

"I agree," he said. "Another few weeks like this and the soldiers shall come upon our fleshless bones."

"Mr. Boylston, really," Mama sighed.

After breakfast, Cassie and I went to the market to see what we might purchase. There was neither meat nor fowl, and the fish had been sold the moment it came to market two hours earlier. In any case, I felt that I could not eat one more piece of fish without growing gills. As we walked glumly through the Whipple property on our way back home, I stopped, for I suddenly had a most intriguing thought.

"Cassie, go on home. I shall stop at the Whipples' for a moment."

"I'll come wit' you."

"No," I said firmly. "Go home." By my tone, Cassie knew not to argue. She frowned, glanced at me once, then curtsied shallowly and fled across the lawn.

Moving quickly, I soon entered the Whipples' kitchen. Within, it was quite warm. Dinah was at the hearth, her face raining perspiration. When she saw me, she set down her pot.

"Hello, Dinah. It smells good in here. I have a favor to ask of Prince. Is he about?"

Prince Whipple and his master had recently returned from our victory in New York, at Saratoga. The town had planned a celebration for them at the end of that week.

"I'll fetch him. He's upstairs." She wiped her hands on her apron, removed it, curtsied to me, and exited the kitchen, returning a few minutes later with Prince. He bowed to me, mortified that I sought an audience with him. For, though a brave soldier, he was a painfully shy man.

"Prince," I smiled winningly. "There's a—tool—I should like to borrow, which I believe you keep in your stables."

"A tool, ma'am?"

"I—I cannot remember what it is called, I'm afraid. If you will allow me to show you the one I mean . . ."

Perplexed, Prince glanced covertly at Dinah.

"It's all right, Prince," I assured him. "It'll take but a moment. I'd be most grateful." Hesitantly, as if it might be a trick, Prince led the way to the stables. The wind had picked up, and I flipped my hood back over my head. Once inside the barn, and having closed the door, I walked over to a bale of hay, reached down beneath it, and wrapped my hand around the thing I sought. It was a French flintlock rifle.

"Teach me how to use this, if you would, Prince."

•   •   •

We dared not practice on the Whipple property. Instead, Prince and I met the following day upon those same plains where, the previous summer, I'd watched the festive crowd initiate its new leaders. I recalled the turbans, and Linda in her red dress and turquoise necklace, the bright sun, and the rhythmic pulse of the drums...

How different the plains looked now. How desolate. There were few trees, and the long grass, grown to seed, was gray and brittle. Only the lone rustle of a vole or squirrel darting for cover disturbed the silence.

I followed Prince to an old Negro graveyard that stood at the edge of Colonel Langdon's property, in a small grove. It was as safe a place as we could find in Portsmouth. I told Prince that no one must know our secret, "not even the servants." By "servants," I meant slaves. And by slaves, I meant Watkins. These flintlocks were not so scattershot as our own Brown Bessies, but they could still misfire or even explode.

In the small grove on Langdon's property, Prince Whipple, war hero of Saratoga, taught me how to shoot. Prince was very patient with me. First, he showed me the different parts of the musket, then how to pour the powder from the horn into the muzzle, to insert the ball, and to use the ramrod to push it all down. Finally, he taught me how to hold and fire. Before we left the grove after my final lesson, Prince turned to me.

"Miss Eliza?"

"Yes, Prince?"

"It is none of my business, but I should not like any harm to come to you. Whom—if I may ask—plan you to shoot with this rifle?"

Suddenly, I realized that Prince had misunderstood my intentions. And yet, how patiently he had aided me! I laughed and said, "Why, a rabbit, Prince. Two, if I'm very lucky."

•   •   •

What Prince had not the heart to tell me was that the Charleville carved a rather large hole out of its victim. When I shot my first rabbit, I exulted—until I fetched it, only to discover that half the rabbit had been blown away. I was obliged to shoot seven or eight in order to feed the four of us. We ate several immediately, the day of the victory celebration. Cassie roasted them in a delicious mustard sauce that got brown and crusty. The rest we salted and preserved. She never did ask me where I had procured the rabbits. Perhaps she already knew.

After dinner, Cassie, Mama, and I walked down to the market to attend the celebration. Papa wished to come, but Mama would not allow it, saying the bitter winds would be the death of him. We heard the sound of drums and whistles while we were still on Front Street. Once in the market square, we nestled together for warmth among the crowd and listened to the various speeches and encomiums of the mayor and other officials. We heard from Colonel Whipple, too, and watched him embrace his comrade in arms, Prince Whipple. At this, the people of Portsmouth went wild—our citizens were in a generous mood, I thought cynically, congratulating themselves for recognizing a slave's contribution to the Cause.

And where was Watkins during all this? I espied him on the other side of the crowd, watching the proceedings with hard eyes. Isaac was next to him, his face animated with pride as he watched one of his own race so honored.

From this point on, I watched John and Isaac. I watched John's eyes grow increasingly angry, though I knew he did not begrudge Prince his moment in the sun. But I knew how deeply he must have suffered to see our townspeople celebrating Prince's patriotism.

I turned away momentarily, and when next I looked, Watkins was gone. I didn't see him again that day, and in the end, I thought it wise to leave him be. He would be too proud to admit his misery to me. Instead, for near a week, I remained safely ensconced in the bosom of my family—either with Mama in the parlor as she sewed or made menus that would never be used, or with Papa in his chamber, Cassie stoking the fires all about like a good little house slave, silent and unobtrusive. To complete this genteel tableau, I took up the needlework pillow I'd abandoned more than a year earlier.

Cassie must have feared that I had broken ranks with her, for I did not once appear in the kitchen during this time.

One night, Papa joined us for dinner, and I almost dared to hope that he was getting well. Indeed, he looked quite cheerful.

"What do you know but I've received a letter from your favorite relation, Mrs. Boylston," he announced.

Mama brightened. "Whom, pray? Phoebe Vassal? Susanna Inman?"

Papa paused for effect, then cried, "Lizzie Boylston!"

"Oh, Richard!" Mama said. "How cruel of you to lead me on so!"

Papa was highly amused, and I giggled.

"Well, Papa, what news has she?"

"A great deal, in fact. She writes that she and Mrs. Adams were in Boston to see the arrival of Burgoyne's troops."

"Have you the letter?" I asked, my interest piqued.

"At table? Why, no."

"Oh, do let me read it. Phoebe!" I called. Phoebe came cringingly forth from her hiding place behind the dining room door. "Phoebe, Papa has a letter he would like you to retrieve. It is . . ." I looked encouragingly at Papa.

"On my desk, directly atop the pile of papers."

"As you heard, Phoebe."

A few moments later, letter in hand, I read:

Dearest Mama and Papa,

I was going to write you about the uneventful days of a country farmeress, but I'm afraid that everything I was prepared to tell you fled from my mind when I heard the news of Burgoyne's defeat. Mrs. Adams and I decided to go at once to Cambridge, and I see now that it was providential that we did.

What a sight awaited us! We stood in the Square and saw a sea of men marching wearily in rows—a veritable Red Sea flowing all the way down the road from Watertown. The sheer mass of men threatened to flood the little village, and we backed off some Yards, fearing that they would march over us. Then they halted and stood there quite some time before being marched in smaller groups to barracks on Prospect Hill and elsewhere.

I took the opportunity to pass by our homes, and you will be comforted to know they are still standing, though the gardens have been sorely neglected. Our homes are occupied by various regiments—whose, I did not stop to inquire.

In Braintree, all is well. Miss Miller—that's the girl you brought me from town, Eliza—and I are kept busy, what with the harvest and the babes that, even now, insist on being born. How these babes came to be I know not, given the absence of men. One would almost believe they were virgin births . . .

"Shocking!" my mother exclaimed. My uncle blushed, but my father seemed to find great amusement in Lizzie's letter. I folded it and set it on the table.

"I must say," Papa commented, "Lizzie has grown on me these past years. Yes, I find her letter quite entertaining. I shall have to write her back."

"Well, do not ask me to sign it," my mother said. "I abhor the girl."

"Abhor is a strong word, Mama. After all, she *is* managing, which I find nothing short of remarkable under the circumstances."

"Perhaps," Mama allowed. "But, oh, so headstrong, so plain-spoken! One would never guess she was the daughter of Judge Lee, though I never did care for her mother. Margaret Lee, I recall, fancied herself a ministering angel. Ran about delivering babies in the dead of night. Lizzie is cut from the same cloth, I imagine."

Thanksgiving came and went without fanfare. We had no guests, and no food to share. The last time I had gone to fetch a rifle, they had disappeared. Prince told me they'd been "shipped off."

"Where, exactly, Prince?"

"To the south, to General Washington." He did not meet my eyes, and I felt Prince withheld something from me. After our humble Thanksgiving meal, I sent Cassie to find out more.

I repaired meanwhile to the parlor, where I read upon a book until all the light had gone and I finally mounted the stairs to my chamber. I felt fatigued and low.

An hour later, there was a knock on my chamber door. It was Cassie, abuzz with information. "Cassie, what is it? What have you learned?"

"Dem arms you asked about, Miss Eliza."

"Yes, what of them?"

"Well, it was like Prince tol' you. Some of 'em went directly to Gen'l Washington."

"This much I know already, Cassie."

Cassie stood there, gazing uncertainly up and down the hallway.

"Oh, goodness. Come in at once." Cassie stepped into my chamber and I shut the door after her.

"Well?"

"Well, what you don' know, Miss Eliza, is that some of dem rifles got sent to Negroes in de Carolinas."

"Negroes? What kind of Negroes, Cassie?"

"The rebellious kind, Miss Eliza."

I stared at her. "Why, whoever in Portsmouth would risk their neck to aid a slave rebellion?"

Cassie stared back at me. "Who you *tink*, Miss Eliza?"

．　　　．　　　．

The idea that John would surely be hanged if found out kept me from sleeping. I tossed and turned, resolving to say something to him at first light. Then, at around midnight, just as I had dozed off, I heard drumming above me. It was a soft, rhythmic drumming at first, but then it grew louder, until it was actually quite loud and I feared Mama and Papa would notice it. Annoyed, I threw on a robe and, taking a candle, moved down the cold hallway and up the stairs to his room.

I knocked. "Watkins! Would you stop that banging? I cannot sleep."

Silence. The door opened a crack. The sight of his face, so close to mine, made my heart leap. His pale eyes gleamed mischief at me.

"You cannot sleep?" he asked, pulling me into his room and shutting the door. "Perhaps it's because I do not wish you to sleep."

He drew me to him, but I struggled to free myself.

"Leave me be."

"Never."

I pushed him harshly, and he fell back upon his bed. I made as if to strangle him. I then took some pleasure in taking a few blows at him until, fending them off, he laughed and whispered, "I surrender!"

Eventually we rose. I grasped his hand and brought him into the hallway. Phoebe's head poked out of her open door, and she stared at us in amazement.

"Go back to sleep," said John. "We are but a dream."

"A shadow's shadow," I added.

Watkins hastily shut the door upon the girl, and we both fell to uncontrollable giggling.

We descended the stairs and entered my chamber, our laughter having died out on the back stairs. Fearful for him and what I had learned, I was without fear for myself. Perhaps Watkins could never have the recognition of the town that he so fully deserved. But he could have me. I had decided it. Before snuffing out the candle, I bade Watkins help me push my chest of drawers in front of the chamber door. His arms were around me in a second; I could feel their fine, downy hairs brush against my back. My hair was loose, and he combed his fingers through it.

"Come to bed, my love," I said. And then I blew out the light.

28

THE BED WAS SOFT, HIS SKIN WARM against my own. I knew not how something so warm and loving could be a sin, though I had been told so often enough. We were both shy, and this made us laugh, which we had to do soundlessly, our mouths open, bottom teeth jutting forward foolishly. Thank goodness no one watched us, for it was less the stuff of drama than of comedy.

Though tentative at first, Watkins became playful, touching and prodding me in places that seemed to amuse and delight him equally. Then the play became more focused, urgent. But always loving and gentle. Afterward I cried, because I had not known men could be so gentle, or so kind.

"Why do you cry?" he whispered in my ear, as I buried my face in my pillow. But the gentle question made me cry harder, and finally I told him about Mr. Inman and Mr. Hutchinson. As I did so, a look of unutterable disgust spread across his noble face. He was silent a long while.

"I'm sorry, Eliza." He shook his head, and suddenly I feared that he would not understand, that he would blame me. Nothing could have been farther from the case: "I am sorry that I cannot fathom the venomous depravity of my sex. When one so fair, so lovely"—he broke off and muttered—"it's well for them they are

not in our midst!" Then he turned back and spoke in a whisper, yet
entreatingly, "Know that we are not *all* like that."

"I do know that, John. Now."

He returned to his chamber in the dead of night. I was loath to
part with him and held his hand until he had to use the full weight
of his body to step away.

"Be careful, Watkins," I said as he left.

"Why say you so?" he asked, suddenly alert.

"Because I love you," I said.

In the morning, I did not see him, and could not believe that
we had taken such a risk—or, apparently, gotten away with it. In
any case, it was not something we would dare to do again.

Soon it was nearly Christmas, and Mama was in good spirits.
Papa had gained strength, and it seemed as if perhaps a miracle
had happened and that he would recover. He was sitting with us
now, at dinner. Above us, a gilt acanthus leaf chandelier reflected
off of dark-green wainscoted walls. It cast a lurid light upon us all,
especially Papa, who looked quite green. Without, it had begun to
snow, and the sky had grown dark, though it was only two o'clock.

"The Peirces have invited us to Christmas dinner," Mama was
saying. "They gave us little notice, but there you have it."

"Must we?" I sighed. Across from me sat Uncle Robert, whose
white wisps of powdered hair blew about as if a wind had made its
way inside. He ignored our conversation and thoughtfully chewed
his food.

Mama looked grim-mouthed, her long, slightly hooked nose
the very model of disapprobation. Her graying brown hair was
piled absurdly high on her head, as had been the fashion a decade
earlier.

"Of course we must," she said. "John Peirce shall be in attendance." I was about to object that I cared nothing for John Peirce
when, fortunately, we were interrupted by the sudden entrance of

Phoebe. At her approach, Uncle Robert curled one arm protectively about his plate.

"—and though it is more a spring gown," Mama was saying, "I see no reason why you shouldn't wear that, with my white silk shawl, for it looks quite well on you."

I was not very hungry and picked at my dinner.

Mama broke off and finally set down her fork. "But why do you not eat, Eliza? Nobody likes a thin girl. Lord knows we have enough illness around here," she added, as if Papa had contracted the consumption to spite her.

"Thin? Why, if our daughter gains another pound, we shall have to buy her half a dozen new gowns."

"Nonsense," said Mama. "She looks very wan to me."

"Phoebe," I called, "bring me a dish of chamomile tea, please. Mama, I'd like to take it in my room, if I may."

Mama's eyes flinched their disappointment.

"But I should so much like to discuss what you plan to *wear*," she said plaintively. "I fear that blue gown of yours is no longer fashionable. I have lately heard that a cap sleeve is all the rage in London."

"Cap sleeve!" bellowed my father. My heart fluttered with alarm, for Papa's outbursts were usually accompanied by a spasm of coughing. "You think John Peirce idiot enough to take on this pretty mooring because she bewitched him with a cap sleeve?"

"Richard, one must be correct," Mama replied.

I met my father's eyes and smiled at him. After a few minutes, Phoebe returned with a fragrant dish of chamomile tea. "Well," I said, rising, "this mooring shall clank her way upstairs. Pardon me." I nodded to my uncle, who merely stared at the spot where his plate had been.

I took my dish in one hand and lifted my skirts in the other. As I rose, I felt the room spin slightly and caught the swaying reflection of the candelabra as it danced in the windowpanes. I mounted the stairs and sat myself on the bench beneath the Palladian window, watching the snow streak diagonally across the road in the moonlight.

·   ·   ·

Two days later, on Christmas Eve, I found myself next to Mr. Peirce in a wainscoted dining room, much like ours. I wore the blue brocade gown, whose unfashionably long sleeves Mama had hastily altered. My stays were drawn tight, and I could barely breathe. I listened with a dull ear to Mr. Peirce's conversation, replying with "indeed?" and "yes" according to the rhythm, rather than the sense, of his words.

John Peirce was handsome, in a forgettable way: tall and slender, long nose, pale skin, pale, shallow eyes, and light-brown hair. He wished to be agreeable, assenting with a vigorous nod to all I said. I was tempted to test the limits of this affability, to say, "Your parents are tedious bores," simply to see whether he would nod with equal vigor. I was certain he would, and this knowledge made me purse my lips to keep from smiling.

Unlike Uncle Robert, who'd had to let his butler go the year before, the Peirces retained theirs—such as he was. The old fellow's venerable wig would not sit straight on his head, and as he poured us wine, a drop of perspiration dripped off the end of his nose.

Mr. Peirce was telling me about a recent trip he had taken to—was it Jamaica? Alas, I paid insufficient attention to know for certain. Upon his return, he had heard of my charitable work among the soldiers and shipwrights. And though he was no lover of the Rebel army, he inquired quite civilly, "And I suppose their gratitude is very great?"

"Yes, yes, it is," I replied, while a sudden wave of nausea forced my lips shut.

Mama and Papa were engaged in a discussion of Washington's latest exploits in New York. Mr. Peirce, his spirit suddenly filled with unreasonable optimism, ventured, "Miss Eliza, I was wondering whether I might call upon—" Alas, at that moment, I caught a whiff of the cold, congealed liver that the butler had begun to serve onto our plates, and my stomach heaved inexorably.

"Excuse me," I interrupted him. I stood up, pushed my chair back, and only just made it into the adjoining kitchen before puking loudly upon the floor.

When I returned to the dining room a few moments later, my face no doubt white and pasty, Papa stood immediately. "It seems my daughter is ill. I regret we must cut short our visit and beg you humbly accept our apology."

•　　•　　•

We bumped along in our carriage toward home. I still felt dreadfully ill but willed myself not to puke again until we'd arrived at Deer Street. After a long silence, Mama finally spoke: "I don't see why you had to ruin a perfectly good evening by getting sick."

"Margaret!" my father intervened, "The poor girl hardly meant to."

"Oh," Mama shook her shoulders in frustration, "but it was so perfectly inopportune—you could not have willed it any more so. How mortifying! Why, it was as if you found something poisonous in the food. Such an insult to their poor cook! Really, Eliza."

"Mama," I objected, "surely you cannot think I would *choose* to run from the table and puke my dinner out for all to hear."

"That's enough," she said, shoving her open palm in my direction, as if to forestall further comment.

"Yes. It is, Margaret. Leave the poor girl alone now," said Papa.

"Thank you, Papa." I kissed his cool cheek in gratitude, then adjusted his scarf and the blanket about his knees, as it was quite cold in the carriage. I could not help but recall the time I'd been pushed into our barouche after the debacle at Mr. Inman's commencement party.

"Well, I for one am glad the evening was cut short," sighed Papa. "The Peirces have little conversation to offer and even less wit." At this, I let out a sudden snort, which made him laugh.

"Oh, the pair of you!" Mama cried.

We soon arrived home. Setting my cape on the table by the door, I called for Cassie. I then removed my bonnet and placed it beside the cape. Mama and Papa had already gone upstairs. I told Cassie I felt unwell and she soon brought me a tisane composed of one of her medicinal plants.

"What is this, Cassie?" I asked. "It smells foul, like stagnant water in a glass."

"Drink 'eet," she said. "'Eet make you feel better."

"I hope so—" I took the tisane from her. "Why, what's wrong with me, anyway? Am I ill? I hope I'm not dying."

"No, Miss Eliza. You in't dying. You wit' child."

I lowered the dish and stared at her. "With child? That can't be."

Cassie leaned in to me. "When de last time dat time of de month come round, Miss Eliza?"

I thought back and could not remember. I then recalled blood on the gown upon my return from Pest Island.

"Before Thanksgiving, Cassie. I should say about two weeks before."

Cassie nodded sagely. "Dat six weeks. You see. You wit' child. Cassie live a long time on dees eart'. Cassie know while you still in bed wit' 'eem."

"You can't have known that," I objected. "You don't know *everything*." But, though I would never admit as much to her, I believed that Cassie did know pretty much everything.

I marched up the stairs and paused at the landing with the dish in my hand. Cassie was looking up at me.

"Why stare you so?" I called down to her. "Go to bed. I'm perfectly well."

When Cassie had gone, I sat myself upon the bench beneath the Palladian window. The house was now dark and silent. It had begun to snow once more, and beyond the window the snow fell gently, covering everything in a mantle of pure white. I sipped my tea and bade my stomach calm itself.

The snow made me recall how Jeb and I used to run behind the house to make snow angels, Cassie shouting dire auguries from the kitchen door. I loved our angels. When I stood up, I was always convinced that I had made a real one, somehow, come to earth to guard us from harm.

Across the road in another house, someone blew out a candle. I tried to shake the picture of that unfortunate dinner with the Peirces from my mind. But the only things that shook were my hand and the teacup it held. Soon I would need to tell my parents that I was with child.

29

THE WEEKS PASSED AND, THANKS TO THE cruel efficiency of my stays, no one was the wiser. January came and went, then February, and finally, March. I still had not told my parents. With each passing day, it grew harder to do so. Watkins and I saw each other but rarely. He and Isaac were now hard at work on the *America*, and I did not feel well enough to ride the ferry. I contented myself with bathing Isaac in the afternoon and hearing him report upon the day's activities at the shipyard. At night, I would listen for Watkins's boots on the stairs. But he dared not venture near my door, nor would I have opened it had he done so. It was as if, having knowledge of one another, we imagined that the veils had fallen from others' eyes as well.

By April, I began to think about where in the world I might go. I knew only one thing for certain: I would have this child, and no one would take him from me. But the relative calm with which I faced my future came to an end one morning around the fifteenth of the month.

Papa had been feeling well enough to sit in his study that week, and he had been within, reading upon a broadside, when suddenly Mama came flying out. She shrieked, "Oh! Oh! Eliza! There is news! Most excellent news!"

Uncle Robert lumbered out of his study at the commotion and looked up the stairway. I moved from the parlor to stand beside him.

"What has happened, Sister?" he called. "Have we squelched the Rebels?"

"Nay. But, Brother, our home has been returned to us. There is a new law. Effective immediately, all homes confiscated before the Troubles shall be reinstated to their families. We can go home!"

The staircase swayed before my eyes. "Excuse me, Uncle, Mama." I curtsied. "I must go tell—I must let Cassie know."

I ran to the kitchen and nearly fell into Cassie's arms.

"Cassie, did you hear? What do we do?"

Hearing the news, Cassie was nearly as distraught as I. She had found a child to love and nurture. She had made excellent friends in the Whipple slaves.

We both wept, not caring if my parents overheard us. I wiped my eyes. "I know there's nothing to be done. We must go. But let us think of this parting as something temporary. I know not how, but I feel, I feel that this cannot be the end of our"—at the word *end*, I faltered. I did not reveal the source of my grief, but Cassie knew well enough what it was.

"Isaac come wit' us," Cassie said.

I shook my head. "And do what, pray? Become Mama's house-boy? Sleep in the stables? No, the best thing for Isaac is to stay here with John—with Watkins. He's happy, and he learns a useful trade."

Cassie grasped my hands. "I'm so afraid, Miss Eliza. I'm afraid his master be lookin' for 'eem, snakin' around town when we gone."

"But Cassie, it's been a year. Surely we would have heard something by now, an advertisement in the paper, at least."

Cassie shook her head. "Snakes—dey lay low in de grass a long, long time, Miss Eliza."

·   ·   ·

The cherry trees were in bloom when I met my John for the last time before we left Portsmouth. Langdon's shipyard buzzed with activity, and the *America* stood there in all its near-finished glory.

I blinked tears back as I spied Watkins hard at work in the hull, Isaac beside him, manlike now in the practiced swing of his hammer. I forced a bright smile as I waved to the boy. He set his hammer down and came running.

"Miss Eliza!"

"Oh, Isaac, I'm so glad to see you." I hugged the child tight, feeling in my arms the warm strength of his little body. "Isaac, I'll see you by and by, but I need to speak to Watkins now. Off you go." As Isaac went running down the shore, the other shipwrights eyed me cagily. Though I was a familiar sight, they must have wondered why I continued to occupy myself with this Negro child. I turned to John, facing away from the men and toward the river. "I know it's not time for dinner, but I must speak to you."

"Ten minutes," he said without looking at me. He returned to work. I remained on the western shore for a while, making as if to gather shells. I walked north against the wind, and when I was well out of sight of the men, I cut across the island. It was very windy on this day, and I regretted that I had not brought a blanket. I sat in the dunes and wrapped my arms about me. About twenty minutes later, John finally appeared. He saw how cold I was and wrapped his arms around me, warm from work, and brought me close to him. But I soon pulled away.

"John, there's news I must impart at once. Our home in Cambridge has been returned to us. We leave on the seventh of May."

"Seventh of May? That is but three weeks away. Nay, not three." He stared at me disbelievingly.

"I know. I know. But there's nothing to be done."

"Why can you not remain here? Just you, I mean?"

"I must explain."

"For God's sake, do," he said. "Put me out of my misery. You don't love me." Here, Watkins twisted out of my hands and laughed bitterly. "Of course you don't. How could you?"

He turned away, but not before I saw that tears had pooled in his eyes. "You're eager to return to Cambridge, and your old life."

I would not humor such words. Instead, I spoke the simple truth: "My old life is dead and gone, and I am glad of it. If I could stay here to prevent you from pursuing danger, I would."

"What danger?" He eyed me with sudden suspicion.

"Sending guns to aid a Negro rebellion. I know you believe you're invisible. And perhaps, to some, you are. But you play with your life, John—and now you play with our lives as well."

I sought and found his rough hands, those hands that had oozed and bled to build our ships of war. Then I looked down and placed a hand on my belly. To John's querying look, I nodded.

He stood there a moment. Then his knees bent, and his hands went to my shoulders. "How long?" he whispered.

"You know how long." I smiled.

"Four months! And all this time you told me nothing?"

"There was nothing you could do, except suffer."

"But I—I could have planned something."

"And given yourself away?"

"You trusted me not," he said bitterly.

"No," I admitted. "With my fate, but not with your own. That is your way."

Then Watkins surprised me by breaking into a broad, proud grin, entirely out of keeping with our conversation. "So, I'm to be a father."

"Yes." I grinned, too.

"Of Miss Eliza Boylston's child. One day to be Mrs. John Watkins." He spoke in bitter jest, but I said, "Yes."

"From this moment you *are* my wife, Eliza. Or—forgive me. I should ask, *will* you be my wife? My hopeless, hopeless wife?" This was no jest, for there was a pitiful cry in his voice, and he fell to one knee upon the sand.

"Yes, John." I bent down and held his face in my hands. "But not hopeless. Do not say so. Trust in God to love his pitiable sinners."

With a hard jaw and steely voice he said, "I shall trust in you."

I pulled him up to face me, and we held each other until a boat from Kittery drew near.

·   ·   ·

When Isaac found out we were leaving, he ran out of the house and did not return for several hours. We were sick with worry until he finally crept into the kitchen at around eleven that evening, ravenously hungry. Cassie scolded him loudly; her voice traveled up the back stairs to my chamber, and I threw on my robe and descended.

"Isaac, listen to me." I knelt down by him. "We shan't be parted forever. We think this best for you: to remain with Watkins. You wouldn't like our house in Cambridge. The work would be low, slave's work—nothing like that of a noble shipwright. And I promise we shall write to you near every day."

"But I can't read," he whined, and let his cup of milk bang on the table.

At this comment, my heart clutched. "Watkins can teach you, perhaps."

"You'll never come for me." He shook his head. "I don't believe you. My old master will catch up with me. Then I'll be done for." He began to cry.

"Who *is* your master, Isaac? It would help if we knew."

This was not the first time we had begged him to tell us, but he would not. This time, however, he bade me kneel so he could whisper in my ear.

"Richards?" I repeated. "Where resides this miserable Richards?" I demanded to know. But that was all Isaac would ever tell me.

•   •   •

It was a busy job, packing, and I tired easily. Everyone pitched in: Mama, myself, Cassie, Phoebe, old Jupiter, and even Uncle Robert. Cuffee and Prince stopped by to join the work party, and Dinah Whipple arrived as well. She would be replacing Cassie as cook to Uncle Robert. When Cuffee and Prince had learned of our imminent departure, they told Colonel Whipple, who kindly offered Dinah to my uncle. Dinah was no cook, being but nineteen, but she learned quickly and, with the Whipple house nearby, she would have guidance. Things could have been worse for Uncle Robert.

At last, on the morning of May seventh, we found ourselves settling into our carriage. Watkins and Isaac had long since departed for the shipyard, which was good, because Cassie and I could not have contained our grief had they been there to see us off.

Papa was wrapped in blankets against the spring breeze. Mama hugged her brother long and hard, for she knew not when she would see him again. We thanked him for his generosity, and for the asylum that had lasted three long years. At the last minute, Uncle Robert approached Cassie. He reached out his hand as if he would take hers. Then, as she proffered it, he sprang back and turned away, mumbling angrily at himself as he retreated.

It was a quiet and contemplative ride back to Cambridge. Each of us was lost in his own thoughts, interrupted only by my father's regular coughing. At one point, Papa said, "Well, we fared rather well, all in all, in Portsmouth."

"Yes. Poor Robert was very kind," added my mother.

"I shall miss Isaac a great deal," I said.

"You seemed to take a particular interest in that child," said Mama.

"Oh, he's a sweet boy, Mama, and very hardworking. You should see how he strives to keep up with the men."

My mother conceded with a shrug, "Well, I suppose in a hundred of them there's one that's willing to work hard." I was about to object when Cassie, who sat so silently among her white masters as to be invisible, placed a forestalling hand on my arm.

We stopped at an inn in Rowley as the sun descended and took refreshment there. It was an old tavern with low ceilings and small, smoky rooms. Before the war, Cassie would have been sent to sleep in the attic with the other slaves. But now such formalities were dispensed with, and she shared my bed, in a pretty chamber with a fair view of the woods beyond.

Once we were alone, Cassie untied my stays, and I was able to breathe freely. The sun was now low over the treetops, and the truth about my break with Watkins was clear to me: it might well be forever. My trust in God left me; all seemed lost.

Cassie was removing the pins from my hair. She continued her work silently for several moments as I gazed out the window, at the treetops. My eyes were wet; my voice choked when I said, still looking away from her, "Cassie, what shall I *do*?"

Cassie considered my question. Then she replied, "You gon' let out your gowns before you choke dat babe to death."

I had meant my question in a far broader sense, and Cassie knew it. But her sensible answer made me smile. She really did seem to know most everything, and this thought comforted me so well that I slept soundly beside her and did not wake till dawn.

Part III

30

AS OUR CARRIAGE MADE ITS WAY THROUGH Cambridge and down the Watertown road, we saw that many of the lawns had grown to seed, and there was a raw openness where ancient trees had once stood. Front doors, stolidly locked when we left Cambridge, were now thrown open to the elements. Windows through which girls such as myself had once primly gazed had been smashed to bits or removed, their muntins melted for bullets. British officers in their red coats strolled up and down the road in groups or pairs as if they were victors, not prisoners.

Some things, however, were much as they ever were: The daffodils had flowered; bits of their dried yellow flowers clung to pale-green stems. Beds trumpeted forth the call of red and yellow tulips, and here and there flourished a rogue swathe of Dutch ones, brightly striated in red and green. We also heard the snipping-scissor sound of Mr. Cardinal and saw his brilliant-scarlet body flit through the elms, which made me think of Maria.

As the carriage came to rest at last before our house, Cassie and I stared at it in amazement. At first, we were loath to enter, but Mama, eager to get Papa into bed, said, "Oh, let us descend!"

We had fully expected our home to have been sacked by Washington's troops. We had expected to lay our eyes upon bare floor where Turkey carpets once had been, and dust where oak chests had stood. But we had not expected blood. Old, brown blood. Everywhere. And gore. Dried, crusted bits of human flesh, stuck to brown remnants of jackets. Stained, bloody, straw pallets strewn everywhere in the front parlor. Abandoned buckets of rusty, foul water . . . I turned to face the street and breathed fresh air, to avoid puking.

"But what has happened?" my mother cried. She peered inside the house but did not enter, then backed slowly away. "We cannot stay here. Mr. Boylston!" She returned to the carriage, to her old consolation of Papa. But the man who could always be relied upon to help us was no more. This man, small and shrunken, wrapped in a blanket, was white and panicky, and could not move without help. Perspiration rained from his forehead.

In the absence of servants, we did what was needed. I inhaled the fresh air from the open doorway one last time. Then, taking Cassie's arm, I ran with her past the tragic hospital remains, up the staircase to our chambers. The furniture, save one large highboy and the poster beds, was gone, as was every scrap of linen. Cassie descended to the cellar, where we had stored our crates and provisions: furniture, linens and bolsters, sacks of grain, jugs of cider, wine, and other provisions—they were gone, too. When she returned, Cassie merely blinked against the light and slowly shook her head.

Well, what would it serve to grieve the loss of our worldly possessions? We did not share the news with my parents, however, thinking to spare them the shock. It would come soon enough.

With the help of Jupiter, who would return to Portsmouth the following day, and Juno, our old stableboy, now a hale young man, we were soon able to locate the few bed linens we had brought with us from Portsmouth. We made Papa's bed, and Juno and Cassie helped him up the stairs and into it. I was able to clean my room sufficiently so that I could remove my stays and lie, breathless and despairing, upon the bare pallet.

.   .   .

The following morning, I found Juno, Jupiter, and Cassie all on their hands and knees, scrubbing the parlor floor. I had slept late, despite having scratchy nibs of feathers pricking me throughout the night, for I had no great wish to wake.

Mama stood over them, pointing to areas of the parlor they had missed. When she saw me she cried, "Oh, Eliza—there you are. At *last*. Observe how slowly they go at it—you'd think they were obliged to clean a palace."

"Well, it would go more quickly if they had help," I retorted. Then I got down on my hands and knees and helped the slaves to clean the gore. Several times I nearly puked and needed to cover my mouth as my stomach endeavored to heave its contents through this opening. Finally Cassie stood up and said, "Dat's enough, Mees Eliza. We can do 'eet. Go and have some breakfast."

But what would that be? There was no grain, no eggs. Not even a stray chicken strut through our fields. Mama, fortunately, had a bit of coin, and she sent Cassie off to market with instructions to procure what she could with it.

At around eleven, Cassie returned from market looking not very satisfied and muttering something about "dose teeves." But she had managed to procure some coffee, milk, and eggs, and so she prepared a pot of coffee and some eggs for me. She then returned to the task of cleaning. Jupiter and Juno threw open the windows and aired the house out, and together we finally managed to remove all signs of the hospital from our living areas. Jupiter and Juno were then consigned to cart the refuse away—somewhere, anywhere. With all this heroically accomplished, Cassie sat down directly on the floor and placed her head in her hands. I knelt by her side on the floor, which now smelled pungently of vinegar. Mama looked about for somewhere to sit as if we had committed a severe breach of etiquette. Then, having nowhere to sit herself, she sat down beside us and cried.

We had been back but a few days when a messenger arrived with an envelope for Papa. This was no farmhand, but introduced himself to Mama as the captain of a merchant ship moored in Boston. Neither Mama nor I knew what news he brought, but the man would hand over the envelope to no one but Papa. The captain stood nervously on the stoop awaiting entry, looking about him as if he might have been followed.

"Cassie!" Mama called, having opened the front door herself. "See if Mr. Boylston will receive this man." Cassie made her way up the stairs and soon returned with a nod. Mama accompanied the captain up the stairs. She descended after about ten minutes, jubilantly waving a fan. When she came closer, I saw that the fan was made of pound sterling notes.

"Look, oh, look!" she cried. "Look what your most wonderful father has done!"

We kissed the money as if it were manna from Heaven. We would eat. Mama told me that Papa had liquidated near everything: ships, slaves, cane fields. This was all that remained of my father's fortune. All of it, minus his debt, had shrunk down to a fan to wave the flies away.

31

"I MUST 'AVE OTHER STAYS," CASSIE COMPLAINED to me about a week after we had returned.

"Well, what do you want me to do about it?" I asked. All Cambridge had come to a halt, yet the life inside me took no note of it. Cassie had already let out my three remaining gowns. Were I to abandon the old stays, none of them would fit. But that was not what we truly argued about. She had wanted me to tell Mama the truth in the carriage on the way home from Portsmouth, where I would be protected by the presence of others. She was distressed that I had waited so long.

"Now you home," Cassie remarked, "nobody see if she keel you."

"Oh, she will not *keel* me," I said. "Hurry up and tie my stays."

Two more weeks passed, and I arrived at the point where I could no longer keep my secret. This time, Cassie shook her head and let the strings drop. "I can't do 'em, Miss Eliza. Hercules heemself could not do dem."

"I know I must tell them, Cassie. I don't see how to avoid it."

"You wait anudder week, you won't have to tell dem. Dey'll *know*."

"I can't tell Mama. I'll speak to Papa first."

She shrugged to say it hardly mattered.

Sunday morning, Mama went to visit a new friend, the Baroness von Riedesel. The baroness, wife of General Friedrich Adolf Riedesel, was taken prisoner after Burgoyne's defeat at Saratoga. She, her husband, and their three children were now housed in John Sewell's old house just down the street from us. I found a reason to stay behind. Cassie, knowing my intentions, had made Papa a particularly good breakfast: eggs, a piece of ham, and even a few bright-red tulip petals strewn about the tray. It was so pretty that he asked me, "Have I forgotten my own birthday?"

"No, Papa. It is a beautiful spring day, though."

"Why did you not go to the baroness's with Mama?"

"I told her I was unwell."

"And are you?" Papa's old shrewdness shone once more from his fevered eyes.

"No. I remained behind because I wished to speak with you." I turned to the window. Sun streamed in, brightened by its reflection off of the river; a song sparrow warbled prettily. Cassie entered the chamber, propped Papa up on his pillows, and removed his tray. Then she left us alone and closed the door. Papa's face was florid; I sat beside him and took his hand.

"My dear Eliza," he said, "you're my pride and joy. Yes, my one consolation in this cold, cruel world."

How I nearly renounced my intentions then! After those loving words, how could I be the agent of such cruel pain?

"I love you so much, Papa. And I hope some day to redeem myself in your eyes. For I do still hope to live a good and useful life."

"Redeem yourself?" he frowned. Such words were tolerated at meeting, but in truth Papa had little use for them elsewhere. "What need have you for redemption, in my eyes or anyone else's?"

"Papa, there's something I need to tell you. I dare not tell Mama. Not yet. I shall do whatever you say. I shall go away . . . Oh,

God help me!" I buried my head in his breast, and he held me and felt my suffering.

"Papa." All fell silent. "I'm with child."

Papa inhaled, then exhaled, as if having received a physical blow. But he whispered merely, "Who? Who's the scoundrel who has abused my daughter thus?"

Had I been a different sort of woman, I might have said it was a case of ravishment. But ravishment was something I knew and could never lie about.

"I love him, Papa. He's a good man. And he loves me."

"Then why not marry as soon as may be? That was very wrong, Eliza, but the remedy is easy enough."

"We cannot marry. I wish we could."

"And why not?"

"I cannot say, Papa."

He cast about the room restlessly. His color rose; his breath became labored, and I suffered inwardly to see him so roused. I feared I would need to call for Cassie.

"You cannot," he concluded, "because he's married. Damned scoundrel."

I said nothing; it was a shortsighted lie, to be sure. Once they saw the babe, they might know something closer to the truth. Papa's chest began to heave. His breath, it seemed, had left him. He asked for a dish of tea.

"Cassie!" I called. She must have been just outside the door, for she entered at once. "A dish of tea for Papa. He's unwell."

"I'm not unwell," Papa rasped. "I'll have the truth around here from now on. I am dying, and I shall soon be out of reach of the world's slings and arrows."

"Oh, Papa!" I reached for him, but he pushed me back and fell into a paroxysm of coughing. I fled to my chamber, while Cassie remained to care for him.

A few days passed with no indication that Papa had told my mother. Then, just as I began to think that all would be well, I woke one morning to find that my chamber door had been locked from without. *Perhaps the knob was stuck,* I thought. I turned it back and forth, but it would not budge. I called out for Mama, but beyond the door was only resolute silence. I called again and thought I heard her footsteps. "Oh, Mama!" I cried, but the footsteps continued on down the stairs. Was it possible she had purposely locked me in? At once, a powerful thirst came upon me. My teeth were foul; I needed to clean them, and to have my coffee. I called for Cassie, but she was below stairs preparing breakfast and could not hear me. I crawled back into bed and endeavored to calm myself. Cassie would soon come to release me.

I went to use the chamber pot but found it missing—what cruel trick was this? Cassie would not forget to return it, knowing how I rose five or six times a night to use it. Could Mama have gone mad and removed it on purpose? With mounting panic I finally threw my night shift upon the floor, squatted down like a cornered animal, and relieved myself upon it. *If this was Mama's doing*, I thought, *I would never forgive her.*

I returned to bed naked and managed to sleep once more, having tucked the bolster snugly about me. I woke up several hours later. The sun had risen above my window and then passed beyond it. I tested the door: it was still locked. I knew now that I had been locked in on purpose. Had Mama finally lost her wits?

Several more hours passed. My room was in shadow. My mind and soul traveled like the sun through every stage of feeling: rage, fear, self-pity—until I reached a kind of resignation. If she wished me to die of thirst, so be it. I had heard tell of parents who had let their wayward daughters waste away in such a manner.

I peered out my window and considered jumping. But I dared not—surely I would break a leg. Mama's rose garden lay beneath my window, too, and, naked as I was, I would be ravaged by thorns. I was lying limply on my side, hands tucked beneath my face, when Cassie entered my room. She stopped and looked at me uncomprehendingly.

"It's past noon. Why you lie 'alf-dead like dat, Miss Eliza?"

"Why?" I sat up, exposing my swelling belly and breasts to Cassie. "I called and called! The door was locked from without! Oh, Cassie!" I rose from bed.

"Why you naked? Why your shift on da floor, Miss Eliza?"

"I . . . I had to relieve myself. There was no chamber pot! She locked me in, and I could not get out. I thought I should perish here."

"Your mudder say you asleep," Cassie replied dubiously.

"Asleep? Oh, Cassie—" I got up and ran to her.

"The door was not locked when I try 'eet."

"Yes, yes it was! She must just now have opened it. Oh, I am parched . . . So, it wasn't you who forgot to return the chamber pot?"

"No, miss," Cassie said gravely, the truth finally dawning upon her. "I descend wit' you." And, not daring to remain alone in that chamber another moment and using the bolster to cover my nakedness, I descended to the kitchen with Cassie. There, I threw off the bolster and, standing quite naked, I instantly drank a mug of cider and cleaned my teeth with salt. Cassie loaned me one of her own clean shifts, which I donned, and then made me a plate of eggs.

"Your papa told her, and now she gone crazy." Cassie nodded conclusively, handing me the plate.

I agreed. What's more, I so dreaded seeing Mama that I didn't leave Cassie's side and resolved to sleep with her in the dairy.

Later that day, around two in the afternoon, I still had not moved from the kitchen when I needed to use the necessary. Without was a glorious afternoon. The tulips were all in bloom, and the salmon-colored quince blossoms had opened overnight.

The maple trees' leaves had unfurled their little green fingers, and though our garden and orchards had been much neglected, they had not been destroyed. With tending they might yet return to their former glory.

I returned to the kitchen. There, I found not Cassie but my mother, waiting for me. I remained in the doorway without taking another step. Where was Cassie? Mama looked me up and down, I in Cassie's shift, as if I were an intruder.

"There you are," she said. I began to speak, but she cut me off, her tone ominous. "You shall have a visitor tomorrow." Mama left the kitchen, leaving me to wonder who was coming to visit, and whither they would take me.

32

IT WAS AROUND NOON THE FOLLOWING DAY, and I was in my chamber. I had just received a letter from John, though it was signed "Isaac." The letter said nothing of great import, merely that he was working hard on the *America* and that Phoebe did not give him a bath every day like Cassie did. Uncle was very low without Cassie and would scarcely touch Dinah's cooking, which brought the girl to tears near every day.

Though the letter contained nothing sentimental, I held it to my breast. Someone knocked upon my chamber door and the sound startled me.

"Come in," I said, setting the letter down upon the bed.

The door opened and in walked Lizzie.

"Hello, Eliza." Lizzie smiled warmly at me.

I curtsied.

Impulsively, she hugged me about the shoulders. There was no question but that she felt my expansive girth between us.

Lizzie was a picture of rusticated good health: Her face was tan and her eyes were bright. Her auburn hair fell about her shoulders, unadorned and unpinned.

"You are with child," she remarked, pulling back from me.

"As you see." My voice quavered but I endeavored to retain a dignified bearing before my sister-in-law. I curtsied.

"How do you feel?" she gazed into my face, her head cocked earnestly.

"Quite well," I said. "Should I feel otherwise?"

"Has the nausea passed?"

"For the most part. My senses are—heightened," I admitted, recalling my revulsion upon arriving home. I realized that I longed to share my feelings with someone—there had been so many new ones—but pride held me back.

"Any bleeding?"

"Bleeding?"

"Yes. You know—down there."

"Of course not!"

"It is common enough." Lizzie smiled. She then cast me an odd look and said, "Shall we sit?"

"I prefer to stand." The truth was, when I sat I could not breathe at all.

"Well, *I* should like to sit, for my journey was rather long." And here she sat on the bed with a sigh, while I remained standing next to the chair.

Lizzie smelled of the outdoors. Her homespun gown was clean, though not pressed. Clearly, she was far more occupied with her garden or the women of Braintree than with her toilet. Beside her, I felt like a fatted goose.

"How many months?" she asked.

"Five, I believe. Or a little more."

"You will not sit because you cannot, am I right?"

"I can sit if I choose to," I said peevishly.

Lizzie merely smiled. "Would you allow me to touch you?"

"Certainly not!"

"I mean simply to ascertain the size of the child. One can plan things better, knowing when it is due. Please." She pointed to my bed. "It shall take but a moment." Lizzie came forward and unbuttoned my gown. When she felt how tightly my stays were tied, she cried, "For God's sake!" and loosed them at once. I let out a great involuntary sigh.

"Heavens above, Eliza. You mustn't tie your stays like this. You'll choke yourself and your babe. Indeed, I should greatly prefer it if you did not wear them at all."

"Not wear them? What do you propose? I have but three gowns, all too small for me otherwise."

"Well," she considered. "Can you sew? Were you to sacrifice one gown, you could easily add panels to your other two."

"How hideous. They are nowhere near the same color or fabric."

Lizzie replied, "No, I agree, it won't do for going abroad. But within your own home I should think no one would take it amiss."

"Go abroad!" I let out a grim laugh. "As if I could do such a thing. Why," I added, looking out my window, "we have British officers here even now, strolling about the town."

"Who I'm sure have never gotten a woman with child," she said, peering out the window. Just then a smart-looking officer with a full gray head of hair strolled by with a young maid on his arm.

Lizzie grinned. I had to admit that my sister-in-law was quite pretty. Working in the sun had brought out her freckles and given her hair a coppery glow. Her eyes were warm and fairly sparkled with an almost mischievous intelligence.

"In any case, Mama would never permit me to go abroad," I said glumly.

"It's a shame. The fresh air would do you good. You're too pale, Eliza. Perhaps you could spend some time each day in your garden. Doing light chores—weeding, pruning, and such. When you find you are out of breath, stop. Now, if you will . . ."

I finally lay back on my bed and allowed Lizzie to feel my belly. Her hands were steady, knowing. She pressed gently, evenly, around the circumference of the babe. She nodded. "Yes, about five months. Or perhaps a little more." I stood and moved to take up my gown, but she blocked my path. She held my stays in one hand. Glancing at the window, she moved to open it. Suddenly, with a great flinging motion, she tossed them out the window.

"What on earth?" I cried.

Lizzie handed me my shift, which Cassie had cleaned and pressed. "Here—you may wear this, with your dressing gown. When you've let out your gowns, you can change then. See, you breathe far more easily already. Some color has returned to your face." I reached for my little looking glass and peered into it. Indeed, the color in my face had risen; I now looked rather more alive than dead. "Mr. Miller shall return for you next month."

"Return for me?" I cried, though I knew, and had known, the point of her visit to me since she arrived.

"To bring you to Braintree, of course. I think you'll like it there."

Though isolated and depressed, I had no wish to leave Papa. Braintree seemed even farther from John than Cambridge, and the thought of meeting the Adamses filled me with dread.

"In fact—" Lizzie continued brightly, "why don't you come next week? It's beautiful just now on the farm, and you shall be able to go abroad freely."

I shook my head. I would go, certainly, but not yet. "I cannot leave Papa."

"Very well. But if you change your mind, write to me."

I nodded. Lizzie curtsied and left.

After she had gone, I called for Cassie and instructed her to retrieve my stays. She dutifully went to fetch them but returned a few minutes later with empty hands, which she spread before me with a shrug.

"Where are my stays, Cassie? They were right beneath the window, on a rose bush."

"I suppose an animal got 'em," she shrugged.

"Animal indeed," I said, staring at her blankly innocent face. Then Cassie burst out laughing, and I joined her.

33

ONE MORNING, I WOKE TO FEEL A distinct motion in my belly—a little leg must have stretched itself straight, for, sitting up and staring in awe, I saw a lump rise up just above my belly button.

"Cassie!" I called. She came running. "Cassie! I felt it! It kicked me!" Cassie placed a hand on my belly, but the babe had withdrawn.

"It come again," she assured me. "Dere no way out—but one."

"Cassie!"

Now that I had felt the babe move, I could no longer bear the thought of strangling it. We set about that same afternoon fashioning two new gowns. It hardly mattered which we chose to sacrifice, since not one of them, once altered, would be fit to be seen in. My blue and green gowns now had twin plum-colored panels down both sides. Hideous! However, they would do well enough to wear about the house.

By June, I found the idea of going to Braintree less terrible than I had previously. It was true that I would be farther from John, and would have to leave poor Cassie and Papa. But I would be free of my mother, who no longer even sat with me at table. When she came upon me in the library or elsewhere, she would actually turn on her heels and retreat as if I were an unwelcome guest. Somehow, the destruction of my once-fine gowns, in service of this growing bastard within me, was the final straw for her.

By any measure, I knew, I had fallen from grace. Yet I did not *feel* I had sinned. At least, not in loving John. I cringed to think of my shallow friendship with Louisa, and my ignorant flirtation with Mr. Inman. But, thinking of John, I felt only the greatest pride and tenderness. Never had I known such a good man, and I did not know at that moment whether my love for him made me better or worse than Mama believed me to be.

My feelings about the war had changed as well. I had compassionated with the wounded boys. Disgust had filled my breast at the arrogance of Cousin George. But it was only through my love for John that I truly understood the evil of oppression. To be silenced in one's opinions, forbidden in one's passions—this was to forbid a man his own manhood, his humanity.

However, there remained a sticking point in my mind concerning this great Cause of ours. There had been, and yet was, so much talk of independence. But what of our slaves? No one took their measure. Few, even among our great leaders, spoke of slavery. I knew not how they lived with their own rhetoric, or with such a paradox.

·   ·   ·

In my remaining weeks in Cambridge, I managed to eke out a sweet, small life, consisting of visits to Papa, meals with Cassie, sewing infants' clothing in the garden, and reading the few but precious letters I received from Isaac. Mama took her meals in Papa's chamber, and we hardly spoke two words to each other.

As my date of departure approached, I decided to broach the subject with Cassie of teaching her to read. Great delicacy was needed, however, for I had no wish to assault those wounds that, while scabbed over, had never fully healed.

"Cassie," I said one evening as we took supper in the kitchen. "You know that we shall soon be separated. I should like to be able to write to you without Mama's interference."

"Naw," she waved her long-fingered hand at me. "Last ting I need is to read and be gettin' de white man's 'eadache. I got a black 'eadache of my own."

I let the matter rest then, but a few days later I brought down several of my old lesson books and that same primer I had used with Toby. We had no other, but as I could do nothing about that, I kept calm and prayed it would not raise the ghosts of bitter memories.

I put the books and primer before her.

"Please, Cassie, if you could find a way to do this for me, I would be most grateful. I shall soon be parted from you, and while it is your choice whether you put the skill to any other purpose, the thought of my not being able to write to you makes me miserable."

"Well, why don' you say so in de firs' place? Now, dere's a reason to be reckon with. All dat knowledge dis, knowledge dat—*now* you're sayin' someteeng. C'mon, bring dat book over here."

"Oh, Cassie!" I hugged her. "You shall soon find that the pleasure of reading is its own reward."

"If you say so." I caught her roll her eyes. That far, she would not go.

• • •

As it turned out, Cassie was as quick at learning as her son had been. I don't know why this fact surprised me, except for the years I had been told that "they" can't learn, and that "they" are slow. Cassie gave the lie to both. She could focus for long moments at a time. It was usually I, or Mama, who reminded her she needed to begin making dinner, or to set out breakfast, or some other errand.

Cassie soon made such progress that, with a little help, she was able to read the headlines of the papers. "Cassie, we must show Papa how clever you are. He won't believe it!"

I took her by the hand and she resisted a little, but at last I managed to drag her into his chamber.

He had been resting with his eyes closed, the paper clasped in his hands, but when he heard the door squeak his eyes opened. "Eliza, is that you?"

"Yes, Papa, but I bring Cassie. She has something she wants to show you."

"Cassie wishes to show me something?"

"No, sir," said Cassie, beginning to back out the door.

"You do, too! Don't listen to her, Papa. Or rather, hand her your paper there, and then listen. Here, let me sit you up."

I propped the pillows behind him and took the paper from his hands. "Here you go." To Cassie I whispered, "Now, take your time. You know these words."

Cassie cleared her throat importantly. My mind flashed back to the time Mr. Inman, wishing to impress me with his absolute power, bade Cassie read the front of the *Odyssey*. What a terrible memory, the more so because I did nothing to intervene but to plead a sudden headache. Today, I thought with grim satisfaction, I would behave quite differently.

Cassie pulled on her petticoats, to straighten them. She shrugged to adjust her frock, and I was about to tell her she was not entering a wrestling match but simply reading a bit of print when she cried, in a loud, clear voice:

"Bree-teesh Aban-don Pheela-delphia."

I clapped my hands together.

Papa said, "Well, what do you know!"

"Oh, Cassie!" I hugged her. "Genius possesses you. That was marvelous."

Papa was laughing now, and I feared he'd bring on a coughing fit when suddenly Mama popped her head in.

"What ruckus is going on in here, pray?"

"Oh, nothing, Mama. Cassie was simply reading Papa his morning paper."

I sucked on a smile and felt myself infused with a delicious spite just as Mama said, "Read Papa his paper! Why, what's the world coming to? Next thing you know, they'll be writing their own declarations of independence!"

But nothing Mama could say dampened our joy on that day. And later, after supper, I came upon Cassie when she thought herself alone in the kitchen. Apparently Papa had given her his paper as a gift, for there she was, tracing her finger across the smaller print and sounding out the words as softly and steadily as a prayer.

34

I LOOKED IN ON PAPA TWICE A day. Sometimes, I read the broadsides to him; other times, I simply held his hand. One evening in early July, Cassie told me that my father wished to speak to me. I thought this odd, as I'd visited with him only several hours earlier. I entered his chamber and found him sitting up.

I was big with child, and Papa stared at me. "I wonder, shall I live to see my heir? I doubt it."

"Oh, Papa—surely—" I began.

"I regret the years in which I deluded myself, Eliza," he broke in, "and I shall not do so now. I wish to apprise you of my situation and my final wishes."

Here, with what scant breath remained to him, Papa gave me to understand that a sizable portion of his property yet remained in Barbados. He had not divested himself of the entire estate, as he had let on to Mama. He had sold the slaves, and most of what remained consisted of a spacious but simple house and about eight acres, upon which many fruit trees and some sugar cane still grew.

"Your mother shall have this house and a small savings I have amassed for her. But the house in Barbados I give to you. I was well regarded there, once, as you shall be, regardless of your . . .

situation. There, people are not so very . . . particular. Nay, in Barbados one had sooner be an adulterer than a rebel."

Papa thought this comment quite amusing and managed to laugh briefly before coughing.

"Thank you, Papa." I kissed his hand tenderly. I knew it was all he had to give. Equally, I knew that I could never leave my homeland for an island in a distant sea, under secure British rule. What use would I have for an old plantation house filled with echoes of atrocities?

As if he knew what I thought, Papa said, "I must say now that I do believe I was wrong to let Cassie's boy go. God punished me well and good for that." Papa sighed and patted my hand. Tears of gratitude came to my eyes.

"Oh, Papa, the Lord forgives, as must I. Please don't leave me."

"If I'm given a choice in the matter, Eliza, I shall not leave you. But there is one more thing."

He had been holding my hand, but he grasped it tighter now, conveying the urgency of his thought. I waited. He needed to catch his breath, and it seemed he never would. Minutes went by before he said, quickly, "It grieves me to see you and your mother grow so distant. Soon you shall only have each other."

"Mama does not speak to me."

"Then speak to her, Eliza."

"I'm afraid Mama does not—love me."

"Nonsense. She's not good at showing her feelings, that much is true."

I thought Mama quite capable of showing disapprobation and meanness of spirit, but I did not say so.

"You think her a cruel woman, I know. But it's because she suffers so. She suffers her losses deeply."

I would not accept Papa's explanation, though I dearly wished I could. I had seen enough of life, enough of generosity of heart—John Watkins, Colonel Langdon, Prince Whipple, Dinah and Cuffee Whipple, and even my own Cassie—to know better.

"Many suffer, Papa. But some would rather die than inflict suffering on others. Yes, some would rather die than do so. Excuse me," I said. "I'll return by and by." I kissed Papa's flushed cheek and fled the room before the tears came.

Mama stood in the hallway, and I nearly ran into her. She wore a blue silk gown I had not seen her wear since before the Troubles. Cassie had done her hair in a style that I recalled from my earliest childhood.

"Mama, where go you like that?"

"To a ball for the king's birthday. The Baroness von Riedesel has kindly invited me."

"But you cannot possibly wish to attend such a thing."

"Why not?"

"You know well enough. Besides, isn't she an enemy prisoner?"

Mama stared at my purple-paneled gown with a cruel smile, as if to say, "Yes, the Baroness is such a prisoner; but then, so are you."

At her withering gaze, I drew myself up. "Oh, go, then! Go! Think of me what you will. I no longer desire your good opinion. Or your forgiveness."

"That is fortunate for you," she replied coldly.

•　　•　　•

It was a hot summer, and as I grew larger, I could not bear to don my gowns, even let out as they were. I remained in my shift: in my chamber reading or in the gardens beyond the house and human eyes. There was consolation in picking raspberries for Cassie or smelling the green beans that grew on the vine. Now that it was summer, we ate better, as Cassie had had the foresight to plant seeds the moment we returned from Portsmouth.

I spent a good hour or so every day with Papa. Nearing death, Papa seemed at last to become a very good sort of man. He threw convention aside. He told me that he regretted having been slow to rally to the Cause. He regretted his behavior toward Jeb, whom he now firmly believed was one of our first heroes. We spent many hours speaking of how I and my child might live a useful life, despite the inevitable obstacles. On one visit, I confessed, "Papa, I wasn't truthful when I allowed you to believe the father of my child is married. He is not. He is by no means such a scoundrel."

Papa seemed pleased by this and nodded.

"I dearly love him and still hope that we can some day live as man and wife." I did not go so far as to reveal to Papa the identity of the man I loved, for this, I knew, would have been beyond his comprehension.

"That relieves me greatly, Eliza. Your life has not been very happy, I'm afraid. I wish you nothing but happiness in the future. I pray that God will remove the impediments that stand between you both."

O, precious acceptance! It was all the sweeter for the delay.

35

BY SEPTEMBER, I HAD GROWN QUITE UNCOMFORTABLE. My ankles were swollen, and I had need of the chamber pot near every hour. The babe kicked me all the time now, as if telling me he had grown tired of his cramped accommodations. I imagined it was a fine boy with very strong legs, and I could not wait to get him out of me and into the world, where I would scold him for kicking me so. Cassie had warned me not to grow attached, not to think of it as anything but a poor creature bound for death.

"What a depressing thought, Cassie."

She looked at me sternly. "'Eet for your own good, Miss Eliza. You have a complaint, you take it up wit' 'Eem." Here, she pointed upward at the heavens.

By autumn, Watkins's letters had trailed off, and he had begun to seem but a beautiful dream. Had he ever been real? Had his strong, tan arms ever held me? Had those scarred yet gentle hands ever touched me? Had I ever caressed those soft curls, or kissed his full lips? My belly told me it was so, yet I hardly believed it. Portsmouth had faded to a dappled shadow in the light of my present reality.

Sometime that September, a tall, loose-limbed man of twenty-eight or so strode up our walkway. Mama answered the door in a dilatory way, as if her butler were momentarily indisposed. The man bowed and introduced himself as one Mr. Thomas Miller.

I had been watching him from the parlor window, but, upon his knock at the door, I scurried to the top of the stairs. He was quite handsome, though large-featured. His brow was thick and dark, his eyes large and wide-set, his nose quite strong and straight.

Mr. Miller appeared to have dressed somewhat too hastily. His cravat was askew, and a button was missing from one cuff. He gazed past Mama and said, "Might I have a word with your daughter? With Miss Boylston?"

"No, that's not possible. She is—indisposed."

I then saw Mr. Miller bend down and whisper something into Mama's ear.

"Eliza!" she called at once. I was now at the base of the stairs; there was no need for her to shout.

"I'm in my dressing gown," I said softly.

"Never mind that," Mr. Miller replied. I approached warily, my arms about my belly, blushing. I had not set eyes upon a man apart from Papa in several months.

Mama introduced Mr. Miller. "Mr. Miller is an acquaintance of Lizzie's. He says he is the brother of the girl you brought to Braintree, Martha—"

"Oh, Martha Miller. I remember her. How fares she? She must be quite an expert at farming by now."

Mr. Miller turned to me without answering. But his tone was respectful when he asked, "Might I speak with you a moment, Miss Boylston—alone?"

He pointed to our sofa in the front parlor. It was our last remaining piece of furniture in that room. At one time, this fact might have mortified me. But no longer.

Mama stood in the foyer watching us as he led me there and bade me sit. Mr. Miller hesitated; he was clearly waiting for my mother to take her leave, which she finally did after a painful minute or two.

"Lizzie—Mrs. Boylston—says I am to bring you to Braintree when—at the appointed hour."

"I see." I did not blush, but Mr. Miller did. We then proceeded to discuss the likely date of our departure, and the details of what I was to bring. Did I have someone to help me pack? he wanted to know. I said I did.

"If you like, I can procure you a cape."

"Oh, yes, that would be good." I had nothing to drape about my enormous girth for the journey.

"Lizzie—Mrs. Boylston—said she might also procure a homespun gown or two from the parish. Nothing so fine as you're accustomed to, I'm afraid, but serviceable."

"You are very kind. I'm most grateful," I said. And I was. But I could not help but think back to the days when I would rather have died than wear that ghastly homespun. The memory made me smile.

Mr. Miller soon took his leave, bowing deeply. He left behind him an impression of a kind, decent man, one who happened to be entirely in love with my sister-in-law, Lizzie, and had not the guile to hide it. I wondered whether she returned his feelings.

Mr. Miller visited me several times more that September. Sometimes it was to discuss practical subjects, but at other times it seemed as if he was content to keep me company for no good reason at all. On one of his visits I said to him, "You're so kind, Mr. Miller, to call upon me. I'm truly grateful. For, as you see, I live quite alone . . ."

"People were not meant to live so," he asserted.

"I heartily agree."

Mr. Miller grinned at an unbidden thought. "You'll like Braintree." He looked about us, at the large cavernous rooms. "It's quite the opposite of . . . of this."

"Noisy and chaotic, you mean?"

He laughed. "Perhaps. At times."

Mr. Miller told me about the farm and the onerous work his sister and Lizzie did every day. He told me about Colonel Josiah and Ann Quincy, and Abigail Adams, whom I would no doubt meet upon my arrival. At this last news, I cringed: how mortifying it would be to make the acquaintance of this great lady in my big, unwed state!

"Oh, but I cannot meet her. That's impossible."

"You shall find her a most gracious and enlightened woman."

"Perhaps. But what shall she think of *me*?"

He considered this. "I believe she shall think that you are very brave."

. . .

Mr. Miller was true to his word and brought me two gowns—simple, country items made of homespun linsey-woolsey, but capacious and quite comfortable. He brought me a cape as well, made of a lovely green wool. Cassie and I packed a trunk. Or rather, I sat on my bed and instructed her. She was moving very slowly and deliberately, as if she were packing my dowry, and I grew impatient.

"No, no, Cassie. There's no need to be so very particular about the folds—it will take forever this way."

"You've got nutteeng for winter. No good stockings."

I shrugged. "Upon the subject of undergarments, I am entirely indifferent."

"You won' be indifferent when you find your feet frozen solid."

"What would you have me do, Cassie?" I cried in exasperation. She had no answer, and I let her complain, for I knew it was her way of grieving my departure.

I grieved, too, for my father, whom I doubted I should ever see again. For Cassie, my one and only friend. And for life as I had always known it.

· · ·

The day finally arrived on which I would leave Cambridge. Mr. Miller arrived at about nine with a coach and four—a luxury in these times, though I knew the ride would be an ordeal. He and Juno lifted my trunk aboard, and the time finally came for me to bid my family good-bye. Cassie and I stood in my parents' chamber, for Papa had not been able to descend the stairs in many months.

"Oh, Cassie, I shall miss you horribly," I said, embracing her for a long time. "Should all go well, I promise I'll visit."

For once, Cassie had no smart reply. She merely wiped her tears and nodded.

I moved next to Papa's bed. He was unable to speak, but his eyes were bright with tears. I kissed and kissed him: his dear hands, his forehead, his cheek. "I love you so much, Papa. I shall write every day."

"Remember what I've told you about Barbados," he whispered. "I am comforted by the thought that I may be of some small service to you after I'm gone."

I buried my face in his chest, kissed him a final time, and departed.

Downstairs, Mama stood in the foyer, a lone, proud guard of all that once had been. Her manner frightened me.

"Cassie!" I called desperately. Cassie came and, fortified by the grasp of her hand, I moved toward Mama slightly, proffering my cheek.

Mama stepped back as I did so.

"You may as well know, Eliza, that I do not expect to see you again. I have tried to reconcile myself to your grievous mistake, but I find I cannot."

I sucked in my breath. Cassie grasped my hand tightly. I said, "Why, even God forgave Eve, Mama. Would you place yourself higher than Him?"

To this, my mother had nothing to say. Suddenly, as Mama turned away, I saw Jeb's portrait lying upon the candlestand in the parlor, next to the sofa. I snatched it up and placed it in my pocket. Cassie saw the theft, but Mama did not.

As I opened the front door, I called behind me, "I pity you, Mama. For you shall very soon find yourself entirely alone in the world, with neither family nor friends to love you. Oh, Mr. Miller!" I cried, turning my back on my mother and releasing my hold on Cassie. "Let us go!"

I cannot describe the black feelings that descended upon me then. Mr. Miller, having been privy to this ugly parting scene, said not a word as he draped the cape about me and nodded to his coachman. I saw the last of Cambridge—its fine houses and strolling couples and brilliant fall leaves—through a thick, wavering pane of tears.

Part IV

36

IT WAS BUT TWELVE MILES TO BRAINTREE, but my discomfort on the journey was extreme. The road was bumpy, and I was obliged to ask Thomas to help me to the shrubs by the side of the road, taverns being few and far between. By the time we arrived at Lizzie's, it was late afternoon, and I was nearly dead with fatigue. Even the babe within me was now motionless, having kicked me furiously most of the way.

Lizzie put me to bed at once in her parlor, where a great old bedstead stood. The bed had been made up with fresh linens and was quite inviting. Mr. Miller brought my trunk inside. A young woman, posture erect and hands clasped, stood by the bed, ready to be of service. This, I soon realized, was Martha Miller. She had grown up since I first brought her to Braintree three years earlier. I hardly knew her.

I lay languidly across the bed in my shift. Lizzie left me then, and I slept. I woke after it was already dark, and I heard Lizzie and Martha talking quietly in the kitchen. Mr. Miller had gone, and I regretted that I had not thought to thank him before I lay down. But I had been so low, so exhausted. I sat up, pushed myself off the bed, and lumbered toward the kitchen. Seeing me, Lizzie smiled and said, "Ah, Eliza. Come join us."

I sat myself upon a rickety chair, half expecting it to collapse beneath me. I then took a biscuit and a dish of chamomile tea, both of which were ready and waiting for me on the kitchen table. I looked about at the many chores that awaited the women in their busy harvest season and felt myself to be yet another chore. As if hearing my thoughts, Lizzie said, "I'm glad you are come, finally, Eliza. It's not a moment too soon."

"I'm most grateful," I said. I sipped my tea and looked out the kitchen window. Beyond the cottage was a beautiful gray-blue crescent of sea beyond the dunes. Ships glided past on their way to Boston. Fishing boats, transport vessels, and merchant schooners all drifted north. Gulls cried and terns swooped up, then down into the dune grass.

Just up the hill from us sat Josiah Quincy's house. It was newly built, and I was told that no expense had been spared on the interior. I thought it unlikely that I would make the Quincys' acquaintance any time soon.

• • •

I took to bed early that first night, and the next morning awoke with dull cramps. It was a Sunday, and as Lizzie and Martha readied to leave for meeting, I wrote a letter to John, not knowing when—or if—he would receive it. The post from Braintree was by no means as regular as it was from Cambridge. When Lizzie found that I wrote a letter meant for Portsmouth, she said, "I'll ask Abigail if she knows of anyone heading in that direction." By Abigail, I knew she meant Mrs. John Adams.

"Thank you," I said. While Lizzie and Martha were gone, I poked about to learn something of the lives that continued here after my Jeb had gone. I did not mount the stairs—that would have been an intrusion, and in any case too arduous for me in my current condition. But I looked in Lizzie's dairy and saw my sister-in-law's many phials of herbs and medications, kept so orderly, with an exact record of their contents used and the dates in chalk upon the door. I espied a fruit tart off to the edge of the coals, covered with glistening apricots . . . How had she managed that? I would have liked to eat the entire thing.

To remove myself from temptation, I stepped abroad and felt the strong sea breeze at once. I heard the raucous seagulls above me. The apples had been harvested, but there were still a fair number of bright-red ones hanging among the branches. These I considered fair game. I plucked one and bit into it, expecting it to be inedibly tart—but no. It was crispy and delicious! I was munching happily away when Lizzie and Martha returned.

Lizzie smiled warmly at me as she approached. "I was able to give your letter to Abigail, Eliza. As luck would have it, someone she knows is heading north." Lizzie then looked at me more carefully and held my face in one hand. "I like not your color. Martha!" she called. Martha had gone directly into the kitchen to prepare us a simple dinner. "I shall stay behind for the second service—you may go without me."

"Nay," said Martha. "I'll remain behind as well and harvest the flax—you may need me."

Lizzie nodded, her eyes still upon me.

I continued to feel Lizzie's gentle hand on my face even after she'd removed it. After our dinner, Lizzie and Martha donned their bonnets and went off to the fields. "Rest, Eliza," Lizzie called. "Let us know if you need us—we'll be keeping our ears open."

"Oh, I doubt I'll need you. I feel quite well now." They both looked at me then, their wizened little faces sharing a single expression I could not read. I washed the dishes, though they had told me to leave them. I then rested for perhaps twenty minutes, but, growing bored, I rose and perused Lizzie's shelf of books. *The Tragedies of William Shakespeare*, Sharpe's *Surgery*, Culpepper's *Herbals*—none tempted.

I decided I would step abroad, as it was yet a fine autumn afternoon. I meant merely to look at the flowers and herbs in the kitchen garden. I had just opened the front door to step into the garden when I felt a flood of warm liquid run down my leg. I did not know a great deal about childbirth, and this alarmed me. Had I involuntarily—relieved myself?

"Lizzie!" I called. She and Martha were just returning from one of the fields, bundles of flax in their arms. When Lizzie saw me, and took in my surprised expression, she dropped her bundle and moved toward me.

"Come," she said calmly. "Let's go inside."

"What's happening?"

"The babe's coming."

I was puzzled. "But I feel no pain. Really, Lizzie, if this is the extent of a woman's labor, then we are a miserably weak lot to complain as we do."

"It will come on gradually," she said.

Suffice to say that "gradually" soon turned to "unrelenting," and thence to "unbearable." It was a torture of such ferocity I knew not why women ever had more than one child. I swore aloud that, were I to come through this one alive, I would never have another. I suffered, shouted shipyard curses—everything I'd heard on Badger's Island and worse. Martha and Lizzie did not leave me alone for even a minute. I labored all through the evening, and, just past midnight on October 14, 1778, I was delivered of a fine, healthy boy.

37

THE CHILD LOOKED WHITE AT FIRST, BUT Lizzie later said she knew at once it was a Negro child. At the time, however, I received only her jubilant cry, "It's a boy! A fine, healthy boy!"

I wept with relief, and, propping me up with pillows, Lizzie helped put the babe to my breast, which he accepted eagerly. He and I both fell asleep, but when I awoke, the babe was gone. I panicked.

"Where is he? Where's my child?"

Martha was by my side at once.

"He is well—just there, don't you see?" Indeed, I could see him. He was in Lizzie's arms by the kitchen door.

"Give him here!" I cried.

Lizzie was having none of my Cambridge ways, however, and I would soon learn that in matters of midwifery—well, in all matters, really—she could be as obdurate as Braintree's granite.

"I prefer to wait until you have regained some strength. He will keep—we give him distilled water with a tiny bit of milk in it. It will do at least till tomorrow. And then there's always Betty, a wet nurse in the South Parish—"

"Wet nurse? Oh, do be clear, Lizzie. My head aches. I can hardly comprehend you."

Martha came toward me and gently wiped my brow with a cool cloth. "Lean back now. That's it."

As I became fully awake, I realized that something had changed while I slept. I felt shivery and could not stay warm. My head ached horribly; the light seared my eyes, and I closed them.

"Am I unwell?" I asked, covering my eyes with my forearm.

"Rest," Lizzie said. "All will right itself in time."

But all was not well. Thankfully, there is a special Providence that makes one unaware of the gravity of one's own illness. I remained in bed a week, as Lizzie silently worked to keep a "slight infection" from carrying me off. In truth I felt very unwell. I lost my appetite and could not sit up to nurse my babe, who I named Johnny. Four, five, six times a day, Lizzie handed me strange teas to drink.

After several days in which neither she nor Martha slept, my fever eased. I knew this not by the abatement of my malaise, but by their relieved faces. Only when it was over did they reveal to me that I had developed puerperal fever, an often-fatal disease in new mothers. When they finally handed me my little boy, he seemed heavier to me, like a fat, delicious dumpling. Thank God for that!

During these early days, Lizzie was strict with me. She still "liked not my color" and was hourly on the lookout for fever. After a second week had passed, however, she allowed me to sit quietly in the kitchen while the babe slept. There, I helped her to grind spices or hang herbs to dry.

It should be mentioned that I had as yet not told either Lizzie or Martha about John Watkins. Perhaps I would in time share my story with them. But to Mrs. Adams? Certainly not. This conviction lasted all of a day—or slightly less. For, that same afternoon, as I was nursing Johnny, in strode a tiny person whom I at first mistook for someone's servant. I marveled at Braintree's easy ways, where servant girls could come upon one without so much as knocking first.

The woman wore a frock of homespun quite imperfectly woven, and her hair had not been combed through in some time. Her petticoat was soiled from various outdoor chores—feeding her animals, perhaps. Only when she looked at me did I see the hard intelligence of her brown eyes and knew who she was: Abigail Adams.

"Oh, what a beauty!" Mrs. Adams exclaimed, seeing Johnny at my breast just as Lizzie entered from the kitchen.

"Abigail!" she cried and hugged her gleefully. She then properly introduced us. Abigail paced the parlor until I had finished giving suck, at which point she said, "I should like to hold him, if I may." Johnny had fallen asleep and lay with his arms akimbo. I nodded to her, and she sat on the edge of my bed and took up the sleeping child.

"I've had five children," she remarked, "but none quite so beautiful as this child. What do you call him?"

"Johnny. After his father."

"Oh, hello, Johnny." She smiled down at him, playing with the fingers of one of his open little hands, which had turned palm-up in sleep. His fingers curled unconsciously around her gently prodding forefinger.

With Johnny, Abigail Adams was perfectly gentle and natural. Yet, when setting her eyes upon me, this esteemed woman reminded me of nothing so much as a hawk. Her small eyes saw everything, even from a great distance.

Speaking of eyes, my child's were of a most unusual color, though I expected they would change and darken. They were the same aqua-blue eyes as John's. Abigail could not help but comment upon them.

"Everyone here has blue eyes except for me," she lamented.

"I don't," Martha said. "Don't envy them, Abigail. For, in the sun, their eyesight is as weak as a ferret's."

"Ha—that's true enough." Her small mouth formed a tiny smile.

As Johnny slept, Mrs. Adams and I fell to talking. "You know," she said, "of the past eight years, I've seen my John only four. And there have been many months—sometimes as much as six in a row, where I've not heard a word from him and knew not whether he was alive or dead."

"What torture that must be. I'm learning . . ." I began, then admitted, "I've not heard from *my* John in many weeks, and it's already more than I can bear."

For a year I had kept my grief locked within me, and I could do so no longer. Abigail, sensing weakness, edged closer to me on the bed.

"Tell me exactly what troubles you, dearest." She placed a dainty yet oddly rough hand on mine. "Spare no detail."

I then proceeded to unburden my heart to Mrs. Adams in a way I had not done with Lizzie. In telling my story, I cried, and when I had calmed myself and thought I might sleep, Mrs. Adams kissed me on the side of my head and said she would return the following day. I dozed until Johnny's cry woke me later that afternoon, to find Martha and Lizzie staring down at me.

"Yes?" I murmured. "What is it?"

The two looked at each other, then Lizzie asked, "How is it that Abigail Adams managed to get you to reveal that which you would not reveal to us, even in the throes of your travails?"

I shrugged. "Sometimes it is easier to unburden oneself to a stranger."

Suddenly I recalled that I had a gift for Lizzie. I let go her hand and smiled. "As it so happens, I have something for you. Call it payment, if you like."

"What could that be, I wonder?" she asked.

I pushed my bolster aside and stepped down from the bed. I pulled out my trunk, opened it, and removed Jeb's portrait. Then

I walked into the kitchen, toward the sunlight that streamed into the window facing onto the sea. Lizzie followed with a puzzled expression. Martha remained in the parlor, with Johnny.

As I handed my sister-in-law the gift, I suddenly feared it might discomfit her. Portraits were expensive and not so common in those days. What's more, to see one's dead beloved could feel like seeing a ghost. But it was too late.

"What's this, Eliza?" she asked, staring at the smooth convex glass above the oval portrait. She held it delicately in the palm of her hand, like an egg. I knew not her thoughts or feelings. But after gazing at it in the brilliant light of the sun, Lizzie closed her fingers upon the portrait and lifted it to her heart. She looked toward me, her eyes swimming in tears, and she said, "Thank you. Thank you, Eliza."

"It belongs with you. You knew who he was."

"Yes," she said simply. Then, suddenly, Lizzie called to Martha, "Martha! Oh, Martha, come see my Jeb!"

Martha appeared at the entrance to the kitchen with the sleeping babe in her arms.

"Come. Look at the handsomest man in the world." A handsome man at this time was a rare sight, one to be greatly savored. Carefully, Martha lifted the portrait and held it by the window. The sun illuminated its details: his fine face, his resolute blue eyes, his thick blond hair.

"He *is* handsome. He has a strong, intelligent face. Is this your brother?" Martha turned to me.

"Yes. He was my brother, Jeb."

Martha handed the portrait back to Lizzie. "Well, what he saw in *her*"—she thrust her thumb in Lizzie's direction—"I know not."

"Oh, you!" Lizzie said, charging at Martha. She knew Martha to be ticklish and went directly for her rib cage.

"Get away from me!" Martha cried, hunching over to protect her tender torso and Johnny, who started but did not wake. And they were soon happily laughing, cutting the heavy dolor of the moment with the bright citrus of youthful cheer.

•   •   •

Lizzie's cottage was small, and Johnny and I were now its great spectacle. Indeed, we might have been Mary and baby Jesus in the holy crèche, so often did my new friends gaze upon us passing from kitchen to garden, or chamber to kitchen. We were the first thing they saw before dawn and the last thing they saw before mounting the stairs at night.

Beyond the cottage was a beautiful gray-blue crescent of sea. I had but to gaze out the kitchen window to see it there, across the dunes.

Within, the eye could feast as well: bushel upon bushel of apples. This bounty was due, apparently, to a certain Mr. Cleverly and his ingenious invention, a watering machine, which he had fashioned for Lizzie the previous summer while courting her. He then seemed to disappear, but my friends offered no further details, and the story trailed off.

"But did you love him, Lizzie?" I asked her one morning that first week of my recuperation. I was sitting up and nursing Johnny. It had now been three years since our Jeb had died, and the idea that Lizzie might come to love another did not seem unnatural.

"Mr. Cleverly was very attentive, very charming."

"She didn't love him," Martha said, coming into the parlor. Lizzie set her bushel down and turned to Martha.

"How do you know?" I asked.

"I just do."

"Would you have agreed to marry him?" I inquired of Lizzie, switching Johnny to the other breast.

"I thought—"

"No," Martha interrupted her. "I would not have allowed it."

"Allowed, indeed!" Lizzie finally got a word in edgewise. "You see, Eliza. Martha truly believes she has the power to determine whom I marry."

"I certainly do," Martha replied without smiling. "I liked him not. Mr. Cleverly, that is."

Lizzie shrugged her shoulders. "My servant liked not my suitor. There's an end to it."

Martha shot her a baleful look, and I laughed. The two women reminded me of an old married couple: quarrelsome, yet deeply intimate.

•   •   •

Two days later, on October 27, I received word from Mama that my father had died. Her note was terse and factual:

> Your father is gone. I have no expectation of your return-
> ing for the funeral, which is set for this Friday. I have sent
> word to Uncle Robert.

The note was not signed. I took the inward blow of my dear Papa's death in silence; all my tears had already been shed. However, I resolved to go to the funeral, though I doubted that I should be welcome at the house. Nonetheless, I wrote at once that I would come, and that, in case Mama was curious, I had two weeks earlier given birth to a healthy boy.

Lizzie wished I would not go. She feared that, under such infelicitous conditions, and without my babe, my milk would cease to flow. She insisted on having me practice a particular kind of massage to make my milk come in at regular intervals throughout the day.

"I shall write to Bessie and tell her to expect you," she said. Bessie was Judge Lee's old servant, who lived with Giles, a former family slave, in Lizzie's ancestral home.

"I don't know what Mama shall do when she sees me. I should *like* to stay at my home, if only to see Cassie."

"Well, then, I'll tell Bessie that *possibly* you'll come."

I thanked her warmly and then returned to the issue of my milk. "But it *is* most inconvenient to have milk dripping everywhere, at all hours," I sighed.

"It's inconvenient to have a child, especially when one is unwed," Lizzie reminded me pointedly. "But I don't hear you complaining about *that*."

"No," I admitted. "I have no regrets on that score." I was entirely smitten with my little boy, who ate and slept so well, and complained so little. Though it had been but two weeks since Johnny had come into the world, I could no longer imagine life without him.

I had not as yet divulged the name of Johnny's father to Lizzie or Martha, nor had they asked. The babe's complexion had darkened slightly since his birth. My friends must have been dying of curiosity, but Lizzie merely said, "I think it best that, in your absence, we have a ready story for our inquisitive neighbors."

"Something at least approximating the truth," Martha added cagily.

I looked at them and sighed. "Well, you shall have your approximation." I then proceeded to tell them everything: about my uncle Robert, and Colonel Langdon, and the shipyard on Badger's Island. And I told them, at last, about Watkins, my handsome, prideful love, son of the governor and his slave. When I was finished, Lizzie looked at me with sincere puzzlement.

"Eliza," she said, "I could not be more surprised."

38

THREE WEEKS EARLIER, I HAD DREADED COMING to Braintree. Now, I dreaded leaving it. The only thought that gave me any comfort was that I would see my beloved Cassie.

Lizzie told me that while I was gone, she and Abigail were to have dinner with the Admiral d'Estaing at Colonel Quincy's house.

"Who's that?" I asked.

"He's a very great man. A French admiral, come to aid our army," Martha explained.

"Who shall care for Johnny, then?"

"Oh, I shall be happy to. I wasn't invited," Martha replied.

Thursday afternoon, I paced the cottage in a state of dread. I had nothing to wear to my father's funeral. Martha had an old black gown, the one she had been wearing when I first brought her to the farm, but it was far too small for me. Lizzie had none. "But only think, Eliza," Lizzie said. "It's November. The chapel shall be cold, and you shall have no reason to remove your cape."

"But afterward," I fretted, "Cassie will surely have made a tea or something back at the house."

Lizzie considered. "Wait—does Colonel Quincy know of your father's death? They were blood relations, were they not?"

"I don't see how he would know. Mama would never write to him. They haven't spoken in many years."

"Well, don't you think it might be proper that he know?"

"Lizzie." I shook my head. "I'm in no state to make the acquaintance of the colonel."

"Allow me to take care of this. All will be well. Trust me." She placed a steadying hand on my forearm and smiled warmly.

Lizzie excused herself, and from the parlor window I soon saw her make her way in the wind and growing darkness, guided only by a sure knowledge of the path, to the Quincys' house. I sighed and caressed my babe, who slept soundly, his thick eyelashes dewy with sleep.

About an hour later, I was startled to see Lizzie round the front of the house with a couple in tow. The man, portly and of medium height, in his mid fifties, wore a raccoon hat and hunting jacket. The woman wore a woolen cape with the hood up and a scarf across her face. She held something in her arms. In a moment, they all entered the cottage, stomping the cold off of them, removing their outer garments and hats. I stood up from the bed, readying myself for mortification, when the elderly couple ran to me, accosted me with hugs, and swarmed my child as if they were his long-lost grandparents. On the bed, without a word, Mrs. Quincy lay a fine black gown.

·　·　·

"What on earth did you say to them?" I asked Lizzie the following morning, as I readied myself to depart. The black dress fit me well, though I was obliged to don Lizzie's stays and have her tie them fairly tight.

"Nothing," she replied. We were in the parlor, awaiting the colonel's carriage.

"Nothing? That cannot be."

"Well, almost nothing. Only that Jeb's sister was lately arrived at our cottage from Portsmouth, that your father had died, and that you wished to go to his funeral. Colonel Quincy said he was very sorry to hear it, as, despite the rift, he had been fond of your father as a child. Indeed, he should have liked to attend the funeral, but Ann objected that his presence would by no means be a comfort to your mother."

"Well, I suppose that is true enough. But, oh, it was very kind of them to visit with us, was it not?"

"That is their way," Lizzie replied. "The colonel can be loud and blustery, but they both are most kind. They do not stand on ceremony."

"I've never seen anything like it."

"No, I don't expect you would have," Lizzie mused. "Braintree is a long way from Cambridge, or even Portsmouth. We are a true country village with all its bumps and warts."

"But what did you tell them about Johnny?"

"I told them that, three weeks ago, I delivered you of a fine, healthy boy, and that circumstances required the father to remain in Portsmouth."

"Circumstances—I suppose that covers a whole host of evils."

"They asked not a single question, Eliza. Indeed, they were so excited to have a babe in their midst, they hardly cared who the mother or father were. They insisted on coming at once."

I shook my head in grateful disbelief. The reactions, the sentiments of these Braintree people—how different from all I'd known before! They were as inhabitants of a distant planet, one I wished never to leave. With a kiss for Lizzie and Martha, one final smothering hug for my child, I was off in the colonel's carriage.

•   •   •

The funeral was a grim affair. From it, I garnered no special consolation, particularly since Mama would not look at me. The service was out of doors, at the cemetery down the road to Watertown.

It hardly mattered. Papa's friends had long since dispersed, and it was only myself, Cassie, and my mother. Uncle Robert had sent his condolences but said that he was not well enough to travel. I wondered what he meant by that but didn't inquire of Mama.

Mama would have liked to serve a glass of wine, but the cellar was empty, and there was no real tea. We had herb tea and cakes made of corn flour and a bit of cheese and some dried figs. Cassie remained in the parlor with us. She kept glancing at me, and at my slimmer girth, as if she would like to ask a million questions. Mama largely ignored looking at me altogether. She ate delicately, her pinkie sticking out, as if she were eating quail eggs. Suddenly she stopped eating, grew still, and stood up.

"Oh, but I entirely forgot." She moved into the foyer and returned holding a letter. "This came for you yesterday."

"A letter? From whom?"

I thought she would say "from that boy Isaac." Instead, she said, "From Colonel *Langdon*, of all people. Know you him, Eliza?"

"A very little," I admitted. "From fishing out on Badger's Island."

"Well, what does he *say*?" she inquired impatiently.

"Mama, allow me to read it first." I moved off into the foyer, but she trailed after me. "You may go to your chamber, if you wish." Apparently Mama had already bade the coachman to bring my small trunk upstairs, which greatly surprised me.

"Cassie!" I called as I mounted the stairs. "Bring me another dish of tea."

"Yes, Miss Eliza." She curtsied. I had not yet greeted Cassie, saving that pleasure for a moment when we would be alone. Upstairs, I shut myself within the grim stillness of my chamber. Then I tore the seal with my finger, my heart pounding thickly in my chest. The moment I looked down, I knew that this letter was not from Colonel Langdon, but from John.

Dearest love—

We received your letter announcing the new arrival to your parish with Joy in our Hearts and a Prayer that we will be able to hold him in our Arms by and by. Our Situation is uncertain. R.C. is being hounded by the Committee of Correspondence. It is rumored that Arrests are to be made. Your uncle readies himself to flee. I know not where we may be headed, but rest assured I shall write when I am able. I send this through a trusted Friend. Your, J.

"Rest assured?" I cried aloud. This letter, far from assuring, filled me with foreboding.

I had feared many things in our months of separation. Would Uncle sell Watkins? And what about Isaac? I needed to write immediately, yet I could not write from my present location. Nothing I wrote would be safe from my mother's prying eyes. Nor did I wish to alarm Cassie—she would be hurt and worried that I had not remained for tea, or to greet her with open arms. But I resolved to return to Braintree immediately. Oh, if only I could run the other way!

Descending the stairs on tiptoe, I grabbed my cape from the back of the chair where it rested and moved out the front door. I called for Juno to fetch my trunk from my chamber and to bring round the colonel's coachman and carriage. Cassie, sensing a commotion, came quickly from the kitchen, her hands wrapped around our teapot.

"Someteeng happen, Miss Eliza?"

"I'm urgently needed in Braintree," I said. "I daren't stop to tell you now. All shall be well," I added, touching her arm and attempting a smile. "By and by, I shall inform you," I whispered.

From the carriage, I looked up at the house and, in the darkening gloom, saw my mother's shadowy form at her chamber window. The shadow disappeared, but by the time it reached the front door, I was already gone.

• • •

"I thought you were to stop the night," Martha said, perplexed to see me walk through the door. It was near midnight, and she was just heading off to bed. Lizzie had not returned from the Quincys' dinner party.

"Something has happened, but I have no energy to discuss it just now. It will keep till the morning." I picked up my sleeping child from our bed and hugged him tight.

"Very well," said Martha resignedly. She kissed me good-night and petted Johnny before heading up to bed.

I stripped out of Mrs. Quincy's damp gown and stays at once, then nursed my child. We both slept, but I woke throughout the night. Around four thirty, I rose for the day. Lizzie had returned, and both she and Martha were already awake. They had fed the animals and clasped their steaming dishes of tea at the kitchen table, deep in discussion. When they saw me, they ceased speaking.

"What do you discuss, so earnestly and at such an hour?"

"Oh, nothing much," Lizzie said silkily.

"How was dinner at the Quincys'?" I asked. I knew they hid something from me but would not press them.

"Fine. Very fine," Lizzie replied. "The admiral and his officers are impressive, and so kind. The repast was such as I have not had in years."

Martha asked, "Why did you return from Cambridge last night?"

I removed John's letter and proffered it to my friends. "I know not what to do," I said. "I know not what I *can* do."

Both Martha and Lizzie read John's letter. Then Martha rose from the table and said, "I shall return by and by." She soon returned with a piece of foolscap, a quill, and a bottle of ink, which she set upon the table. "You must write to Colonel Langdon at once."

"But what do I say?" I looked up at Martha.

"Tell him the truth."

And so I wrote:

26 October, 1778.

Dear Sir. Thank you for your letter of October 24th. W.'s report of the situation in Portsmouth alarms us greatly. It seems something must be done, before the time for action has passed. Where does R. C. intend to go? And what of W. and the child? I must know these things.

Then, for John's eyes, I wrote:

All is well here, though perhaps you've heard the sad news that Papa died. The plant you gave me grows quite lustily and gives me great joy. May God protect you.

I folded and sealed the paper, and Martha ran off to give my letter to Abigail, who would find a messenger to take it to Portsmouth.

Haste and good intentions we had aplenty. But I would not learn of John's fate for another eight months.

39

JOHNNY WOKE AT SIX THIRTY, AND I gave him to suck. Martha returned from Abigail's house soon thereafter, looking triumphant.

"She knows of someone leaving this afternoon. Isn't that auspicious?"

"That's marvelous." I smiled, having resolved not to make our lives harder by sulking. I then noticed that Lizzie was missing.

"Where's Lizzie?" I asked.

Before Martha could reply, Lizzie descended the stairs. She was dressed, most oddly, in a man's clothing: breeches, blouse, and an old cap with her hair tucked beneath it.

"What do you do, dressed like that, Lizzie?" I asked.

Martha came up behind me. She rested a hand companionably on my shoulder. "She goes to place her neck in the enemy's rope, Eliza." Martha approached Lizzie and stuck something on her face. She then backed away to admire her handiwork. It was a mustache! The ruse was now complete: Tall Lizzie, in Jeb's breeches, waistcoat, and blouse, looked convincingly like a young man. Martha had tied Lizzie's hair in a single plait and secured it with a bit of linen.

"But what on earth is going on? What is it you plan to do, dressed in such a costume?"

"It's a long story, Eliza," Lizzie sighed, her breath moving the hairs on the false mustache. "Suffice to say it involves something I learned from the admiral at dinner last night."

"She thinks she goes to save the Cause," Martha snorted.

"No, indeed," Lizzie objected. They were about to get into one of their arguments when I interrupted them.

"Please tell me what's happening. I should like to know." But here, I couldn't help but begin to laugh, for the sight of Lizzie was so absurd.

"Allow me to begin at the beginning." Lizzie glanced at Martha. "Come." She led the way into the kitchen.

"But do remove the mustache," I begged. "For you cannot expect me to listen to you dressed like that."

Lizzie began to pull the mustache off her face when Martha intervened. "Allow me," she said, reaching for the mustache. "I have no wish for you to damage it."

"Well," Lizzie began, once that had been accomplished. "Last night—it is as I said. It was an extraordinary evening. But, as Abigail and I took our leave, I happened to hear the admiral say something to Colonel Quincy. He said it in French, but I understood it, for I learned French as a child."

"What did he say that makes you go to this mad extreme?"

Martha looked pointedly at Lizzie and said, "I fear that we must go back several months."

"I think so as well," Lizzie added.

Martha began. "This past August, at the height of the small-pox, there were two murders in the North Parish."

"Murders?" I stood up and glanced toward the parlor, where my child slept.

"Yes. Two patriots, lodging in the house of Abigail's sister Mary Cranch and her husband, Richard. They were poisoned. I myself discovered the deeds when I was called to prepare the bodies for burial. We had a terrible epidemic of the pox, and the two men died several weeks apart—of this disease, we thought. At first, the Cranches, and even Martha here, believed it to be the pox. Yet I suspected something amiss with Dr. Flynt, and at the death of Mr. Thayer, I knew it for certain. They had been murdered. Poisoned."

"I can't believe this. You said not a word about it."

I was suddenly quite fearful, and my heart pounded—not for myself but for my child.

"I'm sorry, Eliza," said Lizzie, and indeed she looked remorseful. "Thomas Miller had been instructed to say nothing. Your parents would not have chosen to place you in harm's way had they known."

"I wouldn't be so certain." I shrugged, thinking of Mama. "But is there yet danger here? I fear not for myself, but for Johnny—"

Lizzie looked at Martha and then said, "Not with regard to the pox, at any rate. That is gone, thankfully."

"And the—villains?"

"We *believe* they're gone." Lizzie took my hand. Hers was warm. "This is precisely what I wished to explain. The admiral told the colonel where he believed the culprits could be found. Speaking of which," Lizzie added, "it's time I left." Lizzie rose from her chair, straightened her breeches, returned the mustache to her upper lip, and went to mount Star.

"But wait!" I called after her, realizing that she had not told all. "Where do you go? And why must it be you?"

"She thinks she shall discover what they plan to do next. Lizzie takes her gifts of detection far too seriously. But I for one cannot stop her."

Lizzie paused at the door. She gazed at both of us with a tender expression. Despite my confusion, I now considered her the bravest woman I had ever known.

"What if you don't return? Where shall we begin to search for you?"

"We shall place a notice in the paper, Eliza," Martha replied. "Escaped madwoman sought by family. Approach with caution."

"Ha, ha," laughed Lizzie without smiling, for fear of unseating the mustache. She opened the door, letting in the frigid air.

Martha was not very satisfied. "You should take a cape. It's cold."

"I have none that will serve," she said as she climbed upon Star.

"A blanket then," Martha insisted.

"Nay. That would look strange, a blanket upon a man's lap. Never mind. The riding shall warm me."

She leaned down to kiss us good-bye, nearly falling out of her saddle. Her mustache tickled our faces, but we did not laugh at it.

40

TWO PATRIOTS MURDERED. TWO POISONINGS—AND SMALLPOX
as well! All was not well in the North Parish. Still, I was glad to be
out of ignorance, to know the truth. My idyll had perhaps crumbled, but not so my friendships, or my growing love for this town.

The following morning, we received word that Lizzie had
arrived safely in Cambridge. Several days later, however, we
received a more substantial, and more enigmatical, letter:

> My servants Bessie and Giles are well. At the tavern, I met
> Mr. C! Imagine that, Martha. He praised my horse but
> suggested that "to be too busy was perhaps some danger."

Hearing the news that Lizzie had chanced upon Mr. Cleverly,
Martha scowled.

"That is the man who proposed to Lizzie?"

"*Nearly* proposed," said Martha, slapping the letter against
her hip.

"I gather you don't like this Mr. Cleverly?"

"A pompous ass would be putting it mildly."

"She is well out of it, then."

"Indeed, she is." Martha turned as if she would walk into the kitchen, but I persisted:

"What happened to him, exactly? Why did he leave town, and so suddenly?"

Martha proceeded to tell me that Mr. Cleverly had been a friend and associate of the murdered men, Dr. Flynt and Mr. Thayer. He had, like them, been staying at the Cranches' boarding house, visiting Lizzie nearly every day while he worked on his watering machine. But he fled Braintree like a coward the day Mr. Thayer, the second victim, died.

"That very morning, Mr. Cleverly had been about to propose marriage to Lizzie. They stood there in the orchards when Richard Cranch came to tell us of Mr. Thayer's death."

"I can hardly believe it," I said. Nor did I understand precisely what those murders were about. Of what importance had been those two patriots, for some dastardly villain to dispatch them so?

"Believe it," said Martha. "The truth is, Eliza, that you've left one fry pan only to jump into another."

•   •   •

Lizzie was gone for near two weeks. During that time, we lost flesh. It grew quite cold, and we had so little wood left that, to conserve our supply, Johnny and I moved into Lizzie's chamber with Martha. For two weeks we froze and went hungry during the day; at night, we lay in a heap, the bed piled high with bolsters. I slept poorly, fearing that one of us would roll over and smother my babe.

Every day, I expected a letter and would start at the least sound abroad. Or I would sit with my tea in the unheated parlor, so that I could look out the window, the better to see the approach of a messenger. Nothing came, neither from John nor from Colonel Langdon. I saw only the white puffs of my own breath.

On the night of November 14, at midnight or perhaps a little earlier, I started up in bed, having heard something in my sleep. It was a noise like breaking glass. The noise was so sudden, and so unabashedly loud, that I believed it to be one of those details of a nightmare that can seem so real to the dreamer. However, I was just sitting up, eyes open to the darkness, moon hidden by the clouds, when I heard another noise—footsteps.

"Martha!" I whispered.

Martha's eyes were already open. We had left our flint in the kitchen and thus had nothing with which to light a candle.

"Help me, quickly," she whispered, her breath like clouds of smoke. We leapt from the bed at the same moment. Trembling, I whispered to her, "They'll hear us."

"Perhaps. But they mustn't reach us. Help me." Here, she took one end of Lizzie's heavy chest of drawers, and I took the other. We slid it with a great, groaning, scraping sound, against the door. The footsteps below halted, and we stopped; we dared not even breathe. Then the movement resumed.

"There are two of them," Martha said. I looked about the dark chamber for a weapon, lamenting the fact that I had not thought to bring Lizzie's musket up to our chamber. I then knelt down beside the bed and prayed to God to spare my son, if not myself.

"Will you not pray with me?" I asked Martha.

"It's pointless."

I was shocked at this blasphemous reply but had no time to dwell upon it because, suddenly, amidst all the great crashing and smashing below, we heard feet upon the stairs. One pair. They endeavored to be stealthy, but the cottage was old and the stairs creaked. We heard every footfall and held each other in terror. The chest, we knew, would be no great protection for long. Martha's eyes darted toward the window. I did not see how we might escape that way without breaking a limb or being caught at once. And, even were we to try it, what of Johnny?

We were at their mercy, and God's.

I put my hands together and bowed my head. "Please, Lord. I know I have sinned. But do not let them harm my innocent child." Suddenly the footsteps ceased their creaky climb. I rose to my feet, and there was a moment of silence in which Martha and I were locked together as one person. The steps then descended and were lost amid the other pair. Both soon removed to the kitchen. That was the first moment wherein I felt that, whatever these marauders' sinister purpose, it was not to harm but to frighten us. We released our hold upon each other and breathed. Next we heard them, they descended to the cellar. There was the sound of more crockery being smashed. Ten minutes later, they were gone.

We slept not that night, nor dared to move nor push the chest away from the door till break of day, when we rose.

The parlor window had been smashed through. The barrels of cider in the cellar had been cleaved with an ax. Several chickens in the yard had been beheaded, their glassy eyes glancing wistfully toward their distant bodies. In the kitchen, Lizzie's medical sack had been rifled and many costly supplies taken. Teas and powders had been removed from their boxes and poured all in a heap. The entire scene possessed a personal, vengeful quality. What a waste lay before us!

A thought then occurred to me. "This is someone of your acquaintance," I said to Martha.

"Yes," she said. "I know."

41

WHILE I STOOD THERE IN SHOCK, MARTHA ran to Colonel Quincy's, who had his coachman ride to Cambridge to deliver the news to Lizzie. Martha then returned to help me with the task of cleaning up the mess. We were at it nearly all that day, working in silence punctuated only by Johnny's hunger.

It was near four o'clock, and we had been picking up the broken jars and bottles, spilled provisions, and smashed glass for many hours when Lizzie finally returned.

"Oh, God," she said, coming upon us in the parlor. We were on our hands and knees picking out shards of glass from between the plank flooring. "Thank God, you're unharmed." We stood, wearily, and she embraced us both. Johnny woke just then; and we heard his cry from above us. Lizzie went to fetch him and soon returned with my son, who was ready to be fed. I sat on the parlor bed and nursed him.

Finally, when he had settled, I turned to Lizzie. "But who should want to harm you? I cannot conceive of it."

Neither Martha nor Lizzie replied, but I saw a glance pass between them.

"So, you shan't tell me?"

Martha looked away. Lizzie said, "Not yet, Eliza."

I had been strong all day, picking up the shattered bottles and spilled grain, smoothing out the violence that had been done to us. But at Lizzie's words, I felt the truth of my situation. I was not one of them, not one of the inner circle. I was a visitor, nothing more.

"Oh, Eliza," Lizzie saw my hurt at once. "It is for your own good. We wish only to protect you."

"I do not *want* to be protected. I want—I should *like* to face this danger, whatever it is, *with* you."

Lizzie looked at Martha, who shook her head.

"We can't do that, Eliza. Not yet."

"Patience," said Martha.

I said nothing, resigning myself to this virtue of silence if none other.

·　·　·

Soon after these events, the drear misery of winter descended upon us. There was still no word from John, though I had by this time written him many letters. Colonel Langdon, I learned, was not in Portsmouth at all but had gone south to be with His Excellency. I now doubted whether he had even received my letter. But I could feel in my soul that Uncle Robert had left Portsmouth at last, and the whereabouts of John and Isaac were unknown to all but him.

I spoke little of my troubles with my friends, though we each felt the others' grief. Lizzie, I suspected, cared for Thomas Miller, about whom rumors grew daily. And it had been four years since she had heard from her brother, Harry, though Lizzie told us she had heard encouraging rumors about Harry's whereabouts while in Cambridge. As for Martha, she seemed burdened by some leaden weight in her soul.

I took my own model of strength from Abigail, who had not heard from John Adams in many months. What's more, she had to suffer the near-daily reports of his death in the London papers. But

I was not insensible to the fact that there was a difference between Abigail and myself: namely, that she was married to John. They were bound forever by a spiritual connection before God. I, on the other hand, wasn't certain that John still loved me—or even that he lived.

Toward the end of December, it snowed near a foot, rained, then froze solid. The ground was so slick that one could not step out of doors without risk of breaking one's neck. Darkness, cold, hunger, and fear were our loyal companions.

My friends were often obliged to go abroad at night, leaving me to stare into the glowing embers of the kitchen hearth. Low on wood as we were, I dared not light a fire in the chamber but slept on a straw pallet by the kitchen hearth, Johnny snuggled next to me. Whole nights I went without a single candle, too, and at these times tears of self-pity ran freely down my cheeks—my one luxury. And why not? By them I importuned no one but myself.

A bright spot in these dark times was Christmas Eve, when Abigail and her two youngest children, Tommy and Charlie, came for dinner. Nabby had gone to Plymouth to visit her aunt; John Quincy was in Paris with his father. At around four in the afternoon it began to snow, but we were snug within. Abigail had brought wine and a pie. Lizzie stuffed and roasted two chickens.

Tongues loosed by wine, we all spoke freely that night—of husbands, dreams, grief, and the small pleasures of the everyday. The boys focused on the excellent repast and heeded not our conversation.

"Save room," Abigail warned them. "For I have brought a fine plum pie, and I've had to sell your father's books for it."

The boys looked up at her, aghast, as if she might be in earnest. Their worried faces made us all laugh.

• • •

The bright star of Christmas soon faded. January found us hungry, depressed, and continually fearful. Then smallpox invaded yet again, and Lizzie was called upon to care for the sick and dying. Martha accompanied her, and I was left alone once more.

Only Johnny, insensible of the degraded world in which he lived, persisted in flourishing. Oh, he was my little beacon of hope! I so wished John could see him: Having learned to smile, he now smiled at everything he saw. He smiled at the chickens beyond the window; at night, he smiled at the shadows the candle made upon the wall. He always had a smile for me, and there is naught to do when a child smiles than to smile back, though it be through tears.

About a week after the New Year, Lizzie went abroad in the afternoon without a word as to where she was headed. She returned a few hours later lower in spirit than I'd ever seen her. She threw off her cloak and entreated me, "Allow me to hold Johnny." I relinquished him at once.

Lizzie shook her face and puffed her cheeks, which sent him into melodious gurgles of laughter. Lizzie, however, had tears in her eyes.

"What is it?" I asked. "Where did you go?"

"To Abigail's," she said, still making faces for Johnny.

"And did you learn something there?"

"I did," she said, still mugging for my child.

I expected her to continue, but she said nothing more.

"Lizzie, please tell me what has happened."

She took a breath, then let it out. "Abigail has had a letter from General Sullivan about Mr. Miller. Apparently there is evidence of his Tory loyalties from the highest levels. What's more, they suspect he was involved in the murders of Mr. Thayer and Dr. Flint."

"No, Lizzie. Do not believe it."

"I don't *wish* to believe it," she said.

Martha had gone to tend a woman in travail, and so I felt free to inquire of Lizzie's true feelings for Mr. Miller.

"What is Mr. Miller to you? Are you in love with him? I won't mind if you are. Jeb would not have wished you to be alone forever."

"Of course I'm in love with him," she laughed through her tears. "Am, and have been, for many months."

"Then do not believe the rumors."

"Is it a rumor, when Mrs. John Adams says that it is so?"

"In these troubled times there are so many uncertainties, uncertain loyalties. Who is good, who evil? We have but our instincts to go by. Mine tell me that Mr. Miller is a very good sort of man."

"Perhaps you are right," she said thoughtfully. "Yes, perhaps. For my instincts tell me that he is no traitor to the Cause."

At long last, winter ebbed. The sky lightened. The mountains of crusty snow melted, and the ground warmed. The parish, terrorized first by the murders of Dr. Flynt and Mr. Thayer and then by the break-in at our house, began to breathe freely once more. Sunday meeting was held again. People began to stroll the main road, stopping to talk to neighbors. Babes continued to be born.

March came, and we set to work clearing the fields of winter's debris. We pruned the fruit trees and broke the soil. We carried manure and loam in great, heavy baskets and worked these into the soil. Then, in April, we tilled more finely, planting the seeds we had gathered the previous autumn.

We planted row upon row of vegetables: long squash, cranberry beans, brown beans, cabbage, carrots, turnips, beets, onions, and yellow bush beans. It took us a week to plant the potatoes and corn.

In Portsmouth, I had learned to fish and shoot. But never had I exerted myself for this long, or this hard. Abandoning all pretense of ladylike behavior, I threw myself into the work at hand, discovering not only the very great satisfaction that came with self-sufficiency but an age-old secret: that physical pain dulled the pain of the soul.

In May we managed to get the cucumbers and peas into the ground. In the kitchen garden, we planted Lizzie's medicinal herbs: saffron, sage, chamomile, and feverfew.

Johnny kept pace with the growth all around us. In May, he began to crawl, and Abigail's boys built a crib for him so that he would not crawl off while we worked. Soon, he was sitting up, sucking upon a biscuit to ease his sore gums.

That month, there came a bird infestation that threatened our tender seedlings. The town selectmen offered the citizens of Braintree thirty shillings apiece for an old crow and six shillings for a blackbird. One fair Sunday at meeting, after hearing this news, I returned home with a certain resolve in my step. Lizzie and Martha trailed behind me, calling, "Wait up! Why do you run ahead?"

I arrived home, set Johnny in his crib, and removed Jeb's musket from the parlor wall.

Lizzie and Martha were right behind me in the doorway. I turned to them with the musket in my arms, and for a moment they were struck speechless. Then Martha asked, "You know how to use that?"

"Yes. An old Portsmouth friend taught me. Have you bullets and powder about?"

Lizzie hesitated. "Whom or what do you plan to shoot, may I ask?"

"The crows, of course."

She moved to her cupboard, pulled open a drawer, retrieved a powder horn and bullets, and returned to place them in my hand.

"Thank you," I said. I then strode into the garden, my friends trailing uneasily behind.

"Are you certain you know how? I shouldn't like you to shoot yourself, or one of us," said Lizzie.

I did not reply, but focused my attention on properly loading the musket pan and barrel.

"Would you look at that?" Martha observed, impressed. "What has happened to our prim Eliza?"

"Prim, indeed!" I snorted, pointing the musket toward the fence up the hill, where a number of crows perched.

"Should we be afraid?" Martha asked.

I laughed easily, enjoying myself now. "Only if you're a crow." I looked at Martha. "You do look a little crow-like, Martha, now you mention it."

I then pointed the musket in the general direction of the fence, as my friends ducked in fear. "Well," I remarked, "this musket is not so fine as the flintlock I used in Portsmouth."

"Used in Portsmouth? Against someone?" asked Martha.

"Nay." I smiled. "Rabbits. But I like not to kill birds. Well, we must do it, I suppose."

"Yes," said Lizzie. "We could use the money. I hope you share your skills with us, Eliza."

"Of course." Here, I blushed. My pride at knowing something these women did not was great indeed.

●　　●　　●

What would Louisa Ruggles have said, I wondered, *had she seen me in my homespun, with my musket, shooting crows off a fence?* I recalled how I had once taken such pride in being the most fashionable girl in all of Cambridge. How distant that life seemed now!

May passed; June arrived. We worked without cease, and all that time I heard not a word from John or Isaac. Neither had Abigail heard from her John. We drew strength from our mutual widowhood, though neither of us spoke of it.

June was hot and dry. One afternoon, after a morning of tending the gardens, I gave Johnny to suck but found I had no milk. He tried twice, then turned his head aside in disgust and wailed.

The heat of the sun had robbed me of my milk. Lizzie, who had been working several rows ahead of me, heard Johnny's cry. She and Martha wiped their hands and came over to us.

"You've exhausted yourself, Eliza. It's my fault. Come back to the house now," Lizzie said.

I might have argued except that, standing up, I felt quite dizzy. The hot air and the rows of corn spun sideways before my eyes, and I nearly fell with Johnny in my arms. Martha took Johnny from me and endeavored to calm him. Lizzie ordered me to bed at once, then set about feeding Johnny with a bottle of watered-down cow's milk and a smooth mash of leftovers. Johnny soon settled, and I fell asleep to the sound of him banging his favorite pot once more. Martha remained within to tend him, but Lizzie returned to the fields.

I lay in bed, bored to tears, for near a week. Lizzie served me tea, milk, and cider throughout the day. At the end of the week, I felt buoyant enough to float off to sea. Then one morning I awoke to find my breasts aching, and, at Johnny's cry, the milk burst forth and ran plentifully once more.

42

ONE DAY THAT JUNE, I ESPIED ABIGAIL walking down our lane with a quick, determined step. We were already abroad, feeding the animals, and when she got a little closer to us, I saw that in her hands she held a letter. She stopped before us and extended the folded paper.

"It's from Colonel Langdon."

I took the envelope from her and looked down at it; the handwriting was not that of my John. I hesitated before opening it. Abigail and I stood in the kitchen garden. Seeing my hesitation Abigail said, "Let us sit." She moved us toward two low gardening stools, and we sat upon them. I held the letter in my lap, thinking that whatever events it described had already transpired. My not knowing the letter's contents would change nothing.

I broke the seal and read:

Dear Miss Boylston:

Forgive me for not replying sooner. I only received your letter yesterday, upon returning to Portsmouth after a long and unavoidable absence. I myself was in ignorance of the events of this past winter, when thirty-two men were banned from the town of Portsmouth. They fled, and their property was confiscated. Your uncle was among them . . .

"So, the worst has happened," I said aloud, endeavoring to remain composed. Abigail placed an arm around my shoulders. "Courage," she whispered. "All is not lost."
I read on:

Miss Boylston, it grieves me to report that your uncle is dead. He fled to New York, and was two weeks ago found in a hotel room, beside an empty vial of laudanum.

"Oh, poor, foolish man," I cried. "I wonder if Mama has heard?"
"Heard what, dear?" asked Abigail, but I continued to read without replying:

Before leaving Portsmouth, your uncle brought John and Isaac to auction, at Stavers's tavern. The sale had been announced in all our surrounding towns. Apparently, a man from Kittery, one Mr. Richards, attended this auction. When he espied Isaac, a great hullabaloo broke out. This Mr. Richards insisted that Isaac was his, and he wouldn't pay a cent for him, and if Mr. Chase knew what was good for him he'd throw Watkins into the bargain or be arrested. Your uncle took the deal and vanished, with what results you now already know.

I set the letter down. "I feel I am to blame, somehow," I said. I could feel my legs swaying beneath me.
Abigail rose from the stool. "Eliza, you look very ill. Might I bring you something?" Then, as I made no reply, she said, "Yes, you must take something."
"No, thank you." I wavered on my feet.

"I insist. A dish of tea—with rum. I'll return by and by."

Once Abigail had left, I paced in circles in the kitchen garden. Colonel Langdon's words could only mean one thing. Isaac and Watkins were now in the grips of Isaac's former master. I knew not what to do. I could not sit, could not stand, could not *be*.

Abigail returned with the tea and insisted I drink it. My hands shook; my entire body began to tremble.

"You are not well. Come inside and lie down."

"Nay," I said, refusing to comfort myself. For, though I suffered, the idea of fleeing my pain was anathema to me. I sat upon one of the stools and finished the letter:

Miss Boylston, I discovered these events only yesterday, when I returned to Portsmouth to find Johnny and the child absent from the shipyard. By then, the news had spread around Portsmouth, and I have taken the liberty of sending a messenger to Cambridge to relate the news of your uncle's death.

Please know that with regard to the other subject of my letter, my feelings are by no means neutral. You have friends who shall not let sleeping dogs lie. I daren't say more. I remain in Portsmouth for several days but then must away.

Yours most faithfully, JL

"Oh, God, God. The worst has happened. And I was not there!"

At that moment, Martha and Lizzie arrived from the fields. Johnny was asleep in Martha's arms. My friends glanced at Abigail, who gravely shook her head.

"What news?" asked Martha.

I proffered the letter. Lizzie bent down to take it up. She and Martha read it in silence.

"I must go at once," I said. I rose, as if I might leave for Portsmouth that very moment. Then I recalled my babe, still in Martha's arms. He slept peacefully, his breath coming in soft puffs between sweetly parted lips. His long, black lashes were curled and damp with sleep.

"Let us go inside," said Lizzie gently, "and think what's best to do."

"You don't understand." I resisted the gentle tug of her hand. "He would sooner die than live under such a one. Oh, he shall do a harm to himself!"

"Not while you and his babe are in the world," Abigail assured me. "For the thought of you and Johnny would give even the most foolish man pause."

Despite my friends' assurances, however, my legs gave way, and I needed them to help me to my bed. As I lay there, images of John and Isaac danced against the scrim of my closed eyelids. I could hear my friends speaking in low voices in the kitchen. Abigail said I must write Colonel Langdon immediately. Lizzie favored leaving at once. But Abigail had heard of skirmishes in Boston and was frightened of going without a man in tow—someone younger and stronger than either Lizzie's inebriate farmhand or Uncle Quincy's ancient coachman.

I could tolerate but two extremes: the oblivion of sleep, or action. But sleep would not come, and I hardly knew what action to take. Then, from somewhere deep within, I found the will to rise up from the bed.

"Lizzie, have you paper?" I called.

She looked at me, surprised, and moved to her desk, where she found paper and quill.

I pulled the room's one chair over to the desk and wrote to Colonel Langdon.

Dear Colonel,

You will understand my distress at your news, and as I
am eager to be off, I wish to let you know that we leave
for Portsmouth as soon as we can arrange it—I know not
what I can do, but I must be there. We will install ourselves
at Stavers's and await word from you. I hope this letter
reaches you in time, as you mentioned having to depart
Portsmouth. God bless you.—E. B.

Abigail found someone heading north that afternoon and gave
him the letter, along with admonishments about the need for haste.
We readied to leave as well, though Abigail still had her anxieties
about our riding the roads alone. In this, Providence intervened
when the following day we learned that our field hand, Thaxter,
planned to leave us. I had barely noticed his existence since my
arrival in Braintree, particularly since he had an uncanny habit of
disappearing whenever he was needed.

As it happened, Thaxter—whom we had not paid in many
months—had decided to return to his family who lived just north
of Portsmouth. He planned to leave the following week, but with
a little liquid incentive from Lizzie's stash, he agreed to travel with
us that same day.

"I shall tell Uncle that we have need of his coach," Abigail
announced. She had returned to our cottage early that morning
and was present for Thaxter's announcement. She then moved off
through the dunes to the colonel's house.

Martha began to pack our clothing and a sack of provisions
for the road. She would not be joining us, though she would have
liked to, for someone needed to remain behind to feed the animals
and attend the crops.

We set off that afternoon in Colonel Quincy's carriage, stopping at Abigail's for twenty minutes or so while she packed a bag

and gave instructions to her field hands. She gathered up her boys, who had been playing in one of the fields out back. They began to whine and complain until she sent them a look that silenced them, for at once they moved off to pack a few items. Abigail and her family could accompany us as far as her sister Betsy's in Exeter.

We were elbow to elbow in the carriage. It was hot and uncomfortable, and our bodices were soaked through with perspiration by the time we reached Cambridge, where we stopped the night at Lizzie's ancestral home, continuing on early the following morning. Bessie, Lizzie's old family servant, and Giles, their former slave, formed an attachment to Johnny and were loath to let us go, but Lizzie, without giving details, impressed upon them our need for haste.

At last we arrived in Exeter, around ten the following evening, greatly fatigued. I had no breath for speech and retired at once. Yet, brief as it was, my impression of Abigail's sister was highly favorable. Betsy was everything kind and intelligent, and I later learned that she was an accomplished writer.

My sleep that night in Exeter was profound but brief. I woke at dawn, nursed my babe, and then woke Lizzie, who slept beside me. She rose at once, and after a quick breakfast of coffee and eggs, we were ready to depart. Abigail, hearing us, emerged from her chamber, her nightcap still perched upon her little head. "Are you off so soon?"

"Yes, dearest," said Lizzie. "But we will write when we have news."

"Oh, do, please. I shan't rest until I know what there is to know."

We hugged her and promised that we would.

43

"I'M FALLING DOWN," LIZZIE ANNOUNCED UPON ENTERING our chamber at Stavers's tavern. There was but one available, and we shared it. It was in the front of the house overlooking King Street, and we could hear the noise from the street below. But Lizzie was grateful to be out of the coach. "Thank goodness we are arrived at last. I slept quite poorly last night." I nodded but did not reply. I had lost the urge to speak, even to Lizzie. The world seemed leagues away.

Lizzie undid her gown and stays and fell upon the bed; I myself could not rest. I placed my sleeping babe beside Lizzie and moved to the window, where I looked down upon King Street. There, across from Mr. Fowle's old printing house, stood Mr. Henderson's English and India Goods, now closed. Next door was Mr. Brewster's bookstore, at whose display I had often stopped to gaze. And just there was Mr. Bass's establishment, with its display of coats, hats, and fine kid gloves.

Oh, Portsmouth! It seemed an age since I'd lived there. Though only twenty-three, I felt that I'd lived through a hundred years of gain and loss, and was regretful that John had not known this seasoned woman; he had known the girl with her bits of silk still clinging to her.

As I looked out the window, I recalled the pipe-smoking fer-ryman and Captain Jones, and fishing with that impossibly long pole on the eastern end of Badger's Island. I recalled Langdon's shipyard, taking the cure on Pest Island, and our laughter as John and I got to know each other, and my soft bed that one time . . . gone, gone.

"Lizzie," I said abruptly, my voice sounding far away. "Would you kindly walk over to the Whipple house and inform Cuffee and Prince that we are arrived? It is but three streets away, directly up Front Street. The house is blue, and there's an enormous oak tree before it. You can't miss it. Would you have one of them send word to Colonel Langdon that we are arrived?"

"Oh, of course," she said, though she did not move. Her eyes were closed and she seemed to doze. After a few moments she sat straight up, donned her stays and gown, and set off.

While Lizzie was gone, I rested and nursed Johnny. I gave him some crushed blueberries, which Betsy had sent with us in the car-riage. Johnny plucked the berries one by one in his dainty little grip before putting them in his mouth. He fell asleep with a purple tongue and lips, and I fell asleep beside him. I knew not how long we had been asleep, but we were both dead to the world when a hesitant rap on the door woke us.

"One moment," I said, righting myself. It was dark in the chamber now—no moon shone beyond the window—and close. My mouth tasted stale, but I had no opportunity to clean my teeth. I moved to the door and opened it.

Standing before me were Prince, Dinah, Jupiter, and, to my very great surprise, Colonel Langdon himself. Lizzie stood beside the colonel and looked on in astonishment as I was hugged and fairly smothered by the Whipples.

Then they turned to my sleeping babe. Sighs, exclamations, and tender clasping of hands all finally served to wake him, which had no doubt been their aim. They then took him up in their arms, each begging for a turn. None of them seemed in the least surprised by his existence, and from this I concluded that all the slaves of Portsmouth had long known my "secret."

Colonel Langdon, who remained at the threshold, seemed embarrassed by this unbounded display of affection.

I curtsied to him. "Come in, Colonel."

Lizzie added hastily, "It's dark as a tomb in here, Eliza," and lit a candle.

"Lizzie," I said, steering her first to Prince, who stood hunch-shouldered in a corner of the chamber, "this is the soldier who taught me to use a musket."

"A most useful skill, indeed," said Lizzie archly. But Prince, intimidated, did not hazard a reply.

Johnny suddenly pointed to Jupiter, who took that as a sign to take him from my arms. Jupiter grasped him tight and held him high in the air, grinning his broad, white grin. Johnny took fright, frowned, and reached for me.

Jupiter merely laughed good-naturedly. "He thinks I's de Devil hisse'f, Miss Eliza!"

"Jupiter," I said. "I am very glad to see you. But tell me: How is it you remain in Portsmouth?"

"Before he leave, Master Robert, he tells me I ain't worth nothin' and lets me go. Says the same of Dinah—he never did take to her cookin'. Well, I had nowhere *to* go, so Colonel Whipple take me in. I'm a free man, Miss Eliza." Here, Jupiter allowed himself a small, proud grin.

Regretfully, all but Colonel Langdon soon had to return home, and I felt sad to have to cut short our reunion. I knew not when I'd see them again. After several more hugs and many more tears, they all departed.

Colonel Langdon entered my chamber. Lizzie stood at the transom, turning toward the hallway to give us privacy.

The colonel strode anxiously from one end of our chamber to another. I waited. Finally, he said, "Miss Boylston. I see you have earned the love and trust of those who usually find us undeserving of either."

"They were kind to me when others were—less so. Do you wish to sit?" I said, pointing to the lone chair.

"Nay—please," he deferred. I sat with Johnny on my lap, and the colonel sat on one corner of the low bed, his long legs bending at an uncomfortable-looking angle.

"Miss Boylston. I mustn't be so cruel as to delay. I have news as will gladden and pain you at once."

"Tell me," I said. I thought I saw a flinch of anticipation in Lizzie's shoulders.

"Yes. Watkins—John Watkins—"

"Is he well?" I interrupted. "And Isaac?"

The colonel paused in his account, as if deciding how to proceed. "I was going first to say that this Richards character is well known to us. He's a notorious swindler whom Kittery folk call Mr. Wretched. I'm afraid it has not been easy for our boys. Isaac is well." The colonel smiled wanly and pushed a heavy lock of hair off his forehead. "He has grown."

"Oh, Cassie shall be overjoyed to hear it. And Watkins?"

The colonel looked at his feet, then at me. There was much regret in his eyes.

"He is better than he was."

My heart began to pound uncontrollably. "What mean you, sir?"

"The good news is that I have succeeded in procuring him once more for the yard."

By this statement the colonel gave me to know that John was alive, but nothing more. He continued, "When I returned to Portsmouth and learned what had happened, I offered Richards a thousand pounds for them both. But old Wretched refused. It seemed that the very idea I wanted them made him cling to them all the more. I finally offered the scoundrel a king's ransom to have them both returned to the shipyard—hiring them, as it were. Well, *that* the old devil couldn't resist. But the day Johnny returned to me, I saw . . . he kept it beneath his shirt, attempting to hide it . . ."

I rose from the chair. "Kept what from you, sir? What did he attempt to hide?"

"His *hand*," the colonel blurted at last. "His hand has been broken. The bones of all but his thumb were—all smashed."

"Oh, God!" I rose from the chair and placed Johnny on the bed. I felt cold and began to tremble. I turned to Colonel Langdon in desperation. "Are you certain? He can do nothing without his hands."

Langdon approached me and gently took my arm.

"He heals, Miss Boylston. Someday, perhaps . . ."

"Someday! Oh, this evil, evil world. His work—his work is all he has. Without that—oh, why has God put us here to suffer so?"

Lizzie abandoned all pretense of not hearing us and came to my side.

"Miss Boylston," the colonel said, moved by my despair, "he is safe for now, and the hand shall heal in time."

"But *why*?" I said, more to myself than to him. "Why would Mr. Richards do such a thing?"

"Apparently he believed that Johnny knew the whereabouts of certain—armaments." Colonel Langdon looked at me, doubting whether to proceed.

"Have no fear, colonel. I know about them."

"Yes. Well, as you can imagine, they're worth a great deal. The greedy wretch wished to procure them, sell them to his Tory friends. After breaking four of Watkins's fingers, Richards realized that the man would sooner die as give up the whereabouts of the arms."

My eyes closed for a long moment. The thought of Watkins's suffering was unendurable. What reassurance had we that it was over? None.

I finally said, "Perhaps they are with you during the day, but they must return each night to that . . . place . . ."

"Mr. Richards won't harm Johnny now, I am fairly certain. I'm a daily witness of his condition. Should I not like what I see, I could easily find a means of having Richards arrested. Then, as you know, accidents often happen in jail. Most unfortunate accidents."

Here, the handsome colonel gave me a mordant smile, though his eyes were hard. O, for such a backbone! There must be no remorse for the remorseless. I wiped my tears and curtsied deeply. Then, impulsively, I embraced him. "Thank you, colonel. There is a special place in Heaven for people like you."

He nodded, hiding a deep blush in the room's penumbral gloom. Then, after some hesitation, he asked, "Would you like to see him? See Johnny, I mean? I might be able . . ."

"Oh," I burst into tears at the very thought. "Do not promise such a thing. The hope alone should kill me if—"

"No, I won't promise. But I think I know a way." He looked at me as if actually seeing me for the first time since his arrival. "But I have stayed too long. You are exhausted." Then, blushing, this remarkable man quickly took his leave.

The moment he left, Lizzie lit another candle.

"My love is grievously hurt," I said.

"Yes. I heard."

"But he lives. Lizzie, he lives."

I curled up on our bed beside Johnny who, perhaps sensing his mother's misery, whimpered in his sleep.

Lizzie sat on the edge of the bed, caressing the sleeping child's head. "You know," she began, "until this day, I don't believe I truly knew you, Eliza. Though we have been as sisters these ten months,

I didn't understand your character. I am frankly in awe. Well and truly in awe."

I smiled wearily, "You thought me as prim and proper as one of Mr. Copley's portraits."

"Nay—well, in a way, perhaps—"

"You didn't realize the depth of my feelings for—those you would not have expected me to love."

"No," she said. "This much I freely admit."

I took Lizzie's hand and grasped it. "I may be cowardly, but my heart is not. Isn't that odd? Besides," I continued, suppressing a smile, "I thought, I still think, John Watkins by far the handsomest man I ever saw—"

"Well!" she looked at me. "Why did you not say so at once? Surely a woman needs little more incentive than that?"

We laughed. Suddenly, Johnny sat straight up, annoyed at having been awakened.

"Mama!" he cried. Lizzie and I looked at each other in amazement. We had just heard his first word.

44

I CUDDLED WITH MY BABE, AND FED him, and he finally fell asleep for the night at around ten, followed soon thereafter by Lizzie. Their quiet breaths were consolingly regular. But I remained awake. The air was hot and close; the room was utterly black—I could not tell whether my eyes were open or no, and in my nervous state I thought I could hear animals scratching in the walls. I must have dozed off, for I was awakened by a soft knock.

"Who's there?" I whispered. I thought of Langdon's words but dared not hope.

Silence. I got up and approached the door. Perhaps it was a messenger. I opened the door slightly and looked through the crack.

There stood Watkins. His fair, clear eyes took me in for a long moment. Then they moved beyond me, to Lizzie and the sleeping babe.

"A moment," I whispered. I went to wake poor Lizzie. She roused herself quickly, smiled blcarily, and asked, "Who is it?"

"As you see," I whispered.

Lizzie looked toward the door and said, "Oh!" She turned to me and opened her eyes wide, as if to say that I had not exaggerated, that he was, indeed, the handsomest man on earth. She then rose, curtsied without meeting Watkins's eyes, and moved past him into the hallway.

"Where go you?"

"Just here in the hall. I shall keep watch."

"I remain not long," Watkins said to us both. "The colonel waits for me below."

Oh, God! The sound of his voice made me dizzy.

Watkins's right arm was hidden in a linen sling. With his left hand, and very slowly, he took my hand in his. He looked a little older, perhaps, but here was the same animated face; here, the strong, sinewy body I once had known so intimately. His curly hair, which I had caressed I knew not how many times, was now pomaded and tied in a ribbon. One brown-blond lock had escaped and tumbled upon his shoulder. But his eyes were different. In them, I thought I saw a kind of resignation I had not seen there before, not even on the pier after the *Ranger*'s departure. I could think of but one remedy: I moved to the bed and lifted Johnny gently. He remained asleep, on his back in my arms.

"Your son," I said, holding Johnny out to him. "Isn't he amazing? He called me Mama today."

Watkins gazed down at his child. Gently, he cradled Johnny's head in his good hand.

"Amazing, yes. But don't wake him just yet." He glanced lovingly at me.

"No." I placed Johnny back on the bed. John approached me slowly, as if I might flee, his eyes never leaving me. We embraced, saying nothing, and for the longest time we just stood like that in the small chamber in Stavers's tavern.

• • •

John left in the dead of night, Lizzie having stood guard in the hallway the entire time. When it was time for him to leave, she knocked gently. But she did not wake us, for we had not slept. John said he hoped to see me once more before we returned to Braintree.

At breakfast, Lizzie and I sat in one of the tavern's small public rooms, where we were served coffee and a fine plate of ham and eggs. After ten minutes of silence, however, she began to giggle. The harder she tried to squelch the urge, the worse it became.

"Oh, Eliza," she blurted at last, "I must have at least some details. Do give me a morsel and put me out of my misery. For it's certain I'm to be an old maid and must live vicariously."

"You are depraved," I scolded. I gave her no details, though I did say, "Oh, you should have seen him with Johnny. You should have seen his tenderness." She stopped laughing, and her eyes grew tearful at the thought of Watkins holding his son for the first, and possibly the last, time.

Just as we were finishing our breakfast, a messenger approached us with a letter for Lizzie. As she perused it, she stood up from her chair.

"What is it?" I asked.

"It's from Colonel Quincy. My brother, Harry, is alive—and in Braintree. Eliza, we must leave at once." Indeed, she looked as if she would leave that very moment, whether I followed or no.

•　　•　　•

We traveled till near midnight, when we reached the inn at Newburyport and stopped to catch a few hours' sleep. We continued down the coast early the next morning and arrived in Braintree late the following day. I would have relished the opportunity to write Colonel Langdon before I left, but there simply was no time—Lizzie would not rest until she'd seen her brother with her own eyes.

I bore my suffering stoically, as Abigail did. But at least I now knew that Watkins still loved me, and that our bonds had not been irrevocably broken.

As we entered our lane off the coast road, we espied a tan young man walking down the dunes from the Quincys'. He looked hale and hearty, and his golden hair shone in the declining sun.

Lizzie cried, already rising from her seat, "Stop! Stop the carriage!"

At the sound of her voice, the young man turned. "Lizzie?"

"Harry? It *is* you!" She nearly tumbled out of the carriage and ran flying into the young man's muscular brown arms. He spun her around and laughed.

"You are changed," he remarked, holding her at arm's length.

"Am I very ugly?"

"Not exactly." He took another step back, the better to scrutinize her. "You're tan."

"We work in the fields, like slaves." Then she turned to me to see whether her words had given offense. I smiled at her and shrugged. Words did not offend me, where the heart was loving.

"Well, I come bearing gifts that may relieve your labors—at least, for a short while."

"Gifts?"

Harry laughed gaily. "I must return to the Quincys' to thank them and get my things." And off he loped, back up the hill through the dunes. Martha had stepped out to greet us holding a kitchen cloth; she followed Harry with her eyes.

"Oh, Martha," said Lizzie, embracing her. "Eliza has so much news to tell. But first—have you met my brother?"

"Of course. He's been here these past three days—at the Quincys', I mean. I didn't think it meet that he stop here—"

"No," Lizzie agreed.

"He's begun to help about the farm. He says it's in a woefully feminine state."

"Feminine state?" Lizzie smirked. "We'll see how well he fares with all our feminine work!" I had only gotten a glimpse of Harry, but it was enough to know that Harry was a very fine specimen of a man. Five years at sea had hardened his muscles, turned him brown, and bleached his light-brown hair blond. Yet he seemed a mere boy in spirit, lighthearted and ready to laugh.

I handed Johnny down to Lizzie and then descended the carriage, my limbs having grown stiff. The colonel's coachman brought our belongings into the cottage. It was a sweltering day, and as we had traveled since before dawn, we were quite exhausted. Johnny, who'd been asleep on my lap, woke and cried inconsolably.

Harry returned with his sacks just then—what a horrid impression the child must have made! Even I wished to cover my ears. Martha and I set about bathing and changing Johnny. We fed him a bit of mashed pea and potato. After he had bathed and eaten, he finally settled and was soon crawling toward Harry's burlap sacks.

"Hey, there, fella!" Harry exclaimed. He bent down on one knee, and Johnny sat up to listen to whatever Harry might have to say. "Why, aren't you a handsome little man!" Harry turned to his sister, "Dusky, though, what?" Lizzie did not reply, but merely shot him a peremptory glance. It occurred to me, however, that, having traveled from port to port—West Indies, East Indies, even Africa—Harry must have seen a myriad of humanity's variations. Johnny crawled off to the kitchen, where we heard him banging happily on a pot.

"A cozy house, indeed," said Harry to his sister.

"Small, you mean?" She had made us all some tea and brought it into the parlor.

"Nay, cozy. Truly."

As there was but one chair, Harry sat himself on the floor, cross-legged. "Never mind about a chair. The floor is not heaving to and fro—that's already an improvement." Not to be outdone, we ladies sat ourselves upon the floor as well, giggling as we adjusted our petticoats. We no longer wore our stays about the house, so sitting in this manner was not the miserable ordeal it might once have been. Harry sipped his tea and frowned.

"Ugh. Sister, what *is* this? Tastes like horse dung."

"Harry!" Lizzie scolded. "You drink our finest and most patriotic blackberry tea. We've had no real tea since '75."

Martha corrected her: "Recall you not the tea Abigail shared with us in '76?"

"Abigail Adams, you mean? John Adams's wife?" asked Harry, all astonishment.

"Harry," Lizzie said with some exasperation, "I see you're as ignorant as a newborn babe. Of course. This is *Braintree*. Abigail lives not two miles down the road. Colonel Quincy is her uncle. Our Eliza is related to them."

"Oh, goodness me," he said, affecting ignorance. "That would be the lady I met yesterday, with whom I conversed for well over an hour."

"You met Mrs. Adams?" Lizzie cried.

Harry nodded. "And I do believe—I say this with no false modesty—she had a very great pleasure in meeting me."

"Oh!" She hit him upon his head, at which assault he cried out and attempted to shield himself.

Harry then shifted his attention to the sacks. "Go ahead and open your gifts, Lizzie."

"Should I?" she turned to me inquiringly.

"Oh, yes, let's," I said with some enthusiasm. I would not ruin this moment with my own misery, not for all the tea in China!

We set our dishes of tea aside and Harry opened the mouth of one of the sacks. Soon we were exclaiming and crying with joy: Oranges! Flour! Real wheat flour, too!

"Oh, I shall make an orange cake and invite the Quincys," was Lizzie's first comment. Then came Bohea tea—several boxes of it.

"You can feed your blackberry horse dung to the pigs," Harry said to his sister as he handed the boxes to her.

"We have no pigs."

"To the chickens, then—though I doubt whether even they shall eat it."

There was more. Rum, ham, beans, coffee, dried fish. What bounty! Martha's eyes moved silently from Harry to his provisions and back to Harry again, as if she couldn't decide which to devour first.

"What think you, Martha? Is not my brother a most wonderful pirate?"

"It would seem so," she said dryly.

"Oh, but where shall we put him?" Rising from the floor in spirited fashion, Lizzie set her hands on her hips and looked about her. Johnny and I slept in the parlor, and Martha and she were in separate chambers upstairs, as they preferred to be during the hot summer months.

"I suppose we could give him your room, Martha."

"No, indeed," Martha replied. "I want no man so close to us. Let us put him in the dairy, with the cheese."

"Am I ripe, then, Miss Miller?" he roguishly cocked his head at her.

"Rather," she agreed, twitching her nose.

"You could use a bath," admitted Lizzie.

Harry rose up to his full height—near six feet. "Very well, then, ladies. Draw me a bath, since I have no wish to offend." And with these words he began to unbutton his trousers. We all rose at once and ran shrieking from the room. Harry just laughed and laughed.

45

THE FOLLOWING EVENING, THE QUINCYS CAME TO dine, and we feasted on everything good, such fare as we had not tasted in years. The evening was so merry. Lizzie beamed with joy and pride. Harry regaled us all with tales of mysterious islands and primitive peoples. At one point, Johnny woke and would not resettle. Ann Quincy, at her queenly best, said, "Bring that child here at once." After we set him upon her lap, she carried on with our lively conversation, cuddling him while he played with her pendant and snuggling his soft, curly head upon her breast. Then Colonel Quincy motioned to his wife to hand over the babe, and was duly granted it.

The next morning, Harry set about mending a fence whose broken slats allowed all the local cows to wander in and help themselves to our vegetables. Martha watched him, and we watched her do so—Lizzie, Abigail, and I—from the edge of the kitchen garden. Abigail had returned early that morning to fetch a pan she'd left the night before.

Martha took Harry refreshment, and when he announced his intention of clearing away the brambles in the next field, she disappeared into the house to see if perhaps Jeb had owned a pair of leather gloves. He had, and Martha returned with them to offer

Harry. The sight of those gloves pained me; I could make out the creases in the leather where his finger joints had molded it.

"Thank you, Martha," Harry said.

"It's nothing. Those brambles can prick."

"I'm most obliged. Indeed, these shall make the work far easier."

Martha seemed pleased that she could be of service to him. She walked back toward the house with a satisfied smirk.

"But do you think he cares at all for her?" Abigail whispered once Martha had gone inside.

"There's no indication that he even notices her existence," I said plainly. "Not in *that* way," I replied.

"No," Lizzie agreed. "I wonder if I should have a word with him," she said.

"Nay," Abigail replied. "She is proud. That would mortify her."

"Abigail's right, Lizzie," I concurred. "Either he shall fancy her or he shall not, and our urging him to do so won't change things."

"Yes, but it will break her heart if he does not return her affections," said Abigail. So involved were we in our conjectures that we had not noticed Martha creep up on us from behind.

"Of what do you speak, harpies?" she asked, handing each of us a glass of cool cider.

"Oh—nothing," we all said in unison and then blushed. Originality is hard to come by in a pinch.

·   ·   ·

Harry, we were convinced, saw us all as his sisters. But then, one hot day, as we sat in the kitchen garden having a dish of tea, we saw something that made us revise our opinion. Harry was once again by the fence along the eastern side of our property, closest to the Quincy property. Martha handed him a cool mug of cider, as she always did. This time, however, as she turned back to the house, he reached for her hand and held it a moment, unwilling to let it go. Martha blushed and pulled away, to return to her work.

"Did you see that?" Abigail whispered to Lizzie.

"Of course."

"What means it?" I asked.

They both turned to me with hands on their hips. "You of all people should know, Eliza."

They began to laugh. I chased them into the fields, threatening to pour my tea on their heads.

For several weeks after this, Martha and Harry teased each other much as children who secretly like each other do: with insults and gibes. When Harry returned to the cottage in the afternoon, Martha would make a face and say, "Ugh! A pig has wandered in from the road!" When Harry caught a scent of dinner cooking, he would remark, "Oh, no. I hope Martha isn't cooking today—I've run out of Glauber's salt."

"Oh, shut up," she'd reply to him.

The banter didn't fool us one bit. We knew they were falling in love, though the lovers continued to fool themselves for several more weeks.

And what of Lizzie? By all appearances, she had renounced Thomas Miller. She did not speak of him, and when Martha made mention of him—his whereabouts, or the fact of his having dined with so and so—she affected indifference.

I knew otherwise, however, for I had known what it was to pine in secret for someone others believed wholly unsuitable. I often came upon Lizzie pacing her chamber anxiously, or sitting by the window with tears in her eyes. When I asked her what was wrong she would always laugh and dismiss it with a wave of her hand and a glib word.

46

JULY 31, 1779. THE MORNING OF MARTHA'S eighteenth birthday was already hot when we woke at dawn. Lizzie insisted upon baking a cake, which turned our cottage into an inferno. I stepped into the kitchen garden with a basket to gather our blackberries, which were just then yielding a great quantity of fruit. The sea breeze felt good, and I lingered there. When I returned to the kitchen, I was shocked to find Mr. Miller standing close behind Lizzie, behind the worktable. Together, they were stirring batter in a bowl with a large wooden spoon. At the sound of my feet, Lizzie jumped so high I thought the bowl would fall off the table.

Thomas Miller turned quickly. "Mrs. Boylston has been teaching me how to bake a cake, Eliza."

"So I see," I said. And I did—though I knew not why he was in our cottage just then, or in Braintree. I suppose I had imagined him long since departed Boston for the South, or perhaps Connecticut, where the British had lately burned and pillaged several towns.

Johnny was sitting at their feet banging on a pot. When he saw me, he threw down the spoon, grasped the kitchen table leg, and stood up. I knelt down, grinned at him, and opened my arms wide. At that moment, Martha walked into the kitchen with Harry. They both stopped moving at the sight of Johnny, upright and poised to walk.

"Johnny! Come to Mama!" I called.

Johnny let go of the table leg and took two wobbly steps forward before falling on his bottom.

"He walked!" Lizzie exclaimed.

"He did," Martha agreed.

"Oh, my brave boy!" I scooped him up in my arms.

Johnny giggled with delight.

"Well," said Harry after a moment, "I propose we celebrate, Lizzie. As your cake will keep, and as it is very hot, let us all take a swim in the colonel's pond."

"A swim? I have never swum in a pond in my life," Martha said primly.

"Nor I," I added. "And I shan't do so."

"Oh, come with us, at any rate. Johnny will love the water."

"Twenty minutes," said Lizzie, who would not leave her batter to spoil. She poured it into a pan and cooked it, as the men waited most impatiently.

"Is it done, Sister? I'm broiling," asked Harry after a while.

"Nearly. Be patient."

"Aw!" he cried. "Patience is such a waste of time."

After another ten minutes, Lizzie took the cake from the coals and set it upon a rack on the kitchen table.

"Finally," Harry exclaimed and trotted off toward the pond. He was followed by Thomas Miller and we women. Seized with the joy of Johnny's first steps, and the heat, and Martha's birthday, we began to run. Arriving at the pond, the men stripped off their shirts, but at our loud protests they moved around behind the rushes. Then Johnny, who still grasped one of Lizzie's good silver spoons, suddenly tossed it high up in the air over the pond, where it landed with a dull plunk.

"I'll race you!" cried Harry to Mr. Miller.

"Go on!" shouted Mr. Miller, and in the next moment we saw them dive headfirst into the deep, dark pond. They were gone a long moment and then finally bounded up, crying, "Did you find it?"

"Nay."

"Again!"

Back down they went. Lizzie, already drenched in perspiration from her baking, and looking limp with the heat, suddenly threw caution to the wind and made a mad dash into the water, her petticoats floating up over her hips as she cried, "Ah, that's cold!" Her arms were raised above her head, her eyes squeezed shut; her mouth grimaced in painful pleasure.

"Martha, you must come, too!" she soon called from the center of the pond.

Martha frowned. Then, suddenly, she said, "Oh, hell," and ran directly into the water, her impulse accompanied by shouts of shock and dismay. Being a tidal pond, it was quite salty and cold—near as cold as the ocean itself. Both women flapped about screaming and shouting, at last getting their heads beneath the water. Their cheeks puffed out as they held their breath and their noses.

I laughed at their antics, allowing myself a moment of happiness, too.

Martha soon dragged her sodden skirts from the water and approached me.

"Go away," I said, "you're dripping on me."

"Go in, Eliza. It's a rare treat. One you won't soon forget."

"Nay. I cannot swim."

"It's shallow. You'll keep to your feet. Have no fear."

"Nay."

Martha lifted Johnny up and dipped his toes in the water. He shrieked with delight and shook his fat little legs. Lizzie came out from the water, her petticoats trailing like a mermaid's fin. The two fiends, drenched through, together grabbed hold of me and backed me into the water until I fell with a shriek. It was frigid!

"She-devils!" I cried.

Laughing, they splashed me until I was thoroughly wet. I could not help but wonder what Mama would have said were she to see us out in our soaking gowns.

We emerged and fell upon the ground, panting. After a few moments, however, we began to hear a sound that pulled us away from our merriment. It sounded like an agonized groan. Was it man, or beast? The men rose at once, grabbed their shirts from the rushes where they'd flung them, and set off toward the cottage. We followed hard upon them as they approached the barn. The horrible moan could be heard quite distinctly now.

"Stay back. Do not approach," Mr. Miller warned us. Harry had fled into the house and returned with Lizzie's musket.

"Nay, I will see what this is," said Lizzie, and while Martha and I had halted in our tracks, Lizzie moved forward. What she saw made her cry out piteously. "Oh, no, no."

"Move back now," Mr. Miller fairly pushed her back toward us. "Farther," he commanded. I ran into the house with Johnny, and, just as I did so, a deafening shot boomed out.

47

MARTHA PULLED ME AND JOHNNY INTO THE house and would not let me out. Instead, to the sound of the commotion and then eerie silence, she made me a dish of chamomile tea, into which, unbeknownst to me, she had mixed a goodly dose of laudanum. Then she helped me to undress and put me and Johnny to bed, for I had been fiercely trembling despite the heat. Only then did she go upstairs to remove her own wet clothing.

I slept as if dead for many hours and knew nothing of what transpired until later that afternoon, when I learned that Star, Lizzie's beloved horse, was dead. Someone had poisoned him.

It was perhaps four or five in the afternoon when I rose, dressed, and moved to the front door. The men were gone. Johnny was still asleep, and everything was far too quiet. Lizzie and Martha were nowhere to be seen. I walked toward the flax field. There, I espied Martha. She was calmly picking flax as if nothing had happened. In a few moments, I saw Lizzie, dressed in one of Ann Quincy's gowns, approach. She knelt by Martha's side. The sun was low in the sky and cast an orange glow upon the Quincy house above us. Lizzie and Martha spoke gravely to each other, in whispers. I chose not to intrude upon them.

The sun descended farther into the western sky, but no one thought of supper or Martha's birthday cake. It went untouched till the following morning, when we crumbled it up and fed it to the chickens.

I soon heard Johnny's cry and turned back to the house, where I fed him. I know not what made me keep my distance from my friends, but I felt there was some business between them of a very private nature. However, after Johnny had fallen back asleep, as I took tea and a biscuit for myself—having no appetite but feeling that I must eat something—I grabbed up a shawl and went abroad.

My friends were no longer in the field. It must have been past six now, for the sun hovered in a fiery orange ball and cast a broad glow across the dunes and the shore. I walked over the dunes in my bare feet, oddly consoled by the soft sand between my toes.

I espied my friends a distance down the beach. They sat close by one another, not speaking, their heads bathed in the glow of the setting sun, their rich, brown hair—one quite dark, the other chestnut-colored—free and whipping about their shoulders and necks. Their eyes were closed, their faces turned into the wind, into the sun's glow. Lizzie had taken Martha's hand.

I might have been hurt by the way in which they had locked me out of their understanding. Yet I believed that they wished only to protect, not to exclude, me from whatever it was they hid.

"May I join you for a few minutes? I daren't leave Johnny longer than that."

"Of course. Come. Sit with us. You must be bursting with questions," said Lizzie.

"Yes, but they can wait. I came to see if I could aid you in any way, Lizzie."

She shook her head.

"Your presence helps," said Martha. "Just you yourself."

We sat in silence a long time, perhaps twenty minutes, watching the red glow on the water deepen as the sun set behind us. I grew uneasy at the thought of Johnny waking to find his mama gone, and I rose, dusting the sand off my petticoat.

"We'll return by and by," said Lizzie. "There are things you should know."

"Things you *must* know, now," added Martha.

•   •   •

What did they tell me, and what did I learn? Truths I could not have guessed had I lived a hundred years. They say we women lead easy, shallow lives—not so! It is only that men, the storytellers, pay scant attention to us.

Martha began the story as we sat together at the kitchen table. She had made us some real tea, and it was now late. Johnny was asleep for the night. We were bone-weary, but I could not rest until I knew what my friends had suffered.

"My brother, Thomas, I shall discuss first," Martha began, setting her tea down and adjusting her chair. "As you know, there has long been a rumor that he has been in the employ of General Howe." Here, she glanced at Lizzie kindly and put a steadying hand on hers. "Nothing could be farther from the truth. It was a rumor that I myself propagated. But, oh, the suffering this rumor has cost me, cost those I love. The truth is, my dear brother—"

Lizzie interrupted her: "Eliza, Mr. Miller has been in the employ of Colonel Quincy, under direct orders from General Washington, these three years past."

My brow must have furrowed, and I said, "But I don't understand. What does he do, that he must suffer such ignominy, such suspicion—and all untrue?"

"He is still doing it," said Martha. "Protecting us. Protecting Abigail Adams, her family, and the Cause."

"Eliza," Lizzie stepped in. "There is, and has been for some time, a plot afoot to attack John Adams and John Quincy Adams upon their return from France. As we speak, these two illustrious citizens are in Boston. Their ship, *La Sensible*, is in the harbor and will arrive here tomorrow evening. We expect an assault."

"Our men will be ready," Martha added.

"Assault? What kind of assault?" I rose from my chair.

"A surprise attack," said Lizzie.

"Except that it's no surprise—now. *They're* the ones who'll be surprised—by us." Martha added, her dark eyes as cold as her words.

"But Martha, whom do you mean by 'us'?" I did not quite understand.

The two women glanced at each other.

"Thomas," began Lizzie.

"And Harry and his captain," answered Martha. "Among others."

I held my warm dish of tea for comfort. If I understood correctly, there was yet some real danger to us all. But what was the nature of this villainy? Violence in wartime I understood. But a vicious attack upon a noble, innocent creature—

"But what, pray, does this current villainy have to do with that poor, poor beast?" I cried.

"Allow us," Martha forestalled, "allow us first to explain more fully what happened here last summer."

A year had now passed since those terrible events to which my friends had thus far only alluded—the deaths of Mr. Thayer and Dr. Flynt. The people of Braintree had lived in a state of terror for many months. But after a few months, people began to forget. We forgot, too—at least, it seemed so. Now Star was dead, in an act of vicious retaliation. But for what, and against whom?

"Eliza," Martha began, "those patriots who were murdered were not . . . patriots."

"Yes," Lizzie confirmed. "They fooled everyone for a brief time. Or nearly everyone."

"Well, if they weren't patriots, who were they?"

"Enemies to the Cause," said Martha firmly. "Dr. Flynt was no doctor. Dr. Flynt wasn't even his real name. His real name was Mr. Stephen Holland, a counterfeiter from Londonderry, New Hampshire. As for Mr. Cleverly—"

"The one who gave us our watering machine and who nearly proposed to Lizzie?"

"The same," Martha said. "His real name is Benjamin Thompson. My brother believes him to be behind the vandalism at our home. And he already has a wife, whom he abandoned in New Hampshire."

I listened in silence. But at last I voiced my true feelings: "Well, if those murdered men were not patriots but rather traitors, then it must be a very great patriot indeed who dispatched them."

My friends stared at me, wide-eyed, without comment. Lizzie finally said, "It is enough for now, what we've told you. Let us rest, and prepare ourselves for tomorrow."

My curiosity remained inflamed, but I was willing to wait for answers. By now, we were all quite exhausted and retired at once. But I did not sleep well. When the sky began to lighten on the morning of August 2, I had dozed for perhaps an hour or two, no more. Johnny woke, and I gave him to suck. Just as I was doing so, sitting on the parlor bed in my shift, Thomas Miller and Harry entered our cottage, all in a great commotion. With them were three of His Excellency's officers: Captain Wiles, Colonel Livingston of New York, and Colonel Palmer. They bowed deeply. Several of them blushed.

I covered my breast and nursing babe and stared up at the men. All three were quite tall, and all were armed with French rifles and heavy gunnysacks. Colonel Palmer, with his powdered hair and soft pink face, looked far more like a lord of the manor than a Rebel officer. William Livingston, slender, with a long face and long nose, was more British bard than fighting man. Yet, this was the group of patriots who would lie in wait for the expected attack upon John Adams.

I found my dressing gown, donned it hastily, and rose to be introduced. Lizzie, hearing the noise below her, descended and offered to make coffee. I then turned to Harry, light dawning upon my ignorance: "I don't suppose you've been on a privateer vessel all these years."

"Not exactly. Or, rather, she began life as a privateer ship, and I began service in that capacity. But in July of '76, we were . . . commandeered."

"And do you have a position in the Continental Navy, a rank of some kind?"

Martha had just then descended the stairs. She stood where she was and listened attentively.

"Chief boatswain's mate, at your service." Harry bowed.

"Well, chief boatswain's mate," I replied, "you might well go hours without food—let us feed you."

We set to work feeding the men before they went off to continue their preparations. We had some remaining pork rashers from Harry's spoils, and we fried them with eggs and made a large pot of coffee. When the men had finished their meal, we cleaned up, each lost in our own thoughts.

The news about Mr. Miller's loyalty to the Cause was reason for joy; yet none of us felt like celebrating. Terrible things had happened, and could yet happen that night.

Late that afternoon, we removed to the colonel's house, where we would remain till well past midnight. We had few words; the colonel played cards with Lizzie and Martha, endeavoring to distract them from the looming confrontation. Ann, wishing to spare the servants the infection of our anxiety, herself brought us something to eat from the kitchen.

Toward evening, Colonel Quincy looked out his back door and said, "I believe the enemy will come not from a ship but from the woods. Just off to the left there."

"You mean you believe they're already here, in our parish?" I asked.

"I do."

"And where are our men?"

"I cannot say."

"You mean you *will* not say, sir?"

The colonel did not reply but pursed his lips regretfully.

Night came, and darkness. Johnny fell asleep in the chamber that the Quincys called "Dr. Franklin's room," because Ben Franklin had stayed in it on several occasions. Ann brought us a light supper and urged us to eat, but none of us had an appetite. I managed a sip of tea and one bite of a buttered biscuit, much like my friends. The clock chimed eleven, then midnight. We watched through the window at the back of the house, which the colonel had barred with a wood plank. It reminded me of the early days of the Troubles, when Papa nailed planks across our doors and windows, for fear of the Rebels.

Now, *we* were those Rebels, and I was among them.

We watched for *La Sensible* in the moonlight. We listened. Nothing. Nothing, for the longest time. More refreshment was brought. The colonel kept dozing off in a high-backed chair and then waking himself, only to doze off again moments later. At around one in the morning, Lizzie had just wearily suggested that we play a game of euchre when I caught a movement out of the corner of my eye.

"Look," I said, pointing through the window to the sea. Was that a ship gliding silently into our moonlit view, two sails furled? Was that an anchor tossed? A near-full moon meant that we could see the target of this midnight treachery full well; unfortunately, so could our enemies see *La Sensible*.

•   •   •

We rose in unison and moved to the window. Tied to the ship's stern, a dinghy rocked to and fro. For a long while, it remained empty. Then, suddenly—from whence we knew not—one man descended into it, helped by two others. He was portly. His bald, wigless head shone in the moonlight. Another man, far taller and thinner, descended soon after him.

Martha placed a hand upon Lizzie's arm. We saw no sign of anyone else—no enemy afoot. But we dared not release our held breath. The dinghy came closer to shore. Closer. Then, just as a wave took it onto the sand, just as John Adams—it *was* he—had stepped down into the lapping waves to steady the dinghy, from the woods to our left came a rushing, raucous cry and a swarm of fire.

Lit torches descended in dancing blazes to the dinghy. I thought at first it was an Indian attack, though what few Indians remained in the outskirts of our town had caused no trouble of late. But the fire! The raucous cries! I knew not what these meant.

Suddenly the overturned hull of an abandoned canoe upon the shore, one we had seen all day yet not noticed, came to life. It lifted up and flipped over. Rising from it were four men: Thomas Miller, Harry Lee, Colonel Palmer, and William Livingston.

Like the Trojan horse that canoe had sat, immobile and ignored. The men must have been crouching painfully within it for hours. Now at last they lifted their bayoneted muskets. I turned away from the window. "Oh, I cannot," I said. "I cannot watch." I moved away just as Lizzie and Martha pulled the wood plank from the door and rushed outside, heedless of Ann or the colonel's desperate calls.

I heard musket fire; Lizzie cried out. Martha whispered, "There he is!"

Lizzie whispered back, "Who? Who's there?"

"Mr. Cleverly."

"Oh, but Thomas!"

"Harry!" Martha cried. We all heard another blast of musket fire. I covered my ears; my body trembled. Had Mr. Miller been killed? Or Harry? What had happened?

Someone took my hand. It was Ann. "The villains are surrounded," she said. "But Mr. Miller has been wounded."

I had stood up; now my knees gave way. Mrs. Quincy called to a servant, who brought me a brandy, which I drank. Ann and I sat at the base of the stairway, unable to stand and remove ourselves to the parlor. I listened for Johnny, asleep upstairs in Dr. Franklin's room. All was quiet on that front.

In a few moments, Harry and two of his officers banged through the front door, carrying Mr. Miller.

Lizzie shrieked. Both Ann and I ran to her as the men brought Mr. Miller into the parlor and set him on the sofa. His face was black with tar; pain darkened his eyes, too. A wound in his side had turned his waistcoat dark red.

"It's but a scratch," he insisted, glancing down at the blood that had seeped through his waistcoat.

"Allow me," said Lizzie, kneeling next to him.

"Tell me what to do," I said. "Please."

"I need dry cloths and brandy, if you have it. If not, wine will do. I must clean the wound," she said evenly. She lifted up Mr. Miller's waistcoat; Martha, white and silent by Lizzie's side, aided in removing his shirt.

"I fear I bleed on your sofa," Mr. Miller said to Mrs. Quincy.

"Goodness, Mr. Miller, what is a sofa, compared to a man?" Ann exclaimed.

I stared at her for a moment, impressed by her pithy remark. I then flew off to the kitchen as Lizzie examined Mr. Miller. When I returned five minutes later, she was still at work, checking him over as methodically and calmly as if he were any soldier. "The shot has passed clean through," she said with some relief. "No organs are involved."

"Excellent news!" I said. I set down the bottle of brandy and handed Lizzie several rags. She applied a compress to the wound, which made Mr. Miller groan in pain. She continued to press upon the wound, but as she did so the pain she caused herself seemed worse than that of the patient's, and she burst into tears.

A knock at the front door silenced us all, so oddly regular and civilized did it sound compared to our turmoil within. The door opened. In walked Mr. Adams and John Quincy Adams—alive, if not entirely well. Mr. Adams spoke quietly for a few minutes with Colonel Quincy and Ann. I saw him pass a hand wearily over his bald head. He then grasped his son's shoulder and said, "Forgive me. But we should like to go home now."

"At once," said the colonel. He rushed abroad to call for his coachman.

I watched the weary father and son depart. I was glad for Abigail, but I felt a pang of envy in my breast for their imminent reunion. We soon took our leave; I did not wish to wake Johnny and so left him to sleep through to the morn. I knew he was safe with the Quincys.

I returned to the cottage with my friends, who supported Mr. Miller beneath his arms, he protesting all the way: "Nonsense. I am well. I am quite well."

"Hush," Lizzie hissed at him, "the spirits will hear you."

Once arrived at our cottage, my friends did what they knew how to do so well: They nursed their men. Martha heated water for a bath for Harry. We found him within, sitting on a stool, bent over and filthy, head in his hands. Lizzie used some of the hot water to bathe Mr. Miller as he lay stretched out on my bed, Lizzie taking care not to disturb his bandaged wound. The two men were clean as babes when the women blew out their bedside candles.

48

I WAS RELIEVED AT THE SUCCESSFUL CONCLUSION to the terrifying events of the previous day, which might so easily have taken a more sinister turn. My friends' great trial was nearly over. Yet mine was not. John Adams must be protected at all costs, yet what of my poor John? What practiced band of patriots lay in wait to vanquish those who would harm him? I knew well the answer.

It was quite early the following morning. Mr. Miller was still asleep in bed, but Lizzie was awake and in the kitchen when I descended. I smiled at her as I endeavored to hide the dark feelings in my breast.

"What's wrong?" she asked the moment she saw me.

I pursed my lips so that no evil would escape them. "I am very happy for everyone," I began, and then burst into tears.

"Come here," said Lizzie. "I know what you're thinking. We have not forgotten him." She hugged me tight. After I had composed myself somewhat, I asked, "Mr. Miller—is he well?"

"He shall be well, I believe. I was up for hours. There is as yet no redness or swelling at the site of the wound. That is auspicious."

At the word *auspicious*, I suddenly remembered a dream I'd had the night before.

"Lizzie, I had the strangest dream last night. I dreamed of my father's plantation."

"Have you been there?" she asked, pouring two dishes of tea for us both.

"Oh, no. Never. But in the dream, I saw it clearly. It was a house much like Colonel Quincy's. Airy and light-filled. It too sat upon a hill—not by our waters but overlooking the Caribbean Sea. So blue, so warm, surrounded by white sand and palm trees. We pulled up to find the house uninhabited yet open to the soft breezes. I sensed an air of possibility all about, and I thought, *I shall have to procure some furniture.* What make you of it, Lizzie?"

"I know not," she said honestly. "But it sounds lovely. Quite— free of care. I almost wish I were there myself."

"It was another world."

"The enemy's world, though," she reminded me. "Entirely against our Cause."

"Yes," I replied thoughtfully. "I suppose."

After I had finished my tea, I made my way up the hill in the fog, to retrieve Johnny. The Quincy house was dead quiet as I entered through the back door, now unlocked. One servant was up and preparing breakfast for the Quincys, who had not yet descended. I ascended the stairs with a familiar nod to her.

Johnny was asleep on his back, splayed out on the bed. A bolster was twisted, surrounding him so that he would not roll off in the night. I lifted him gently; he was warm with sleep.

Returning with him to the cottage, I gently set my child upon the bed next to a still-sleeping Mr. Miller. Johnny squirmed, put his thumb in his mouth, but did not wake. It was near six—a late start for us. But this morning, the chores could wait.

"Is it well Mr. Miller sleeps so long?" I asked Lizzie.

"Oh, yes. His body heals itself. Yet I'll watch him closely throughout the day."

Her air of indifference did not fool me. Nor did it fool Martha, who, coming in from feeding the animals, had overheard her.

"Indeed, you should watch him very closely, Lizzie. I shouldn't leave his bedside, if I were you."

Lizzie darted a warning glance at Martha.

I smiled. "Lizzie, if we can't tease you now, when can we?"

"Never."

"But I'm so happy for you, truly," I said, my low spirits lifting at the news that Mr. Miller would recover. "What's more, I'm delighted that Mr. Miller is precisely who we thought him to be, and not an evil manipulator like Mr. Cleverly or Dr. Flynt."

"Well," replied Lizzie, "I'm not certain General Howe will feel as we do. The general had thought Mr. Miller quite a dedicated subject of the crown. Even our dear Abigail was fooled."

We heard the creak of the stairs and turned to find Harry, descending. Normally a bold rogue, Harry now looked sheepish. What had he been doing upstairs? We had left him quite cozily ensconced in the dairy!

Entering the kitchen, he would not meet our eyes. Lizzie pursed her lips and endeavored to stifle a smile. But the attempt failed, and she burst into laughter.

"Shut up, Lizzie," said Martha. "Nothing untoward happened. As you see, I have not yet changed my gown."

"A great deal can happen with a gown on," she replied. "I have safe delivered many a product of such an encounter."

"Lizzie!" Martha blushed scarlet.

"Oh, don't torment the poor girl," I said. "For I see no mark of sainthood upon your fair brow."

"No, indeed," she said, pinching her lips tight as she glanced toward my sleeping babe. I smiled good-naturedly as we all helped to put some breakfast upon the table.

Suddenly we heard footsteps and turned to find Mr. Miller, walking toward us in a bloodstained nightshirt. He sat down on a stool in obvious discomfort.

Lizzie shrieked. "What on earth? What do you think you're doing?"

"Why, joining you for breakfast, if I may."

"You may not. Your bandage leaks. I must change it. You should remain in bed another day at least."

"One night by his side and she henpecks him like a wife," Martha muttered. "Take care, Tom. She'll soon have you fetching and carrying."

Lizzie swatted Martha out of her way. "Come along, Mr. Miller. Let's get you out of that bloody shirt. And I must change your bandage."

Mr. Miller obeyed. He turned around and headed slowly back toward the bed, where Lizzie removed his shirt, her face turned modestly away.

"You will look upon me someday, you know," said Mr. Miller brashly.

"Yes, well. Not *today*," Lizzie replied.

She asked me would I fetch another shirt from her upstairs chest of drawers. I did so, as she went about changing his bandage. In a few minutes, she had succeeded in helping him back into bed. Finally Lizzie went to fetch him breakfast on a tray, but by the time she returned, he was fast asleep.

• • •

It was a day of quiet industry and contemplation. We had all been through so much together, and yet some of what we suffered could not be shared. Thus it was with great tact that we allowed one another time and space to make sense of that which had been revealed.

Much later that day, after the extreme heat had passed, Martha, myself, and Lizzie took tea in the kitchen garden, where we had brought our garden stools. Johnny sat on my lap, and he was banging a spoon against a block of wood. Harry had gone into town to follow up on the arrests of Mr. Cleverly and his band. Mr. Miller was awake and sitting up in bed.

Unbidden, Martha began to weep.

"Why, Martha, what is the matter?" asked Lizzie. I had never seen Martha weep, and I suspected that Lizzie hadn't, either.

"I promised him I wouldn't say, but I fear I can't keep the news to myself."

"What news?" Lizzie and I asked in unison.

"Nothing. Nothing at all, compared to yesterday." Martha endeavored to laugh. "Harry leaves for New York Monday next."

"Harry leaves? He didn't tell *me*," said Lizzie.

"He's not afraid of the British, but he is apparently quite terrified of his sister. Yes, Lizzie, he's been given orders."

Lizzie paused, searching for a tactful way to phrase the question we both had on our minds: "And . . . do you have an understanding?"

"There has been no time for words. But—" Here, Martha sent Lizzie a look that went beyond my understanding.

"Yes," Lizzie replied to Martha's silent question. "You must speak to him."

"It's certain he loves you," I said. "We've seen how he looks at you."

Martha sighed. "Yes, he loves me," she agreed. "If only love were enough."

• • •

I might have questioned Martha further but just then a shadow caught my eye, and when I looked up I saw Abigail turn into our yard. With her was Mr. Adams. When they saw us they let go of each other's hands like young lovers caught by disapproving parents. At once we showed our respect by standing.

"Nay, nay, stay where you are." Mr. Adams waved to us. "I would not have you stand on my account."

Martha and I sat down, but Lizzie approached Mr. Adams. She said, "Mr. Adams, I don't believe you've met my friend Martha Miller, or my sister-in-law, Eliza Boylston. The handsome fellow on her lap is her son, Johnny."

"Well, how'd ye do, Johnny," said Mr. Adams, and came over to where I sat. He reached out his arms for the child, but of late Johnny had become shy of strangers. He frowned at Mr. Adams and turned into my shoulder.

"I'm so sorry, Mr. Adams. I don't know what's come over him. He's a friendly child, usually."

"Don't concern yourself, my dear," said Mr. Adams. "I have that effect on most people."

"Oh, John," Abigail reproached him.

"Would you like some tea?" Lizzie asked. "It's the real thing—my brother Harry's spoils of war."

"It's our patriotic duty to drink the spoils of war, wouldn't you say, Portia?" Here, John looked so lovingly at Abigail that I blushed, though she did not.

"I'll make a fresh pot," Lizzie said.

"We stay not long," said Abigail. "Don't fuss. John wished to see Mr. Miller, as did I."

Turning to Lizzie, Mr. Adams said, "I'm very glad to hear that Mr. Miller's wound is not life-threatening. I owe him a very great debt. *We* do, that is." He looked at his wife.

"What *I* owe him is an apology," said Abigail. "Excuse me. I'll be but a moment." Mr. Adams moved to accompany his wife to the bedside of Mr. Miller.

"He's in the parlor," said Lizzie. "Please don't incite him to any patriotic activity just now, Mr. Adams."

"No, I think we've had enough of that for the time being." Abigail looked pointedly at me and Martha.

She returned a few minutes later, leaving her husband by Mr. Miller's side. Her little face was aflame with anger. In a hushed voice she addressed us:

"I simply can't believe that no one thought it meet to tell me that Mr. Adams and John Quincy arrived."

"We *could* not, Abigail," said Lizzie, looking down at the ground.

"We took our orders from Colonel Quincy," Martha added.

"But why?" Abigail's voice rose in distress.

"Shh," said Lizzie. "We've no wish to disturb our men. They've all been through a great ordeal."

"That's just the point," said Abigail hotly. "What if they'd not survived? What if my John, or John Quincy—oh, I cannot even think of it."

"But what good would it have done for you to be in agony all that time? We ourselves could hardly bear it. Isn't it better this way? Wouldn't you have done the same, in our place?"

Abigail contemplated this new idea. "If I were you . . . I should not have wanted you to suffer in anticipation. I suppose I would have trusted in my fine soldiers. Oh, Lizzie," she turned to her friend. "I am so heartily sorry I misjudged Thomas Miller. That must have caused you indescribable pain."

"You were meant to be deceived, Abigail. But let us forget the past—it was all for the best. And here we have our men, safe and nearly sound."

"I am so contented to see my John." She sighed and allowed herself a small smile. "Though he tells me he is to go to Cambridge to write the Commonwealth's Constitution. He's like Odysseus.

But if he expects me to sit home knitting his shroud, he's wrong. We nearly argued about it, but I had not the heart last night."

Lizzie went in to make the tea, and as she opened the door, we heard John Adams's hearty laugh coming from the parlor. I wondered what he could have been laughing at. I followed her into the kitchen.

Soon, with the teapot and dishes on a tray, we offered a dish to Mr. Miller, who was sitting up. He glanced at Lizzie with unabashed adoration, which made her blush. Then we all stepped into the garden. Martha brought up the rear carrying a candlestand, upon which she set the tea and a plate of biscuits.

"Oh, how delighted I am to be on dry land," said Mr. Adams, after sitting down, a dish of tea on his lap. He stretched his short legs out before him and tipped his face into the late afternoon sun. "You've no idea of the tedium of a ship. I've a mind never to leave Braintree again."

"You leave tomorrow," said Abigail flatly.

"Saturday," he corrected her.

"And did you have a good trip otherwise, Mr. Adams?" I hazarded.

"Dismal," he replied. "If I had to spend one more minute with Dr. Franklin, I should have gone stark raving mad. The man is always right!"

"As are you, dear," said Abigail, patting his shoulder. "How very inconvenient for you."

We laughed at Abigail's wit, but Mr. Adams merely waved her comment away, content for once to let her have the last word.

•   •   •

The Adamses had just said their good-byes when Martha stood up and cried, "Oh, dear! I entirely forgot!" She ran upstairs and returned with a letter in her hands. "This was under the door when we returned from the Quincys' last night. It is addressed to you, Eliza. Forgive me, I—"

"Don't apologize, Martha. There were far more important things to think about last night."

I sat back down with the letter in my lap, hesitating only a moment before breaking the seal. It was from my mother.

August 2, 1779, Cambridge

Dear Eliza,

The fog has finally lifted from my grieving eyes. No longer can I in good conscience allow the crime upon you to go unpunished. I write to tell you that tomorrow I go to Portsmouth—Cassie says I do wrong, but who is she to say so? She has grown most impertinent! There, I hope to bring the father of your child to justice. It is right; it is just. For, when the villain is hanged by his Neck, your Reputation shall be returned to you. Then may you take up your life once more in Cambridge. —Mama

Martha, who had been reading over my shoulder, sucked in her breath.

"I can't believe it," I said.

"Might I share this with Lizzie?" Martha asked.

"Yes. But I must go to Cambridge at once. Oh, I fail to understand! She never expressed the least interest in Johnny's father. She's gone mad."

I handed Martha the letter. She moved silently into the kitchen, and I followed her. Lizzie read in ominous silence. She then met my eyes, as if searching for my own understanding of the letter.

"Mama knows perfectly well that it was not a case of ravishment. She—but I must ready myself at once."

"A moment, dearest Eliza," said Lizzie, touching my arm. "Let us think what to do."

"I know what I must do. I must go to Cambridge."

"Yes," she confirmed, "but I believe you told us that Colonel Langdon has offered to help?"

"He did," I agreed. "Yet I fear that whatever he had in mind to do, the time for it has run out."

"Before you go," Martha held my arm a moment, "perhaps—perhaps you ought to share this news with someone else who might be able to help."

"And who might that be?" I replied with a bitter, hopeless laugh.

Lizzie and Martha looked at each other.

"You'll catch him easily, if you make haste," said Martha.

49

THE ADAMSES HAD GONE AS FAR AS the meetinghouse by the time I caught up to them. The little couple strolled calmly, hand in hand, enjoying the darkening light and the calm that had finally fallen over the town.

I coughed, and Abigail turned around.

"Oh, Eliza, it's you. You frightened me. Have I left something behind?"

"No, no." I curtsied. "I wished—Lizzie, Mrs. Boylston that is, and Miss Miller, thought I might do well to speak to Mr. Adams upon a most urgent question. I have only just now received a letter—"

"By all means," said Abigail, moving away slightly, to give us privacy.

Mr. Adams turned to me.

"Shall we sit? I find my legs are yet a bit wobbly. Would it be terribly inconvenient if I sat upon the steps, just here?" he pointed to the meetinghouse steps.

"Of course not. I shall join you, if I may."

I sat upon the steps, and this great man sat down next to me with a relieved sigh.

"I should say at once, Miss Boylston, that I have no idea of being the least help to you. I know a little of your story—a very little. But naturally whatever is in my power, I shall do."

Mr. Adams, do whatever was in his power? I tried not to think of the many times Mr. Adams might have said those very words to the likes of His Excellency George Washington, or to the king of France. Who was I to ask anything of this man? Yet I inhaled and soldiered forth. I told Mr. Adams about the letter from Mama, and about Colonel Langdon's former intent to help John and me.

Listening, Mr. Adams's demeanor changed from the affable country rustic I had met but an hour earlier. His face became grave, his voice low and steady when he said, "From everything you say, the situation has become critical."

I nodded. "Mr. Adams, I'm most grateful for your solicitude. But I have no wish to involve you in my troubles. You're just now safely arrived yourself, and Abigail cannot do without you—"

Mr. Adams cut me off. "That is a very pretty speech, Miss Boylston. But I've been involved in troubles almost since birth. I hardly know how to occupy myself without them."

How gracious he was! This was hardly what I had expected of the man whom all our broadsides drew as a loud and vulgar clown.

"Rest assured," he continued, "that if I do manage to help you, I shan't budge from my beloved farm to accomplish it." Then, his thoughts seemed to change tack: "By God, we've not gotten this far without—without our human web, as it were. We are all a part of it, in however small a way—you, Lizzie, Martha, even Watkins, from what I gather—" Here, he broke off, as if he'd revealed too much. "The web is sturdy, Miss Boylston. Upon its strength I'd stake my life. Yes, my very life!"

Mr. Adams was silent for a moment. He then asked in a whisper, "But this Richards fellow—has he a wife and family?"

"A wife, I'm told. A cruel mistress to her slaves."

"Hmm. I shall have to see whether . . ." he trailed off. "Well." John Adams cleared his throat and turned to face me. "Are you prepared, my dear?"

"In what way, sir?"

"Prepared to get what you wish? If we're successful, and we get them, you must realize that your troubles will just be beginning."

50

THE ROAD TO CAMBRIDGE WAS HOT AND dusty: I coughed much of the way. At another time, I might have enjoyed the views outside the carriage, of boats both small and large, of fishermen and merchants. I would have delighted in the birdsong and the occasional wild creature I saw darting in and out of the bushes. But on this day, I felt only deep, engulfing fear.

Along the way, I recalled my remarkable conversation with Mr. Adams. I know not quite how to describe him. The best description was perhaps that of his wife's: He was like Odysseus, born for trouble. Indeed, I had thought I detected, upon hearing my dilemma, a lift in Mr. Adams's spirits, a welcome engagement of his natural energies. They had idled far too long—a full nine hours!

But as we approached Cambridge, my thoughts grew darker. I had little faith that Adams could do anything from Braintree. But even if he could, even if this "web" of his managed to free John and Isaac, they would be hunted like animals. How long might they remain undetected in Braintree?

I suddenly recalled my dream of the night before: that mythical place across the ocean, bare, clean, and filled with light. All these months, when I dreamed of John's escape, I had unconsciously dreamed of us living with Johnny in Braintree, among the friends whom I so dearly loved.

I saw that dream for what it was now, as I rode in the carriage on the way to my ancestral home. Braintree could not be our home. And, for all I had come to love the Cause, I knew that this war was not *our* war, nor would its victory be *our* victory. This could never be *our* America, mine and John's. I looked out at the coast and the sea through eyes that saw the truth.

· · ·

Three long hours later, having stopped not once, we finally arrived in Cambridge. The chestnut tree that stood upon our front lawn was in full flower. Bluish-lavender Rose of Sharon trees bloomed on either side of the door. A second bloom of bright-pink roses and dusty catmint made a fine display on either side of them.

At first, the house looked just the same as when I'd left it near one year earlier, after Papa's funeral. But as I descended the carriage and walked up the path, I noticed that its once-pristine white paint was peeling, and the once-neat lawn had gone to seed. I looked toward the stables: they were empty, neither horses nor men within.

A hammering sound came from the vicinity of the orchards. There, just beyond the apple trees, I discovered the frame of a house going up. Mama must have sold off the back lot. The estate that had once seemed an infinite wilderness in our childish games of hide-and-seek was now quite finite.

Mama noticed the carriage and, by the time I came round to the front, was standing in the doorway. For a moment, she just stood there looking at me. I approached, but soon stopped at half a rod's distance: How old she'd grown! There were thick streaks of gray in her hair. Her gown had biscuit crumbs all down the front.

She looked wilted and decayed, like a plant eaten by disease from within.

"You've come," she said. "I had no notion that you would."

"I came immediately upon receiving your letter," I said coolly.

"You are too thin," she observed. "They have worked you to the bone."

"Only such work as I wished to do," I replied. Then I reproached myself. There was a purpose to my visit, and I would do well not to lose sight of it. "Well, it's good to be home, anyway," I said, entering the house and endeavoring to smile.

The coachman followed with my trunk. I looked about the foyer and then at the front parlor. Our few remaining pieces of furniture were gone. In my father's study, silhouettes of dust remained on the parquet floor where the sofa and table had once stood. Only the books in the cabinets remained. I moved past Mama, after the coachman and my trunk. Passing her, I noticed a distinctly unpleasant odor: it was the rank, sour smell of unwashed clothing.

As I began to mount the stairs she said, "I am glad you are home, Eliza. Most glad. We shall have time enough to talk—you must be exhausted. Cassie!" she called.

Cassie soon appeared from the kitchen; seeing me, her eyes widened in shock. Her face seemed longer, sadder, and older, too. I ran and fairly flung myself into her waiting arms.

"Oh, Cassie!" I cried.

We held each other, and after a few moments Cassie pulled back and looked at me questioningly, though she did not dare to utter a word in my mother's presence. Clearly, she knew not why I was there, without my child, nor why the coachman hoisted my trunk up the stairs. But she finally said, "I make you a dish of tea." She moved toward the kitchen, but I stopped her with a touch upon her arm.

"Wait a moment. I have some things for you both . . ." I ran up the stairs to my trunk. Opening it, I found the boxes of tea, the sugar, and a bag of flour my friends had given me from Harry's spoils of war.

"Your mama will be very happy to see all dis," she said, but the items did not seem to cheer her.

"There's more—I shall unpack it all later."

Mama had mounted the stairs and stood watching us from the doorway. "But where did you get these goods?" she asked suspiciously.

"It's a long story," I said. "I'll gladly tell it by and by."

"Well, but such tea will be a delight, after all this time," said Mama, putting aside her scruples. "Cassie, do make us some." Cassie nodded, and I took the sack of sugar and moved off to the kitchen with her. Once I knew we were alone, I drew her to me and whispered, "Cassie, it's most urgent that I speak with you. But not within these walls."

"I go later to de market. Come wit' me. I go around four. Dey sell cheaply at de end of de day. Sometimes dey even give away de food."

"So it has come to that," I remarked thoughtfully. Of course, we had been accepting handouts from the Adamses and Quincys for nearly a year. But I suffered to think that we fared far better than Mama and Cassie. "Very well. I shall accompany you."

Fifteen minutes later, Mama and I were sitting out back in the kitchen garden—she had placed her one remaining tea table and a set of chairs out there, finding it more pleasant to enjoy the occasional breezes that came up from the river. At night, Cassie brought the table and chairs inside, in the event of rain. But it had hardly rained at all that month.

"Oh, isn't this wonderful?" said my mother, closing her eyes and sipping her Bohea tea.

"Yes, we've been quite spoiled—in some ways. Lizzie's brother, Harry, returned from sea one month ago. He'd been gone many years. He brought us two sacks of British goods."

"That was very lucky for you."

"It was," I agreed. "And so, how fare things here?" I endeavored to sound cheerful. "I see you sold a parcel of land."

"Yes. It was—necessary. The owners built themselves a fair-sized house, though of course it will not have the gardens we do."

"Have you met them?"

She shook her head. "But I hear from Papa's lawyer that it is a colonel and his wife and two children. They are not likely to know our circle."

"No, indeed," I agreed, doubting whether anyone of Mama's former "circle" remained in Cambridge. All had long since fled.

After tea, I went upstairs and rested in my own chamber. I lay upon the bed and stared at the ceiling and asked the Lord to give me strength for what would come. After a while, determined to resist my sinking spirits, I rose and sought out Cassie. I found her by the hearth, drenched in perspiration, making a cake with the flour I'd brought her.

"Cassie, you're melting. Let us go to market."

Cassie pulled the cake from the coals, wiped her brow with an elbow, lifted the pan with a rag, and set it upon a heart-shaped trivet. At the sight of Cassie continuing to do what she had always done, stuck in the iron grid of service and lost dreams, my heart suddenly lurched, and a decision took hold of me.

Cassie moved from the fire and took a moment to tidy herself. Then, emerging into the hallway, she called, "Miss Margaret! I go to market. Eliza come wit' me."

Mama was in the library, doing I knew not what. She replied, her voice too shrill, "See if they have a halibut. I fancy a halibut for my daughter's return. And have we gooseberries for a sauce?"

"Yes, ma'am."

At an earlier time, my mother would have thought it most rude to speak from such a distance. Cassie sighed, but not at Mama's solecism. I looked at her, expecting her to say something, but she did not. Only when we had left the house and had gone half a block toward town did she stop and turn to me.

"Your Mama not too well, Eliza."

"What do you mean?"

"In de 'ead." She pointed to her own. I stopped walking and touched her elbow.

"Please explain yourself, Cassie."

Cassie was reluctant to speak ill of her mistress, but at my insistence, she let out a sigh and began. "Some days, she confused. She tink it maybe de year 1770. Some days, she believe Jeb away and return soon."

"That cannot be," I frowned. "She seemed perfectly well to me, except"—here I broached the subject of my mother's hygiene —"she *smells*."

Cassie nodded gravely. "She won' let me bathe her, Miss Eliza. It been many monfs . . . you stay a little longer, you see for yourself what she like."

"Perhaps it is but a temporary state, a breakdown from which she'll recover. She has been through a great deal, what with Papa's death."

Cassie merely shrugged, unconvinced.

"But Cassie, listen. I have information I must impart. Urgent information that shall cause you no little pain."

From the corner of my eye I perceived a bench by the blacksmith's shop, half a block away. I motioned for us to go sit there. I took Cassie's hand—whether to steady her or myself I knew not.

We sat down. "Here's what I know . . ." I began.

I told Cassie about my uncle's death and the confiscation of his home. I recounted the news of Isaac's discovery at the auction house, his return to his former master, and John's sale to this same master as well. At my news, Cassie inhaled, bent over, and put her hands to her mouth.

"*But*," I added quickly, "there are those who help us even as we speak, Cassie. People of great weight and connection."

I had endeavored to impress her, but by Cassie's demeanor I knew her to be wholly disbelieving. I then addressed the other urgent matter: "Do you know that Mama wrote to me with the intention of finding Johnny's father?"

Cassie nodded. "I thought so. Oh, Miss Eliza! I don't know what anyone can do. Your Mama, she'll get Watkins for sure, now. She talk of nutteeng else for weeks and weeks. It keep her alive."

"Yes, it seems so." I sighed, "Though I can't imagine why."

"You can't?" she looked at me.

"Not really. What good will it do her to punish Watkins?"

But Cassie shrugged, as if she felt I must discover this for myself.

"Cassie," I continued, touching her shoulder so that she would look at me. "I have no intention of going to Portsmouth with Mama."

"You don't?"

"No. I merely stall for time. These people who help us, if perchance they do succeed—"

"Don' ask me to hope for dat, Miss Eliza," Cassie interrupted me. "Please don't."

"But if perchance they *do*," I persisted. "Well, you must know we could not remain here."

Cassie waited for me to say more.

"It's a dangerous time to travel, but I have only one place I can think of to go. There will be terrible dangers, difficulties."

I looked about me, but there was no one save a few children who raced past us, playing a game.

"Cassie, I have a question to put to you. An important one."

"Yes, Miss Eliza?"

"My question is, Do you wish to come with us? You and Isaac? I know not what we shall find. I know not how we shall live, though

John is a goodly shipwright—or was . . ." I trailed off uncertainly. "Isaac is skilled now as well. But your only certain possession shall be your freedom. That—and to live among friends. That's all I know, and all I can offer."

Cassie had closed her eyes and now seemed to be praying. I knew not to whom or what she prayed, nor did I ask. When she was finished, she stood and began to walk along the road toward the market, saying nothing. I trailed after her.

"Cassie? Cassie, dear. What is it? Please. Share your thoughts with me. Share your true feelings—for once."

She turned to me. Her face was wet with tears. "I pray for dees every day since you were a little girl. *Every day*. Do it come true today? I ask myself. Every day."

"Oh, Cassie," I said. "Then we shall have each other. Surely that is no small thing."

"No, Miss Eliza. 'Eet's no small ting."

51

WE ATE OUR SUPPER AT THE TABLE in the kitchen garden. The air had cooled somewhat, though it was still quite hot. My mother ate little but spoke with animation about everything we would do together now that I was home. Certain of these activities seemed reasonable, such as her suggestion that we attend a concert in town. Perhaps the sale of the parcel of land had given her a little security. But then she said, smiling mysteriously, "And of course there shall be a Harvest Ball, and but—oh!—we must order you a gown from London at once."

I sat back in silence. Cassie, coming out to clear our plates, met my eyes briefly. Her look was knowing, and I nodded dispiritedly.

Mama's mood, on the other hand, had grown nearly jubilant: "Eliza, I can't tell you my relief that you have returned from Portsmouth at last. My brother was very naughty to have kept you so long. I shall scold him soundly anon." At these words, I smiled, excused myself, and ran into the kitchen, where I let out a moan.

"You see now," said Cassie, appearing by my side in the kitchen.

"Yes, I see. Oh, God, Cassie. She has not mentioned Johnny— or Lizzie, or Braintree, or any of it. It's as if none of that ever happened. She is far gone, and yet she wrote to me with such odd lucidity on the subject of Johnny's father."

Cassie nodded. "Dat truth 'ees a thorn in her side, Miss Eliza. She need to pull it out."

"Dat truth" reached my sluggish brain at last: Were Mama to dispense with father and child, it might be as if no time had passed. Nothing would have changed. My virtue would be reestablished, and I could return to her barren bosom and life in Cambridge once more. O, hellish fate!

I moved out of doors and said resolutely, "Mama, let us order that dress as soon as may be. I am thinking perhaps a lilac color."

"Lilac is quite beautiful, Eliza, and looks well on you. But it is hardly appropriate for winter. I don't know—" she tapped her pointy chin with the fingers of one hand. "I'm betwixt and between—dark green might suit in the event of a winter soiree."

"You're right. I hadn't thought of that."

Mama nodded with satisfaction. She sipped her tea and ate another bite of cake. I nattered on. I told Mama I was looking forward to the Harvest Ball, and to Christmas. Though it was August, and sweltering, I spoke fondly of a white Christmas.

"Do you remember when Jeb and I made snow angels? I was so happy then," I blurted, then regretted it at once.

"I do," she said guardedly, her eyes flitting toward and then away from me.

"I always thought those angels were real, but of course they weren't. You had a beautiful family, Mama. I have many happy memories."

She stared into the apple trees, her hands now clasped together. "Yes, I did, didn't I?"

Mama seemed so contented to have me home that I allowed myself to think that perhaps she would forgo her mission in Portsmouth. But as if hearing my thoughts, she said, "You know, Eliza. I have had sufficient time since writing you to realize that, as the court will certainly want your testimony, you will need to come with me to Portsmouth. There is hardly a point in my making two trips when one will suffice."

"Of course," I said, hiding my disappointment. "When did you wish to go?"

"I had planned on leaving first thing tomorrow. But as you seem quite tired yet, perhaps we'll head out on Friday. Would that suit?"

"Let us depart on Saturday. There are things I would yet do—in Cambridge. There was a particular bonnet I wished to buy . . ." My tongue felt suddenly heavy with lies, and I could not continue.

That night, sleeping in my old bed, I allowed myself to pretend that I was a child once more. I would wake to a cheerful houseful of noisy children. Maria would descend with her notebook, and Jeb would send a kite over the railing for me to chase. Or Maria and I might, after breakfast, play a game of chess in the library, watching the Vassals' maid shake out the carpets. Waiting for Mr. Cardinal to appear. How pleasant the illusion was! I understood why Mama had chosen never to wake from it.

Early the next day, I descended and took my morning coffee alone. Mama rose late. She breakfasted and allowed Cassie to bathe her. The previous evening, I'd managed to convince her that it would be prudent to bathe before donning a new gown. She had assented, much to our relief.

After breakfast, Mama said she wished to help me unpack. But I told her that it was unnecessary, given that we would soon leave for Portsmouth. I would merely remove what items I needed for the next few days.

"How very sensible of you, Eliza." She smiled.

I was so surprised by my mother's approbation that she must have noticed, for she looked at me in a way she had not for many years. She took my hand. "I love you, Eliza, despite what you might think. I always have. Even more than the others. Perhaps that's why

I expected so much of you. Anyway, it was Mr. Boylston's particular wish that I make that clear to you."

I stared at her in stunned silence. She had surprised me in many ways, but this outburst of kindness was the deepest surprise of all. When I thought of a reply, a lifetime of unspoken words came crowding in on me. So did a great deal of hurt and anger. I replied simply, "I love you, too, Mama."

Her shoulders felt so thin as I embraced her, the cage that held her heart so fragile. How strange, I thought, that she should begin to love me now, now that she wished to do me the greatest harm of all, and I planned to abandon her forever? O, when would this torture end?

Later that day, Cassie and I walked to market; the vendors erected makeshift tents to keep off the burning sun, but on windy days, such as it was on this day, the tents swayed and threatened to crash to the sides of the stalls. I looked about the town at the old vendors and shopkeepers I knew, many of whom remained, though their clientele was not what it once was: We all looked quite plain in our homespun gowns. The silk gowns and bonnets were all gone.

At home, Mama and I partook of our scant dinner at the garden table. Just as we began to eat, I put my fork down in unfeigned disgust.

"Mama. Cassie eats all alone in the kitchen, and, honestly, I don't see the point. Why can she not eat out here with us? It is stiflingly hot within, and having her with us would be far more companionable."

"Companionable? A slave?" Here, I thought she would launch upon one of her diatribes, but Mama cast me a flinty look and said, "Oh, yes, very well. But tell her to hurry up. I find I'm quite hungry. Cassie!"

Cassie came running to serve us, but Mama growled, "Hurry and pull up a chair. And bring your plate. You shall eat out here, with us. And *do* endeavor to add a bit of conversation to the meal, Cassie, for it won't do to sit there like a stone."

The look on Cassie's face I shall never forget: it was as if she had just seen the parting of the Red Sea.

52

WE DRANK OUR TEA, BUT CASSIE WAS too flummoxed to eat. She had never put a fork to her mouth before Mama, and she looked as if God might strike her dead were she to do so.

"Mama, shall we stay at Uncle Robert's in Portsmouth?" I asked.

"Heavens, no," she replied. "No, we stay at Stavers's. I hope it shall be of short duration. But these days the courts are in such disarray, I should imagine we'll remain there for several weeks." Mama soon excused herself from the table. She rose, hesitated, then curtsied shallowly in Cassie's direction. Cassie nearly fell off her chair, and I thought, *Given a hundred years, Mama might well become a decent sort of person.*

The moment she was gone, I whispered, "Cassie, have we any writing paper about? And do you know a messenger? You must call upon him at once."

"I go look, Mees Eliza."

Hastily, we cleared the table, then set about finding paper. Cassie met me in the foyer after scouring Papa's study—she handed me an old note from his attorney in Barbados, affirming the sale of several slaves, dated three years earlier. Using his old pen and ink, I crossed the note out with distaste and used the back of the paper:

Dearest Lizzie.

I find myself in direst circumstances. Mama brings us to Portsmouth on Saturday. It was the best I could do, given her wish to leave immediately. But as she has no carriage, we are obliged to go to town for the Flying Stage Coach. We leave Boston at ten o'clock. I know not when we expect to arrive in Portsmouth—Sunday afternoon, perhaps. Give my love to those who feel its absence.

Yours, Eliza

I was repacking my clothing upstairs when Cassie returned half an hour later with a sad-looking Negro boy of about thirteen, accompanied by a bony old horse. I saw them out the window and cringed lest Mama should see them as well.

Cassie appeared before me and I gave her the letter. Quickly, she moved to give the letter to the boy, who untied the horse and took off in the direction of the bridge. Ten minutes later, Mama descended the stairs and regarded me with a level gaze:

"Who was that?"

I shivered. My mouth was growing accustomed to it, but my body was unused to lying. "Oh, I sent word to Lizzie that we would be out of town some weeks. In case she needed to reach me."

"Why would she need to reach you?" Mama asked warily. How pointed, how shrewd, she could be on the topic of my life, if not her own!

I shrugged. "Mr. Miller suffered a grievous wound in a skirmish, and I should like to know if he takes a turn for the worse. He has been a loyal friend." This explanation seemed to satisfy her, though she did say, "Well, *I* should like to know, in future, if you plan to send messages."

I felt the old-familiar rope tightening about my neck. This time, however, it had a salutary effect: it distilled me of remorse for what I was about to do. No remorse for the remorseless. That was the Rebel credo, was it not?

I slept very ill Wednesday night; fear was my steadfast companion. Thursday and Friday passed with excruciating slowness. I knew not when, or if, someone might endeavor to find me. I sat in the front parlor pretending to read, listening for horses' hooves.

Mama kept asking, "Why do you not go into the library? Would it not be far more comfortable? There is a breeze from the open door."

"Nay, I am content," I replied, though I was sitting upon a garden stool.

"Very well, suit yourself."

Saturday morning came with still no word from anyone. I thought of Harry's ship, the *Cantabrigian*, readying itself to set sail from Hogshead Point that Monday. Would we be passengers upon it?

I rose but could not settle and paced about restlessly. Cassie emerged from the kitchen with an old leather case, wearing her wool cape. She looked absurd, and already perspired beneath it. However, it would be just the thing for a sea crossing. Mama did not notice it, being occupied with all our last-minute chores.

"Have you means to pay for the coach?" I asked her.

"Why do you inquire about such matters?" she replied. "Of course I do."

"Never mind. I simply thought it prudent to ask."

I stepped outside, onto the stone landing. I looked up at the ancient trees that had made it through the arboreal massacre of '76. I looked back at the house and through the open doorway at the foyer, now empty. At one time it had contained a beautiful carved mahogany table and a splendid china vase of flowers. I saw the staircase, once the envy of all Cambridge. How long ago that life seemed!

I heard horses' hooves and whipped round, but it was only the coach that Mama had hired to take us to town. There could be no delay now, no further means of stalling.

For a brief moment, I thought of pretending some kind of fit. No, I was far too poor an actor. It was all I could do to lie with words.

Cassie and I walked down the path toward the waiting coach. I shut my eyes for a moment and imagined: Where were they now? Where were John and Isaac? Had anyone reached them? Had John done something foolish? Perhaps our friends arrived too late for rescue. Surely John would not leave Isaac . . . no, no. He would be more likely to attempt an escape for the both of them . . .

It had been too long since I had nursed Johnny, and my milk came in, seeping through my bodice. Mama was fussing in the hall-way when all at once she caught sight of the waiting carriage out front. "Eliza! Why did you not tell me that the carriage awaited?"

"It only just arrived, Mama."

"Well, then, let us be off."

She moved out of doors, then suddenly spread her hands up above her head. "Goodness! What is the matter with me! I have left my hatbox upstairs! I'll be but a moment. Coachman!" she called. "Take our trunks at once!"

When Mama had gone, I turned to Cassie. There was some-thing I wished to say to her about our journey. Just then, a tall man who had been moving haltingly in the distance approached our coachman, but I was bent toward Cassie and so did not see his face. I then felt a sudden tap upon my shoulder and nearly jumped a foot in the air.

I looked up. Beside me stood Mr. Miller. Down the street, before the Vassals' house, a small carriage waited, along with two hot and dusty-looking horses. Mr. Miller bent down to whisper in my ear. He said but three words:

"We have them."

53

"CASSIE, DID YOU HEAR? DID YOU HEAR?"

Cassie was by my side; she heard. We gripped each other, laughing in disbelief, and moved with Mr. Miller toward the waiting carriage. I turned back and looked at my house. Mama was within, retrieving her hatbox. I had planned to leave her, to flee without so much as looking back. But I had looked back. Now she was at the door.

Had I felt no remorse, I should have been forgiven by all who knew my story. But as I stood there beside Mr. Miller, carriages waiting, questions waiting, I *did* feel something, regardless of whether I wished to or no.

Mama had done little to earn my love or loyalty, and yet, standing at this crossroads, I discovered to my surprise that she had them. It would have been simpler had things been otherwise: Life without her in it was indeed a consummation devoutly to be wished. Yet what kind of monster would I be to abandon her, alone and unwell, without so much as a servant to tend her? It would spell her slow but certain death.

"A moment," I said to Mr. Miller. I turned back to the house. Mama had just shut the front door and hurried down the path with her hatbox.

"I can't believe I nearly forgot this," she said. "But I suppose you may as well know—I've become a little forgetful of late, Eliza. Muddling things up." Here, she placed a hand to her head. I was about to say something but she continued more cheerfully, "But, oh, well, perhaps it shall pass."

"Mama." I stood there, making no attempt to move.

"What is it, pray? The carriage awaits."

"I have something to ask you, and I must do so now."

"Whatever nonsense is this, Eliza? We shall miss the coach in Boston."

"It was never my intention to board that coach, Mama. You see, I meant to leave you. Meant to, intended to. Cassie and I, we leave for Braintree this very moment. The question is, Shall you come with us or not?"

"Come with you? Whyever should I wish to do that? And what do you do with my Cassie? We go to Portsmouth," she insisted. "You yourself agreed."

"No." I smiled sadly. "I lied. All this business about helping you to bring my ravisher to justice—it was a means of stalling you while we endeavored to procure his freedom. And, oh, Mama—we have succeeded! But even had we failed, you must know that I love the father of my child. The father is John Watkins, and we shall be joining him immediately, in Braintree."

"John Watkins?" Mama murmured to herself. She looked about her, as if no longer sure where she was. "That cannot be. Watkins is a slave. Your uncle Robert's slave."

"It *can* be, Mama, and it is. Your brother is dead. He sold John to another, from whence he was rescued by loving friends—thank Heaven. Before you tell me that I shall be an outcast, know that I have come to care little for our so-called society. My sustaining joy is the thought of my family, growing and prospering. I wish to hear the playful cries of children, as you once did. I long to see my husband's face each morning when I wake. I have a boy, Mama. He is very fine, bright and good-natured . . ."

I broke off and reached for her, but she took a step backward in horror.

"Mama," I begged, weeping now. "I know I have disappointed you. I never thought of myself as a particularly good person, but neither am I wholly bad. My heart has traveled great distances, to places where you said it could not go. Now I find that it has traveled back to you. Of this one gift am I proud. You should take it."

Mr. Miller approached. "I dislike intruding, Eliza," he whispered. "But we must depart at once. Do you wish to stay and join us later? It might be arranged."

"No, indeed," I said, drying my eyes. Cassie took my arm. The three of us headed toward the small carriage.

Mama faced the other, muttering, "Well, but I shall send someone for Cassie by and by."

"You won't find her, Mama. You must choose, and choose now. Time has run out. You have not the luxury of your fond delusions any longer. Shall you remain here, with your illusory comfort, or shall you come with us?"

Mr. Miller's carriage had been backing up slowly and now stood expectantly before us. The coachman came round and helped me up, then helped Cassie. It would be a tight fit, and I knew not where we might put all the trunks, which were still in the hired carriage.

Mama looked up at me, a sudden panic of understanding in her eyes. It was almost as if she had not known what was happening until this moment.

"But Eliza—where do you go?" she asked.

"Back to the cottage. And thence—God willing—to Barbados." I grasped Mr. Miller's hand as he mounted the carriage. "Come, Mr. Miller."

Mama turned away from us. She paused, turned back around, and looked at the hired coach waiting to take her to Portsmouth. She glanced back at the house, up to our chambers above, and down to the roses and catmint and the Rose of Sharon trees that bloomed so luxuriantly.

Her moment of indecision lasted a long time. But at last she mounted the hired carriage bound for Portsmouth. She set her hatbox by her side and looked directly ahead, not at us.

Involuntarily, I cried out, "Oh, Mama!" Cassie took my hand and pressed it in hers.

Then, to her coachman, Mama called in her high, imperious voice: "To Braintree. The Quincys! And be quick about it!"

54

HE WAS PLAYING PEEKABOO WITH JOHNNY IN the kitchen garden when we arrived. His handsome face darted in and out of the shadows of the mint that grew in wild profusion and scented the air. Every time Johnny saw his father's face emerge, he gurgled a high, phlegmy giggle.

I espied Isaac behind the cottage, shooting crab apples off the fence with a slingshot. He had grown a head taller since last I'd seen him. When he heard our two carriages arrive, he stopped and gaped.

"Isaac!" I cried. He came running and I hugged him tight. Then Cassie grabbed hold of him and wouldn't let go.

Then John saw me. He stopped playing, picked Johnny up with his one strong arm, and approached as if I might disappear. I looked at him: my free man—or nearly so—in Braintree, among my dear friends. How beautiful he was, and how right it seemed for him to be here. So perfectly right.

Mr. Miller helped Mama down from her carriage and set to removing our trunks. He then paid the coachman, and off he went.

I recalled our brief conversation on the journey from Cambridge. Cassie and I had said nothing for the first half hour, merely clasped each other in shock and amazement. At last, round about Boston Neck, I asked Mr. Miller if Isaac and John were truly well, truly in Braintree.

"Yes, yes," Mr. Miller assured us. "They are both quite well, and no doubt enjoy the company of the Adamses as we speak."

"But I have so many questions. Mr. Richards? What about him? Oh, I'm so fearful he follows upon our heels and that John shall be caught."

"Eliza," Mr. Miller forestalled me gently. "Mr. Richards and his wife are gone."

"Gone?"

"Fled the country. They got word that they were about to be arrested. It seems that Mr. Richards didn't sign the Association Test."

"Ah," I said. "Well, thank God for that."

Now Mama stood there, in Lizzie's kitchen garden, looking utterly lost, just as Lizzie herself emerged from the cottage. Seeing my mother, Lizzie's eyes darted in my direction, her pupils huge, uneasy question marks. But then she approached my mother with great good cheer and curtsying, said, "Welcome, Mrs. Boylston. It has been too long! I'm sure you're tired from the journey. Would you care for some tea, or cider?"

"I am parched," said Mama. "The road was very dusty. I should like some tea, if you are making it."

"Of course."

Lizzie curtsied once more and came at last to hug me. Her face next to mine she whispered, "Thank God you're back. We were so worried; you have no idea. But you must be falling over."

"Oh, I'm all right."

Lizzie ruffled Johnny's hair. "He was such a good boy while you were gone!"

"Your Thomas has been very good to us," I replied, "and he not yet entirely healed."

"Well, you may praise him all day if you like, for he stops awhile. Martha has cooked something very special. But—your mother?" her eyes widened. "That is a surprise."

"There will be time to talk, I hope," I said. I smiled at her, then handed Johnny to Lizzie. I glanced back at John, willing him to follow me as I hurried into the house and up the stairs.

"Excuse me," he said to the general crowd. I had not introduced John to Mama, nor had he greeted her. That would be too much to expect from either of them. She had been polite to Lizzie, and would hopefully be cordial to the rest: that was all I prayed for.

John followed me. I had lain down on Lizzie's bed, and he lay down next to me. I shut my eyes and held him, endeavoring to cover the surface of his body—arms, legs, torso, ankles, feet—with my own, leaving no place unjoined. We lay like that, just feeling each other. Just breathing in and out.

Finally, John spoke. "I have been here but a few hours," he said, "and yet I can see why you would find it hard to leave. These women are—extraordinary."

"Indeed. But, John, what *you* must have been through," I replied. "I have as yet asked no questions. You must tell me every detail, when I have rested."

"Of course. There'll be time, my love. But I myself did almost nothing. I had but to use my legs to run and follow Colonel Langdon to the ship. Indeed, I was too weak, too low, to do more. I shall never share the depths of my resignation with you—" Here, John broke off. I said nothing, only waited for him to continue. "But never mind that. I'll say instead that the coordination of the plan was like nothing I've ever known. Not even the smuggling of Langdon's arms."

"Mr. Miller tells me the Richardses are gone—fled the country."

"Yes. I believe both Adams and Langdon had their hands in that, though neither will admit it. They are both quite closed-lipped in that regard."

"You have that in common with them, then," I replied.

John smirked, as if it were absurd to compare him to them. He changed the subject. "Your mother is here."

"She is."

"I had not expected—"

"I know." My eyes closed; suddenly I was overcome with exhaustion. The room had begun to spin about me, and I felt faint. "I can't speak more just now. Forgive me. It is all too much."

"There will be hours and years for us to speak, Eliza. Sleep now. That's it."

The room was dark, and my love's arms were around me. He did not move. In his arms, I felt at peace at last, and fell asleep. When I woke, he was gone, and I sat straight up, panicked at the thought that perhaps I had been dreaming.

I hastily descended to find Mr. Miller sitting behind little Johnny on the floor. Mr. Miller's long legs were splayed as he beat a pot with wooden sticks and sang a silly song. Johnny was laughing wildly.

John sat on the parlor bed and watched Mr. Miller and our babe. He seemed content to watch them, and when I sat down beside him he took my hand. Mama and the women were elsewhere, perhaps in the kitchen. That was good. Two worlds lived in Lizzie's cottage now, and I knew not how I would make them one, so I didn't try. Instead, I thought: *They will have to make themselves one, somehow.*

John was very quiet, watching his son and Mr. Miller play. I asked him, "What is it you're thinking?"

"Selfish thoughts, I'm afraid." He smiled at me, but those aqua eyes were liquid and near tears. "I missed a year of my son's life."

"He shan't remember it."

"Yes, but I shall."

The ruckus of banging pots and off-key singing had grown so loud that no one had heard the persistent knocking at the door.

Suddenly the little baffled face of Mrs. John Adams appeared, followed by the bewigged and powdered head of Mr. John Adams himself.

"Hallo!" Abigail called. "Are we to let ourselves in, then?" In her hands she held a pie.

"Oh, sorry!" Lizzie motioned for Martha's brother to cease his banging. Martha came barreling out of the kitchen at the same moment and nearly collided with Mr. Adams.

"Pardon!" she said and then burst into embarrassed laughter, as did Mr. Adams. He pat at his limbs to see that all four remained in his possession.

Just then, Mama, regal and pathetic in her frayed silk gown and erect bearing, emerged from the kitchen. I had no choice but to introduce her to the Adamses, which I then did.

"Mama, allow me to introduce Mr. John Adams and his wife, Abigail. You have heard much about our esteemed citizens, I'm sure."

"Indeed," said Mama. Thankfully, she curtsied.

"Well, well. Welcome to our humble parish, Mrs. Boylston," said Mr. Adams cheerfully. "Did you have a good trip?"

"Not very," grumbled Mama. "The roads were dusty."

My heart clutched; I knew not how Mama would behave, nor how she would be received. *Two worlds,* I thought, *and I alone cannot make them one.*

Suddenly Mr. Adams let out a hearty laugh. "An honest woman. And annoyed, too. Well, why shouldn't she be? It is hot, the roads are dusty, and for her troubles she finds herself surrounded by the likes of us!"

Mr. Adams thought this was vastly amusing, but Abigail nudged him.

"Hush, John," she said.

Lizzie went to fetch tea, and Mr. Miller at long last broke off his singing to help carry the garden stools into the kitchen garden.

Martha had made us a fricassee of chicken with our own peppers and a salad of beans. Mr. Adams carried the table from the kitchen into the garden, refusing to let Mr. Miller help him, as Mr. Miller's wounds were not yet healed. He had trouble once he got to the front door, however, and Abigail grabbed one end of the table in exasperation. It was a comic sight, watching the two of them argue about how best to get the table through the door. At last, they succeeded, much to our relief.

The Quincys soon arrived, bringing wine. Once more, I made introductions, and once more, Mama, though dour, was civil enough. She seemed to realize that she was outnumbered.

But I soon nearly forgot Mama, her feelings, her thoughts, or even her behavior. Abigail pointed to a pie she had set upon the table, and I laughed with joy at the sight of it.

"What have you made for us, Abigail?"

"An apple pie. Some of yours were already ripe—I took the liberty of purloining them for the occasion. It *is* an occasion, is it not?"

"Oh, Abigail, it is!"

We had not enough chairs for all of us, but it mattered not. Throughout the evening, Abigail and John argued over one chair, pushing each other off of it at unexpected moments; they seemed to enjoy this fight for chair mastery, and it was hard to tell who had won until, finally, at the dessert course, we heard a thud, and Mr. Adams disappeared momentarily. We rose in wonder, to find him splayed out on the ground. Abigail exclaimed triumphantly, "There—at last! The chair is mine!"

"It seems you've managed to do what no one else has yet accomplished, Abigail," said Martha.

"What is that?"

"Unseat the great John Adams."

At this, we all laughed.

• • •

That night, Mr. Adams told memorable stories: of France and Paris, Benjamin Franklin and Thomas Jefferson. But he also listened with great interest to my John, who spoke about the *Ranger*, the *Raleigh*, and the *America*. I burst with pride at John's modesty, his simple eloquence, and his ease among these illustrious citizens. *He was born to mingle among such company*, I thought. At one point, he even glanced Mama's way, though she studiously avoided meeting his eyes.

Cassie observed us all in silence. But her head pivoted this way and that, as if she were watching a game of catch.

Isaac chimed in with his own panegyric upon John Watkins: "Watkins taught me everything! The men of Portsmouth loved him!"

But as my John spoke, Mr. Adams grew increasingly thoughtful. Finally, he said, "I'm most aware of the sad irony, Mr. Watkins, that while you built the ships that are to win us freedom, you were not free to enjoy that which the rest of us fight and die for. It is a fact of our times for which I am heartily ashamed."

"You need your own country," Lizzie suddenly blurted to us, then glanced at Mr. Adams to see if she had given offense.

I smiled at my John. "Imagine that," I said. "Our own country."

"It is hard to imagine. Perhaps I shall be able to dream of it while I sleep." He returned a gentle smile.

Mr. Adams gazed at Isaac, and at Johnny, who sat on Martha's lap. He said, "True equality, I fear, shall fall to the next generation to accomplish."

"Speaking of accomplishments," I finally managed to bring up the subject I had wished to address for some time, "I feel the need to thank you, Mr. Adams. I have no idea how the miracle happened. I should dearly like to know."

Mr. Adams pursed his lips. He glanced at Mama, quickly calculating whether she would be a risk, then let out a sigh. "Braintree was in dire need of grain, as you know all too well. Portsmouth, as it turned out, had a . . . a great deal of grain, housed on board a French brig. I was able to wrest from Congress approval to have Colonel Langdon send the grain immediately to us, upon his new ship the *Hampton*. I dare say no more."

Mr. Adams, meanwhile, looked about the table and then raised his wineglass. "To Colonel Langdon."

"To Colonel Langdon!" we all cried.

We made many other toasts as well—to His Excellency, to Mr. Adams, and to the barrels of grain that, I suspected, would leave many a loaf tasting of gunmetal.

•   •   •

We all knew these were my last hours in Braintree. But for the rest of the night, we kept sadness at bay. We felt it a sacred duty to celebrate our triumph, for the Lord knew how many defeats we had suffered.

After dinner we danced, and everyone joined in. Mr. Miller and Isaac banged on Lizzie's pots and chanted strange noises, in very poor imitation of the Natives and their victory dances. Mr. Adams, Abigail, myself, Martha, Lizzie—even the colonel and Ann Quincy—joined in the dance. Martha had been holding Johnny, but when she entered the dance she placed Johnny upon Mama's lap. "Here you go," she said. Mama frowned, but oddly, Johnny did not cry. He reached for my mother's nose as she reluctantly began to bounce him on one knee.

Round and round the table the rest of us went. Our hands and faces lifted to the ceiling, then bowed to the ground. We all chanted in unison, Mr. Adams chanting loudest of all and cutting a most absurd figure. At one point during the victory dance, he made such a sudden and violent gesture that his wig nearly flew off. This brought a roar of laughter from the rest of us.

Years later, I would ask President Adams and First Lady Abigail Adams, "Do you remember that time we danced like Indians in Lizzie's cottage?"

"I recall no such thing," replied the First Lady. But I caught her eye, and we laughed.

At around midnight, two men approached our door from the direction of the water: Harry and Captain Wiles. We ceased our dancing at once, but this time there was no burst of laughter.

Only Harry's voice broke our silence. He said, "We shall be ready to depart by noon tomorrow." He turned to Captain Wiles for confirmation.

"Ten, if the winds oblige," Captain Wiles assented.

Ah, yes. The winds. The winds that would blow and scatter us across the earth like autumn leaves.

55

IT WAS EARLY, AND VERY STILL. NO light shone through the window. No one else was yet awake. But I sat up, holding the blanket across my breasts because Martha had entered Lizzie's chamber and stood by the bed. She was heedless of the fact that by my side slept the runaway slave Watkins. Johnny was on the other side of me, sleeping sweetly.

"Eliza," she whispered. "Eliza, wake up. I've something to tell you."

"Give me a moment. I must dress and have some coffee, if possible. Oh, I was so tired—you cannot imagine."

I began to rise from my bed but Martha forestalled me. "I have something to confess."

I paused. "All the more reason to make some coffee. Go on, then." I stood up, stark naked, and reached for my dressing gown. "I don't wish to wake them," I whispered. Martha followed me down the stairs.

For several weeks, I had suspected Martha of involvement in the deaths of Dr. Flynt and Mr. Thayer. But now that she seemed ready to tell me the truth, I wished to know the whole truth, not just a part of it.

"Who destroyed our supplies and Lizzie's beloved Star?" I asked, bending to put the kettle on to boil.

"Cleverly has just now confessed to it."

"But why did he wish to do such a thing? Why did he wish to harm us?"

"Reprisal," she said curtly, her mouth tight. "For what I had done."

"And what had you done, Martha? Was it you who killed those men?" I inquired mildly, now that we sat with our coffee, side by side at the table.

"Yes."

"I thought so."

I was silent. Martha glanced at me in surprise. "How calm you are, Eliza, and at such dreadful news as this."

I sighed. "Our laws and precepts—everything and everyone I once revered, Martha, have long since proved themselves unworthy. Much as I should *like* to judge the sins of others—we all know how well I am suited to the task—I now find that I am incapable of doing so."

My friend smiled wanly.

"That is most generous," Martha replied. "More than I feel I deserve. But let me say only that I acted not alone, but rather with the knowledge and consent of my brother, the colonel, and General Washington himself. The men were an immediate threat, and I alone had the means."

"I am very sorry for you, Martha. Truly." I reached for her hand and grasped it. "While I can't pretend to understand how you feel, I do know that it must be a terrible burden. I meant to leave my mother alone—Lord knows she deserved it. Yet, at the last moment, I found I could not do it. I am weak and admire your strength."

"You know that is not weakness. That is compassion—a luxury *we* could not afford." Martha's voice was hardly above a whisper when she added, "I see not how I shall ever recover."

I sipped my coffee and considered Martha's words. Finally I replied, "Even Cain was allowed to recover. Did the Lord not give Cain a mark to protect him from others' condemnation? Martha, though you bear a mark, you shall—you must—recover."

"But I have taken two lives," she said.

"I am an unwed mother whose babe is as brown as her homespun."

"Yes," Martha said thoughtfully. "That's pretty bad. And yet, oddly, we like you so much better now than before." Martha suddenly flashed me a beautiful smile, though her eyes brimmed with tears.

•　　•　　•

Later that day, we gathered on the beach: Lizzie and Mr. Miller, myself and John, Cassie, Mama and Isaac, Abigail and Mr. Adams. A ways down the shore, Charlie and Tommy Adams played catch with a purloined apple from Lizzie's orchards.

Harry stood off a ways, to the east of us, before the moored ship, beside Martha. They were speaking earnestly to each other, though we heard not their words. Then Harry got down on one knee before her. To give them privacy, we forced our eyes away, up to the gulls and terns, then down to the plovers running to and fro with the tide, like tiny shadows. I looked up, finally, at John and nodded. It was time to set off.

Embraces, tears, promises to write . . . We waved until our wrists hurt and salty tears burned our eyes, the figures of our beloved friends growing smaller and smaller, and finally becoming grains of sand on the distant shore. Once our separation was complete, and we saw only the iron-gray water, it went easier upon our souls.

For the most part, our little band of thieves—Harry and Cassie and Isaac, myself and John and Johnny—made for a jolly party. For a long time Mama kept herself apart, and I did not try to bring her in. At one point early in our voyage, she had begun to talk about Watkins—though he was but half a rod from us—at which time I took the opportunity to make things clear to her. Things that I had been thinking about ever since we left Cambridge.

"Mama. I fear I must make the situation clear to you, so that we have a good understanding. Assuming we survive this voyage, you must know the house we sail towards is my house—mine and John's. I shall say this only once, so listen carefully."

Mama's mouth gaped open but she said nothing. Cassie stood by me, also silent, all ears.

"You enjoy, or have previously enjoyed, the liberty of saying what you like to me. But in my house, though you may complain all you like about the land or the food or the war, breathe a word of disrespect to myself, my husband, or my son, and you shall find yourself sold to the first trader of old crones. Do you understand me, Mama?"

"I do," she murmured. "I understand you full well."

"Good!" Here I smiled gaily and patted her arm.

For several days after this conversation, Mama did not speak, either to me or to anyone else. However, she soon began to complain about the wet bedding in her bunk. Then she expressed shock at the weevils in the potatoes, followed by a diatribe upon the unhygienic state of the necessary. Such was to be her way from now on: casting her jaundiced eye upon the world and leaving us in peace. That was all right by me, for we allowed that old women had earned the right to complain. We soon ceased hearing her, in the way we no longer heard the roar of the ocean waves.

Meanwhile, John, having built boats but never sailed one, grew more joyful and confident by the day, as he crewed the ship alongside Harry. His hand ached him. It was stiff and swollen, but he now had some use of it.

We arrived in New York after a week, where we said a tearful good-bye to Harry.

"I feel certain we'll meet again someday," he said to us. "Until then . . . I hope to hear from you, Eliza."

"Of course. My pen shall be faithful." I had already written my friends several letters, which I gave to Harry to post for me.

New York to Barbados was a long, miserable journey. Most of the time I kept my eyes on the horizon, the sea, the birds overhead, or the dark waves, in which I saw, or imagined I saw, the heavy tails of great dark leviathans. Several times during our crossing, I did see a tail flop lazily over, or caught a sudden, tall geyser. And upon sight of the beast's great vanishing tail, I thought: *Never again would we suffer as we had during those days of America's war of independence.*

The winds were against us, and twice we nearly capsized. We were heading to St. Vincent on the French ship *La Gabriel.* St. Vincent was an island about one hundred miles from Barbados, recently overtaken by the Admiral d'Estaing. Though ill and greatly fearful most of the way, we all arrived at St. Vincent in one piece, some time in mid-September.

Of our weeks on the ship, I have little to say. It was tumultuous and sickening. It was Purgatory. I could neither read nor talk. I could not even open my eyes, but lay either on my cot or rolled in blankets on the deck, the wind slapping me until I felt bruised.

Cassie fared no better. She had not the wherewithal to care for young Johnny, but remained on deck as well, preferring, much like myself, either to be swept off to sea or to freeze solid in the brutal winds. At one point I remarked to her that she had finally succeeded in becoming white.

She shot back, "I may be white, Miss Eliza, but you *green*."

Interestingly, and with a great show of exasperation, Mama took it upon herself to help with Johnny. The roiling seas that made Cassie and me so deathly ill had no effect upon her whatsoever. She was able to remain belowdecks with Johnny while we froze above.

One day, having descended briefly for something, Cassie returned to the deck, her face aglow with delight and tears in her eyes: "Your Mama read to de child, Miss Eliza! He sit on her lap wit' one finger in 'ees mouf, like she de best gran'mama in da worl'."

"Ha, ha," I replied, tears now in mine, "I pray he's never the wiser."

·   ·   ·

When there was no more light and the winds howled, we were obliged to descend. Once below, I was unable to open my eyes but had to lie till morning with my eyes shut. I had but two gowns, and already there were traces of puke on both. My hair was perpetually sweaty with chills. My stomach heaved, and I groaned constantly.

And yet John's joy could not be put down by something so small as a woman without her sea legs. As I lay there flat on my bunk, eyes closed, he sang. Sea shanties and war songs, which were diverting for a few minutes but quickly grew annoying.

"John, kindly be quiet," I would say. And he would place a hand to his mouth and reply, "Oh, pardon!" Silence would reign for perhaps two minutes and then, suddenly, he would bellow, "*Johnny* Todd he *took* a notion for to *cross* the ocean *wide . . .*"

·   ·   ·

I shall herein gratify the prurient reader who wishes to know whether we were married, and whether we shared a bunk. The truth is, John and I kept separate quarters in the ship from New York to St. Vincent. Apart from the fact that Mama was with us ever since we had left our shores, I had felt an instinctual desire to begin anew. That we were doing so was literally true: We had nothing but ourselves, our friends, and our child to bring to this new life. But I wished for this to be morally true as well. Everything had to be different. With freedom came responsibilities.

By day, when I was well enough, we spoke to each other. There was so much to know and to tell. John's fascination with me seemed inexhaustible. How had I come to love him? he wanted to know. I said, "When first I saw you disembark from the ferry, and you looked at me with those astonishing eyes of yours . . ."

John loved hearing this story. Over and over he made me tell it, the way a small child enjoys the story of his own birth.

Sometimes John and I lay together in my bunk and said nothing but simply held each other, Johnny in bed between us.

"Eliza," he said to me one evening, upon a reasonably calm sea, "if nothing exceptional ever happens to me again—or if we perish in a storm at sea—know that I consider my life complete right now, at this very moment. Oh, you cannot know, but I have so much more than I ever imagined I would!"

"You shall yet have more, my love. A house that is yours, and an exceedingly pretty wife . . ." This latter I spoke with a smirk.

"Ha ha. Indeed, I have grown fond of your fair hair, which sticks to your head like glue. And the tart smell of sickness on your frock."

"You've gone mad," I laughed.

Meanwhile, Cassie, seeking to give us what privacy she could, engaged herself with Isaac. Now that she had escaped the heavy thumb of service, having no one to interrupt her or call upon her (though Mama would surely have liked to), she lavished upon Isaac all her maternal feelings.

"What a leetle peeg 'ee 'ees, Miss Eliza! I don' bathe him, he never bathe himse'f. 'Ee never brush 'ees teef. 'Ee don' wan' to speak proper language, neither, but swears oafs like a pirate!"

"Oh, Cassie." I smiled. "Be patient with the poor boy. He has been in a shipyard, among the roughest sort of men. Nor can you expect to imbue him with ten years of wisdom in ten weeks."

"Oh, but I try, Mees Eliza. I try! We get to Barbados, 'ee gon' be a propah gentleman."

.   .   .

Sometime in our conversations—I could not tell you what day or even month, as all days at sea blended into one long rising and setting of the sun—John asked me why it was, exactly, that I loved him.

I looked at him, at his grave demeanor, and understood that I could not trifle with him, that his soul was wide open to me.

"From a small child," I began, "I felt, rather than understood, that I lived a lie. Oh, I did what I was told. I enjoyed the luxuries I had been born into. But after Maria died, and then Jeb, I could be happy in one room, and that was the kitchen, with Cassie. Being useful—"

John nodded, but he did not interrupt.

"I wished to hear Cassie's stories. True, wrenching stories. I could no longer abide anything else. The dinners, the parlor discussions, Mr. Inman—" I shivered. "But with you . . . you, John, were true from the start. Oh, the thought of being happy in all the rooms once more, not merely the kitchen!"

I could see that my love was moved, but he chose to lighten the moment with a joke:

"I hope that the bedroom shall be particularly . . . happy."

"Mr. Watkins!" I cried. "Well, you'll just have to wait and see, won't you?"

"I've seen." He grinned.

I punched him in the arm, and we laughed before the sudden bump of a wave threw us apart.

•   •   •

On the morning of September 21, 1779, we arrived at Kingstown, St. Vincent. No sooner had we disembarked, weak and disheveled, than we were met by a small coterie of French soldiers in smart blue uniforms. These turned out to be the Admiral d'Estaing's men. With the greatest solicitude they brought our little gang and our luggage to the headquarters of the general. Apparently, through that same "web" of which Mr. Adams had spoken, a letter had made its way from Braintree to the captain of *La Gabriel*, who dispatched a sailor to deliver it up to the house the moment we arrived.

We were given several hours to bathe and rest before meeting the esteemed admiral himself, and thus were in presentable, if not exemplary, condition in time for dinner. The admiral provided us a light meal of fish and fruits, as our heads reeled and our appetites had not fully returned.

John and I were married on the island's beautiful shores the day after our arrival. I might have been embarrassed by the presence of the esteemed general, but my dearest Abigail had paved the way by writing to the admiral of John's extraordinary character and contribution to the Cause. During the brief ceremony, I happened to glance in the admiral's direction and saw his smiling eyes. But then the French, I've heard, are less fastidious than the Americans are on this score.

By the second day, we grew eager to set off for our new home. Hearing that we desired to push on, the admiral hired a trader and his boat to escort us through the treacherous waves to Bridgetown.

We said affectionate good-byes—everyone kissing on both cheeks twice, four times . . .

Johnny especially did not want to leave the admiral, having spent much of the time in his lap, being caressed and teased. Before we left his shores, the admiral told me in private that he believed Johnny would be a great man someday.

"Oh, I agree he is everything marvelous, but that is a mother speaking. How can you know it so absolutely?"

"I have known many people in my life," he said cryptically. "Good and bad and indifferent. This little child—he is a good one."

Well, who was I to disagree with the great Admiral d'Estaing? His efforts helped America win the war. *He* was one of the good ones. And for this virtue he was beheaded, a decade later, by his own cruel compatriots.

I kissed him tenderly and we soon left the shores of St. Vincent, arriving, at long last, at Bridgetown on the twenty-third of September.

•   •   •

The plantation looked nothing like the portrait that had hung above the fireplace mantel in Papa's library. But it did bear some resemblance to the house in my dreams. The manse stood on a rise amid a stand of palm trees, overlooking Carlisle Bay. Before the house, a broad, circular drive made of smooth stone welcomed our carriage, and the horses' hooves kicked up a gentle cloud of white dust. Behind the house were acres of rolling land, dotted with palm trees and abandoned shacks, and cane fields grown to seed.

At first, the home, too, appeared abandoned, but about ten minutes after our arrival, there materialized a very fine-looking Negro caretaker. He introduced himself as Moses and eyed Cassie with unabashed interest. She returned his look with a withering stare.

"What 'ee lookin' at, you tink?"

"You, of course," I said. "I suspect you shall soon be courted, Cassie."

"Oh, go on, Miss Eliza."

I set Johnny down in the entrance, upon fine plank floors of very red mahogany, and off he went on his own two feet, half running, half careening toward the open doors and the gold light beyond. Mama followed protectively after him.

Isaac whooped and hollered with joy, and went running past little Johnny, calling, "Come on, Johnny—want to play ball? I saw one just there, beyond the driveway."

"Baw," pointed Johnny, and went toddling toward the older boy.

The French doors, opened to the sea, let in a filling, warm light. Moses took our trunks into the house and up the stairs, but not before casting Cassie another assessing look. This time, her glance was not quite so icy, for Moses was a young and handsome fellow, with a sweet smile.

"I suppose we shall have to procure some furniture," I said with a sigh. Cassie just shrugged.

Finally I turned to my new husband. "Can you believe it, John? Can you believe we are here, alive—and free?"

Still gazing about him, John wrapped both arms about my waist. "No," he said. "I'm sure I dream and shall soon awake."

"Oh, I hope not," I said.

Acknowledgments

NOT ALL AUTHORS ARE AS SMART AS they seem—at least, this is true in my case. It was a smart move, however, for me to seek help from those whose expertise allowed me to create this illusion. I would like to thank Peter Hogan and Jessica Hogan for providing honest critiques of early drafts. Valerie Cunningham, founder of the Portsmouth Black Heritage Trail, kindly read over the Portsmouth chapters; her book *Black Portsmouth: Three Centuries of African-American Heritage*, inspired me to create the slave characters in this novel. The Cambridge Historical Society, the Massachusetts Historical Society, and the Portsmouth Atheneum all provided invaluable archives. Thanks go to my ever-supportive agent, Emma Patterson of Brandt & Hochmann, who made the business end of things go smoothly. And finally, to Jodi Warshaw, senior editor at Lake Union, developmental editor Jenna Free, and Gloria Greis, director of the Needham Historical Society, all of whose insightful comments helped to make this novel as good as I sincerely wanted it to be.

Author's Note

WHEN ASKED WHICH OF MY CHARACTERS ARE real and which are fictional, I usually pause before replying. The easy answer is that they're all fictional. The more complicated answer is that they're all real. In writing historical fiction, I have found, "real" characters come to life by virtue of my fictionalizing them, and fictional characters come to life when I impose on them rather strict historical parameters. Of course, my characters are free to act however they wish, but they cannot take a carriage ride on the day of a blizzard, buy a piece of meat when the price is too high, or go to their church if war has forced it shut.

Historical characters are bound by these laws and also by their own actions to the extent that I was able to learn them. For example, John Adams won't appear in Braintree when he was actually in France. Nabby Adams won't join Lizzie and Eliza for Christmas dinner if she's in Weymouth on that day.

Our Own Country takes place during roughly the same years as its predecessor *The Midwife's Revolt*, and thus, some readers will already have met certain of the characters: Eliza Boylston and her family are entirely fictional. While the name Boylston is meant to evoke prominence, her family is not related to the "real" Boylstons of early Boston fame.

Readers of *The Midwife's Revolt* know my Braintree characters quite well: Colonel Quincy, uncle to Abigail Adams, John and Abigail Adams and their children Nabby, Tommy, John Quincy, and Charlie, are all real, as are incidental servants, pastors, and innkeepers.

John Watkins and Cassie Boylston are entirely fictional, as is John's father, the "former Royal Governor of New Hampshire." Logistics would have us point the finger at Benning Wentworth, but while Governor Wentworth did cause a scandal when he married his dead wife's maid, he did not, so far as anyone knows, sire any children from his slaves.

In Cambridge, all the leaders and Tory families mentioned existed. The Inman family existed, too, as did George Inman. Poor George Inman fares badly in my treatment of him: in "real" life, he was merely guilty of being a Tory and an officer in the British army. There is no indication in the records that he committed any crimes against women.

In Portsmouth, John Paul Jones appears at a time and place that is factually correct. Others who existed, though perhaps not entirely as I imagined them, are Colonel John Langdon, the future governor of New Hampshire; master shipwright John Hackett; Colonel William Whipple; and the Whipple slaves, Prince and Cuffee. My Dinah Whipple is fictional, although I based her on the real Dinah Whipple, a freed slave who married Prince Whipple.

The house on Deer Street actually exists. I found it while driving around Portsmouth one snowy day, looking for my setting. Freakishly, it was exactly where I imagined it to be, at the crest of the hill on Deer Street. It was as if, like the house, my story was already there, needing only to be told.

About the Author

JODI DAYNARD IS THE AUTHOR OF THE bestselling novel *The Midwife's Revolt*. Her short stories and essays have been widely published in journals such as the *New England Review, Fiction, Other Voices,* and in the *Paris Review*. Ms. Daynard has taught creative writing at Harvard University, M.I.T., and Emerson College. The third novel in the *Midwife* trilogy will be published by Lake Union in 2017.